The
Road
Builders

The Road Builders

Joy Chrisman Welch

Bellamy-Fleming Publishing
Clay City, Kentucky

BF
Publishing

Cover Design by Wizard Graphics

The Road Builders
Copyright 2015
By Joy Chrisman Welch

Published by
Bellamy-Fleming Publishing
A Division of Parkway Publications, LLC
All rights reserved.

Editorial and Sales Offices: Bellamy-Fleming Publishing
295 Forge Mill Road, P.O. Box 710, Clay City KY 40312-0710
(O): 606.663.1011
www.bellamyflemingpublishing.com
Janice@bellamyflemingpublishing.com
Jerlene@bellamyflemingpublishing.com

ISBN: 978-0-9969676-0-0

This book is printed on recycled paper.
Printed and manufactured in the United States of America.

Acknowledgements

I want to thank all the people who have helped to bring *The Road Builders* to fruition. My readers, Bo Chrisman, Judy Grim, and Julie Shultz, as well as my daughter-in-law, Meiko Welch. Their input and encouragement has been, without question, priceless. I also want to thank my husband, Paul. His support made *The Road Builders* possible.

I would be remiss if I did not thank my editors, Jerlene Rose and Janice Odom. They have been patient with my OCD angst over this first novel, and patient with my attention to story more than punctuation. Thank you.

I also thank the voices of my characters who did not give up on me through the time of writing. Carrie was persistent, and I suspect will continue to be so. If I wrote something that she would not have said, she didn't let me sleep until I changed it.

And, I give thanks to God, who is the author of imagination.

Chapter 1

She called them road builders, people of another age. Grandma and I packed our reed basket and left our secluded hollow, crossed the ridge to where we stood above long strips of gray. She told me these were roads, deserted highways that took them everywhere. This one was an afternoon's walk from Stears Branch.

Today, we laid belly down like always on the cliff's ledge. Sprays of gravel fell downward, bounced on an outcrop of rock and hit the empty road below before skipping across sections of smooth pavement and into broken cracks. I squinted into the southern sky against the hot afternoon sun.

"Carrie, it stretched from far to the north in a place called Michigan, all the way to Florida. Back then it was lined with vehicles, nose to nose."

"What happened to Michigan?"

"Can't rightly say."

She leaned on one elbow and looked at me.

"I was one of them," she whispered, as if in speaking aloud the road below us might hear.

"You was what, Grandma?"

"I was a road-builder. Not that I built the roads. It was because of people like me that they kept building, kept repairing them."

A faded green sign pointed "Exit 63" in tall yellowed letters.

I said, as I had a hundred summer afternoons before, "Tell me again about the road builders."

With the sun warming our backs and sweat beading on our upper lips, she expounded on all matter of highways and wheeled travelers.

"Wasn't a time that part of that interstate down there didn't have some piece of road tore up. Sometimes the traffic just slowed to a standstill. Damn near every vacation we went on, we were stopped somewhere along I-75 for hours."

I rolled from my belly and looked at her. "Grandma, don't swear."

If Grandpa scolded her, she said one more bad word just to spite him, but I could say it, and she would nod that she wouldn't.

"We drove that old 2004 Chevy four-by-four. Wasn't what you'd call luxurious, but honey, it's what got us here to this valley. It was

7

worth every one of its 156,000 miles. It'd probably still run if we were able to get the gas."

I knew of the old truck. It sat behind our barn and housed the dogs that hung out at our place. It was a good place to keep warm in winter, and sometimes when I wanted to be by myself I'd go and shove out the strays and pretend I was driving up one of Grandma's roads, but I was younger then.

Today, after the story was told again, it grew quiet between us. I grew anxious to have her finish the story because it always ended up the same, and I needed to hear, wanted to hear. She was slow in the telling, but I knew she wanted to tell it, ponder on it and remember the other times as much as I hungered to hear it.

It has been eleven years since Grandma and Grandpa brought me to Stears Branch. You see, Grandma raised me. I wasn't yet six when we settled here. My Momma, Grandma says, was the prettiest woman who ever lived. She was supposed to have followed us, leaving right after she and my Daddy got our dog and their papers, but they never arrived.

"I begged them to come with us right then," Grandma said. "Told them wasn't anything or any old dog so important that they should risk staying behind."

She would recite the same words every time we came to the ribbon of gray. Every time we reached this part of the story, Grandma would dip into sadness at the loss of my Momma.

"It was probably my fault, you know," and she would always add, "I didn't make them listen. I thought they needed to do it on their own, make up their own minds, your Momma and Daddy."

Grandma stared at the road, like her staring could make the four-by-four give up its puppies and bring back my Momma, her little girl. She liked to imagine that Momma was up north somewhere, with Clays Ferry Bridge down, and her thinking no one able to get across the river. She prayed for Momma's safety every breakfast and every night, last thing before her and Grandpa crawled into bed. I can remember from when I was little, even up to when I was nearly grown, Grandma standing at the window, watching, listening in case my Momma and Daddy showed up, she could be the first one out the door, first one off the front porch to meet them.

Grandpa'd say, "You're wastin' your time, Janie. If she could have, if there was any chance of her making it, she'd already been here."

8

When I was eight, Grandpa put up markers for Momma and Daddy back behind the house in a little clearing beneath the apple trees where yellow flowers bloomed in spring. Two wooden crosses with their names clearly carved, Emily and Jonathan Baxter. He said he did it so they'd not be forgotten souls.

Grandma just said, "They'll never be forgotten," and she didn't speak to him, not a word, for nearly a month. And for a longer spell, seemed like months, it was quiet between them, with Grandpa stomping out the back door and Grandma inside crying.

Grandma shifted, stretched her bad leg, and a loose rock dropped over the side, collected with others on its way down, and when they all hit the bottom, lifted a cloud of dust.

"They dynamited out these hills. See the drill holes over there?" And she pointed to where drilling lines scarred the cliff sides every two feet. "It's how they made these roads straight. They were always coming up with ways to get through these hills."

"That what made the earth mad?" I asked.

"That's what a few crazies said."

"Grandpa said that's what you believed."

"Your Grandpa always thought he knew what I believed. He didn't know anything," and she said that with bitterness.

"He said you kept a scrapbook with dozens of newspaper stories about earthquakes and wars, and all that kind of stuff."

"I did do that. Funny, everyone thought it was California that was going to get it. I guess it did, but I didn't hear whether it fell off the side of the world like everyone predicted. Guess we were all sittin' on more fault lines than we could count. Caught all us common folks off guard." Grandma smiled at me with that.

"Course, your Grandpa made fun of me storing up heirloom seed, too, but that came in real handy when the time came. No, I wasn't nearly as weird as your Grandpa thought. Truth of the matter is, he must not have thought I was all that crazy, 'cause he came with me and you, now didn't he?"

It was true. We'd gotten away from the city just in time and well supplied. To hear Grandma tell it, she really didn't get strange. She'd just got this uneasy feeling. She told me she read books about end times, said she didn't know if any of them had an ounce of truth in them, but they scared her, nonetheless. And then, there was all that stuff in the Bible.

9

"We already passed 2012. Some believed the Lord was gonna come first and take all the good Christians out, so they didn't have to suffer the Tribulation. If he came sometime that year, he didn't find any worthy, 'cause I didn't hear of anybody being raptured."

Grandma laughed at that and picked up another stone, larger than the others and threw it into a sink hole between the two lanes. The sun had moved farther in the west, and I knew we needed to head back. Neither one of us liked walking the hills in the dark, but Grandma wasn't ready to move yet.

"Grandma?"

"I know, we gotta go. Sometimes I miss it."

"Old times?"

"Yeah, real beds and sheets. Computers. Microwaves. I wonder if anyone in the city, those that are left that is, still have electricity. They can keep their cell phones, but I think I'd kill for a diet Pepsi, with lots of ice."

"That'd taste good on a hot afternoon, huh?"

"Oh yes."

We were starting to get up, and out of the corner of my eye I thought I saw something moving in the north. "Grandma," I started to say, but she saw just as I did and pulled me by the arm flat against the ground. Its sound, a loud rumbling noise, bounced and echoed off the rock walls.

"What kind of vehicle is that?" I whispered.

"Shhh..." she warned.

The vehicle stopped right below us, in front of the four-foot wide crack. Dark smoke billowed from the double pipes that poked out from beneath it. I watched Grandma's face, stone cold and silent, as she watched the door open. I followed her eyes. It was a man, not old like Grandpa – not much older than me.

He looked into the hole, kicked at the jagged edge, then turned and looked at the cliff where we lay. His eyes studied the rock wall long and hard, straining to see what was at the cliff's edge. Grandma pressed my head harder as I pushed against her hand to see the stranger. She gave me a "Carrie, stop it" look, and I laid my head again into the sunburned dust. Against the pressure of her palm I turned my head sideways so I could see her face. She was as still as the stone beneath us.

What seemed like forever passed, and I heard the vehicle door slam.

10

The motor raced, revved. Grandma's hand let up and I raised my head in time to see the vehicle make an awkward U-turn, stirring dust and rocks as it sped back in the direction from where it came.

"Who was it?" I asked her.

"Don't know."

"You know everyone from the ridge."

"Wasn't from the ridge, or the hollow, or from anywhere around these parts."

"How can you be so sure?" I could still see the dark smoke, like a small dark swirling cloud in the distance.

She looked at me, perturbed that I questioned her. I rarely did, but this was different. I had to know, because if it came from somewhere else, they might know, might have heard what happened to the others further north. Last group of stragglers to wander into the hollow was eight years ago, but they didn't come from the north...they stayed for a season and then moved on. No one had come into our protected home place, not one that we knew of, since that time. I thought she might be happy, too.

"What do you supposed he was doing?" I asked.

"I don't know. I just wonder how he got here, unless they've rebuilt the bridge."

"Is that so bad?"

"Don't know. I suppose he could have come by the ferry. "

She got up, brushed the dust from her faded skirt. The sun had already dipped behind the western ridge. We ended up walking in the dark, and I wished we had the stranger's vehicle to take us home.

*****

"I'd started to worry about you two." Grandpa said.

"You had good reason," Grandma answered. She was in what Grandpa called "one of her moods."

"We saw a vehicle," I said.

"An '82 El Camino, yellow, only it looked about half rusted out in the back. Couldn't make out the tags if there were still any on it."

"There was a man...."

Grandpa interrupted, "How do you figure? If it was somebody in the surrounding territory how'd they get fuel, and if it was from the other side, how'd they get across the river?"

11

"Maybe they rebuilt the bridge," I said.

"Surely we'd a got word. I suppose they could have ferried over, just that you don't hear much of that. The ferry is a kind of dangerous place, isn't it?" Grandma asked.

Grandpa nodded.

"What do you suppose it means?" I asked, but they didn't answer. Then I said, laughing, "Grandma, I think you're over reacting."

"Don't speak to your Grandma that way," Grandpa's voice was raised.

It was the first time I could ever remember of him speaking harsh to me. We ate our boiled eggs and bread in silence. Grandma looked older, wore out, and at her nagging, Grandpa went out to check on things. He used to do it every night, checking on each of the outbuildings, the old truck, the fields in front, the woods around back, walking around the perimeter of what we called "our place," but in the last few years the two of them had quit worrying about interlopers. That had been a thing of the past, when they feared people were on the move, when they feared folks were hungry and desperate. Things had settled down, until today.

Chapter 2

Six days have gone by. I have marked my calendar above my bed. It has become a long line of days and weeks ever since Grandma taught me to mark time at age five. It was how we knew how long it has been since we came here. There are eleven years of marks.

Today is Sunday, day of rest. I can hear Grandpa's low snores and Grandma's voice soft with song rising with the sun into my dusty loft. It has been a long time since I heard her singing. Her voice had gotten lost somewhere between then and now...

"Many things about tomorrow, I don't seem to understand,
But I know who holds tomorrow..."

Her voice softens, lowers, forcing me to strain to hear the last words, then stops. I hear logs being thrown on the old rock hearth, the ashes stirred to bring up the fire and the smell of apple wood smoke. I hear her ladle water into the old pot and know that she is brewing roasted chicory, the bitter, coffee-flavored root that Grandpa digs every spring. Over the crackling new-born fire, her melody rises wordless, heavy, weary. I hear her shuffle and know she is limping. Her knees still hurt from last week's walk.

All week there have been silences, her anxious silence, his fearful silence, both pondering silences. Grandma has stopped her naggings and Grandpa his tricks. Grandpa made his way across the ridge, watched the ribbon of road two afternoons and saw nothing. He met with neighbors two miles on up the hollow, and then went one day's walk across the ridge to the northeast to inquire about strangers. Someone heard motors the week before, but no one knew anything. New lines among the old etched between Grandpa's and Grandma's brows.

After Grandpa reads from the big old Bible, the one that had been Grandma's mother's, after he reads from the Psalms, Grandma recites our lineage. She calls out the names of her grandfathers – Solomon, Joseph, and Arden, and then women of the family – my Momma, then Edith, my mother's dearly beloved grandma, her mother's great-great grandma, Meona. She recites the same stories, in the same tone of voice, solemn with its importance while holding the pearls, a reminder of the past – our only remaining treasure.

13

Afterwards, we sit on the porch peeling apples to dry for winter. She is showing me, as she does every time we peel apples, how her own grandma used to peel them, one long continuous line of thin peeling.

"It's important," she reminds me. "We gotta keep connected with those times: Grandma's dried apples, my own Mommy's smiles, and Papa's last Christmas, and your Momma's wedding."

"And, you can't forget how your eyes are blue like your great-grandma's, or forget pictures of the day you were born. Lord, I wish you could have seen them, how you sucked your thumb even back then."

They are pearls of remembrance that keep Grandma settled, and it is important to her that I set the stories to memory so when she is gone I won't forget. It has been years since she has gone on and on about the past, like she won't be here much longer. Tired or not, I think she is making too much of it all. That is why when I heard it first I should have told her. I heard the motor, but as soon as I had decided that's what I had to do, she heard and dropped her knife.

"You hear that?" she asks me.

"Uh-huh."

"Get into the house. I'll get Jim."

She hardly ever calls Grandpa by his given name, and while the words are coming, she is leaving, running around the back of the house.

"Get inside, I said," she says with a sternness that is unfamiliar.

I don't. I watch as the vehicle, the same yellow El Camino, comes barreling up our narrow lane, dust billowing out from behind it like a March tornado. Our house is the first in Stears Branch, and the cabin must have come as much of a surprise to him as his vehicle was to us. He brings it to a stop not twenty feet from the step where I sit. When the dust settles, I can see his face through the front window distorted by dirty film. I haven't seen many people other than the dozen or so who live near us, and certainly no man so near my own age.

He is crawling out the door when Grandpa comes with Grandma around the corner of the house holding a 12-gauge shotgun that hasn't had shells for in as long as I can remember. The boy stops, raises both hands above his head. He is lean with a scruff of red wind-blown hair that stands on end. The sun lights up his face and the scared, wild look in his eyes.

"Don't shoot," he calls.

14

Grandpa doesn't lower his gun, keeps the empty weapon sighted on the stranger.

"I've not got any weapon. I'm unarmed."

"How am I supposed to know that?" Grandpa calls.

"Look," the boy says. "Where'd I have it?"

His arms are still up in the air. He is dressed in a light shirt and jeans as wore out as any in the hollow.

"I'm gonna turn around so you can see I'm not hiding anything, so don't get spooked."

Slowly he moves away from the vehicle and turns around so Grandpa can see he's telling the truth. Grandpa lowers the gun.

"So, what you doin' in these parts with a vehicle, and where'd you come from, and where'd you find gas for that car?" Grandpa whirls one question after the other leaving no time for the stranger to speak.

"My name is Gary. The car's my uncle's. I'm trying to find my Daddy. His family was originally from these parts, and I thought he might have come back here."

"What's your daddy's name?"

"Gary Combs, Sr, Sir."

"I've never heard of him."

"Anyone else around here I can talk to?"

"If I don't know him, I suspect no one else around here does either. You'll not find him here."

"Grandpa, don't be so rude," I say from the porch. "We've not had word from the outside in forever. Grandpa, ask him to come on in."

"Carrie, get in the house."

"Grandpa, please. Grandma, talk to him. The stranger might know something about Momma or Daddy."

"I don't think so, honey," Grandma says. "He's too young, not much older than you."

"But what if he does?"

Grandpa stands with the gun to his side, one hand on his hip. The boy has lowered his hands, stuffs them in his pockets. The car is idling.

"Sir, I'm gonna turn the car off now. It's wasting my gas. Is that okay with you?"

Grandpa nods, and it's the same as inviting him in.

"Ma'am," he says to Grandma. "I'd appreciate a drink of water if you have enough to spare. I know there's been rationing, but I'd be willing to pay for a drink."

15

"Water's free," and she moves up the steps and into the house. I can hear her tipping the bucket, pouring water into a cup. She walks out, and her expression is hidden behind blank eyes. I try to see what she is thinking, but she doesn't want me to know, not me or the stranger, and I'm not sure Grandpa, if he is looking, can tell either. Grandma and Grandpa have become closed, and this stranger isn't going to get anything out of them at this rate. He walks too easy and self-assured to be entering enemy territory.

Grandma comes back out and hands the stranger the cup then steps back. Her arms are crossed over her chest. The stranger lets out a grunt of approval.

"This is the best tasting water I've had. It's sweet, like...well, can't really say. Just doesn't taste like the water from home."

"Spring water," Grandma says. She is a talker, but she is saying nothing, and I feel like someone has to say something nice to this stranger.

"Where's home?" I ask. I know Grandpa wants to know, too, but he just keeps staring wordless at the fellow. Grandma always said he was suspicious about most folks, and I can see it in his eyes now.

"Originally?"

I nod.

"From Lexington. Was born there. After the Tribulation, there wasn't much to keep folks going, so my Mom headed for her family's place over towards Ashland. Not as much backwash. My uncle was there with his family. Mom and Dad divorced a long time before the Tribulation. I was only three. I don't really remember him. I've been looking for my Dad ever since I was about fifteen."

"Tribulation?" Grandma asks.

"Yeah, that's what my Mom called it. I remember how scared everybody was. Anyway, water wasn't safe from all the flooding, so folks added Clorox to it. Food got scarce. Wasn't electricity for a long time. My Mom lost her job because the building she worked at was basically destroyed, and our house was condemned. There wasn't anywhere else to go. That's why we left."

We are all standing in front of the porch, the stranger with cup in hand, Grandpa with the gun, and Grandma with a mixed expression on her face. She's scared, and I can't say why...this guy doesn't have a thing to hurt us with that I can see.

Grandpa finally speaks up and asks, "So, what makes you think

16

your daddy's around these parts?"

"It's where my grandpa lived. They had land somewhere around here. I got word that folks were living in between the road and the mountains. I thought that maybe...just maybe, I'd find him."

"So, how come you left your momma to go chasing after a dad you didn't even know?" Grandma asked questions point blank sometimes. It didn't have to be none of her business for Grandma to ask.

"She died. Left me with my aunt and uncle and their kids. They had enough to deal with without having to take care of me. Plus, my uncle, well, I guess he knew how things were and all, with me needing to find kin. He told me to take one of his cars, just bring it back when I was done."

"How'd you get gas?"

"That's easy in Ashland."

"And in between here and there?"

"Carried it in the back," he says and motions with his thumb to the back of the El Camino. "On the other side of the river, and even on southeast of here, you can get gas if you got the money or something to trade for it."

I like the sound of the stranger's voice. It is not raspy as Grandpa's, not so...I can't really say, he just sounds more like the books Grandma used to read to me.

"You educated?" I ask.

Grandma says, "Carrie, you're being impolite." And I laugh right out loud in front of them all, because I don't know what impolite is if it's not holding a gun on a stranger or asking just as rude questions yourself. Grandpa is ready to take me to task, I can tell by his expression, when the fellow answers.

"Well, yes and no. I went all the way through elementary school in Lexington, then school kind of, well no one went to school for a while until things got cleaned up. When we were in Ashland, I went on through high school, finished by the time I was fifteen. Not many of us did, though Mom said it was important."

"Grandma taught me," I tell him, and he nods. "Grandpa, can't we just all sit on the porch? We've stood here forever."

Grandpa hesitates, and it's no secret that he isn't too happy about me inviting the stranger onto the front porch.

"That's okay," the stranger says. "Since you don't know anything about my Dad, I'll just try to get further in, if you don't mind me

17

crossing your property. I'd like to see if anyone's ever heard of him."

"Like I said before, if I haven't heard of him, I doubt anyone else around here has. I know this, he hasn't come through here since I've been here. Still, if that's what you want to do, I'm not gonna stop you. You can cross my property. Just make sure you leave when you're done."

"Thank you, Mister.....I don't think you told me your name."

"I didn't."

"We're the Kelsey's," I say. "We didn't mean to be rude. My name is Carrie, this is my Grandpa Jim, and my Grandma Janie. My Momma's married name was Baxter, Emily Baxter, and my Daddy's name was Jonathan. Before everything happened, we lived in Lexington. Have you ever heard of them?"

"I'm sorry, can't say that I have. But then, I was only nine when we lived there. My Mom might have, but then she's gone. Before she died, she still kept in touch with friends that stayed behind. They might know something about them. You never heard from them?"

"No," is all I say.

"When I get to Lexington, I'll see what I can find out, you know, what might have happened to them or where they went."

"I'd really appreciate it. We'd all appreciate it."

"Sure. Well then, I'll head on. How many folks live behind you guys?"

"Three families," Grandma says.

"Okay, about how far?"

"Not far," I say.

He nods and hands the cup to Grandma. Grandma takes it like it's a copperhead. She's scared of snakes.

"Thanks again for the water," he says, and then turns back to his car.

I want to say, "Stay. Stay just a little longer and tell me what happened to Lexington." I can't tell whether Grandma and Grandpa just don't want him around or if they really don't want to know.

How could they not want to know? Why not want to know? All the years that Grandma lived there, why not ask about some of her friends? Maybe the stranger has heard of just one. Maybe his mom's old friends knew Momma. There could be a link, someone we could find. I know Grandpa thinks they're dead. He says they are gone. He doesn't want to stir up old feelings. But Grandma, she believes. She

18

believes they are out there somewhere...and if she believes, then I can't figure out why she won't ask. 'What's wrong with you?' I want to scream at her. 'Our only hope to find your baby is getting in his car right now, and he's going to drive away, and you are not going to do one thing about it.'

The El Camino's engine starts, and the stranger is backing up, then moving to the path beside the house. He lifts a hand and smiles at me as he passes. I smile back. It's a tight squeeze between the woodpile and the apple trees, but he slips through, then all we can see is the billow of dust behind him. When the dust settles, the yellow El Camino has passed into the trees behind the house and out of sight.

Chapter 3

Grandma.

Carrie is asleep upstairs, but down in Jim's and my bed, there is an uneasy silence that doesn't permit sleep. The boy's coming has brought the past into the present. Most days, the present doesn't have time for the past, but tonight, after his coming, the past creeps into the now and keeps me awake.

Before the floods, there were quakes. We don't know what happened...not really...polar shift new-agers said, liberals said global warming, solar magnetic storms crushing the earth. I do know this one thing – we had quakes, then the water. People used to talk about how California was going to break off and slip into the ocean. Every time I heard of a quake out there, I was glad we were in the east...no earthquakes here, at least not in 200 years. And, while all of us were fretting over California's potential demise, thanking God we weren't there, Jim said us non-geological types were sitting right on the edge of catastrophe.

We were watching Thursday night TV when we felt the first tremor. I looked at Jim and said, "You feel that?" He nodded. We kept watching TV, and it came again. This time it was harder, and the pictures on the wall shook. Carrie's baby picture fell to the floor.

"I bet there was a wreck out back," I told Jim. "It felt like the time the guy hit the embankment. Remember? I thought it was an earthquake."

"It shook that hard, twice?"

"You're right." I got a scared, sick feeling then.

"We have earthquake insurance?"

I indicated that we did and went to the phone. I dialed Emily's number. It rang twice. I heard Emily's voice.

"Did you feel that?" I asked her.

"Yeah," she answered. "Scared Carrie to death, and the dog is nearly climbing the walls."

"The show we were watching has just been interrupted...you have the TV on?"

"We were about to go to bed."

20

"Turn it on, quick. Oh God, Emily, it *is* an earthquake."

I heard her tell Jonathan to turn on the TV. There was silence on her end, then she said, "Mom...it's all over the place."

"You guys get over here now."

I got off the phone. I remember how we sat watching. Could be major damage the newsman said...leave buildings higher than three stories, seek shelter with friends or relatives, or if nowhere to go, go to the nearest emergency shelter and he provided the addresses of the locations.

"Why'd you call them over here?" Jim asked.

"I want them near me if something is going to happen. She's all we have."

"This is probably the most we'll feel."

I still had this sinking feeling in my stomach. This wasn't going to be all we felt. I went into the extra bedroom, into the closet that was lined with boxes, my crazy closet as Jim liked to call it. He humored me with my bags of seeds, dried beans, dried milk, water purifier, and the rest of the things I thought were needed for emergencies.

"What are you doing in there?" he asked, his voice rising above the television.

I couldn't answer. My throat just closed up on me. *Was I over reacting? Was this just some minor tremor coloring my deep seated fears about the end of times?* Jim once told me I was watching too many movies about catastrophes, but until that day there'd never been another thing like that, at least not for us. All those folks in California, maybe they knew how to live with fear, always wondering, staying there all the same, but I couldn't. I called out to Jim, "Any word of California."

"Yeah, come here. Look at this."

I came out and watched as the live news reported from the west coast, talked about the tremors felt out there. They were talking about the significance of it happening at both places at once.

"What does he mean, both places?"

"Here in the southeast, the New Madrid fault stretching from Cairo, Illinois, on south, and at the San Andreas fault in California."

I heard Emily and Jonathan's car. They carried the little one in. She had fallen asleep on the way over.

"Put her in our room," I told Emily, and little tow-headed Carrie rose up sleepily and said, "Hey Grandma."

21

"You go back to sleep baby. Emily, lay her on my bed." When she came out, Jonathan, Jim, and I were all staring at the television. Tremors were still being felt all up and down the fault line that followed the Mississippi River.

"I'll be back in a couple of minutes," I told them.

"Where you going?" Jim asked.

"To get gas."

I walked out the back door and grabbed two gas cans. Down the street, at the Speedway, there were only a couple of stragglers left. It was after eleven p.m., and the attendant sat at his station with ear buds in. I filled up the car and two five-gallon containers.

At the counter, I asked, "You feel the tremors a little while ago?" I handed him my credit card.

"Huh?" he said, then removed the buds. He ran the card through the scanner and pressed in $98.52.

"You feel those tremors?" I asked again.

"Who didn't?"

"Funny, there's not much going on here. I'd have thought people would be filling up."

"Why?"

"Just precaution, I suppose. You know, like when there's a winter storm warning?"

"Well, you and the ones before you have been about the only ones with a fill-up. Kind of quiet tonight except for the shakes."

"Thanks."

He handed me back my card. On impulse I headed to the bank. There was a large crack in the foundation of the building, the north side plate glass window was cracked all the way down. I thought bank alarms should be going off, but all was quiet. One street light stood at an eschewed angle. I was relieved that the ATM machine worked, and I got all it would let me, the $500 a day limit. Folding the bills neatly, I tucked them into my wallet. There wasn't a soul to be seen, not a bird skittering across the parking lot, nothing. It felt like a ghost town already, and my heart trembled at the thought.

I was almost back to the house, had just passed through the last traffic light and approached a four-way stop when the earth trembled again, shook like there was no tomorrow. The lights from the corner gas station went out, all the street lights went dark, and all there was to be seen were my own headlights and the lights of the other car at the stop sign. Neither of us moved, our two beams of light crisscrossing each other with the shaking up and down by the tremor. The ground rolled beneath the car, tossing it like a small boat trying to ride out rough seas, and finally it stopped. The other car went through the intersection, then me. There were two cracks in the pavement a hundred or so yards ahead following the double yellow lines. It was dark. Electricity was out on our end of town.

Jim met me with a single beam of light when I stepped inside the door. "Took you long enough. Carrie's crying. Where are all the other flashlights?"

I went into the kitchen with Jim following me. He guided my way with his light he shone before me. I opened the lower door on the hutch and pulled out another flashlight.

"Oh my God," I said. The kitchen floor was scattered with broken dishes, pots, and glass.

"You think that's bad, look here," and he pointed the beam of light to the ceiling. There, where the ceiling and wall used to meet, was a four-inch wide gap and two cracks opened a foot downward.

"We better collect some water," I told him.

"You guys have a radio?" Jonathan asked.

"No. You need electric like with the TV," Jim said.

"In the little bedroom, second shelf of my closet, right there in front along with a pack of batteries," I said.

"Better pee now," I told Emily. "We may not have water much longer." She was holding Carrie who had stopped crying. "We're having an adventure," I told the five-year old. "You like adventures, right? After you go pee, how about you help Mommy find some candles?" She nodded and wiggled from her mother's hold.

Jim went after the five-gallon buckets from the garage. In the dark I pushed broken dishes to one side, reached for what pans were at hand, and began filling. I knew we'd need water, was half way surprised we still had any. I thought the pipes would have gone first, then I thought of the gas lines. The house took on a chill, the furnace having quit when the electric went off. *Check the pilot light – gas lines.*

"Jonathan," I called from the kitchen. "Can you put out the pilot light?"

Jim had just come in and at the same moment remembered the pilot light. "We got to turn off the gas now, in case the gas line ruptures." His face was drawn tight. I remember how pale he looked in the yellow beam of the flashlight. He ran down the basement steps, sounded more like he rolled down the steps. I heard the furnace door being removed, and was grateful that I didn't smell gas.

"Done." In the silence of the house, I could hear his whistle of breath release in time with mine.

"Over seven point six here," Jonathan called from the living room. "Office buildings and hotels collapsed in downtown Louisville. Worse in Owensboro and down the Ohio River into the Mississippi, all the way down into Tennessee. They say we can expect more here before dawn."

"Jim," I said. "We have to get out of here now."

For once he didn't laugh at me. Don't know what hit him, all the times he made fun of my doomsday survivalist stuff, but now he was ready to go.

Emily found candles, and she and Carrie listened to the radio by candlelight while Jonathan helped Jim and me pack the truck. Jonathan had already decided once we were packed, he and Emily would go by his dad's before heading out with us.

He called, talked to his father in quiet tones. "Pack the Bronco we'll all go together... I don't know."

I suspected his father had asked where we were planning to go. I mouthed "Jackson County."

He told his dad, and then nodded "yes" to me.

We packed most of my closet in the truck. Jonathan and Emily had things at their own place to fill their minivan, plus the dog.

I went over my list: dried beans, powered milk, yeast, rice, seeds, aspirin, toothbrushes, bandages, towels, batteries, needles, thread, blankets, sheets, paper, pencils, wire, and string. I gathered every piece of clothing I could find and stuffed them into black garbage bags. Jim said two five-gallon gas cans weren't enough if it was going to get as bad as I feared.

"We could have used a generator," he said. "Take out those books, they take up too much space."

"I'm taking Grandma's Bible, the children's books, and these boxes of crayons." I held up a box of pictures and our passports, "I'm packing these, too."

"Why those?"

"I don't know, but I don't want them lying around here if the house is ransacked."

24

"You act like we're never coming back."

"Not that. Just how much you think is going to be left when we get back, the way it looks now."

He agreed. He got things I hadn't thought of: coin collection, axe, knives, hammers, nails, tools, gun, shells. When we were done, the sky had just begun to lighten with the dawn. The tires were low to the ground beneath the heavy load.

We were thinking maybe we had acted too hasty when the third big quake hit. Down the street, two blocks over, there was an explosion that lit the sky, and within seconds black smoke mushroomed upward into the yellow sky. Gas lines, I thought, and all of us watched in horror. Other doors flew open, and our small neighborhood stood on their front steps in fear and disbelief. A water main broke just a hundred yards from our house and shot a geyser into the air. The earth trembled, shook so that the ground felt like an old Coney Island roller coaster shaking our senseless bodies against its wooden frame. Sirens began to sound, and I ran to my neighbor where she stood with her daughter. I hugged her, said goodbye. Jim locked and dead bolted the doors. It seemed a useless task as window facings pulled away from the brick façade.

"Come now, with us," I said to Emily.

"We got to get our things."

"What things?"

"The dog, our stuff. You know, like you got."

"There's no time now, honey."

"Jonathan's mom and dad," she said.

"Then let Carrie go with us. You follow. We got to get her out of here now."

"Mom, no. It's not as bad as you're making it."

The ground beneath us was still shaking, our very voices quivering with the earth's vibration

"Emily, please."

"We're wasting time here," Jim said.

Emily handed Carrie to me, and I handed her to Jim, who put her into the car.

"Where's the car seat?" Emily asked.

"No room," Jim said.

"At least buckle her in," Emily said.

"Emily, please come with us. I'm scared for you."

25

"Mom, we'll be okay. We'll meet you at the Athens-Boonesboro exit. Thirty minutes, no more."

"You don't have time to get there from here in 30 minutes, let alone stop by your house. It's dangerous. You don't have time."

"We can't just leave without his parents."

"Call them. Use the cell phone."

I heard Jonathan's voice above the spewing water. "We'll be at your place in less than an hour."

"Thirty minutes," I said.

Jonathan ignored me. "They're taking Carrie with them. Yeah, I know. You just have things ready. Okay, then."

"Meet us at your Grandma Kelsey's in Jackson County. Go straight there, right Jim?"

He nodded. We didn't know where else to go. It seemed like the safest place. Emily agreed.

"When will you get there?" I asked.

"Soon as we can."

"Hurry."

"We will."

"I can't leave you." I wrapped my arms around her crying.

"It's okay, Mom. You're going to scare Carrie. Remember, it's an adventure."

"No, it's not," I told her. "I love you. Do you hear me? I love you."

Emily leaned inside the car, hugged Carrie. "Now, you be good for your Grandma. We'll see you in just a little bit." She hugged the child again.

"Take care of her for me, Mom."

That's the last thing she ever said to me, the last words out of her mouth before she jumped into their mini-van and headed downtown.

26

Chapter 4

Carrie.

Grandpa is fit to be tied. The stranger has been in the hollow for two weeks now. He came back the same day as he showed up asking to sleep in the barn, and Grandma said she didn't think it was a good idea. Grandpa just said "No," and the fella left right then. He went back up to Harold and Jolie's. He's been there ever since. We've heard him in the car a couple of times, taking Jolie's children rides. He was here two days ago asking if he could leave his El Camino here.

Grandpa said, "Don't know as I see the need for you to do that."

The stranger asked us to call him Gary, then explained, "I'm running out all my gas with taking the children rides, and I'd be obliged if you'd let me tell them that you won't let me take it through the fields anymore. They'll believe that."

"I suppose I can agree to that. You can just move on back to Harold's place on foot straightaway," Grandpa said.

"Harold found a bee tree on Tuesday. Jolie's invited you all to come on to their place tomorrow evening and have a sample of the sweet cakes she's concocting. Harold's thinking I can tell you what is going on farther north. I've been telling him how there are plans started to building back the big bridge. The Thompsons and some of the folks from across the way will be showing up."

With that, Gary just turned around and walked off. Grandpa wanted to ask where he heard the news about the bridge and ask him how he got on this side without being bushwhacked. Under any other circumstances Grandpa wouldn't have given Gary the time of day, forbade us all from going. He'd already told me that I couldn't go over there, and if he caught me sneaking off to Jolie's, he'd whip me until I couldn't sit down. He's never whipped me, not once. I think this time he meant it.

We never made it to Jackson County. Grandpa said we were lucky to find this little deserted valley. Stears Branch was high enough in the hills it wasn't hit with the floods. There were old stone foundations all the way up the hollow, some little, some pretty big, and it's how we put up all the cabins back here. You could tell someone had tilled the

27

flats because the trees and rocks were cleared. Since there was no one here when we arrived, there wasn't anyone to tell us why they left. Grandma wondered if the ground was cursed.

It is a mile and a half back to Harold and Jolie's place. They are our closest neighbors. You can't see it from our house because of the trees. They stayed with us for a winter when they first came into this valley, having made their way north from the town that got flooded when the dam broke in and around London. They lost everything except the few things they grabbed as the waters rushed across and through every low lying place that lay dry since the Corp of Engineers made the reservoirs.

Grandpa and Harold found an old stone foundation farther up the hollow. Jolie already had one boy about four named Tommy, and she was expecting Kathy. There wasn't enough room in our house, so everyone that could pitched in, and they had a their own cabin before the next winter.

Grandma helped her with birthing Kathy. She's nearly ten now. Jolie has two more, so in all there are four children. Grandma says it's two too many.

For the most part, all of us here in this part of the world pretty much keep to ourselves, except for Jolie's children or when someone has killed a wild hog or something like news of rebuilding the bridge comes up. So, when we get to Jolie's, everyone from Stears Branch is there, that is except for Aries Pendleton, who is too old to make it. She hardly gets out at all, and Grandma says it won't be long until she'll be going on to her reward.

Besides Stears Branch, the folks from over the next ridge have come. Jolie has a house full. Outside are children I haven't seen since they were babies, and inside are babies I don't think I have ever seen. I've never seen so many folks in one place at one time, ever. It appears that everyone is all troubled about the bridge that Gary is talking about.

Jolie has out-done herself. The place never looked so clean. She says it is hard for her to keep up with four children and all the work you have to do when there are no modern conveniences, but truth is, she just doesn't like cleaning. She has made cakes with corn meal and honey, a sweet gooey concoction, and there is honey in the comb on the table and a pot of sassafras tea on the fire.

Jolie's littlest one, Moe, has sticky stuff all over the front of her blue dress. It's a hand-me-down. We don't throw nothing away here...

28

not anything. I've had coats made out of old quilts that Grandma cut the best parts out of and put together. Moe is wearing Kathy's dress. We're all careful with the things like cloth. It's hard to come by and hard work. Joey, Jolie's third child, is chewing on honeycomb, and I want to help myself to some of the sweet stuff, but also want to look my age. It's not like I'm a child.

Grandma nods greeting to Jolie. I know she notices how clean everything is, but she doesn't embarrass Jolie by gawking over it. She just says, "Things look real nice, Jolie."

"Thanks, Janie. This here guest of ours has made himself real useful. He and Harold found the bees last week and with it startin' to get cool, Harold thought it would be a good time to get them."

"Bring the bees back with you?" Grandpa asks. Harold nods his head proudly that he did.

"Put them in that hollowed out stump behind the house and put a top on it. Sure will be nice to have some bees close by instead of hunting all over creation for honey."

"You suppose they'll stay this time?" Grandma asks, and he shrugs. We only had luck with bees once, kept them a couple of years, and then out of the blue one spring they just swarmed off. Never did return.

Grandma nods to Gary.

"Hello, Mrs. Kelsey."

Grandpa is ignoring Gary.

I say, "Hi."

Gary says in a kind of husky voice, "Hi, Carrie."

I can feel my face get warm and Jolie is watching me with a big grin on her face. Grandpa and Grandma both stare at me with disapproving looks. I'm not sure what I'm supposed to say. I get off the hook because the Thompsons from the next place come through the door.

"Jim, Harold, Gary," Mr. Thompson says all in one word.

"Come in, come in," Jolie says reaching for Reva's hand in welcome.

I think Mr. and Mrs. Thompson are about the same age as Grandma and Grandpa. I'm not sure how they got to Kentucky. They came from a lot farther south. They had a son about thirteen years old when they came to the hollow, and he left about five years ago. He didn't get along with his dad and said there wasn't much to do around Stears Branch. One day he just up and left. Mr. Thompson acted like it wasn't nothing, but poor Reva stayed at our place two nights and two days.

29

Grandma says that Reva is a fragile woman. She's small and delicate with coffee and cream colored skin and a soft voice that sounds like a whisper.

When all that happened, with their son running off, Mr. Thompson came down to our house and after some words, took her home. I guess they've been okay since then. No one talks about the boy. His name was Frank, after his dad. Mr. Thompson never went after him, and he never came back. Grandma said it nearly grieved Reva to death.

"I stopped by Aries'," Mr. Thompson says. "She's interested in what's going on, too. Said she wants someone to stop by and let her know what this here boy has to tell us about the outside." He says all this like Gary isn't even in the room. "If we're not here too late, I'll go by there after we're finished."

"How you doing, Reva?" Jolie asks.

"Oh, can't say one way or the other. At my age, well...everything seems like a big job. Just about wore out with getting things ready for winter. It's comin' early you know."

The women from the other ridge agree. They are a strange brood with their dress and their hair. Grandma says they are Holiness women, calls them pious. Other than their clothes, dresses dropping past their knees and long sleeves, I think they look pretty much like the rest of us.

"Well, if there's anything we can do to help you out," Jolie says to Reva.

"That's real kind of you."

"You put up any apples yet?" Grandma asks.

"No, my heart just hasn't been in it the last couple of weeks. Should have already had them done by now. I just can't get over being tired all the time."

"Yeah, probably should have. It's starting to turn cold, and they won't dry when the frost starts falling every morning. We got a good crop this year. If you need, I can send some by Carrie."

"We'd appreciate it."

I didn't mind taking her a bag of apples. Mr. Thompson is no help at all around the house, just sits around whittling. He only raised half a garden this year, and it seemed like Reva did most of the work as it was, on that half garden. He'll be the death of her, Grandma says, and Grandpa agrees, but he never calls Mr. Thompson to task for it. Says it's none of his business.

"Carrie and I will maybe do some herb gathering tomorrow, and if we find some teas, we'll send those, too. That may help your energy a little. Would you like that?"

Reva nods. Grandma is the resident doctor. Not a doctor really, not a healer either. She can't stop blood from flowing, or stop the thrush, like some old timers used to do. She just knows about the plants that grow in the hollow, which ones perk you up, and which ones help you sleep or stop a cough. She gave Jolie some that was supposed to keep her from having so many kids, but it didn't half work, or else Jolie didn't take it, because she has a house full.

"Well, the night's not getting any younger, and I don't want to walk back late, so boy, if you got anything to tell us about the outside, tell us," Mr. Thompson says in a puffed-up voice with his southern accent.

"Harold, here, said you'd want to know about the bridge," Gary says.

"That, and more," I say.

He nods understanding before he continues.

"I read where they started doing the studies for the foundation work for the bridge. They're not replacing the upper one, that one snapped, but the way I understand it, a smaller one, probably off the lower cliffs. The river is still up from where it used to be, so they can't use the base of the old bridge that was at the bottom."

"I remember that one," Mr. Thompson says. "It crossed right down on the river and then the road wound up the side of the hill on both sides. I used to see it when I was driving my rig north."

"The interstate replaced it with the four-lane bridge at the top," Grandpa says.

"Six lanes," Gary corrects. "The one at the bottom, well, it's under water. The ferry crosses the river where it used to sit. Some engineers started plans, oh, maybe a year ago, to rebuild the bridge about a third of the way up. They will connect it to the old US 25 before it curves up and around to link into the big road."

"They have equipment for that?" Grandma asks.

"Sure," Gary says.

"What good is one bridge going to do without the road on either side?" she asks him.

"They're working on the road, too," he tells her. "They're taking part of the old road that led to the bottom and have already patched holes on the north side."

31

No one says anything. They just look at each other in silence. Finally, Mr. Thompson says what I think my grandparents are thinking, "So what's that mean...I mean, what about all of us. What is gonna happen after they get across?" There is fear in his voice.

"The road being rebuilt doesn't mean anything. It doesn't have to be bad," Harold says. "Could be good. You all know there are things we'd like to have, don't have no easy way of getting 'em here, no way of communicating with people out there," and he motions with his palms up indicating outside of Stears Branch.

"I like it the way it is," Mr. Thompson says.

"Well, I wouldn't mind having a little electricity, a little television, lights, dishwasher. You know, some of the things we used to have," Jolie says.

"Ice and diet Pepsi, right?" I say to Grandma and smile.

"They aren't everything," she snaps back to me. "Besides, they'd have to stretch new lines. It'll take a long time to accomplish all that, and that costs money, and where are we going to get that kind of money."

"It wouldn't cost you any money, at least not for the lines and poles. I'm sure there are investors. I don't know why someone hasn't come in here before now," Gary says. "For a long while they were afraid of the depot's contamination. I suspect you all were protected by the mountain."

"I heard it wiped out all of that town," Harold tells us, and the adults all nod.

"There have been officials coming in and checking every year, and I've heard it's been clean for the most part for at least two years. I understand people keep a watch for new leaks, but I came through that way on my way here, and I got here okay."

"Officials?" Mr. Thompson asks. "Officials of what?"

"The government."

"We're still the United States?" he asks.

Gary looks at us like we're from another planet.

"We really haven't had much news from outside," Grandma explains. "When it all happened..."

Jolie interrupts, "...whatever happened."

Grandma begins again, "When it all happened, whatever happened, we came here and were protected, found shelter. Not many folks got here, or if they got across the bridge before it snapped, didn't stay in this part of the country. And with the bridge being out and water being up, there wasn't anyone getting across. By the time the water went back down, well, I guess family thought we were dead."

"What she's saying," Grandpa, interrupts. "Once the batteries died, we didn't have word from the outside to amount to anything. Not who runs the government, who or what survived. We just did what we had to do for us to survive. Later, there didn't seem to be any need to disturb our peace by inviting anybody in. I'm sure there are other places just like this pocketed all over these hills, too small to be of any importance to anyone except ourselves."

"How'd you take care of yourselves?" Gary asks.

"We did what we had to do, learned to do things we didn't dream we'd ever need to learn to do," Grandma says.

Most nod agreement, but one of the women, a tall blond haired lady from two ridges over says, "Still, we're about to run out of it all, except for food we grow or hunt. We always have food we grow, but it seems like every dress or shirt we have is threadbare. Don't know what we'll do when the threads give way."

We all know what she means. Seems like we are one season away from wearing skins for pants in spite of Reva's cotton, and God-almighty, I don't wanna do that. If it's not wore-out, it's hand-woven and hand-made.

"Here, let me draw you a map of what it looks like on the outside," Gary says.

Jolie clears bowls and plates from the table and gives him a charred stick, "Go ahead and write on the table," she tells him.

He draws lines with the stick, indicates land and marks seas and rivers.

"What's that?" Mr. Thompson asks.

"It's called the Gulf of the Mississippi. They called it that because it used to be the Mississippi River. All the land above the Ohio River to here," he says pointing from the Ohio valley basin northward, "was flooded to begin with, right after the quakes." He moves his hand over a large portion of the left side of the map. "Here," and he motions with his hand, "stayed above water. The Kentucky River backed up, flowed backwards with the force of a tidal wave. It's what knocked out all the locks and bridges, docks, and shore-side houses all the way to here."

He touches a point on his map, and looks at me saying, "Lexington was spared the flooding when it came through – highest point in the

33

central part of the State. But it was cut off from both the north and the south, and to the east, and extended west to Versailles. The Great Lakes spilled their waters over the Ohio Valley all the way to Dry Ridge. For years central Kentucky was an island. It took two years for the water to begin to recede. It was tough then. I remember it."

"How many died?" Grandma asks.

"All those above this point, I'm sure. Wasn't enough warning for folks to get out of its path. I heard tell of roads being crammed with cars trying to get away from the quake zones, but there were a lot of parts of the country who weren't getting quakes. They didn't have a chance. They were sitting there watching their TVs while the earth wobbled and tipped the Great Lakes so their waters swallowed everything in their path in a matter of minutes. No warning."

"And what about here?" Grandpa pointed to the depot.

"Everyone between the river and the mountain on the south side and east, about twenty miles, died from nerve gas poisoning."

Grandpa shakes his head.

"What about the other side of this, what did you call it, the Gulf of the Mississippi?"

Gary nodded. "I don't know much about it, except each side set up its own, I guess you would call it, government, or disaster relief. It was a matter of communication logistics. Once communication was re-established, there didn't seem to be a need to combine the two. We've had the same leader on this side for about six years. The one before that died when I was fourteen."

"What about wars? Other countries?"

"Communications with them was slow, with every country trying to recover from their own catastrophe. No world conflict. There wasn't time for wars. All over the world people were like you, just trying to survive. You know places that were cold are hot now, and places that were hot are cold."

"What about the stock market?" asks one of the men. He is with the blond-haired lady from the other ridge.

"I'm not sure what you mean," Gary says to him.

"You know, who controls the money? Are there banks? What do you do for money?"

"There are banks. Some people barter. In fact, many barter for one thing or another; but, there is money."

"So what is the money backed by?" he asks again.

"Silver certificates. Paper money backed by silver, like a hundred years ago, and coins certified real. I have seen banks, but my family mostly barters, like services for stuff. "

"What's it look like?"

I watch Gary pull out a worn leather pouch from his back pocket. He opens it book style and pulls out two pieces of paper. We all take turns looking at it, except for Reva. There are numbers in each corner and a picture on one side.

"If the paper money isn't silver certificate, it won't spend," Gary says. "It has to say it right here," and he points to the place on the paper money.

"Looks the very same as I remember it. Looks exactly the same," Harold says to my Grandpa. "Wonder what happened to Fort Knox?"

If Gary knows, he doesn't answer. The adults agree that the money seems the same, and hands the bills back to Gary who puts it back into the pouch. On the other side of the pouch are pictures.

"Who are the pictures of?" I ask.

"My Mom," he says. "Here's one when she was young, and this here is my Dad, who I'm looking for." He hands the picture to Grandpa and Mr. Thompson, then asks, "Do either of you recognize him?"

They both say no.

"I suppose then, after I've helped Harold get in some more wood for winter, I'll head on my way. It'd be nice to just stay here," he looks at me as he says this, and then says, "but I got to find him."

I nod my understanding.

"Where do you think you'll go from here?" I ask.

"Probably north to Lexington to work for a while to replenish my funds and gas and to get some leads. I'll see if any of the old timers recognize him. I know where he worked when we lived there, worked a horse farm on the west side of town."

The talk of the map and the world to the north grows quiet. Children touch the map, wonder smearing charcoal markings of land masses and water, while the faces of adults hold one of two expressions.

Reva, who has remained silent, speaks up in her soft southern drawl, "What about down here?" she asks, touching the charcoal smeared peninsula below the new Mississippi Gulf.

"I haven't been down that far, Ma'am, but I have been told that part of it lies under water. It is hotter than it was before. The equator changed. Jolie said you raise cotton here, and I guess that's because of

35

the climate change. It's hotter now than it used to be here, more like where you came from, that right? So if the area you are asking about is not submerged, it's probably like a jungle."

Reva nods, and Mr. Thompson puts a hand on her shoulder. No words are exchanged, and I wonder if she thinks that is where her Frank went.

"It's getting late. I suspect we ought to head back down the road," Grandpa says, interrupting the solemnness of the moment.

"You haven't tried my honey cakes," Jolie says. "They're made with the corn meal you ground, fresh walnuts, and that fresh, wild honey."

"They do look good, but I don't think so," Grandma says.

I say, "Oh please," and Grandma looks at Grandpa who says okay.

Gary walks outside, and I take a cake and follow him. I can feel all eyes on my back. I can see with these eyes in the back of my head that Jolie is smiling and Grandpa is frowning.

"When you get to Lexington, will you do me a favor?" I ask.

"If I can."

"Will you ask around about my Momma and Daddy?"

"What did you say their names were?"

"Emily and Jonathan Baxter."

"Sure, I'll ask."

"And, if you find out anything, will you come back and tell me?"

He pauses for a minute looking at me straight-on with his blue eyes, then says, "Sure. It'd be easier to find something out if you had a picture of them. You have one?"

"I'll find one," I promise. "I'll see you have it before you leave. When do you think you will be leaving?"

"Well, I feel beholden to Harold and Jolie for their hospitality, and their boy, Tommy, doesn't do much to help around here. But, I suppose we'll be finished getting in enough wood in a week or so."

"You don't need to stick around for that," I hear Grandpa say behind my back. "If Harold needs help, we'll help him. We've always taken care of our own folks in the hollow."

Gary turns looking at Grandpa and says, "I'm sure you do. You have taken real good care of each other back here. I just feel like I owe him something, you know, for putting me up and all."

Grandpa ignores Gary's response and says to me, "Carrie, come now. We're leaving."

36

Grandma and I go down the steps first, Grandpa follows. I look back over my shoulder to where Gary stands on the porch. He is smiling at me, and I start to smile back, but then Grandpa is scowling.

"Maybe I'll see you again before I leave," Gary calls, "to get that picture of your momma and daddy."

I wave and say, "I'll find one." Grandpa gives me a rough push.

"That won't be necessary," Grandpa says to me.

"Why not?"

"Carrie, don't sass your Grandpa."

"Grandma, I'm not sassin', just asking."

"Sounds like sassin' to me," he says to my back.

It is dark on the way back. The low hanging trees hide the stars and the young moon from our path. Grandpa pushes past Grandma and me, and I step in wet leaves and mud.

"Shoot," I say.

Grandpa stops and turns, "Watch your mouth, young lady."

"Grandpa," I start to say.

"Listen, I've had about all I can take from you. You can shelve it right now, do you understand?"

I tell him I do. I don't though. I don't know what he's talking about. I don't understand how a picture of Momma and Daddy can get him so churned up, and I can't figure how one boy from the outside our hollow can stir up so much trouble.

We walk the rest of the way to the cabin in silence. Grandpa stomps on ahead. The cabin is dark, and inside the fire has died down to low embers. Grandpa keeps his back to Grandma and me when we come in. He has a stick and is stirring up the ashes in the fireplace. He adds two logs and pushes them to the back of the fireplace and against the glowing coals, then adds dry branches that ignite the coals into yellow flames. It is important to keep the fire going. We don't have many more matches, and we keep the embers going winter, summer, spring and fall. Grandpa knows how to restart a fire without matches, but it is a pain.

"Clean off your shoes," he says to me, still not turning around.

"Okay," and go back to the back step to scrape the caked-on dead leaves and mud off the bottom of the soft soles of my shoes. It is an endless task, so I remove them and set them just inside the door so the dogs won't drag off my only pair of shoes. The way Grandpa is acting tonight, he'd make me go all winter without fixing me new ones.

37

My hands are sticky with Jolie's honey cakes, and I wash them in cold water before climbing to the loft. At the top of the ladder I call down, "Grandma, good night."

"Sleep tight," she calls back to me.

And in our nightly routine, I call back to her, "Don't let the bed bugs bite."

"Love you, Carrie," she says to me.

"Love you, too, Grandma."

The loft is cold and drafty, and I pull off my dress and pull on my nightgown quickly. It is dark outside and very little light filters through the window. Crawling beneath the covers, I try to shake the image of Gary's face from my mind so I can go to sleep. Sleep is long in coming.

Chapter 5

It is cold and dry this morning. The sun is bright and Grandma tells Grandpa that it is a good day to gather.

"May be the last good day to do it, and I'm out of some things we'll need for winter. Plus I was thinking I should get Reva some ginseng to perk her up, and maybe stop in to see Aries to see if it's her heart acting up again."

Grandma looks up from her cup of chicory then back down into the steaming brown liquid before continuing, "It's about too late to get motherwort, but if we can find it, I imagine Aries can use some tonic to help get her through the winter. What you think, Jim?"

Grandpa ignores Grandma and speaks to me. "What are your plans?"

"Plans?" I ask trying to figure out his point.

"She's not got any plans but my plans. I intend to take her with me," Grandma says. "I'm not getting any younger. My bones get stiff on mornings like this, and someone's gotta learn to recognize the plants, what to dig."

"I was just asking. You didn't need to jump all over me."

"I was just explaining. She needs to know what to gather, and what they'll do. Lord, Jolie won't ever learn. Don't think any of her children are smart enough to learn it either."

"Grandma, that's not nice to say."

She looks at me and shrugs, "Any of them know how to read yet? Can you tell me that?"

"Tommy's not too bright, but Kathy's trying. So is Moe."

"They should all be reading by now. I want you to go with me today, understand?"

"Sure, Grandma. Have I ever not wanted to go?"

"I suppose not. We'll see if we can find motherwort for Aries," she repeats to me, as if she hadn't explained that once already. "Then we'll drop by to make her some tea before we head back, and some ginseng, though we'll have to dry it before giving it to Reva. She's likely to let it mold otherwise."

"What about coneflowers?" I ask.

"We should have already gotten them. Probably too late. What's

39

left, birds have gotten. But, if we see any, we'll gather the seed. You coming with us?" she asks Grandpa.

He shakes his head. "Think I'll help Harold get some more wood in. The sooner that Gary leaves the better."

"Grandpa, he hasn't done one thing to make you talk that way."

"Carrie, I warned you last night about talking back to me."

"I'm not talking back. I..."

"If I hear one more word about that boy, you'll stay up in your room instead of going with your Grandma." Grandpa sets his cup down with a thud. "And Janie, I don't want you to go anywhere near Harold and Jolie's place, do you understand?"

"You made yourself clear last night," Grandma says to him. "I'm not arguing with you on the point, so don't talk to me like I am."

"I just want you to understand..."

"I understand," Grandma says. "Carrie, you'll need more than that shirt. Go back up the ladder and get a jacket."

"It'll warm up."

"Until then, I don't want you getting sick. You'll wear the jacket."

I shrug. Both Grandma and Grandpa are acting touchier than need be. I get up from the table, and both of them are scowling at me. I haven't done anything wrong. I want to say that, but the mood they are in, it'll be called back-talking, and I don't want to be cooped up in the house today.

Grandma gathers her bags, two long floppy-handled, pocket style baskets made of woven reeds: one for roots and one for leaves and stalks. She carries them over her left shoulder, along with the walking stick that Grandpa made for her, in her right hand, to help her climb the steep hillsides.

Grandma brought aspirin and Tylenol, but we ran out the winter that Harold and Jolie were with us. Grandma studied her herb book all that winter, saying the names out loud, asking Grandpa if he ever heard his daddy talking about this or that, and would he know it if he saw it. That April we gathered sweet violet, peach bark, witch hazel, and squaw vine.

By the time we were here a full two years, Grandma's pantry was filled with all sorts of seeds and dried roots stored in reed baskets, or in little pots she made from creek bed clay. If we had a cough, she gave us tea from catnip. If Reva or Grandma got a case of the nerves, they drank lady slipper tea, and if any of us had a cold, Grandma made a tincture with coneflowers.

She gathered motherwort for Aries Pendleton last fall, and it kept her through the winter. So, today we will gather motherwort, if we can still find it this late. It's a good time to look for ginseng because of the berries, and that is what we will dig for Reva.

"Gives you energy," Grandma says to me again as we make our way across the grassy field, and I nod agreement. She tells me that every time we go to dig. Most of what we need today is in the woods, and at the far side of the field we turn and wave to Grandpa who stands watching from the back step. We both know why he is watching.

"Don't go back by Jolie's," he told Grandma for the tenth time before we left, and she said back to him as we went out the door, "Do you really think I will?"

They think it is not good for Gary and me to see each other.

"Which way, Grandma?"

"Up over this hill. I remember I saw ginseng earlier, some three-pronged ones last year just past the big walnut tree. Should have berries on it and easy to spot."

"Getting walnuts, too?"

"Don't feel like carrying them back. We'll send Grandpa after them later."

"Squirrels may have them all by then."

"Could be. Seems we have lots of reds this year. Pesky little things."

"I love them."

"Your Grandpa likes to eat them," she says. "You do, too. Watch for snakes. It's cool, but some may still be crawling."

We climb the steep hill in silence, our eyes scanning the ground for motherwort and the tell-tale signs of ginseng. We leave the berries on the ground to encourage regrowth, reseed for what we have taken. Not that we could rid the land of herbs, not our little group of folks in this hollow. Grandma says at one time people just about stripped these woods bare of roots, gathered every Lady Slipper and ginseng root they could dig. Sold them for money. Lady Slippers have replenished now, and when April gets here, the woods are covered in yellow and pink.

I follow Grandma towards the place of the big walnut. She is not her usual self. I can hear her ragged breathing. We stop several times for her to get her breath.

41

She says, "There, Carrie. See the motherwort over there? Here's my bag. Go get some of that. We need that." And while I go to where she has pointed, looking for the long slender stalks with delicate arrow-shaped leaves, she sits on a log that has fallen and made her a bench.

She is flushed. I haven't seen her face so red when we've walked in forever. She used to be fat, when we first came, and I remember her breathing back then. Thick and labored, Grandpa called it. But she's a little woman now, skinny and wiry from walking these hills, and she hasn't done like this in a very long time.

"Grandma?"

"Huh?"

"You okay?"

"Yeah, just got a little warm is all."

"Not that hot out. You sure you're okay?"

"Just catching my breath."

"It's not much further," I say.

"Just over this rise here, and maybe a quarter mile or so. No, it's not far."

"I thought so. You going to be able to make it?"

She gets up with that, face still flushed, climbing up the rest of the ridge. The tree she is talking about is on a little ways, beyond the hill we have just climbed, down the other side in a flat place. Despite her being out of breath and red faced, she doesn't stop again until we see Jolie's oldest and Gary under the walnut tree.

"Hey," Gary hollers over to us. I wave back.

A flying walnut whistles between Grandma and my head, and smacks the tree behind us.

Grandma stops, leans on her walking stick. "Tommy, good Lord." Then she whispers, "How'd they get here!"

"Same way as us, Grandma, except from the back side of the hill."

"I didn't hear them as we came up,"

"Me either."

"We're picking up walnuts," Tommy shouts at us.

"I can see that. How come you're at this tree?" Grandma asks.

"Everybody knows about this tree," Tommy says.

They have an old sack almost full, its thin fabric just about to split beneath the weight of the nuts.

"Looks to me like you're going to lose your day's work," I say.

"Yeah, got about as much as it's gonna hold," Gary says. "You gathering walnuts, too?"

"No. Digging roots."

"Roots?"

"Ginseng," I say. Grandma is scowling, red face and all. "Over there, see it? Grandma, give me the digger."

She gives me the hand-made root digger, an old rock-climbing tool her brother made a long time ago, shorter handle now, still pointed on one end to pull up rhizomes, the other end flat to dig the soft dirt around the roots.

"There," I say as I point to the plant. Gary and I head in that direction.

"Wait on me," Grandma hobbles along catching up to us.

I kneel and begin digging around the base of the plant, using my fingers when I can see the light beige root. "Manroot," I say holding up the four-pronged root.

"Wow," Gary says. He takes it from me, turns it in his hands, inspecting the wrinkled tuber. "This is ginseng?"

"Yeah. See there's a pretty good patch of it here."

He hands it back to me, and I put it in the root basket on Grandma's shoulder and begin digging another.

"How much do you think we need?" I ask Grandma.

She is beside me, on her knees too, working the leaf rich dirt with her hands. She has found a smaller piece, covers it back for another year's growth.

"Not much." Her voice is tense, and she looks up frequently from digging to where Gary has knelt, working to loosen and find a root.

"What's it for?" he asks.

"Energy," I tell him.

"How do you know that?"

"Everybody knows that. People have used this for centuries," holding up another large root.

"But how'd you know that?"

"Grandma taught me. She knows all about this stuff, right Grandma?"

Grandma looks up from her work, but doesn't say anything. She has clammed up again. I get up and move farther up the patch away from her. Gary follows.

"I don't think your grandparents like me," Gary says so Grandma can't hear.

43

"They're just not used to strangers," I say, trying to excuse their behavior.

"No, I'd say it's a little more than that. Your Grandpa tried to shoot me."

I start laughing so hard I lose my balance in the dried leaves. I attempt to right myself and look back towards Grandma. She looks up and I brush the leaves from my dress pretending to continue to dig.

"What's so funny?" Gary asks.

"Grandpa didn't have any shells, silly."

Gary looks at me in disbelief, and gives me a hand to steady me. His hand is strong and I hesitate in letting go. I see another five-pronged leaf a few yards away, rise, and move to the plant with purpose and begin digging.

"You kidding?"

I shake my head, and glance up to see if Grandma is listening. She is digging at the moment, and not paying attention to me.

"How do you get your meat then?" Gary asks.

"Grandpa made a bow and arrows. Just like Indians used. It's beautiful. And we set snares."

"Really?"

"Yeah, and I'm pretty good with a sling shot."

"I'm impressed, but I'm still pretty sure your grandparents don't like me. I bet your grandpa wanted a shell or two that day."

"Gary."

"Well, most folks from your hollow, they're friendly enough...just not your grandparents. They don't trust me."

"It's not that."

"What is it then?" He pauses before he says, "You?"

"Oh no, not me. I'm not that way. I trust you."

"That's not what I meant."

"We've got enough," Grandma calls from where she has been kneeling. "Come on, it's time to head back."

She stands and brushes off the dirt from her skirt.

"I'd like to talk to you again," Gary says softly.

"I'm not sure I should."

"Why? You don't want to?"

"No. I want to talk to you. Really."

"Try to get away tomorrow morning. Meet me."

"Where?"

44

"At Jolie's."

"Grandpa says I'm not to go over there. Not while you're there."

"Where then?"

"You know Mrs. Pendleton's place?"

"Kind of. Aries'?" he whispers. "The place behind the Thompson's?"

I nod. "Grandma is probably taking some motherwort over to her this afternoon. I'm to go with her."

"Motherwort?"

I laugh, "That's a lesson for another day."

He smiles, "When will you be at Aries', I mean, Mrs. Pendleton's?"

"Early afternoon," I whisper back.

"Carrie!" Grandma calls.

Tommy looks up from his walnuts. His hands are stained black from their hulls.

"Carrie, come on right now!"

"Coming, Grandma." I get up, put the roots in the pouch of my jacket, and turn to where Grandma is waiting.

Behind my back I hear him whisper, "Later."

"What were you two keeping secrets about?"

"Secrets? No one was keeping secrets."

"Then what were you whispering about?"

"I was telling him about roots and herbs."

"You had to whisper to tell him about that?"

"We weren't whispering. We just weren't yelling like Tommy would have. He's never heard of using roots for medicine."

"It's all we have," Grandma says.

"That's what I told him, and we weren't whispering."

We climb up and out of the flat place, climb the rise to the ridge that separates our house from the big walnut. I turn, and Tommy and Gary have disappeared, taking their walnuts and heading back the other way. Grandma turns and looks too, then looks at me.

"Your Grandpa isn't going to like this."

"I know. We couldn't help it."

"We should have turned around and went back the moment we saw them, before they saw us."

"They saw us first," I correct her. "We going to head back to Mrs. Pendleton's now?"

"We're going to go home first."

"It's longer that way."

45

"We're going to go home first," she repeats.

I want to talk to her about Gary, ask her about boys. I want to ask her why I feel all stirred inside when I see him. It's not a good time, but I'm wondering if there is going to be a good time before he leaves Stears Branch, and once he leaves, what will be the use? She told me about girl things when I was twelve, but never ever has she talked about boy things. Suddenly, I want to know about such things.

I am lagging behind, turning to look back across the hill we have just crested. Grandma stops, waits on me, and when we are face to face, she says, "We're not telling Grandpa anything about this morning. Understand?"

I understand fully well.

Chapter 6

We didn't get to Mrs. Pendleton's yesterday. We are going today. Just like Grandma warned, we didn't say a word to Grandpa about the walnut tree. He said, "You two were gone long enough." And Grandma didn't say anything. She just took what roots we had and spread them out on the table.

Then Grandpa said, "Well, to be gone all morning, you sure didn't come home with much." And to that she said, "Well, this is all we got." She was real prickly last night. Grandpa and I both let her alone.

This morning she gathers up her doctoring stuff – tinctures, herbs, and teas and packs them in the medicine bag. It hangs heavy on her shoulder, and we walk in silence. It takes a good half-hour to get back to Mrs. Pendleton's and that's if we walk a good clip and don't piddle at Jolie's. We move by Jolie's fast, neither of us saying a word to the other or even looking up at the house. None of them are up or stirring, not that it is that early. Grandma thinks that we've lost the whole day if we sleep in. We walk alongside of the corn field, beyond the stand of trees, and past the little trail that leads to Reva's. Another half of a mile past Reva's is Mrs. Pendleton's house. She likes Grandma, and as we come into sight we see her standing on the front porch waiting.

"I thought you'd be here yesterday."

"How'd you know that?" Grandma asks.

Aries hesitates and says Harold said to expect us, and with that Aries gives me a knowing look.

"Sorry Aries," Grandma says. "Took us a little longer than I thought, and we had a little problem."

"Wasn't that boy now, was it?"

"Who said anything about a boy," Grandma snaps.

"You know, Janie, that Gary boy that's staying over with Jolie."

Again, Grandma snaps at Aries, "No. That wasn't our problem."

Mrs. Pendleton ignores Grandma, gives me a knowing look and smiles a wide, wrinkled smile.

"Look at you, Carrie. I swear you're prettier every time I see you."

"Thanks, Mrs. Pendleton. You say that every time I come. I think it's because there aren't any other girls my age to compare me to."

"I'm not so old I don't remember pretty. Now you two come on in."

47

We climb the two stone steps and follow her into the little house. It is just two rooms, front door and back. It's smaller than one room in our house, but she has always said it was all she needed and as much house as she had energy to take care of.

"You got a good fire going, Aries," Grandma says.

"Gary came by yesterday afternoon and stoked it up, brought in some wood so I could keep it going. He's a good boy."

Grandma just grunts and goes into the kitchen. I hear the back door slam. From the back porch she calls in to us, "Well, the least he could have done was to fill your water barrel."

"I didn't even think to ask. He would've, you know. He's a good boy," she says it again, winking at me.

I hear the door squeak open, and Grandma comes back in. "Seems he could've seen." She is carrying a small kettle and hangs it over the fire.

"Carrie, Aries' barrel is looking a little green. Think we need to empty what's left in the bottom and clean it out. Think you can handle that?"

"You don't need to do such a thing," Aries says to Grandma. And then, says to me, "The young need to have a little fun. Not much excitement been going on around here. Time to have a little fun, that's what I think."

"She's here to help today."

"It's no problem at all, Mrs. Pendleton."

On the back porch is a big wooden barrel. It's not for rain water. That one sits on the other side beneath the corner of the roof that slopes down. It catches wash water. This one's for drinking, and it smells foul. I can hear Grandma inside apologizing for having not come sooner. I hear her say, "There's just been so much going on, but that's no excuse."

"This hollow sure has been hopping," I hear Mrs. Pendleton say. "You probably got your hands full."

I can't hear what Grandma says, but Mrs. Pendleton's old rattly laugh reaches out the door to where I am standing over the smelly barrel. I call from the back porch, "I'm gonna have to use a brush on this. You have one?"

"Hanging right there in front of you," Mrs. Pendleton calls back.

I look up, and it's right there in front of my face. Grandma would have said, if it was a snake it would have bit me. "Thanks," I call back.

48

I tip the barrel on its side to empty the last of its contents, then reach down inside as far as I can reach, scrubbing the thin layer of green. It smells like an old pond. "Grandma, this barrel stinks."

She comes out and inspects it. "Wish I had some Clorox. Just do the best you can."

I nod, and she goes back inside.

She tells Mrs. Pendleton, "No wonder you're not feeling so good. I'm surprised you don't have dysentery. I'm really sorry we haven't been back here sooner."

"Nah, Janie," I hear Mrs. Pendleton say. "The water's not what's got me down."

I lean all the way over and stick my head inside to reach the bottom. I just about gag with the smell. The bristles of the brush fill with long green filaments. I pull them off and throw them over on the flower bed, then brush some more.

"I'm going to go and get a couple buckets of water to rinse this out," I call inside the door, and with a bucket in each hand, I head back towards the creek.

Mrs. Pendleton has the best water of all of us. The creek that passes by our house forms a deep pool that flows out of the side of the rock behind Mrs. Pendleton's house. No matter how dry it gets, there's always water to have. One hot summer the creek about dried up down next to us, started turning as green as Mrs. Pendleton's barrel. But here, under this cliff, a steady stream poured, cool and sweet as a spring morning.

I fill one bucket, then the other, and walk the two hundred yards back to the house. I hear something in the woods, so I stop and scan the trees. We used to have problems with stray dogs turned wild. They were mean devils, and if they attacked, you weren't supposed to run. It was good I was never attacked, because I know I would have run. I am ready to run now, but I don't see anything...and for sure no dogs. What was there has either gone or is standing still, and right at that minute I think of Gary, so I smile in that direction and keep going.

The first rinse water I poured out of the barrel is crayon green. The second is better. I go back again to the spring, watching the trees the whole time. It must take fifteen minutes or more to fill the buckets and get back to the porch. The water runs clean this time. I roll the barrel back on its end and stick my head inside the door.

"Grandma, the barrel's clean. I'm going to go ahead and fill it up."

49

"Okay, honey."

As I jump off the back steps, I can hear Mrs. Pendleton call, "You don't have to do that honey. I'll get that boy to take care of it later."

I call over my shoulder, "It's okay, Mrs. Pendleton. I want to." I half run, half walk back into the trees.

"Hey," I hear him call. I don't need to look up to know who it is.

"I thought that was you."

"I thought you were coming yesterday. I waited half the afternoon for you."

"Yesterday you spooked Grandma," I say laughing.

He laughs, too.

"Yeah, I'm real scary."

"You sure are. Nobody knows what to make of you."

"It's just your grandma and grandpa that don't know what to make of me. No one else has any problems with me."

"True. I'm sorry for how they've been acting. They're nice. They really are."

"Yeah, I think you're right. Sure would be easier to talk to you though, if they trusted me."

I shrug and stretch to reach the bucket beneath the clear running water. Gary touches my arm and I shiver.

"You cold?"

"The water is like ice." I shake loose. "I'll have to do the filling. If Grandma doesn't hear me, she'll come looking, and then we will both pay," I say to him.

He nods and takes the extra bucket. When they're full, we walk back towards the house. He hands me the pail when we get to the edge of the trees. I walk the rest of the way to the barrel and pour the water in and head back to the spring. He walks in step beside me as soon as I am out of sight of the house.

"I'm gonna be heading out in a couple of days," he says.

I feel my heart quicken and get an anxious spot in my stomach. "Why?"

"Well, there's not much more to learn here. I mean, it's been a dead end so to speak."

"Oh."

"Well, not exactly."

We are at the water again, and he is holding the buckets. I feel my face get warm. For a few minutes we don't say anything. We fill the buckets, and this time he carries both buckets to the edge of the trees, then I take them on up to the porch. I scan the trees to see if I see him, and I can't. I wonder if he is waiting or whether he has gone back to Jolie's. I pour the water into the barrel. The barrel is a quarter of the way full. I can hear Grandma and Mrs. Pendleton talking. Their voices are soft and relaxed. The smell of tea floats outside. I take the back steps in one jump and run back towards cover. He is waiting.

"I'm gonna go to Lexington," he says, and I feel my heart beat even faster. "I'll look for word about your mom and dad."

"I'd be so grateful," I tell him. "How long do you think you'll be?"

"I dunno."

"I've never stopped wanting to find my Momma and Daddy."

"Yeah, I kind of know how you feel. I've felt that same way. Oh, I had my Mom, but I always wanted to find my Dad. Just seems like there is a hollow place inside."

"I know. Grandpa's just kind of set it in his mind that my Momma and Daddy are gone, and well, Grandma kept hoping, or least used to."

"It's been a long time, Carrie."

I like the way he says my name. It is sort of a husky whisper. No one here in Stears Branch says my name like that. It's either Grandma calling, or Grandpa fussing, or Tommy pestering. I can't remember how my parents called my name, and I feel myself grow sad.

"It's been too long. I hardly remember my Momma's face. I've got to look at the old pictures that Grandma brought with us, but the pictures are faded and creased. I'm scared she's just going to disappear from my memory if I don't find her soon."

"I doubt she'll just vanish."

"I've lost all my own memories. My memories of her now are Grandma's." I feel tears start, and I say real quick, "I gotta get back with this water."

I stand and pick up the buckets.

"Here, I'll carry them."

We walk in silence, and again I take the buckets at the trees' edge. I am walking slowly this time. The memory of my mother, her fading picture is in front of me.

"You about got that barrel full?" Grandma says, coming through the back door. She helps me pour one of the buckets into the barrel.

"You're kind of slow."

51

"They're heavy," I say.

"What's the matter?"

"Nothing."

"You just look like...like you lost your best friend."

"Sorry, I was just trying to remember Momma is all. It's getting harder."

She hugs my shoulder. "I'll help you finish up," she says.

"No. I'd just as soon be alone right now."

"Oh."

"I'm not meaning to be ugly, Grandma. I just have some thinking to do right now."

"It's okay, honey."

Talking to Gary has made me think of Momma. I feel sad and dishonest all at the same time. I told Grandma I wanted to be left alone, but I don't want to be alone. I want to be with Gary, and I have lied to my Grandma.

"What'd she say?" Gary asks.

"She doesn't know you're out here, if that's what you mean."

"Good."

"I lied to her," I tell him.

"What'd you say?"

"That I didn't want her help, and I wanted to be alone."

"What'd she say. She suspicious?"

"No," I snap back.

"So, you want me to leave you alone, too?"

"No," I say again, but this time without the anger.

At the edge of the spring, where the water fills a small clear pool lined with soft green moss before it runs on towards the creek, I sit and dip my feet. It is cold, and the late October sun has not reached through this patch of trees to warm the ground. I shiver. Gary sits beside me, puts his hand on my shoulder. His touch heats the cold.

"How old are you?" he asks

"Sixteen. I'll be seventeen in January."

"I turned nineteen last May."

It sounds old, but not old. He moves closer. I am staring down into the water, and he is looking at my face. I watch him from my side vision without moving my face or eyes towards him. I cannot look at him straight on now, and I don't know why.

"You're real pretty," he says.

"Sure," I say.

"No, you really are. I've seen lots of girls, and you're very pretty. Prettiest, I'd say."

"Really?"

"Yeah. You've got just a few freckles, and your hair is like, well ...like sunshine, and your eyes are the prettiest blue I've ever beheld."

"Yeah," I say and smile. I am still looking at the water.

"No, I'm serious."

Again, I say, "Yeah."

"You ever been kissed?"

I swallow hard, then say, "Sure, Grandma kisses me every day, and most days Grandpa, too."

"No, I mean have you been kissed by a boy?"

"Like sure...who, Tommy?"

"Yeah, like Tommy."

"No way," I say laughing.

"He's about your age."

"He's about five from my perspective."

"Well, yeah, I guess you're right. I just thought he'd be the natural one for you to hook up with if you stayed here in the hollow."

"I've never considered being with anyone, and especially not Tommy," I say laughing, and then I look up at him. His eyes are steel gray in the sunless creek's edge. He looks real serious, and then breaks into a grin and laughs with me. He moves closer to me, his face just inches from mine. I think he is going to lean over and kiss me, but then I hear Grandma's voice from the back porch. She is calling. Gary's face gets white, and he stands.

"If she finds me with you, I'll never get to see you."

"When are you leaving?"

"I'll talk to you later. I'll keep watch on your house and when I can get a chance I'll meet you, okay?"

I shake my head, and pick up the buckets. He is gone before I can say yes. I slip my leather sandals on, the ones that Grandpa made for me, and head back towards the clearing of Mrs. Pendleton's house.

"I was beginning to wonder if you were okay," Grandma says. She has come into the woods to meet me. I avoid looking back to see if Gary is out of sight.

"I'm okay," I say.

"You sure?"

"I'm sure."

"You haven't done much damage in filling this barrel."

"I know, but it's big."

"Here, I'll carry one of those. Won't take quite so long if I help."

Mrs. Pendleton is standing on the back porch. She watches me with curious eyes and scans the trees behind us.

"I was thinking you got lost," she says to me.

"Nah, just taking my time."

"I can see that," she says laughing, and then looks towards the trees again. "I sure appreciate you two's work."

"Two?" I can feel panic rise from my belly to my heart, and then on to my face.

"You and your Grandma."

"Oh, yeah," I say and dump my bucket into the barrel.

"Lord, this water smells good, Janie."

"Your barrel was in pretty bad shape," Grandma says.

"Well, Carrie, you did a good job."

"I want to get another couple of buckets before we leave," I say.

"Oh, this is enough for now. You can come back in a day or two if your Grandma will let you. You look worn out now."

"Yeah, I kind of feel that way, but I've no good reason to. Like Grandma says, I just need to ignore it."

"Well, your Grandma is a pretty good doctor and all, but not sure she is right about everything."

"I wish you'd take my doctoring a little more serious, Aries. We'll come back in a day or two to see how you're feeling, okay?"

"I'd like that for sure, as long as you bring Carrie with you."

"If you want me to," I say, "and if Grandma says it is okay."

Grandma laughs and promises I can come along.

The walk home is as silent as our coming, but this time it is my silence. Reva is out hanging clothes on the line, brown home-sewn pants, a faded dress, and dish towels. Cotton grows here now, and up beside Reva's we all grow a little patch each year. It was Reva who somehow had the sense to bring cotton seed. It was Reva who showed us how to plant, raise, pick and clean cotton, and it was Reva who showed us how to spin thread. It was slow, hard work, but we learned.

All our making do with what know-how we brought with us is what has kept us going. And all our making do is what makes me nervous about Gary, with him being where everything is store bought like before. I think I must look pretty pitiful beside the girls he's seen, despite what he told me about being pretty. Just thinking about what he said makes my face hot, and I look the other direction so that Grandma can't see the pink on my cheeks. To think, he almost kissed me and would have if Grandma hadn't hollered, and I feel disappointed. God, if Grandma had caught us, I'd be dead.

We pass Jolie's, and the kids are out playing. Moe runs to meet us. Her brother, Joey, throws a dirt clod at her and almost hits Grandma. He ducks behind the house quicker than a snake. Moe hollers at her mom, but Jolie must be inside working on dinner because we can't see a sign of her anywhere. I don't see Tommy either.

"Hi, Grandma Janie," Moe calls to Grandma.

"Hi, sweetie. What you doing out this morning?"

"It's not morning no more. Can Carrie come over and play?"

"I don't think that would be a good idea."

Grandma looks over at me, and I wave at Moe. She is only six years old, and she looks up to me more than the others. When I go over, I work with her and Joey on letters trying to help them learn to read and do numbers. Jolie doesn't put a whole lot of stock in book learning, at least not here in Stears Branch. She always says "What's the use? Where they gonna use it?"

"Maybe Grandma will let me come over tomorrow. We can work on writing again."

"Not sure that's a good idea. They've got company, you know."

"Yeah, I forgot," I lie.

"Company?" Moe asks with a confused look on her face.

"Yeah. That boy that's staying with you," Grandma says.

"Oh, he's not company no more, Grandma Janie." All Jolie's children claim Grandma as their own.

"Well, don't think it would be a good idea."

"Maybe later," I tell Moe, and that seems to be enough to please her. She turns and heads back to her house. I see Tommy at the barn. He is by himself, and I wave. He waves back.

"Why can't I come by and work with Jolie's kids tomorrow?" I ask when we have passed the house and barn.

"I don't think your Grandpa will allow it."

"You can tell him it's okay."

"Not sure I will allow it either, missy."

"He's probably going to be leaving pretty soon."

55

"And how do you know that?"

"Don't know for sure. Just figured he's getting tired of it here."

"You do, do you?"

"Yeah."

"He just might want to stay here. How'd you feel about that?"

"No, he wouldn't want to stay around here. Why would he?"

Grandma doesn't answer that one. She just grumbles and picks up her pace. I can see the stand of trees in our back yard, the wooden crosses that rise beneath them. I sigh and wonder if I will ever know what happened to Momma and Daddy. If Grandma's paying attention to my sighs, I can't tell. She just looks ahead. I can see Grandpa next to the barn. He's sharpening the axe. It's getting past time to bring in winter wood. Probably should have already had it all done. We have a cord or so to cut before we'll have enough to last through winter. I think he's getting too old to do it by himself, but you can't tell him that. Sometimes he looks like he is a hundred years old.

Chapter 7

Grandma cooked up sweet potatoes and greens for supper, mixed with scrambled duck eggs. I set the table for three. Chicory and collard greens smells mingle in the air. I love greens, and Grandma has always said that was a good thing – it keeps the blood strong. The soil here is sandy, and it grows good collards, but you have to wash them until your hands wrinkle to get all the sand off the leaves, elsewise they aren't fit to eat with grit in your teeth. I washed them tonight, long and hard, and my hands are green from the stain.

We will probably only have fresh greens straight from the garden a couple of more times before a hard freeze gets them and we have to bring them in, then it will be potatoes, squash, and dried beans for the winter. I hope Grandpa kills a good size deer this fall. We could get along without it, with the duck and fish that are plentiful in the creek, but venison is better.

"How's Aries?" Grandpa asks across the table after I've said grace.

"She's got something made her pretty sick," Grandma tells him. "Probably from bad water."

"Whatta you mean, bad water? She's got the spring."

"Her barrel was the greenest I'd ever seen it."

"This time of year?"

"Well, I can't remember when any of us has been back to help clean it out. Carrie did it today."

"Hmm," he says and spoons a big bite of potato into his mouth. "I'd thought Jolie's kids would've cleaned it out."

"They don't help Jolie," I say, and Grandpa nods agreement.

"Why'd Jolie not stop in to check on her?"

"Probably basking too much in what's going on in her own house."

All of us know what she means. That sets Grandpa off into a bad humor. Talking of Gary, even without speaking his name, does that.

"I'll be glad when that piece of trouble leaves," he says.

"Jim, I can't rightly say that he's a piece of trouble. He's not done a thing to earn that title," Grandma says. I hold my breath and wait for the explosion.

"Well, I do, and things haven't been the same since that yellow El Camino made its way down the road."

57

"I don't know that you can name one thing the boy has done to warrant your ire."

"Who's side are you on?" Grandpa bellows, jerking his head up to glare at Grandma.

"There's no sides to take, Jim. I think Carrie is right, you're making too much of all of this."

"I think that you need to keep that kind of talk to yourself."

His voice goes quiet when he says that, and I think he sounds dangerous. I am wondering what Mrs. Pendleton has said to shift Grandma's opinion.

"Aries needs me to go back tomorrow."

"You're not going back tomorrow. We got enough to do right here."

"I need to see if her diarrhea has cleared up."

"I don't see why she can't take care of herself."

"She's over ninety years old." Grandma eyes him hard. "I just hope there's someone around when I'm ninety to help me out. It sure as hell won't be you with your attitude."

Grandpa scoots his chair out and walks out the door. Grandma gets up and begins clearing off the table, banging the wooden plates in the dishpan. Getting up behind her I scrape leftovers into the slop bowl and go out back to feed the dogs. When I come back in Grandma has quit slamming pots, and water is soaking in the potato skillet. Grandma gets one of her books from the shelf and pulls a chair close by the fire to read. I go to the ladder and climb half-way up.

"Grandma, I'm going on up to bed."

She looks up from her book, "Already?"

"Uh-huh."

"You feeling sick?"

"Nah, just feeling a little tired, I guess."

"Tired?"

"I must have carried a dozen buckets at Mrs. Pendleton's."

"That's stretching it a bit, but you did carry quite a few. Didn't think it would make you feel tired enough to go to bed quite so early. Grandpa's tirades wear you out, too?"

I smile. Looking down at her white head, her face glowing yellow from the fire beside her, she's got "worried" written all over her face. I want to tell her that I'm not tired, I'm just mixed up, but I don't want to put any more worry lines on her face. I just want to climb down these rungs and tell her I think I'm falling in love, and I got to spend some time thinking about what that means. I always heard them talk about love, loving each other, and my Momma and Daddy being in love. I'm trying to figure it out for me. But I can't tell her. She'll say I haven't known the boy long enough to be in love, and then she'll tell Grandpa. He'll say I don't know anything about being in love, and that will be the end of that.

"I'm feeling fine, Grandma, really. That barrel cleaning just done me in."

"Well, you won't have to do it tomorrow," She laughs. "We won't even have to go tomorrow if you aren't feeling well. We can wait and go back in a couple of days."

"No!" I almost shout at her. She looks up at me startled. I take a deep breath, then more quietly say, "No, I should be fine tomorrow, and you know Mrs. Pendleton didn't look too good today. I'd never forgive myself if something happened to her. You know what I mean, Grandma?" And Grandma looks at me with narrowed eyes and nods that she does.

"Goodnight then, honey,"

With that, Grandma turns back to her book. I watch her for a second more before climbing the rest of the way up to the loft. Being deceitful doesn't feel good.

Chapter 8

Morning comes, and I don't have any more worked out in my mind than I did last night. I hoped sleep would give me some reason to know why I was feeling the way I did. I dreamed about Gary all night long…woke up feeling my face hot with the thought of him.

From downstairs I hear Grandpa grumbling about something. Even though I can't make out what he is saying, I have a pretty good idea what it is about. He's going to be the death of me. And if he doesn't kill me, I'm not so sure the constant worry is not going to be the death of him. I renew my vow: I won't say a thing in Gary's defense. I climb down the ladder already dressed. Grandma is at the sink, and I ask if I can help her finish the mush.

"You're a good help. Use the last of that jar on the right."

I take down the jar and get one of the wooden spoons. I add the cornmeal in a slow, steady stream into the boiling water so it doesn't clump, then stir with my other hand as fast as I can. The fire feels good against my legs. It is cold in the house.

"Frosted again this morning," Grandpa says. He is drinking his cup of chicory, watching me, and I pretend I don't know.

"Heavy?" Grandma asks.

"Bad enough that you'll need to get the rest of the greens in today."

"And you'll need to dig the rest of the potatoes."

"That's pretty much done."

"Both the sweets and the whites?"

"Uh-huh." Then to my back, "You're not saying much this morning."

"Not too much to say."

"That's pretty unusual for you. You'll need to help Grandma get the rest of the collards in."

"I will."

"You've not been doing much around here lately, kind of distracted," he says.

I turn around and look at Grandma, because that's not true. I wait for her to defend me, and she does.

"Jim, you don't know what you're talking about. She's always a good helper, and it's no different the last few weeks. I can't believe you'd even say that, I really can't. What's gotten into you?"

60

"All I said was she's not been herself."

I want to turn around and say, "Who's not been himself?" but I think better of it.

"No, that's not what you said."

Grandpa grumbles something under his breath that I can't make out. I got this sick feeling that everything around here is just about to explode, like it did when Grandpa put up the crosses. We all eat our mush in silence. When Grandpa finishes up, he pushes his bowl to the center of the table, gets up, and walks out the door without even a word or a nod. Grandma doesn't say anything about it. I want her to fuss at him and make it like it used to be.

"Grandma?" She looks up at me.

"What honey?"

"Can we go through some of the old pictures?"

"Whatever for?"

"I want to see the pictures of Momma."

"Maybe tonight."

"Can't we do it this morning?"

"We've got work to do this morning. I feel bad enough that we aren't going to get back to Aries' until tomorrow at best, and if we don't get what's left of the garden in today, we won't get there tomorrow."

"How long will it take?"

"The pictures or the garden work?"

"The pictures."

"Carrie, I don't understand what the rush is about."

"That boy," I say, then say his name, "Gary. He's leaving soon, and he promised to take a picture of Momma with him to see if he can find out about her."

"Carrie," and she sighs as she says my name.

"Grandma, don't you understand. I can hardly remember her anymore. It seems like a thousand years ago, and I don't remember. I only have your memories, and mine are disappearing. I can't let them disappear. Gary can help."

"Is that what he says?" Her voice sounds hard.

"Huh?" I ask, more in response to her tone than her question.

"You know what I mean," she says again, and I feel like I am caught.

"Back at Jolie's, he said if I got him a picture of Momma and Daddy, he would see if he could find them. He'll be leaving soon, and I won't have another chance."

61

"He was just telling you that just to get your..."

"What are you saying?"

Grandma looks away, doesn't look straight at me, sighs and says, "All right, say he is willing to help you. If he is telling the truth about the bridge and road, you'll have plenty of chances of your own."

"Like when the bridge is done, Grandpa is going to up and let me go looking for Momma?"

"I don't like that tone."

"Grandma, please."

"When do you plan to give him your mother's picture?"

"I don't know. I never see him," I lie.

"Uh-huh." I don't think she believes me. "What do you think your Grandpa'd say if you asked him?"

"That's easy, 'no'. And I don't want him to know we are going through pictures."

"So you want me to go against what you know he would say?"

"No, I don't want you to go against Grandpa. Just convince him."

She laughs at that and gets up from the table. Just then Grandpa walks in.

"You two still in here?" he asks.

"We're moving," she tells him. Her voice has a knife-sharp edge, and I really don't think it has to do with me.

"Well, the day isn't getting any younger, you know, and Carrie will have a lot of greens to wash."

"We don't wash them when we store them for winter," Grandma says and goes into the pantry.

"What's gotten into you?" he asks Grandma.

"Nothing," the voice comes from the pantry.

Grandpa looks at me and I shrug. "What'd you say to upset her?"

"Nothing."

When Grandma comes out, she is carrying a bag for greens. She doesn't look at me or Grandpa, just says, "We're wasting time."

The air outside is cold, colder than most Octobers. I have put on my sweater and the chill steals right through. The sky is a cold blue and the trees, red and yellow and brown, stand in bright silhouette against the blue horizon. Jolie's house is hidden by the autumn colors, and this morning it might as well be a million miles away.

"Come on," Grandma says again, and I follow her down the back stoop, three steps behind her until we pass the barn and into the garden.

62

Brown-striped stalks of corn stand in long rows. Lonely remnants of pole beans hang waiting to be pulled to save the seed. There is a row of wild lettuce, the last of the cool season. It has grown too tall and too tough to eat. *I will gather the seeds from its flowering tops.* The collards stand strong against the frosts of the last two days. Grandpa is right. We need to get it today or we will lose the rest of the crop. In the root cellar it will keep for four weeks or more. It will be the last of our fresh green vegetables, and we will eat every last leaf. None of it will go to waste.

Grandma motions me to the row next to her, and we pull by the roots the deep green leaves, shake them free from clinging sand in the frost-filled air before tying in bundles and putting them in our bags. There is enough to share.

"Grandma, let's take a couple of messes to Aries this afternoon.

"Think not," she says.

"There's more than we can eat before it goes bad."

"Not today, Carrie."

"I'm sure it would help Reva's blood, too; get it up and strong before the cold sets in."

"You've taken up doctoring now?"

"No," I say, raising up from my row. She is bowed before me over her row. She doesn't stop, doesn't turn, doesn't say anything more. I return to my row. When she gets to the end of hers, she turns and heads back. When we get shoulder to shoulder she stops and raises up.

"Carrie," she says. "I'm scared."

"What you got to be scared of?"

"I don't like the way I feel about what's going on in our hollow, and I fear things are going to change, and not for the good. Not my good."

Grandma's face is ashen and lined. Evidence of tears has streaked her cheeks.

"What you have to be scared of?"

"You."

"Grandma, I don't understand."

"No, I don't suppose you do. How could you. You've been here nearly all your life and been sheltered from everything on the outside. Now the outside comes barreling in, and all you can think about is some wild red-headed boy."

"His name is Gary, Grandma, and he isn't no wild boy."

"Carrie, you don't have a clue what a wild boy is."

63

"And what makes you think he's the only thing I'm thinking about?"

"I'm not blind. It's in your eyes, girl. Where was you planning on meeting him?"

Before I can deny it, she bends over the row and moves on. I am standing from behind, watching her stooped shoulders. I am torn in half. I have loved this lady my whole life, and she has kept me safe for all of it. Now she is an un-giving wall of resistance.

"Grandma, it is beyond me why you are not helping to find Momma."

"Your Momma and Daddy are dead, Carrie."

Her words slap me, slap me harder than her cold wet hand could have. I feel the stinging of tears in my eyes. I rise and run from the garden, away from her and the world she is binding me to. I don't look back, and she doesn't chase me. I run past the corn and past the barn. Grandpa raises up from his tasks and hollers, but I don't answer. I run up into the trees, up the steep hillside. I run until I can run no longer, my breath ragged in my chest, cold air burning my lungs. When I get to the walnut tree I fall, fall onto its leaf-covered roots. The ground is chilly and damp, but I don't care. Everything that has sustained me for eleven years has let go and let me down.

I cry.

"You okay?"

I know his voice, and I wonder how he found me. I don't want him to see me crying.

"What happened?" he asks.

"Nothing."

"It's not nothing."

He kneels down beside me, his face close to mine. His hands are on my shoulders, and he pulls me to his chest.

When I am rid of the tears, when the front of his shirt has taken their wetness, I look up into his face. It is marked with worry.

"You okay?" he asks again.

I nod wordlessly. His embrace does not loosen, and he is warm against me. He has been chewing on a sassafras twig, and his breath is sweet. I focus on his mouth; his teeth are white. I feel him shift, move closer, feel that sweet breath upon my cheek, and then his lips, gently pressed against the line of my jaw moving slowly until reaching my own mouth. An urgency rises up between us, and I press back, not the goodnight kisses from Grandpa, but a driven push against his partially parted lips. I can feel his hands move from my shoulders to my back, pulling into a tightness that will not let me go. I do not want it to let me go. When it is over, when his face moves away from mine, I lean into him wanting more.

"Wait," he says.

"What?"

"I have to tell you. I'm leaving."

I feel my heart sink, the momentary elation of new sensations vanish.

"Why?"

"Carrie, go with me."

"I can't."

"Yes, you can."

"What about Grandma, my Grandpa?"

"Carrie, I'll bring you back."

If I leave this place, I will never come back. I can never come back. Just like Grandma predicted. It will all be different. Nothing will be the same. All things will be changed.

"Carrie." There is pleading in his voice.

Gary leans again into me, takes my face into his hands, looks hard into my eyes. I can't hold his gaze. I look away at the lonely manroot, it's yellowing leaves, berries already fallen to the ground. He pulls my face back towards his, holds my face with the pressure of his lips on mine and moves to my neck and finally pulls at the sweater so his lips touch my shoulder. The shimmering inside frightens me, and I push away.

He hesitates.

"I'm sorry," I say.

"Carrie, I think I love you."

"You barely know me."

"I thought you felt the same way."

"I think…it is so confusing. I do."

"Then come with me."

Gary moves back, is sitting on his knees, both hands holding mine, his face pleading as much as his words.

"Where are you going?" I ask.

"North. I'll help you search for your parents."

"I can't."

"I don't understand."

"What about my grandparents?" I ask again.

"There's nothing for you here."

"They're here."

"Two days from now, after midnight. Shortly before the moon sets, when it is dark. Can you get out without being heard?"

I nod.

"Watch for me from your window. I'll stand at the left corner of the barn."

"Gary, I'm scared."

He stands and pulls me up, and when he does he pulls me into a kiss I fall into.

"Two days," he repeats as he lets go.

"I don't know," I say again.

"If you don't come, I'll know your answer."

He turns and disappears into the woods. When I come off the hill and into the pasture, I see no one. Grandma is no longer in the rows of collards and Grandpa is gone. I am glad. I can't look at them now with the taste of sassafras lingering on my lips. I feel like I have taken sides with an enemy, but an enemy of what, I don't know. In the garden I see the last row of greens has been picked except those left for seed. I cross the yellow green stubble to the wilted pumpkin vines. I gather two pumpkins at a time and store them in the root cellar. *At least I can do this before I leave.*

Night comes quick. I can smell the sharp smell of wild onions and cooking greens. It mixes with cornbread and pushes out the door into the night air. No one speaks at supper. There is an unspoken, agreed upon, truce. No barbs, no reprimands for running off into the woods. There are no demands for explanations, no "I'm sorrys." We eat in silence. I climb the ladder into the loft after the table and dishes have been cleared off. There are no goodnights spoken among any of us. No goodbyes.

Chapter 9

The night is black. I find him at the edge of the barn, and silently we open the door.

"What's wrong?" he asks me. "Why'd you stop?" He turns and looks back at the house. "Who is it?" he asks.

"Grandma."

"You sure?"

"Yeah," I tell him. "If it was Grandpa he'd already been down here after us."

"You don't have to go, you know."

"I know that."

"So why are you crying?"

I don't know how to explain it. He doesn't have a grandma or grandpa. Grandma and Grandpa have been all I've had for eleven years, given me all that they could, spared me hurt, loved me. Loved me, and I think, "This is how I repay them." I don't say it out loud, because Gary would say, "Okay, stay. It's okay. If you got to stay, then stay."

Grandma always says that decisions aren't easy, some harder than others. This is one of the hard ones. She's crying. I can't see her doing it, but I know she is. She's up there thinking I'm breaking her heart. I'm not. I'm bringing back Momma to her. Then we can all be happy. *Maybe...this is the hardest decision of all.*

I look back at Gary. Silently he is opening the door to the El Camino, putting it in neutral. I am at the back bumper. He puts his shoulder to the front door frame. He whispers, "Push." I push as hard as I can. I can feel Grandma's eyes on my back. They are hot with tears. The car edges forward, then bounces back. I almost lose my balance.

Gary looks back and whispers, "You all right?"

I nod.

"You sure?"

I nod again.

"On the count of three, push. One...two...three."

I hold my breath and push with all my strength. I feel the car bounce forward again, then move in a slow hesitant roll. Gary is steering with one hand, pushing with his shoulder. I put my head down, push again.

67

The car moves more easily now, even over the small holes in the dirt road. I am having to walk fast just to keep up, almost a run.

"Hurry," he says. "That little hill is just up here."

I run along beside the passenger's side, grab the door. He slows the car down so I can get the door open. It almost stops by the time the door swings wide. I put my shoulder against the door facing and push again to help regain our momentum, and when I feel the car speed up, I jump inside. We are at the hill and Gary jumps in behind the wheel.

"Just a few more hundred yards," he says. He isn't whispering now. "I think we can roll far enough so your Grandpa doesn't hear the motor start."

The bottom of the small hill rolls out in front of us, gradually. I see shadow trees pass by, then we come to a clearing. The moon has set, there is no light, the stars hidden by the trees. We are guided by instinct. I hear the key click in the ignition, hear the engine turn over, then start. It is loud, and I look back through the window toward the house, toward the window where Grandma is standing. Gary flips on the headlights. They are knives of light that cut through the pre-morning darkness. A raccoon is in the road, stops and stares at the lights reflecting in his own eyes so they look like beams of light of their own, then he scurries off into the shadows.

"That was about his last night out," Gary says laughing.

"He's probably never seen a car."

"Probably not."

We ride in silence another mile to the old two-lane paved road, turn left and cross the cement bridge where Grandpa taught me to fish with wooden poles, safety pin for hooks, and wiggling night crawlers submerged into this spring-fed mountain creek. It provided us with bass and sometimes trout. "Good eatin'," Grandpa would have said. I grieve over the memory.

Gary drives for what seems like forever on the two-lane road. The sky turns gray, then a trout-belly pink before the sun can be seen pushing the pink away with its light. The morning star blinks goodbye to me. The road is empty. I have never been this far away from home.

"You hungry?" Gary asks me.

"No."

"Sure? Jolie packed me some of the stuff she had the other night, some turnips..."

"Jolie knew?"

68

"Of course she knew I was leaving."

"No, I mean, did she know I was coming with you."

"I didn't say that out-right, but I think she suspected as much."

"Great."

"What was wrong with Jolie knowing?"

"She has the biggest mouth. Hard telling what she'll say. She'll probably tell Grandma that I confided in her. Geez."

"Oh," he says softly.

All I can think of is Jolie running first light down to the house and blabbing to Grandma how she knew all along that I was intending to leave with Gary, how maybe I'd said as much. I didn't. But for some reason she'll say that. And then there will be Grandpa standing there as mad as he can be at Grandma. He'll think she knew all along. It won't be the way it was, but Jolie will make it look like it was. I tell this to Gary.

"I didn't even decide for sure until last night," I say to him.

He shakes his head in agreement, "I didn't think you'd come."

"You were at Jolie's for a little over three weeks, you probably got to know her well enough to know she talks...it won't matter what the truth is, she will tell it the way she sees it, and then Grandpa will blame Grandma."

"How many people live up there anyway? They're going to find out."

"That's not my point. It's just that Jolie will make it look like she was my confidant and all. That will hurt Grandma."

"We can turn around and go back right now if that's what you want. I mean, we've only been gone what, about an hour or so. I wouldn't have you troubled, and if it means taking you back...that's no problem for me. You just say, 'Turn around, Gary,' and I'll turn around."

"No." I'm afraid I will change my mind. "Grandma already knows, I'm sure. Grandpa too, probably. The damage has been done, and if I go back now..."

"You'll never leave."

"Probably," I agree.

"No 'probably' about it."

We have coasted down a long stretch of mountain into a little valley. Empty, fallen-down houses line the road. Old gas stations, broken fences. We roll along the two-lane road alone, swing around a few curves, past a cemetery, two churches, one that says "We're waiting

69

for Jesus to return. Are you?"

When we hit a stretch of rolling hills surrounded by tall chain-linked fence Gary says, "Roll up your window now, Carrie."

I roll up the window and ask, "Why?"

"We're getting close to the depot."

"I thought you said that it was safe now."

"There are still barrels of nerve gas and mustard gas buried, some that may not have ruptured with the quake, some that could still leak through rusted containers. Each of those mounds over there," and he points to fields on our right, "they're full of barrels. I wouldn't want us to take any chances. That stuff is deadly."

"What're you doing?" I ask as he fiddles with a switch on the dash.

"Turning on the recycle air button until we get through this area."

"Recycled air?"

"The car isn't air tight, but turning this button shuts off the vent to the outside. You need to watch for buzzards."

"Okay."

I have suddenly become the look-out person for buzzards. The landscape is hilly, the road winding in and out of overgrown trees, cedars and oaks growing together to form archways. Kudzu has overtaken old electric poles, grown over everything that didn't move out of its way. The hills are green and lush; the sky empty of buzzards.

"Why won't it kill the buzzards?" I ask, staring out the front windshield.

"They've adapted, I guess, from eating contaminated carcasses."

"Wouldn't other animals adapt, too?"

"Probably, but some things adapt easier than others. Watch for dead animals in the fields, too."

"And what happens if some poisonous gas leaked out and there were no dead animals lying around to warn us?"

"Then tell me if you start getting a headache."

"Now what good would that do at that point?"

"Can't say that it would do any good at all," he confesses. "Scared?"

"Not really."

"Good."

We pass buildings so covered with vines their windows are barely visible.

"That's an old elementary school. There's the old depot."

On the right side of the road are rows of more kudzu-covered

70

buildings, and in front of them a field lined with row after row of white crosses. I look at Gary and he answers my unspoken question.

"Markers for all those who died from the gas leaks."

"Oh my God," I say. "Who buried them?"

"Emergency workers, volunteers, relatives, I guess. Took months to get in here to ever get a body count. That wasn't counting those who died from falling structures. By then, no one could tell what the cause of death was. I suspect it was a labor of love to come and put this memorial up. Little more left than bones, and..."

He doesn't go on because my face has turned white, and I feel clammy, like I will be sick.

"I'm sorry," he says. "This was a bad place. But then, there weren't too many safe places to be found anywhere. There's probably memorials like this all over. You know, the quakes, the floods, combined, wiped out over half the country's population.

"I didn't know."

"Wiped out millions, and that doesn't count the ones who were missing. The thing replaced the best farm land in the country with an ocean."

"Is the big bridge near here?"

"About fifteen miles north of here."

"Can we go that way?"

"Sure," he says.

We merge onto a bigger road, and enter into a town before we turn left at an empty intersection. There are no other cars on the road that is intersected with cracks. The yellow El Camino bumps over each crack with a jerk. Empty buildings stare out from broken windows. Fields are grown tall in grass. We pass buildings, once tall, now crumbled, but still standing taller than I could have imagined. Then, we get to the big road, the six-laned highway that I have seen before with Grandma, only farther south.

"This is the road you first came in on, isn't it?"

"Yeah, how'd you know?"

"Grandma and I watched you. Watched you from the cliff. It's that way from here, I think."

"Yeah, I remember that day. I got almost to Livingston. I thought I saw something, thought it was an animal. Rocks fell."

"Grandma was so mad at me that day. I wanted to lift my head to see you."

71

"That was you?"

I nod, and he laughs. "Go figure," is all he says.

"How far from here to there?" I ask.

"Oh, I can't say for sure. I suppose it was maybe twenty or thirty miles south from here, by way of this road. I couldn't go any further that day."

"Because of the crack?"

"Yeah. Couldn't get across that spot. There are others in between here and there, but that was the worst. I planned to go back and get some sheets of wood or something to span the gap and make my way farther south. That's when I decided to check out the valleys in between. Thought I might get some help."

"And did you?"

"It's where I found you."

We turn right onto the six-lane highway, cross cracks just like Gary said, smaller and passable. We round a curve with high, cut-out rock on either side, go down another long hill, and there it is, before me, and I am rushed with memories that I had forgotten I had. My stomach lurches, climbs into my throat and pounds at my heart. Gary stops the car.

We get out, and I follow him to the edge, the jagged, torn edge of bridge, rusted rods, broken concrete and kudzu covered. A river runs farther down, green and ribbon-like past rock cliffs and rugged angular trees. On the far side are the jigsaw pieces of the rest of the bridge. Beneath the pieces not yet put back together, men, small in the distance, carrying tools, driving equipment. I am crying. I move closer to the edge, look down at tumbled rocks.

"I remember this," I tell him in a whisper. "I remember the day we crossed the bridge, the cars, so many cars. I had never seen that many cars and trucks. I was sitting on Grandma's lap eating sausage biscuits. She kept feeding me sausage biscuits," I smile at the memory.

"Grandpa kept saying, 'You're gonna make the girl sick. She doesn't need any more sausage biscuits.' Cars were stopped, they couldn't move any farther. They were honking their horns. We were on that side," I say, pointing to the other side of the expanse that used to be the bridge.

"And Grandpa was honking the horn, too. When we were half way across, but couldn't move any farther, there was a big truck, the kind that Grandma used to complain about. I remember it now, how it was bent in half, right here where we are standing, and there was only one line of cars able to get through. Everyone was trying to get over, so they could get across the bridge. Grandpa pushed the nose of the Chevy into a tiny break in the line, and someone let us in. Grandma was praying out loud, and we could feel the truck start to shake. I got scared and dropped my biscuit.

"We started moving across the bridge, over half way across when... Oh god, I remember this bridge rocking back and forth, and people started screaming. I heard all the screaming. They started stopping and getting out of their cars. Grandpa didn't stop. He gunned the motor and just kept going, kept blowing his horn, and so did cars in front. The noise was so loud, and it sounded like rocks were cracking, like thunder, loud cracks of thunder.

"Then we were at the big truck. The man inside, his eyes were wide with fear. I could see his lips moving. He was trying to move the truck, but it wouldn't move, and other people were yelling at him to move, to move. We passed him, and then the road opened up. We moved part way up the hill and stopped. Through the back window we watched the bridge ripple in the middle, raise up high and then the center dropped and cracked in two. Cars and people fell head over head, over and over. There weren't any cars left on the bridge. They were all gone, all at the bottom. And the truck, that big truck, slipped.

"Grandpa got out of the car, stood beside the open door, and Grandma and I watched from inside. The truck's back end hung over the edge, back tires in the air spinning, and the driver gunned the motor. It roared and black smoke came out of a stack on the top of where he sat. Black, foul smelling smoke. His front tires spun round and round throwing gravel everywhere, then he slipped some more. Grandpa yelled at the guy to jump. 'Get out of there,' he yelled, but I don't think he could hear him over the roar of that big old truck."

I look at Gary, "I didn't remember any of this until now."

"Did the truck pull it out?"

I shake my head that he didn't. "Wouldn't open that door and jump. I remember crying and Grandma telling Grandpa to get in and get the hell out of there. He just watched, and between my crying I could see on the other side, cars everywhere, bumper to bumper, turned every which way with no place to go. And, I remember thinking...I remember it so clear now, that Momma was on the other side, somewhere back there where all those cars were all jammed up, and I remember thinking

73

I'd never see my Momma again, and I was scared."

I am crying those tears again now, long lost tears pouring down my cheeks, forgotten tears from over a decade ago. I don't care if Gary sees me crying, don't care if I look like a baby, don't care what he thinks right now. All the feelings from back then heap up on me, fresh and new, like it was happening all over again, and I am a five-year-old who has lost her mother. And, then I am crying for Grandma, and if I cross this very river, this river that took me from everything I knew before, then everything I've known since will slip away.

I sit on the dusty graveled edges of the super highway, at the remnants' edge of the big bridge and wonder how it could cause so much grief.

"I'll still take you back if you want. I'll do it right now. It's okay you know."

I want to say "Take me back." Part of me wants to tell him that, but there are metal ropes stretching beneath us, across this wide expanse of river, stretching from the other side to this, and there has been work done, some kind of work on the other side, I can see it. I think maybe that means there is hope, that I can get back on this side if I go across. The metal ropes are connectors from this world to that, from Grandma to Momma and back. If I don't go on I'll never know, and then I will likely die old and alone, never knowing, like Grandma. Gary will take me back, I believe him.

If I go back, I know what will happen. Jolie's kids will get bored and leave the hollow. She and Harold will grow old and die. So will Reva and Mr. Thompson, and Mrs. Pendleton, sooner than the rest. Tommy will get tired of pestering me, grow tired of trying to get me to marry him, and will leave. Grandma and Grandpa will finally die, and I will be alone in Stears Branch, all by myself. I laugh at my silliness, and laughter chases my tears.

"What's so funny?" Gary asks, confused by tears turned to laughter.

"Just me," I tell him.

"Tell me," he says.

I get up from where I am sitting, brush dust from my back side.

"How do we get across?" I ask.

He looks at me, his head tilted to one side, trying to figure me out. I laugh again, because I can't figure myself out.

"This can't be the only way across," I say.

"No, this isn't how we get across."

"So, how do we do it?"

"Back track about three miles, then follow the river to a crossing spot."

"What're we waiting for?"

Chapter 10

Grandma.

I saw you. Yes, I saw your face for just an instant in that pre-dawn darkness as you turned for one last look at home.

By the dimmest light of the setting moon you knew I was watching, because you stopped, just for a minute you stopped, turned and saw me. There was a sorrow mixed with something else in your expression, something I had long forgotten. I saw you, and in you I saw your mother, the same determination.

I was powerless at that moment to stop you, to call out your name or wake your grandfather. He would have stopped you, I know that. He would have moved faster than he had the years to stop you, to prevent you from doing what you have done, what you believed you had to do. I had no hold on you, no way to keep you here. What was I to do? There was nothing for you here on this narrow stretch of dirt, trees, and grass. There was no one here for you but us, and we grew backward and antiquated.

I watched you from the window, watched you and the boy push the yellow El Camino. You strained, and then I saw it begin to roll, rolled out of sight into the dark cover of the trees. I kept watching the darkness until I heard the faint sound of the motor starting. You were gone, and I thought to myself it was too late to hurry down the ladder, too late to wake your grandpa. And what do I have to tell him? Lie that I slept through your leaving? Even if it was true, his anger cannot be salved. In his mind I conspired with you, encouraged you. I didn't, but it doesn't matter. He will not believe me. It is my fault, he will say. I wasn't firm enough with you, didn't discipline you enough. He may be right. I don't know anymore.

Carrie, remember I told you I was scared? How can you not? It was only days ago. I told you things were changing, and it was not good. Why didn't you listen?

I knew that day at the ribbons of road our life was going to change. Change came in the form of a red-haired boy in a yellow El Camino. Then he was here, red hair standing on end, dusty face, dusty handsome face, hands up in the air like Jim was going to blow his head off.

Jim and his rifle with no bullets and so rusty, even if he had bullets, it wouldn't have fired. Your Grandpa knew, too, that the boy meant change. That was why he was so protective. I'm not sure who we were protecting the most, you or ourselves.

On the bedroom wall are charcoal markers of days, then weeks and months. There are enough marks now to look like some ancient petroglyph in parallel lines, indicators of all we have known here these past eleven, almost twelve years. First my marks, then yours, circles around the first of each month. Stars beside those dates we chose not to forget, as if we ever could. First lost tooth, first period. Your birthday, your Momma's. We have marked our lives on these dormered walls, and I have no desire to mark more.

The sound of the El Camino is long gone. The sky has grown light. Red and orange colors replaced the night. I remember my father's ominous prophecy, 'Red in the morning, sailors warning.' How did he know? I lay on your bed, soft pallet of straw and old ticking. I smell your childlike perfume of homemade soap and sweet sweat, and it reminds me of summer mornings.

I will never move from this place.

Two hours ago he wakened by an inner alarm. I was charged as expected, found guilty without trial, and he has gone, your Grandpa, to find you. When he does, I don't know what he will do to you or the boy. I doubt, even if he finds you, he will ever return to this place. Nor will he ever forgive me for letting you slip away.

Chapter 11

Carrie.

Gary grins a funny grin, faded freckles showing up across his nose. All this time I hadn't paid much attention to his looks. I did, but then I didn't either. His eyes are as blue as the midday sky, and his hair reflects glints of sunshine on copper. He is as handsome a man as I've ever seen, but then again, I haven't seen that many. Grandpa, Jolie's husband, Mr. Pendleton before he died, Mr. Thompson, Tommy and Joey, and then occasionally, those from the other ridge. Still, I thought if I'd had lots of boys to compare him to, I'd still think he was a good looking fellow, and having thought that, I wonder if he can read my mind, because he is grinning even bigger.

"What're you looking at?" he asks me.

"You," I say, and then walk to the El Camino. "I think I'd like to see what Jolie packed you. My stomach is growling."

"It's not dinner time yet."

And I say, "We never had breakfast."

"True enough. Look back behind the seat. That's where I put the box of food."

"She must have liked you," I say, pulling out the box with a loaf of corn bread, honey, some dried apple butter, sweet cream butter, and a dozen or more autumn apples.

"I think I helped her out by keeping those kids out of her way. God, I can't imagine why they had so many. She told me she was having another one come the new year."

"Another baby on the way? Guess there wasn't much else for her and Harold to do."

Gary starts laughing, and I think I have said something wrong. I am embarrassed, because what I said must of not come out the way I intended. I turn back around and sit down. I don't look at him directly, but look out the window. I can tell he is still thinking something is very funny.

The El Camino is running, and Gary does a U-turn. We head back in the other direction and pull off the big highway to a two-lane road. The road curves first one way and then another down towards the river,

78

but there are no big cracks. There are empty houses, windows with broken out glass, grass grown up in the yards. There are no people out picking apples, no one on front porches. There are no children running wild along the narrow strip of road. No dogs chasing the car, and no sign of cows or horses.

"Why didn't people re-settle here?"

"When folks were re-settling, this was probably under water, then covered with mud, and probably too snaky."

"Still looks snaky."

"Probably is. Where's that breakfast?" he asks.

I lean over the back of the seat and pull out the bread. I pour honey onto a square and pass it to Gary. He holds the car onto the road with one hand and eats his bread with the other. Honey drips down his wrist, and when he finishes the bread, he licks it off. I have put the apple butter on mine. Less messy, and I have two hands free to eat, so I stay clean.

"Jolie was a pretty good cook," Gary says.

"I agree," then add, "but Grandma was better."

"Oh, was she now?"

"Yeah, she always thought Jolie was a little bit lazy. She took shortcuts in making stuff, just to get it done quick. Now, Grandma took her time, and she would have strained that honey better. She would have saved the comb for Grandpa to lick, then melt it for candles. We always needed candles. Every now and then she'd let me have some of the comb to chew on. She said it was like chewing gum."

"What was it like, living without a store to get things?"

"Can't say I know what living with a store was like. We did okay. We never went hungry that I can remember except that first winter. Oh, sometimes we had to be careful with what we had, but I really don't remember being hungry."

"You ever had a candy bar?"

"No, but Grandma talked about them. She loved Mallow Cups."

"Hmm, don't remember them. Now my Mom liked Hershey Bars. They're still around. Place in Pennsylvania makes them."

"Grandma liked Hershey Bars, too."

"Some had nuts and some didn't. My Mom liked the ones with nuts. You ever had chocolate?"

"Sure. Grandma had cocoa for a while. We would fix hot water, honey and cocoa and would drink it. We finally ran out."

79

"A lot of things you didn't have, living back where you did."

"We had all we needed."

"Maybe, but didn't you miss white bread, or Pepsi, or, I don't know, it just seems like you wouldn't have had much."

"Like I said, we had all we needed, and then some." I feel myself getting defensive at his tone. "Grandma brought yeast. It lasted for a pretty long time, then she made starter with it. She always has starter. We didn't always have white flour. We always had corn flour. Everyone grows a stand of corn, eat on it all summer, then we'd save enough for seed. The rest we ground for meal. We had beans, apples, and potatoes. A cow wandered into the hollow early on, and Reva kept it in their barn. She knew how to milk it, but gave the milk to Jolie because of the children. She always shared butter and milk with us.

"Then there were blackberries, and then a couple of times a year the men would rob a bee tree. You helped Harold smoke that tree didn't you?"

Gary nods that he did, then laughs, "Got stung, too, but Jolie didn't tell that part."

"We had ducks that showed up and because we fed them, they stayed and so we had eggs. Grandpa killed a deer every year. Don't see what being out in civilization could have added to what we had."

"I suppose not," Gary says.

My voice betrays my irritation, and he allows us to ride in silence. The road twists and turns as we head to the crossing point Gary has talked about.

Every now and then we see a house, set back off the road and clothes hanging out on lines to dry. There are dogs here, and they chase along the road at our tires, barking as we move beyond them. They stand at the edge of their territory warning us not to come back. Their barked warnings are meaningless.

We are heading downward to the ferry. Grandpa had been to the ferry once. He came back and told us of it. Heathens and ruffians, he said. He had no inclination to go on to the other side, and no inclination to return to the river or the ferry. Nothing over there interested him, he said. His finality of "nothing over there that interested," had closed the subject. We respectfully left the discussion closed.

The sun passes the noon hour and begins moving westward in the sky while we head east. A small creek joins our journey to the right and rushes along beside us. It widens and slows down until it turns a different direction, leaving us to ourselves again.

"We're almost at the river," Gary finally says. "We will probably have to wait for the ferry. It only crosses twice a day. That means we'll wait until almost dusk when it heads back over to the north side of the river."

We cross a creek. The road spans it with thick logs and boards, and I wonder if it is the same creek we followed before. The El Camino rattles across the boards. On the other side is a two-story house. It's clapboards are gray with age, and warped. There is a porch that stretches from one end to the other, and on it sit people I think must be waiting for the ferry to take them back to the north side of the big river. They watch as we pull up, not surprised, no indication of curiosity about strangers pulling into the lane. They are different from us in our hollow.

"See you're back," says an old man who comes through the front door.

Gary nods.

"Got someone with you, I see," he says again with a brown toothed grin.

Gary nods again.

"Right pretty passenger."

"Got room for the vehicle to cross over tonight?" Gary asks.

"Sure."

"Same price as before?"

"Fifty cents more with another passenger," he tells Gary.

"Deal," is all Gary says.

"What's your name, missy?"

"Carrie," I say.

"You kin to this red-headed fellow?"

"She's my cousin."

"Huh. Guess you found relatives after all. Didn't think you would. Most of those living back between the two rivers are kind of close lipped, if you know what I mean. Keep to themselves."

"That they do," Gary says.

I say, "Didn't see no reason to do otherwise, sir."

He laughs. "What'd you say your last name was?

Gary says, "She didn't. When does the boat leave?"

"Same as last time."

"Have any good water?" Gary asks.

81

"Cold inside," he says, watching us as we climb the front steps.

Inside, the room is nearly bare: two tables with four chairs each and a counter that stretches across one wall. Behind it are shelves lined with pretty colored glasses.

"We'd like two waters," Gary says to the girl behind the counter. She looks like the woman on the front porch, only younger and with more teeth.

"That's five bucks," and Gary takes money out of his pocket, gives the girl five silver coins. She pours water from a large metal pitcher into two blue glasses. Gary takes them.

"Thanks," he says. "Over here," and motions to the table nearest the window.

We sit. The water is stale looking, not clear and fresh like Grandma's. It smells of fish and some other smell I can't identify. It isn't cold.

"Is the water safe?"

"Yeah. It doesn't taste great, but they put bleach in it to get rid of the contaminants. Expensive, but it's water."

I sip slowly. He has spent five whole dollars on this foul tasting stuff. I don't want him to waste his money on me. I think I won't be able to get it down when he says, "Better get used to it. Water gotten from this river will all taste like this, and around here and where we're going, the water comes from this river."

I think I don't know how I am going to drink it, but I do. We leave the glasses on the table and go back outside to sit on the porch with the other people.

"When do we leave?" I ask.

"Several hours."

"What do we do in the meantime?"

"Wait."

His manner has changed since getting here. In just a few minutes he changes from friendly to distant. He has turned silent, and I am angry at him for putting down mountain people, but in this place I don't call him on it, not now. I am uncomfortable in the straight back chair. The old man on the steps whittles on a piece of wood, spits brown juice to one side, then whittles some more. A little girl comes out and sits at the old man's side.

I am homesick. I am scared. I want my Grandma. I want familiar faces, faces that smile back at me when I smile, not the grin that makes me squirm that I am receiving from the men who run this ferry. I am

82

afraid I have made a mistake and don't know how to remedy it.

I have waited too long for the "I'll take you back if you want" request to be honored.

The porch we sit on smells – smells dusty and dirty, and not at all like home. It smells foreign. We speak in whispers.

"Who are these people?" I ask.

"The gray-haired man owns the ferry. The girl inside is his."

"His daughter?"

"His wife."

"He's old, and she's not much older than me. Is the little girl hers?"

Gary shoots me an impatient look.

"She's too young to have a child that age."

"She's old enough."

"Why would she want to be with..." and I start to say with an old man like him, but my voice carries louder than I realize, and Gary shoots me another look that says, "Keep your mouth shut."

The old man grins at us, and with his booted foot gives the child a kick off the step. The little girl falls on her knees and starts to cry.

"The rest of these people crossing?"

"Don't think so," he says. He pulls something out of his pocket, a pack of cigarettes like Jolie's husband used to have and lights it up with a match.

"I didn't know you smoked."

"Now you know," is all he says, and I think I don't know him at all. I wonder how many other things I am going to have to learn about him before I find my Momma.

Another man and woman leading a mule with two children on its back walk up. They nod to us and I nod back. The woman smiles at me, and I try to smile. She has a boy and a girl, the boy about the age of Jolie's littlest one. They are clean, have combed hair. I touch my own hair to see if it has flown every which-way and tuck the straggling strands behind my ears.

"When does the ferry leave?" the man asks.

"Not too long," the old man tells him.

"How much to take the four of us across."

"Two-fifty," he tells them.

The man and woman whisper to each other, and the woman pulls some change from her pocket and hands it to the man.

"Good looking mule there. Pretty good size. Better add another

83

dollar for the mule."

The woman dips deeper into her pocket and gives the money to her husband, who hands it to the ferryman.

"It's pretty heavily packed now," the ferry man says while putting the money in a pouch at his side, "and I got this here vehicle to go. If the boat sets too low on the water you'll have to leave the mule."

"Can't say that I can do that," the man says.

"Up to you, but you've already paid for the fares. No refunds."

I watch the man's chest rise with taking a deep breath. I think he is going to say something, but the woman puts her hand on his arm and shakes her head, then tells the boy to tie up the mule to the porch post. She climbs the steps and comes to where Gary and I are sitting.

"Hard bargaining sometimes," she says. "My name is Donna Wilson. You been waiting long?"

"My name is Carrie. This here is Gary. And yeah, we've been here for a while."

"You two married?" Donna Wilson asks.

I feel my face flush, "I'm too young to be married."

"She's my cousin," Gary adds quickly.

"Oh," she says, and her two children come up beside her.

"Hold me," the littlest one says, and the woman picks her up.

"Here, you can have my seat," Gary says rising.

I watch him walk to where the other men are standing. The woman sits on the chair that Gary has offered. The boy sits on the porch floor beside his momma. The littlest one lays her head on her mother's shoulder.

"It's real hard traveling with children," she says.

"Where you from?"

"Over in Estill County."

"Where's that?"

"It's kind of hard to explain from here. You know where the depot was?"

"We went through there this morning."

"Well, it's east of there. We were on the other side of Kirby Knob, the mountain protected where we were staying."

"Why are you leaving?"

"You're just full of questions, aren't you?"

"I'm sorry. You're right. It isn't any of my business, but you were talking about how hard it was to travel with children and all. I just

84

supposed there must be a pretty good reason."

"It's okay, I really don't mind your questions. Just haven't talked about it much up until now. He thought we ought to go on north, better opportunity and more folks there." She nods towards her husband, "I'm not sure. I kind of liked it the way it was. But he's right in that there's not much for the children where we were living, and well, even when we got to where there were more folks, it still wasn't going to give the kids what they needed in the long run. He was schooled, you know. He went to the University, and he wants more for them. It's been real hard for Bill, them not having a proper education."

"Grandma taught me. I can read and write. Grandpa was an engineer. He taught me algebra. We had some books that Grandma made sure we brought with us, and what books we didn't have, we wrote and made up our own."

"We got out with the clothes on our back, so to speak."

"Where were you from, before?"

"From the other side. Bill and me went out on a date. We were parking, know what I mean?"

"No, not really."

She smiles at me a sort of quirky smile and goes on. "We were on a back road, it wasn't yet midnight. We felt the quakes start. I was only nineteen and scared to death. Every road there abouts was cracked wide open. I called home, and my dad told us to hold tight, but to get away from the gas station we were calling from. We went up to a little church. Must have been a hundred folks there, most of them praying."

She is rocking the little girl back and forth. The little boy is listening to his mother, nodding like he's heard this story before. I think for a minute that the lady is going to cry. She looks up and away from me, back towards the river.

"You hunting your folks, too?" I ask.

She shakes her head, "No, they didn't make it out. Not with the flooding."

"How do you know?"

"There wasn't hardly a place between Ohio and here that wasn't under water. We headed along the Mountain Parkway and crossed the river into Beattyville before the big backwash of water. We raced ahead of the flood, moving to higher ground until we ended up in the foothills. Getting there, though, I can't find the right words to tell you what it was like. The water behind us roared like a train gone wild."

85

"My Grandpa's name is Jim," I say. I don't know why I tell her. Just saying his name makes a hollow place in my heart. It is getting dark, and I think we will soon be getting on the flat-bottomed boat that will take me even farther away.

Gary comes up the steps, "He's getting ready to board. Come on."

"Cousins?" she asks me as I get up to follow him.

"Yeah, he came to help me find my Mom and Dad. I haven't seen them since the...I don't know what you call it, but I haven't seen them since I was five"

"Carrie."

We head towards the shoreline. There are seven of us crossing besides the man who owns the ferry: one of the men who was on the porch, the family of four, and Gary and me. Gary starts the El Camino and pulls it across the ramp into the middle of the boat, turns off the engine and pulls up the hand brake. Then the mule is led to the front portion and double tied, neck and belly, to the wooden rail. The rest of us follow on foot. Gary has gotten out of the car and is waiting for me.

"What'd you tell her?" he asks me. "You know you shouldn't be saying anything about what we are doing."

"Why not?"

"Just not the thing to do."

"Now you sound as suspicious as my Grandpa. So, what did you do when you got to our hollow, huh?"

Gary lowers his voice, "That's different. You just have to know who you can talk to and who you can't, and I don't think you know the difference."

"She's a nice lady," I say, defending myself and the lady.

"So she seems."

"Well, she lost her folks just like me. They got separated during the quakes." My voice has gotten louder, and he shushes me with his finger across his lips.

"You just need to be careful," he whispers. "That's all I can tell you. Not everyone can be trusted. You're out here all by yourself, and you don't need anybody to try and take advantage of your situation."

"I thought I had you with me, and what's my situation?" I whisper back.

"Like I said, you're out here all by yourself. You don't have any money, and you haven't a clue about your folks."

"And like I said, I thought you were with me."

"I'm just one person. What kind of defense do you think I will be for you against, say those three guys that were on the porch?"

"But we haven't had any problems."

"We're not on the other side yet."

I can feel the ferry move away from the shore line. The old man is pulling on a thick rope that stretches from one side of the river to the other. The other man is next to him.

"Hey, boy," he calls to Gary. "I need a hand over here. You too mister. The boat's too heavy for the two of us to pull by ourselves, and the current is fast tonight."

Gary and the man named Bill go to the front of the boat and grab hold of the rope. All four men pull the thick rope, and the ferry moves slowly at first, moves into the river. The bow turns down stream, and the ferry owner yells at Gary to pick up the slack or they will lose it. The rope that is overhead grows taut against the current.

"We should have waited," the lady says nervously to her son. He holds onto her leg in fear, and the toddler begins to cry. Water splashes up on the deck. I want to run to where Gary is pulling to ask him if we will sink. The mule loses its footing and slides against the side of the boat. The movement causes the boat to rock, and I grab hold of the door of the El Camino. Gary looks up from his position to where I am standing, then puts his shoulder back into pulling harder. The worst of the current is in the very center of the river, and it seems like forever before we are out of its strong pull. I am relieved when I can feel the ferry scrape the river bottom, but the four men continue to pull until the ferry docks against the north side. The ferry owner drops ropes with rocks tied onto the ends to keep the boat from dragging further downstream and hollers at Donna and me to get off. Gary starts his vehicle and moves it slowly to dry land. Bill unties the mule. In its terror, the mule drags him off the boat.

"It's gonna cost you more for my trouble," the ferryman says to both Gary and Bill.

"We paid you the required full fare, regardless of your trouble," Gary says.

"Well, the two of us will have a hard time getting this ferry back in the water."

"How's increased fare gonna get you back easier," the lady says.

The ferryman turns around fast and looks at her, "You stay outta this."

87

"We don't have any more money," she says.

"Well, then, maybe this kid here can help you out."

"Like I said before, we already paid our fare. I don't have any more money to give you, not for me or for them. Your getting back isn't our problem."

"Well now, I'll have to remember that the next time you're wanting to get across," he says, and he climbs over the railing and onto the ferry. He lifts the rocks and begins pulling on the winch. We watch as the back side of the ferry pulls down stream and we see the old man and younger man strain against the current. On the far side are the other men and the old ferryman's young wife.

"Come on," Gary says. "Get in the car."

"It was a pleasure talking with you back there," the woman named Donna says.

"You all had better get on your mule and get away from here as fast as you can. I can't say I trust the three of them not to head back across," Gary says to Donna and her husband.

"Why?" I ask.

"They're not the most scrupulous folks, is the nicest way I can put it. Think they'd just as soon shoot you in the back as look at you."

I watch the ferry halfway into the river. It is lighter, and though there are just two men, it moves more quickly than it did when we were coming over.

"I'd offer you a ride if it wouldn't mean leaving your mule," Gary says to the man.

"It's okay. We'll manage."

"Then you need to move on out now. Like I said, I don't trust them."

I watch as Donna climbs onto the mule's back, and her husband lifts the two children, putting one in front and one in back. Her husband leads them at a slow run. Gary and I watch as the ferryman finally docks on the far side. It is dark, and though we can see two other men head down the hill to meet them, we can't tell whether they get on the ferry or not.

"Come on," Gary says. "Let's not tempt them by standing here gawking at them." It has gotten cold at the river's edge. The motor is running, and in another moment we are bearing up the road. We pass Donna and her husband. The hill is steep, and he has stopped running, catching his breath. They are less than a quarter of a mile up the north side. Donna waves.

"Where do we go from here?" I ask.

"Northwest."

At the halfway up mark, I turn and can see the river above the tree tops, see the house, the lights burning from the front room windows casting light onto the front yard. I can see the girl and child standing on the front porch. I wonder what they are watching, then I see the ferry in the moonlight. It is half way across the river.

"Gary," I say, my voice low.

"What?"

"The ferry is coming back across."

Gary slows down, pulls into an old turn-off. He gets out of the car and stares down at the ferry. I stand beside him. A soft glow of silver light reflects on three men's faces.

"What are they after?" I ask.

"Those folk's mule and a little revenge, I suspect."

"Why the mule?"

"Mule or horse is just about as valuable as a car, and doesn't need gas."

"Are they in danger?"

Gary shoots me this, "Are you stupid?" look.

"What's going to happen?" I ask.

"They'll probably catch up with them in a couple of minutes. It looks like they got a four-wheeler between them."

"What's a four-wheeler?" I ask.

"An all-terrain vehicle."

"What?"

"A small jeep-like vehicle. Don't ask me what a jeep is okay? It can climb sides of hills and go over embankments. Not as fast as a car. Wouldn't be able to catch us, but a mule, a wife, and two kids? They will be up with them in less than two minutes after they dock."

"So, what do we do?"

"Nothing."

"Nothing?"

"What do you suggest?"

Gary is looking at me, even in the shadow of the trees I see the exasperated expression on his face.

"Going back to help them," I say.

"There's just two of us. How do you propose we save them?"

89

"If we don't, what's going to happen?"

Gary stares down at the river. The ferry has reached this side and is behind a stand of trees. We can't see them now, but the start-up sound of the vehicle reverberates up the side of the hill. He looks at me, then back at the road behind us. He hesitates and then says, "You get over there in that brush. Here's my wallet. Stay put. Don't, and I mean don't, come out until you hear me tell you to come out, you understand?"

I nod that I do. "What are you going to do?"

"What I can. You wanted me to rescue them, right? Now get over on that side and stay there."

I cross the road into the shadow of the underbrush.

"I can still see your face, get farther back. Good. Remember, stay there until I say so. And if I'm not back by daylight, go north to Lexington."

I watch as Gary climbs back into the El Camino. He spins the vehicle around and heads back down the hill. I can hear the four-wheel vehicle roar louder than the El Camino. The vehicle roar has stopped. I guess that we are only minutes up the hill from where we passed Donna. It feels like time has stopped, and I don't hear any voices, not angry voices, not frightened voices, just the sound of a squirrel overhead cutting on acorns.

My legs grow stiff with my squat position. I shift, stand up, and squat again. I look down the road and see no headlights coming up the hill. I think to myself that a watch would be helpful if I had one, but I don't know what it would help.

I hear one shot fire off, a second, and finally after a forever time I hear a motor. Where it comes from, I can't tell if it is the El Camino or the four-wheeled vehicle. I come out from my hiding place, cross the road, and look over the stone fence to the river below. I can't see Gary, Mr. Wilson, Donna or the children.

At the far side of the river I can see the ferry, three men climbing onto the shore and the mule between them. One looks to be limping. I don't see the vehicle. I'm scared.

In the middle of the road, my return to my hiding place is halted by two yellow lights. I stand frozen, unable to move in either direction. In the light I can't tell the car or the driver. I am blinded. When the vehicle stops, I see it is the yellow El Camino. I breathe relief and smile.

"What'd I tell you?" Gary jumps out of the window and into the double lines of light.

"Gary," I say.

His face is rage red in the headlights. "I told you to stay under cover until I told you to come out, didn't I?"

He has me by the shoulders and is shaking me. I don't know what to say to him. I start to cry and yell, "Stop it." He stops and drops his hands.

"Why didn't you listen to me?" he says.

"I did."

"No, you didn't. When I came up the road, there you were, right in the middle. I could have been one of those thieves."

"I heard shots. I didn't know what to do."

"Yes, you did. I said stay put. I said I'd be back," he yells.

"It was forever," I say.

His face softens, and he becomes the person I met three weeks ago. He runs a hand through his hair, and it stands up with the stickiness of his perspiration. I laugh through my tears.

"What's so funny?

"Your hair," I say, and I point to the tuft of hair that is sticking up. He pats it down.

"Get in the car," he says softly.

Inside the El Camino are Donna and the two children. I squeeze in, and the older child moves onto my lap.

"Front seat only," Gary apologizes, and I wonder where Donna's husband is. I twist to look through the back window. Nothing but three bundles, a large gas tank. No Donna's husband. I look at Donna's face. It is pale, eyes wide. The children carry the same expression. Her dress is torn, one sleeve is missing. Her sweater is gone. There are dark splatters on her arm, scratches that have oozed red. Gary's face is vacant, no sign of what happened. We ride up the road. Even the children are without words or whimpers. I am afraid to go where they have gone.

It's getting late," Gary says. "We will need to stop pretty soon for the night."

"Where?" I ask.

"There is an exit a few more miles up the road."

"Will those men follow? Are we safe?" I ask.

"They won't chance coming into town."

"Are there beds?"

"We'll sleep in the car. Donna, I can fix a bed in the back for you and the children. Carrie and I will stay in the cab, or vice-versa, which ever works best for you. I can make a cover over the back with a tarp to provide some warmth and protection. Just seemed that it would give you more room."

"Whatever will be fine," she says to him in dull, flat tones.

The road merges with the highway, and we move on at a faster speed. There are other vehicles on the highway, and where the roads cross the highway, lights shine illuminating other cars and people walking.

"Where are we?"

"Just outside of Lexington."

We pull off the highway in an area where a large building stands with glass from top to bottom. There are people milling around. Some stare, others glance in our direction with nervous expressions and look away. I realize I am hungry. I ask the boy if he is, and he nods that he is.

"I have to pee," the least one says, and Donna says she will take her. She hands her out the window to Gary. Under the lights I can see Donna's dress is stained with red blotches. As she climbs out the window I see that she has no panties on, and I turn my face away.

The boy slides off my lap, and I turn to get the parcel of food from behind the seat. I hand him a piece of cornbread, and he devours it. I nibble on a piece and hand a piece out to Gary. He shakes his head that he doesn't want any. When Donna and the little one get back, Gary says he will take the El Camino around back, out from beneath the lights.

"Meet you there," Donna says, and she crosses the grass to the rear side of the opposite lot.

Gary climbs in, and we circle around to where he backs the El Camino up to an isolated sidewalk and climbs out. We wait for Donna. When she arrives, I hand her a piece of bread. She gives it to the little girl.

"Here, Susie," she says, and I hand her another. She says, "No, it's okay. I'm not hungry."

"You decide if you want the front or back?" Gary asks.

"Just as soon have the back."

He attaches a tarp to the front with rope and then stretches it to the

92

lower end of the tailgate. Before he attaches the other side, Donna climbs under the tarp. She spreads out part of her bundle, a multi-colored quilt, and I hand her the child she called Susie and then the boy climbs over the back. Afterwards, Gary ties down the ends.

"Do you think you'll be warm enough like that?" Gary asks through the tarp.

"We'll be fine," Donna says.

I can hear the little boy whispering to his mother and hear her low voice reassuring him. I don't hear the little girl at all.

"We'll sleep sitting up here, if that's okay with you. You mind sharing the front?"

I say no. Once inside, when the motor has stopped running, and I have wrapped myself in my sweater, I ask him, "What happened?"

He is leaning on the driver's side, his legs stretched onto the middle hump. He has been facing the driver's side window, and with my question he turns to me.

"I don't want to offend you, but I can't talk about it right now."

"What about Donna's husband, Bill?"

"Dead," he says, and he turns his face back toward the night sky.

Chapter 12

Morning comes cold. There is a thin film of frost over the windshield. During the night I edged to the middle of the seat, and now I find myself beneath Gary's arms. The sky is still dark in the direction of Lexington. A pale haze begins to creep up the eastern horizon. I lift up and look back through the rear window. Delicate icy patterns blur the view of the tarp that hides Donna and her children. There is no stirring beneath the cover, no rustling children ready to get up.

I turn back into Gary's warm body, feel his chest rise and fall with his slow breathing. My movement makes him stir, and he folds his arms around me, draws me closer. His eyes do not open, his breathing does not change. I can hear his heart, steady and strong. I think if I close my eyes again, I will forget about last night and the events that he does not want to talk about and Donna does not want to divulge. So I close my eyes and wait.

Minutes pass, and I cannot forget the night – the unshaven faces of violent men, the pale faces of Donna and her children, the drawn, weary face of Gary. Only my face was spared the evidences of terror. I feel guilt. I sense Gary stir, begin to waken. I keep my eyes closed. His hand strokes my hair, and I can feel his breath, warm with wakefulness against my face, feel his lips brush against my cheek.

He whispers in my ear, "You awake?"

I pretend sleep. His hand moves away from my head and rubs my back, slowly up and down its full length with gentleness, then with firmness pulls my body closer into his. He rests his chin on my head, and movement stops. We stay in that position, neither of us moving, neither disturbing the peace that has enveloped us.

When I think we will stay this way forever, he speaks again.

"I think we need to get married," he says. I try not to move. I don't know how to answer.

"I know you're awake. Why won't you answer me?"

"I don't know what to say."

"Say you will."

"I hardly know you," I say.

"You can learn to know me."

"Isn't that supposed to come first?"

94

He laughs. "Probably, under most circumstances. But this isn't most circumstances."

"After who I saw yesterday, I don't know."

"Who do you think you saw yesterday?"

I hesitate. "First, it was the you I thought was you – sweet, funny. At the ferry, you were cold, hard. You frightened me. Then last night, you were someone who just closed me out. You were here, but yet you weren't."

"So, which one do you think I am?"

I sit up and look into his face, more rugged than before. I say, "I'm not sure. You tell me which one is really you."

"The one who wants to marry you, that's who."

"That tells me nothing."

"Well, the one who wants to marry you thinks he can take care of you. The one who wants to marry you thinks you will be safer if you are married to him. The one who wants to marry you is the one who has fallen in love with you, and gets scared out of his pants when he thinks you're in danger. The one who wants to marry you wants to spare you the horrors of nights like last night, wants to keep those kinds of things from happening to you. Do you want to marry that man?"

By the end of his brief tirade, his voice has risen. I put my finger across his lips. The tarp in the back shows movement beneath. Donna's little boy sticks his head out from under and calls, "It's cold out here. Can I come in?"

I look at the exasperation on Gary's face and motion the child to join us. He climbs out with a quick jump and slides in through the door I opened. His thin arms are mottled blue with the cold.

"Come here," I say, and he snuggles up between Gary and me. "You're an icicle."

We sandwich the boy between us. "How'd you get so cold?"

"I dunno," he says.

"I never heard what your mom calls you," Gary says.

"I'm Billy," he says. His teeth have quit chattering.

"I thought you, your mom and sister would stay pretty warm back there," Gary says.

"Mommy left last night."

Gary jumps out of the El Camino and strips back the tarp. No Donna and no little Susie. One bundle was left in the back along with Gary's

95

spare gas tanks and a folded piece of paper. Inside I say to Billy, "You smell like gasoline."

"Yeah, I know."

Gary climbs back into the car with the folded piece of paper. "Your mom tell you she was leaving?"

"She told me to stay put."

"She say anything else, like where she was going?"

"No sir."

"How old are you, Billy?" I ask.

"Six, Ma'am."

"Well, Billy, I think you are the bravest six-year-old I've ever met."

"Thank you, Ma'am. I try to be."

I watch Gary reading the note. He looks up at me, and I wonder which Gary I am going to see. He looks down at the note again, folds it up and puts it in his pocket.

"Well now, Billy," he says. "Looks like you're gonna be spending a little time with Miss Carrie and me. Is that okay by you?"

"Sure. You're both real nice, mister, and you tried to save my Daddy last night."

"Yeah," Gary says. "Tried to save your Dad. I'm sorry, Billy. Real sorry I didn't get there in time."

"Mister, are you gonna be my Dad now?"

"I don't know."

"That's what Mom said. She said to listen to you just like you were my Dad."

"Well, I'm starved, and I think we should take Miss Carrie out for breakfast. What do you think, Billy?"

"I think it sounds good, sir."

"Great. One thing Billy."

"What's that, sir?"

"Call me Gary, okay?"

Billy grins. Gary starts the El Camino. We turn out from the parking lot behind the building that says Holiday Inn.

I ask Gary, "What's Holiday Inn?"

He laughs. "Guess I'm gonna have two to educate now. It was a place too expensive for us to stay in last night, so we slept in a car."

"Oh, like that tells me anything."

"It's a place where travelers pay to spend the night, in a bed no less."

96

"Oh..."

"Yeah, Oh..."

"Gary, is there any place where we, where I can wash up? I feel stinky."

"I think you smell great."

"I'm serious. Where can we wash up?"

"Now you're saying I stink."

"I didn't say that."

Billy starts to laugh. "You guys are silly," he says, and all three of us laugh.

We turn left out of the parking lot. Gary says we are heading into town. I ask if we can wash up before he finds us the place to eat breakfast.

"There's a gas station just a little ways up. You can wash up in their bathroom. You do remember what a bathroom is?"

"Funny," I say.

"Well, do you?"

"Kind of."

He pulls the El Camino into a station that says "Shell" and goes inside the building. When he comes out he is waving a key.

"Come on, you two."

On the side of the building he unlocks a door and swings it open to a dingy, smelly room.

"What's this?" I ask.

"A bathroom."

We all three enter, and Gary pulls the door behind us, so that we are squashed in the small room.

"Here is your everyday sink," he says pointing to the dirty white bowl and, turning so we are squeezed face to face, he points over my shoulder. "And this is your modern toilet."

I turn to see a yellow stained seat with a similar stained back.

"Grandma told me about these things," I say to Billy. I maneuver around Gary and turn on the water, cold water, and splash it on my face. Gary turns his back to us and begins to relieve himself.

Back to back, I ask, "What are you doing?"

"What do you think I'm doing."

"I hope not what I am thinking, or I am going to be embarrassed to death."

"Your turn, Billy," I hear Gary say to the boy, and then I hear

97

another stream of water hitting water in the yellowed bowl.

"Good job, Billy."

"Your turn," Gary says.

"I don't think so. Not with you two standing there watching."

"So, you were watching?"

"No," I say quickly. I am pulling paper squares out of the dispenser, and I look up in the mirror to see Gary with a big innocent looking grin on his face.

I dry off my face, wipe off my neck and down my arms. It's cold. There is no sweet smelling soap, but I do what I can with what I have. I remind myself it's what Grandma taught me. But Grandma had it a whole lot better than this.

"You two wash your hands, and then get out of here so I can finish."

I stand back and push Gary to the sink. "Cold water," I say.

"That's all Jolie had."

"Well if you'd befriended my Grandparents, you would have had hot."

"Now *you're* being funny," he says.

I watch Gary use double hands and pour water on his head, scrub with his knuckles, and then rinse again with another two hands of water. Billy watches. Then, Gary gets another two hands of water and pours it over Billy's head.

"Hey," Billy complains.

"Scrub that gasoline smell off you boy. Tonight we'll let you sleep in the cab with us. How's that sound."

Billy says "Good." More paper towels are pulled, and Gary rubs the boy's head dry. He pushes his own hair back from his forehead with his hands.

"Now, let's leave this place so the lady can do her business in private."

"Yeah," Billy agrees, and the door opens then closes behind them.

I don't know what to do with relieving myself. I don't want to sit on the filthy thing they peed in, but I am about to burst, so I stand on top of it, straddling the hole and pee. And, I pee some more. I think I am never going to stop peeing, and I realize it has been over 24 hours since I last peed. I wonder how I kept from wetting on myself, and then wonder what Gary did.

When I am done, I wash my hands again and look at the girl in the mirror. She looks like me, same face, same eyes and mouth. But I'm not the same girl who ran off from Stears Branch. With everything that happened in the last 24 hours, I don't think that girl is ever coming back.

Outside, the two of them are standing near the El Camino. A long black hose stretches from the car to a pump, and vaguely I remember such things, back before Stears Branch. Gary is pulling bills from his wallet and handing it to a man in green pants and shirt. He nods and wads the bills in his pocket.

"This is a gas station, isn't it?"

"Uh-huh. Billy, you ever see a gas station?"

"No Gary," he says. It sounds the same as saying 'no sir,' but Gary doesn't correct him. He just pats his head and says we need it to make the car go.

Inside the car I ask, "Is it expensive?"

"Yeah, it's pretty high here, but not as bad as it was."

"I didn't bring money. I mean, I don't have any money."

"It's okay."

"But it's going to be expensive with the three of us."

"Probably."

"So what are we going to do for money?"

"Right now we're gonna get a hot breakfast, right little buddy?"

Billy is grinning from ear to ear with the promise of breakfast, and I am wondering how we are going to get by if we spend every cent Gary has in the first day we are here.

"But how are you going to afford it?"

"We're celebrating."

"What are we celebrating?"

"Our up-coming wedding. You *are* going to marry me, aren't you?"

I watch him, dazed, as he jumps in the car. "Come on you two. Get in. Breakfast is waiting."

Gary pulls back on the four-lane road that leads into town and the landscape flies by in a blur. Cars appear out of nowhere, and we slow down. Most of them are nicer than Gary's El Camino, but he doesn't seem to notice. He sits behind the wheel with a contented look on his face. Last night's haunting fears have vanished. He thinks I have agreed to marry him. I haven't told him different. We pull in front of a small building, mostly windows and green siding.

"Get ready for a treat," Gary tells us both. He pushes the door open, and the people behind the counter chime in together, "Good morning."

It's clean, and the lady behind the counter says, "Find yourself a seat. I'll be right with y'all."

Gary guides us to a table with soft, padded benches. The lady takes a water to the next table, two ladies in sweaters and pants. At our table she holds a small tablet and pencil.

"Now what can I get for the three of you?"

"Coffee for me," Gary says. "Milk for the boy, and an icy cold Pepsi for the lady."

Before I can ask Gary what he thinks he is doing, the lady has brought the coffee, milk, and Pepsi. She looks at me and says, "Honey, sorry, we don't do free refills on sodas anymore."

"That's okay," I say. I didn't know what else to say. I whisper across the table to Gary, "Who is she?"

"She is a waitress," he explains. "It is her job to take orders and bring us our food. Now let me do the ordering. She'll be back in just a second. You like waffles?"

"I never had waffles," I say.

Billy chimes in, "Me neither."

The waitress returns, leans over the table towards Gary and says, "What's for breakfast?"

"Three waffles all around, some bacon, and eggs for my wife here and our little friend."

The waitress straightens a little, smiles at me, and says, "It'll be right up."

"Gary, why'd you tell her that?"

Billy says in a real loud voice, "I thought you all were cousins."

I laugh. Gary turns red. "I lied," he tells Billy.

"You're not supposed to tell lies," Billy says.

Until Gary came to our hollow, I never knew what lying felt like. Now I do, and I can't say I like the way it feels. I agree with Billy. The two ladies at the next table, the ladies who wear pants, turn to see who it is that has been telling lies. The one with the black hair smiles at Gary. Seems like women all over the place like to smile at Gary, and I'm not sure I like that.

Billy begins to drink his milk. "This is good," he tells Gary. I look at my Pepsi, and I think of Grandma.

"What's the difference between this Pepsi and the Diet Pepsi my Grandma always talked about?"

"Sugar, honey," the waitress has come back to our table bearing

100

plates of food, hot, sweet smelling food. "You never had Pepsi before?"

I shake my head that I haven't, while she sets plate after plate before us. There is a whole platter of bacon, three plates with round indented pancakes, and four big sunny-side-up eggs.

"Well, if you don't like the Pepsi, just let me know. I'll replace it with a milk at no charge, honey."

"Thank you," I say and smile back at her.

"Dig in," Gary says.

"We gotta' say grace," Billy interrupts. I smile. At least I know what grace means, and Gary doesn't.

"You go ahead," I tell Billy, and I bow my head as he gives thanks.

Gary follows my lead, and looks up at me from his bowed head, I frown and motion for him to close his eyes.

"What's that all about?" he asks when Billy is finished.

"He says prayers of thanks before he eats. I bet he says prayers at bedtime, too, don't you Billy."

"If you eat before saying your prayers, God will make you get sick for not being thankful," Billy explains to Gary.

"That true?"

"I don't know. You feel sick?"

Gary's waffle was half gone before Billy started his prayer.

When the waitress refilled Gary's cup, he asked, "Where's the courthouse now?"

"Same as before, straight down this road, all the way into town on the right. You can't miss it. Used to be fountains in front, but there's water rationing. Too precious for fountains. Still, you'll have no trouble finding it."

"Thanks."

The waffle is good. The eggs taste about like duck eggs. I've never had bacon, and it is okay, but salty. It is the Pepsi that surprises me. I choke at first, snort it right up my nose. Gary laughs, and so does the black gentleman behind the counter. He stops flipping eggs to laugh. The waitress comes back to our table.

"You okay, honey? I can't believe you've never tasted Pepsi."

"She's from the other side of the river," Gary offers.

"Oh."

"Now who's giving too much information," I accuse. I am embarrassed, and I am angry at myself that I am embarrassed. "Who you lookin' at?" I say to the lady at the next table.

101

"Carrie," Gary says.

"I've had enough. I'm not hungry anymore. I'll be in the car." I get up and walk out the door. I can hear Billy say, "Why's she mad?" and Gary says, "I dunno."

From the car I can see Gary and Billy finish the waffles and bacon. Gary turns up my Pepsi and drains it before picking up the bill and going to the counter. Billy tips up his milk, and waves at me through the glass. I wave back, but I don't smile. I can see the waitress is talking to Gary and see him shaking his head with a smile on his face. He and Billy come out the door and head for the car. I'd like to lean over and lock both of them out. They are having entirely too much fun.

"Did you get enough to eat, Billy?" Gary asks.

"Yes sir, I mean, Gary. That was good. He drank your soda Carrie. Was that all right?"

"That was fine, Billy. I didn't like it anyway."

"Sorry it made you choke," he says.

"That's all right," I tell him.

Gary is smiling, can't keep it off his face, and I am fuming. He says to me, with that same smile on his face, "Seems like I've seen a different Carrie. Wonder which one I'm gonna marry."

He doesn't make things any better with his smart lip. If I had a stick I would hit him with it.

"Where we going now?" I ask.

"To the courthouse."

"What're we going to do there?"

"Get a marriage license."

"Then what do you think we're going to do?"

"We're gonna go look for a preacher."

Chapter 13

I watch Gary drum his fingers on the steering wheel, look at me for a moment, and then say, "Before we go to the courthouse, we need to get some things."

"What kinds of things?"

"Things like blankets, coats, dresses for you, and clothes for the boy."

"You ashamed of what I am wearing?"

I look down at my simple dress. Yes, it is wrinkled; I slept in it. Yes, it is a little worn, a bit small, but it is all I have. The best I have. Grandma and I were going to work on some things this winter.

"No, I'm not ashamed of you. My clothes aren't any better than yours, but how did you feel when those women were staring at you?"

"What's your point?"

"I just think you will feel a little more comfortable in some newer clothes."

"Where you going to get the money?"

"I didn't say we were going after new clothes."

He turns off the road that leads to the courthouse, drives past two big stores, lots of cars, more places to eat, and stops in front of a building that says "Goodwill" in big blue letters.

"We can buy hand-me-downs here," he says.

Inside are rows and rows of dresses and pants of all sizes, and people of all shapes and sizes rummaging through piles of clothing. We move towards the back.

"What size are you?" Gary asks.

"I don't know."

"Well, you're not too big for your age and not too tall either."

He goes up to a lady behind the counter, and I hear him ask for help. "My friend here could use some new things, and neither she nor I have a clue of what size to get. Do you think you can help us?"

"Well, what sort of things are you looking for?" she asks.

"About anything. I know she'll need a coat, some shoes, she's got little feet. I'd like to see her get at least one real pretty dress for a special occasion."

"What do you have in mind for the special occasion?"

"Something white," I hear him say.

She smiles. "Well, let me see what we can find."

The lady is tall and lean, with black, close clipped hair. Her lips are full, and I think of Reva, only she is taller – more striking. If I found a word to describe her at first sight it would be "strong." Her eyes are black, shiny, and friendly.

"You look to be a four, maybe a six. I can't tell. Guess it will depend on the dress, right honey? Now what color would you like?"

"I really don't care," I tell her. "I'm fine with what I got on."

"Well, it is a pretty little dress, but I think you've about outgrown it."

"Here, how about this one?" She holds up a light blue print, soft material, white collar, white belt. "People don't mind white after Labor Day anymore, and I think this will be warm enough for winter, even with the short sleeves. Let's take this one back to try on. Then, here's a red one. Not sure it's your color though. How about a pair of pants? Girls wear pants all the time, and they are awfully comfortable, especially if you are traveling."

Before we head back to try on clothes, she has pulled eight dresses, four shirts, and two pair of pants off the racks. I see Gary in the front of the store with Billy holding up jeans and shirts for the boy. He sees me with the sales lady and waves across the room. He holds up a yellow shirt and points to Billy. I nod yes. It is a pretty shirt for a little boy.

I am ushered into a narrow hallway and into a small square of a room. "You try these on, and I'll be back to check on you in a minute."

I never saw so many dresses at one time, and for sure, not all for me. I liked the blue one she picked out first, and I hold it up. It looks like it will fit. I do the same with a yellow and a green one. I don't like the red either, so I put it back on a knob on the wall.

"How we doing?" she asks as she returns. "Do they fit?"

"I think they will," I tell her.

"Well, did you put them on?"

"No, I just held them up."

"Honey, that's no way to try on clothes. You got a man out there that wants to see you dressed fine, even if they are second hand. We'd better make sure they fit."

She helps me pull my old dress over my head.

"Oh my," she whispers. "I'd better go back to see if we can find you some proper undergarments. That all you have?"

"Yes Ma'am."

"Poor child, where you been?"

I'd like to get mad at her, but she is kind and she doesn't say it in a way that she talks down about me. So I let it go. She returns with panties and brassieres.

"You're not too big, but not too small either. Some girls like you got it just right honey. Don't worry about paying for these under garments. They're on me. Be just you and me's secret, okay?"

I am thankful for her generosity and secrecy. I didn't know what I had was so poor looking until I saw the pretties that she brought me.

The blue dress fits. So does the yellow. I like the pants, especially the blue jeans like Gary wears. I think I look real smart in them, and the white blouse with the dark blue sweater.

"Can I wear these out?" I ask.

"Sure, sweetie."

She leaves and comes back with a dress all white, lace sleeves and bodice. She tells me "my young man" picked it out for me.

"You're pretty as an angel," she says, looking over me after we have put the dress on and zipped the back. She fingers my hair, gathers it up away from my face, and says, "You'll make a beautiful bride."

"Maybe," I say.

"Well, you better not say maybe. That young man out there has not only picked this dress out for you, he has found himself a suit and that little boy, too. Is he your little boy?"

"Oh, God, no. I'm not old enough to have babies. His mother left him with us last night."

"Really? Now why on earth would a mother leave her child?"

"I can't say I know."

"Well, I think we should get all of these. Now let's go back out and see what else the boys have found."

She leaves my old dress on the chair, and I pick it up.

"You don't want that old thing now, do you?"

"Oh yes, Ma'am. I've got to have it." I start to tell her that my Grandma made it, and I got to have something to remember her by. But I don't say it. She takes the dress and folds it carefully and hands it back to me. I think maybe she understands.

Gary and Billy are waiting for me at the tall counter. The clerk piles my clothes on top of Gary's and takes her piece of paper and begins adding. I think I will have to take most of the clothes back, because we surely don't have enough money to pay for all of this. Gary can't take his eyes off me. I know why. Those two women in the restaurant don't have a thing on me now, and I know it.

The clerk is smiling at Gary and clears her throat to get his attention. "That'll be two dollars," she says.

Gary's face shows surprise. "You sure you added it right?"

She looks at him and smiles at me. "I'm sure I did."

Gary pulls two bills from his wallet and hands it to the lady. There are four large bags, and I think there isn't room in the El Camino for all this stuff. He carries two large ones, Billy the small one, and me with another large one.

I say to the clerk, "My name's Carrie Baxter. Thank you for all your kindness to me today."

"Well, Carrie, I was glad to do it. Have a happy life, you hear?"

"I will, Ma'am."

Outside, Gary is packing the back of the car, folding the tarp over our new clothes so as not to lose any to the wind. There wasn't enough room inside for Billy, Gary, me, and the clothes.

"Where we going to wear all these things?" I ask.

"I don't know. One thing I do know, you are beautiful."

"He said you look hot," Billy says.

"I did not," Gary denies.

"Did too."

"Okay, I did, but it's true."

"Well, I think I need to say 'thank you,' because that sounds kind of like a compliment."

"It's just one o'clock. The courthouse stays open until four, I think. Let's head down there."

We backtrack to where the restaurant was, turn left instead of right. Old trees line the street making a living tunnel of reds and golds, and I wonder aloud how they managed to survive the earthquakes that hit here.

"West and to the south sides were hit hardest. Most of these old houses stayed intact. Built to last, my Mom said. The trees here were old back then, and I guess they just didn't give up their place. Their roots ran too deep."

"They're beautiful," I say.

The trees clear, make way for gray and brown buildings with

106

windows staring down on us. Our street splits into two, and we go straight. Other vehicles fly by us. We travel slowly down the paved road, stopping at lights that blink red and going on green. I remember this, remember the moving and stopping, and when we come to the wide plaza that includes the courthouse, I am sure. A tall statue of a man stands in front of fountains that are dry.

"I think we lived somewhere close to here," I tell Gary.

He looks through the mirror on his windshield, turns his head and moves into the lane closest to the right and turns in front of the plaza. Like the lady said, the fountains no longer spray. Across the street a concrete creek lays dry. There are no places to park the car, and we turn onto another street, and then another, until there are spaces for vehicles.

"You cold?" Gary asks.

"A little."

"How about you?" he asks Billy.

"I'm fine, sir."

"Gary," he reminds him.

"I'm fine, Gary," Billy corrects himself.

Gary slides the El Camino between two yellow lines, and we walk to the building, walking alongside of more people than I ever knew existed. Everyone seems preoccupied, bags over their shoulders and with their heads down, small contraptions held to their ears.

"What are they doing?" I ask.

"I think they are talking on phones," Gary says.

"Grandma told me about those. Everybody used to have one."

"Well, here that's still the case."

"You have one?"

"No," he tells me. "I don't know anyone else who has one, so I can't see any need."

"Grandma thought they were a nuisance."

"For once, I think I agree with her," he says smiling.

We are standing in front of tall glass doors. "I think this is the main door."

"What, exactly, are we supposed to do here?" I ask.

"Two things. First, we get a marriage license. Second, we ask where the Hall of Records is located."

"In that order?"

"Yeah."

At the counter Gary asks the gentleman where we might get a marriage license.

"Not here son," the man says.

"Is this where we would find death certificates, or, you know, find someone who is missing?" I ask.

"Not here, Ma'am. You all must not be from around here."

"This is the court house, isn't it?" Gary asks.

"Well, yes, it is, but it is not where you're going to find records, or a marriage license. This is where court is held, judges' offices, things like that. You need to go on down to the Annex."

"Where's that?" Gary asks.

The gentleman rises, comes from around the counter. To a uniformed officer, he says, "Henry, you watch my desk for a moment. I need to help these kids. Follow me."

Billy, Gary, and I follow the large dark man back out the door, past the fountains and statue towards the main street. He points back down the street.

"There, see that structure, big drive opening? The door to the left is the door to the licensing offices. They should have everything you're looking for. Where you parked?"

"Around the corner," Gary tells him.

"Good. I wouldn't recommend pulling into the parking structure. It's not safe, really. The back drive collapsed following the last aftershock, and even though it isn't to be used, there's no guard. Sometimes folks use it anyway."

"Thanks for your help," Gary says.

"No problem, kid. Good luck."

I say, "Thanks."

We walk the short distance between the courthouse and annex. I can barely keep up with Gary's long strides. Billy runs to keep up.

"Hold up," I tell him.

"Sorry," he says, and he slows down.

We pass the large dark opening, and there are cars parked there just as the gentleman said, and from the next level up, people lean over the ledge laughing and calling out to passing pedestrians.

Inside, there is a long hallway. Signs above doors stand out in bold letters: VEHICLE LICENSING, FISH AND GAME LICENSES. There is a plaque on one wall, and it tells us that the marriage license office is on the next floor. With that, we head up the stairs. There, at the top of the stairs is the door marked MARRIAGE LICENSES. I pause on the top step. Billy passes me, and Gary stops.

"Are you coming?" he asks.

I just stand there.

"Well?"

"Come on, Carrie," Billy says. "We're gonna get married."

Gary moves back to the stairs, puts his hand on my arm. "It's okay. We'll get the license. If you don't want to get married, we'll just tear it up. I mean, it's not like we're gonna do anything today, okay?"

I feel like turning and running back down the steps, but if I bolt, I have no idea where I'll go.

"Come on," Billy says again. He runs back to where I am standing, and pulls me towards the lettered door, pushes it open with his thin arm, and we are inside. Gary follows.

"May I help you?" the older woman asks. It seems to me the first thing everyone in this whole town says is "May I help you."

"I have a couple of questions," Gary says.

"Well, I'll do my best to answer those."

Her hair is curled close to her head and colored like gun metal. I think she is old like Grandma, but her skin is not lined or rough.

"Well...I'd like...we'd like to get a marriage license, you know, to get married; but, if we get one, does it mean you are married right then?"

Now Gary sounds like he is from the other side of the river.

The lady smiles, "No, it isn't valid until it is signed by a duly authorized minister or by a Justice of the Peace. Even then it isn't fully validated until the marriage is consummated."

Gary nods. "We'd like to get a license."

"I will need documentation of your identity and age. Do you have that?

"Yeah," and Gary pulls out his wallet and hands the lady a card. She looks at the card, and back up at Gary, then hands the card back to him.

"And the young lady?"

"She doesn't have any," Gary says.

"How old are you?" she asks me.

Gary says, "Eighteen."

I turn to look at Gary.

"I asked the young lady. Honey, how old are you?

109

"Sixteen, almost seventeen."

Looking back at Gary, she says, "She needs a parent or guardian's signature as indication of parental consent, and even if she was eighteen, she'd need documentation of that."

"She doesn't have parents. They died in the quakes. She was living with distant relatives over the river until coming here with me."

"Is that true?" she asks me.

"I don't rightly know Ma'am. I lost my parents in the quakes, and I don't know if they are alive or dead. We got separated. I came here looking for them."

She glares at Gary, "That's quite a bit different than what you just said." Then to me she asks, "Are you with him of your own free will?"

"Gary's just trying to protect me. We've already come through some bad places, and Gary thought he could protect me better if we were married. I don't have anyone else here. No one, Ma'am."

"I can't give you a license. You have no identification. You are under age. This boy can be charged and arrested if he has done anything to harm you or taken advantage of you. He's over 18. Are you aware of that young man?"

"Yes Ma'am."

"First thing you need to do, young lady, is get some identification. Where were you born?"

"Here in Lexington."

"You will need to go to Frankfort and get an official copy of your birth certificate. Do you know your parents' names?"

"Of course," I say.

"Where in Frankfort?" Gary asks.

"Records Department, off US 60. It will cost you ten dollars in coin, not paper money."

Billy slips out from behind Gary and asks, "Ten dollars?"

"Is he your child?" the lady asks Gary.

I say, "No, I'm too young to have a boy Billy's age. Billy's..."

"Not you," she says. "Mr. Combs, is the boy yours?"

"My mom asked Gary to take care of me 'til she can get back," Billy offers.

Gary frowns at me, and then takes Billy and me by the arm and pushes the door open.

"Thanks for your help," he says, then thinks to ask, "Is there any place around here to stay?"

110

"Homeless Shelter is farther up the street, but they may be full, or there's the Hope Center for Women for her, but that's farther away. If the Shelter's full, they can tell you how to get there."

When the door closes behind us, Gary whispers under his breath, "Thanks for nothing."

"I'm sorry," I tell him as we leave the building.

"It's not your fault."

"Yes, it is. I should have lied about my age."

"She wasn't going to buy it. Besides, you didn't have identification of who you are or proof of age. She was right."

We walk back to the car in silence. On the front window held in place by the windshield wiper is a white slip of paper. Gary pulls it off and curses beneath his breath.

"What?" I ask.

"A ticket," he says. "A damned parking ticket."

"What's that?" I ask.

"Apparently I parked in a 'no parking' zone."

"So what does it mean?"

"I owe twenty dollars in coin to this stinkin' town."

"What are we gonna do now?" I ask.

"Go down to the Homeless Shelter."

Chapter 14

"That's a lot of money, isn't it Gary?" Billy asks. He hasn't stopped talking since we got into the car.

"Billy," I say. "Gary's trying to concentrate. Be quiet for a few minutes, okay?"

"Sure Carrie, but where is Gary going to get all that money? My dad said that money was hard to come by, and I just can't stop thinking about where Gary's going to get..."

"Billy, shut up." Gary's voice is firm, and Billy sits back against the seat. His eyes well up, and tears spill down his cheek.

"Carrie," Gary says to me, "do something with him."

"Up there," I say. "Doesn't that say *Shelter*?"

Gary turns into the circle drive.

"Wait for me here," he says as he turns off the car and climbs out the window. An elderly gentleman has come through the doors, well dressed in a dark gray uniform. Gary stops him, and I can see his lips moving, but can't make out what he is saying. He points to the car. Billy is still crying.

"Billy, you've got to stop crying. Someone is going to think we're hurting you."

"What's going to happen to us, Carrie?" he asks between sobs. "Where are we going to go, and when is my Mommy coming back. We need to go back to that place where we was this morning, 'cause she's gonna' come back, and we won't be there, and she won't know where to find us."

He cries even harder, and I don't have a clue what to do. "Come here," I say to him, and he wiggles across the seat. I pull him close, wrap my arms around him. His tears are muffled in my sweater. "It's going to be okay, Billy, I promise."

He lifts his face, "You promise, Carrie?"

"I said 'I promise,'" I say, looking into his eyes. He looks like his father.

"You gonna help me find my Mom?"

"I'll do my best."

Gary walks back to the car, sticks his head through my window, "We can stay here for a little while. He said they'd get us a place of our

112

own as soon as one comes open. They have stuff like that for people who are down on their luck. He says he can get me work. Doesn't pay much, but it will be something. I told him we were married."

I look at him, "You what?"

"I had to. They would've separated us and put Billy in foster care. Would you have wanted that?"

"What about what that lady said, you know, about you being charged?"

"I don't think she is going to follow up on it, Carrie. Why would she?"

"I think she thought you were taking advantage of me."

"That's exactly what she thought."

"So you don't think she'll try and follow up on it. I mean, she sent us down here, didn't she?"

"I guess it's a risk I'll just have to take."

Billy raised his head, "What's foster care?"

"Nothing for you to worry about," I say, and press his head back against my chest. Then I whisper to Gary, "What's foster care?"

"They'd take him away. Carrie, while we're here we'll stay in separate quarters, you and Billy with the women, and me on the men's side. We'll be able to take meals together. You're going to have to act like we're married. Are you willing to do that?"

"What do you mean?"

"You know, act like, I dunno..."

Billy raises his head again, "You know, Carrie, that mushy kissy stuff."

Gary's face turns red.

"Is he right?"

"Yeah. At least while we're here, you need to keep up appearances. I swear to you, Carrie, I'll not ask you to do anything you don't want to. I mean it."

I remember the almost kiss at the spring, the kiss under the walnut tree, and it is my turn for my face to get red. I think it isn't such a bad thing, and he promises to not make me do something I don't want to do, but I'm not quite sure what that means. But I do believe him.

Gary goes to the back of the El Camino and pulls back the tarp. "Some of this I'll keep locked up in the cab of the car. Like the white dress, and our suits, are you okay with that?"

"Sure," I say.

Each of us carries one of the black bags into the building. Gary introduces me to Captain Davis. He has a stern face, is younger than Grandpa, minus the smile or laughter I remember when Grandpa played a prank. I don't think Captain Davis knows how to play pranks.

"Mrs. Combs, if you and the little boy will come with me, I'll introduce you to my wife, and she can get you situated in the women and children's quarters. How old is the little boy?"

"Six, sir," I say.

"You look way too young to have a six-year-old."

"Oh, I am," I say in a rush.

Gary jumps in, "He's not our child, Captain Davis. He's my sister's boy. She has asked me to keep him for a couple of weeks. I'm sorry I didn't make that clear."

"That's not a problem, son. We'll work on getting you a place of your own as soon as we can. What brings you to Lexington?"

"My wife, Carrie, wants to see what happened to her parents. She was raised by her grandparents across the river, and she needs to know what happened to them."

"I can understand that," he says. "Lots of people lost family. We'll be serving up supper in about an hour. Until then let's try and get you settled."

Mrs. Davis's face is serious, but not as stern as her husband's. I would feel better if they would at least smile. Before we go to separate sleeping quarters, Gary leans over and kisses me lightly on the lips. I kiss him back.

"I'll see you at supper," he says. I nod.

"Mr. Combs," the captain says as an afterthought, "since the boy is your nephew, maybe he ought to stay with you in the men's quarters."

"Whatever you think is best," Gary says, and Billy runs to Gary with his small bag on his shoulder. They pass through a green door, and I feel deserted.

"Mrs. Combs?" the Mrs. Davis says. I don't respond. I am still watching the green door, and I don't recognize my new name.

"Mrs. Combs?"

"Huh? I'm sorry, I was distracted."

"How long have you two been married?"

"Not long." I say, and it's the truth.

"It must be hard being a newlywed and having the responsibility of someone else's child."

"Not really," I say. "He's been through so much."

"I understand," she says. "Now come with me."

We enter the yellow door. There are narrow beds, covered with white sheets stretched tight in neat lines like the rows of stark crosses at the depot. It is an unnerving picture, and I shudder.

"You all right, dear?" Mrs. Davis asks.

"Yes Ma'am. How many women stay here?"

"It varies. More when it is cold, less in the summer. We will be filling up rather quickly. Weather has turned cold early this year. Most Octobers are a lot warmer. Usually doesn't turn really cold until after Christmas. Now where are you from?"

"Across the river."

"You can put your bag under the bed. Do you have any valuables in there?"

"No Ma'am."

"It should be safe enough then. We have lockers if you need one, but the women seem to honor each other's clothes."

"Where's Gary going to stay?"

"Oh, just across the hall. You won't be too far from him. How long did you say you'd been married?"

"I don't think I said. We've not been married a year yet." I say, again not lying. *I've got to ask Gary how long we're going to tell them so we keep the same story.*

"There are showers over there," she says and points to the back of the large room. "Sinks and commodes there as well."

"Thank you." *I have to remember to ask Gary what a shower is.*

"We have supplies, you know, feminine hygiene items, if you need any."

I act like I know what she's talking about. She looks at her watch.

"Supper will be served in about thirty minutes. I'll leave you to get washed up. If you have any questions, any one of our staff should be able to help you."

I watch her leave through the doors. I count fifty beds. Five rows of ten, not two feet apart. Each bed has a white sheet, pillow and a red blanket folded neatly at the foot. It looks just like the blanket that Grandma puts on my bed every November. Two days and one night has passed since we pushed the car down the lane. Two days since I looked the last time at Grandma's face, pale in the upstairs window. It feels like two years, a forever ago. I want to cry, but there is a woman

115

two beds over watching me. She stares from beneath straggly brown bangs. The edge of my bag of clothes pushes out from beneath my bed. I am glad that Gary left the bag of fancy clothes in the El Camino, because she looks at me and then at the giant black bag. Ms. Davis said my things would be safe, but it doesn't feel like it.

I jump by a touch on my shoulder.

"I didn't mean to startle you," a soft voice behind me says. "My name's Claire. She won't bother your things. She's not quite all there." Claire sits on the bed beside me.

"Are you sure?" I ask.

"Yeah, I'm sure. Her name is Mave. She's been here for years. Shell shock from the earth quakes, I suppose. She's too pitiful to be out on her own, not pitiful enough to be in a state hospital. The Davises allow her to stay because there is nowhere else for her to go. What's your name?"

"Carrie."

"Carrie what?"

I start to say Baxter and then catch myself. "Carrie Combs."

"Pretty name."

"Do you live here?

"I did, for a long time. Then I sort of married Jack."

I must have a puzzled look on my face, because she goes on to explain, "I work here now. After I met Jack, I moved out. I decided I needed to do my part, kind of pay back the kindness that was shown to me when I was alone and scared."

"Will all these beds be full tonight?" I ask.

Claire scanned the room. "Probably about half, but when it gets cooler, more women will come in off the street. Let me show you the bathroom, and we can get you ahead of the crowd in the dining room. Where's your husband?"

"Behind the green door."

She laughs, and stands. "Come on."

I follow, and inside the bathroom is a row of sinks and beside them rows of metal boxes with the towels made of paper like the ones at the Shell station, only a lot cleaner. There are closed tiny rooms. Claire pushes open a swinging door to show a toilet.

"In here are the showers," she says, and we walk into a room with small knobs protruding from walls.

There are two naked women, one young with rolls of fat, the other

116

old and skinny standing beneath the knobs with squirting water. I have a vague memory of standing under such a knob when I was little, but it is a faded memory. The women pay us no mind and seem not in the least embarrassed by their nakedness. I follow Claire back into the room with the beds.

"In the cabinet on the far wall," she points to the windowed wall, "are towels. You can have a clean towel and washcloth every three days, so you will need to keep track of them. I used to fold them over the foot of my bed in the morning, and by the next morning they were dry."

Through the doors, and back into the hallway, I find Gary and Billy waiting for me.

"The dining room is at the end of the hall," Claire says to me. "I've gotta get home to Jack. He'll be waiting for his supper. I'll be back here in the morning if you need anything." With that she nods to Gary and leaves through the front doors.

"Did she get you settled?" Gary asks.

I nod. "I never saw so many beds in one place."

"Yeah, I know what you mean. There must be a hundred on our side."

I add in my head, "That's twice as many as the women's side. How can they get so many beds into one room?"

"It's tight, believe me."

Billy's hair has been combed down. So has Gary's. I didn't even look in the row of mirrors to see what I looked like. Instinctively I run a hand across my hair.

"You look fine," Gary says. He has read my thoughts, and I wonder how he can read me so easily. "Come on, the line is going to get long."

It is. I wonder where all the people have come from, because once inside the gray doors, a line stretches around the wall to where we stand. I think there must be two dozen or more children, from little ones, to two that look to be near my age. And, I have never seen so many men and women, all sizes, all ages, all colors.

"Carrie," Billy says, pulling on my sleeve. "Look at that man. He's black as coal."

"Sh..." I whisper. "It's not polite to stare."

"But, Carrie," he says again. I don't think he knows how to whisper.

"Talk soft," I tell him.

"But, I never saw a man with black skin."

117

I wonder how far back in the hollows he must have lived to have never seen a person of color. We had the Thompsons, and in our hollow color didn't matter, not to Reva and not to us. Funny but he didn't notice the lady at the Goodwill store or the gentleman at the courthouse. But this man is darker, and his skin glistens, like he had worked hard all day and just come in. He smiles at Billy, and I bend down to Billy and whisper, "Smile at the gentleman."

"Don't teach him to be so familiar, Carrie."

"Why?"

"Just better to keep to ourselves."

"Politeness doesn't invite company."

"Yes, it does."

"Am I to be friendly or not," Billy asks, looking to Gary and then to me.

"Friendly," I say.

"Not, Billy."

In defiance I smile at the gentleman.

We reach the food table, and we each do as the person before us, pick up plate, spoon, and fork. The food smells good – potatoes, meat with tomato sauce on top, green beans, and milk to drink. Billy's eyes grow big at the large squares of chocolate cake with dark icing. The smell of cocoa reminds me of cool nights around the fire with Grandma's concoction. We find a table with three seats together, and again Billy lowers his head in thanks. I elbow Gary, and he bows his head as well. Billy's words ring out to those around us, and in respect the diners nearby bow their heads.

"Thank you God for this mighty good looking food. And take care of Mommy and Susie where ever they went, and God, take care of Daddy. Amen. Oh yeah, thank you for Gary and Carrie for taking good care of me, and finding this place where I can sleep on a bed again. Amen."

I can hear the guy at the next table chuckle, but Billy doesn't notice, because he is digging into the soft white potatoes.

"Is your room okay?" Gary asks.

"Room? Like my own room?" I am sarcastic for a moment, then realize how ungrateful I must sound. "It's fine," I say. "Just lots of beds."

"Yeah, but better than the car, right?"

"You're right. There's this place called a shower room, knobs sticking out of the wall on all sides. Water spewing out."

"To take a shower, Carrie, to clean up." I can hear an impatience in his voice, but I don't think he understands.

"Well, there's no modesty at all. I'll not take my clothes off in front of all those women. And it's got to be cold, spraying that water right out of the pipes."

"The water is heated."

"Oh. I still don't want to get naked in front of someone I don't know at all. Point in case."

I look towards the strange woman from my side of the yellow door who goes through the food line and sits at our table. She nods at me and begins eating with soft grunts.

"Who's that?"

"Mave," I say, then whisper, "Crazy Mave. Her bed is two over from mine."

"That true?"

"One of the staff told me. Crazy, but harmless." Mave looks up from her food and stares. Billy's excitement breaks the visual hold.

"There's two kinds of pots to pee in, Carrie." He finishes wiping clean his plate. Licking the last of the icing from his spoon and looking at me with chocolate smeared on his cheek and adds, "One like where we got gas this morning, and another one you stand up to, real close and just pee right in. Gary showed me how to do it, only it was easier for him, because he's bigger. I had to stand on my tip toes to keep from peeing on myself."

The guy at the next table laughs right out loud this time, and Billy turns and smiles at him.

"First time in the big city?" he asks Billy.

"Yeah, and this place is great. But, I'm sorry, I'm not supposed to talk to you. Gary doesn't want me to be polite."

Gary turns red, says to the man, "You got to be careful in a new place."

"Yeah, I know what you mean. It's okay, no offense taken." Gary nods.

"Can I go over there to where those little kids are sitting? Please Uncle Gary?" I decide Billy is smarter than we give him credit.

Gary says, "Okay, but wipe the chocolate off your face." To me he adds, "I'm to go for an interview in the morning. Will you and Billy be okay?"

119

"Interview?"

"For a job. We need to get some money. I'm getting low."

"Where?"

"Not too far from here. Captain Davis said there was a garage a couple of streets over that might hire me as a clean-up man. It's not much pay, and won't be all day, just afternoons. Maybe I can get on as a mechanic if they like me. Hopefully, it will be in coin, but I think the silver certificate paper spends fine here in the city."

"What are we going to do while you are working?"

"I don't know. There's a library here, maybe teach Billy how to read?"

"Books?"

"A whole room full of them, and puzzles, and games for children. Plus they'll probably serve lunch, too. Captain Davis said there was a schedule out in the hallway. I didn't notice when we came in; but before we leave for bed, we'll look for it. He also said if we were here long enough, you would be asked to help out. You okay with that?"

"Not sure what I can do, but I'll do my part. I always do."

"That's what I told him.

"Gary?"

"Huh?

"What's feminine hygiene products?" I ask. I am finishing up the last of my bite of cake.

Gary spews his milk across the table, and Crazy Mave frowns. The man behind us laughs right out loud, and Gary's face is redder than I ever saw it, redder than his hair.

"It's stuff for women."

I look at him perplexed. "What kind of stuff?"

Crazy Mave stops eating and watches us. She may be dim-witted according to Claire, but she seems to know more than me about these things.

"You know, the things a woman needs when..." Gary stammers.

"When she bleeds," she says to me from across the table.

"Oh," I say, and I think to myself she is talking about rags. I haven't considered what I am going to do when that time comes. I didn't think of it at all, didn't consider that I might be gone long enough for another cycle to arrive, and now it is my turn for my face to grow red.

Gary stands with his tray in his hand. "You done?"

"Yeah." I get up to follow him to the large trash cans near the door.

At the cafeteria doors, Gary stops. "We need to talk."

"I know."

"We need to get some things straight."

"I'm sorry about back there," I tell him.

His face flushes again, "It's okay."

Billy sees us and comes running. "I made some new best friends."

Chapter 15

Gary left right after breakfast. He looked clean shaven, neat, and it was easy for me to pretend that we were married. I walked him to the door, and he gave me a hug. I said, "Good luck."

Billy cried and said, "Uncle Gary, you're coming back aren't you?"

"Yeah, Billy, I'll be back. I couldn't leave you and Carrie, now could I?" It was a statement, not a question. Billy looks up at me, grabs hold of my hand, like he thinks I'll move out the door behind his Uncle Gary.

I don't think it is an act. In the last forty-eight hours his life has changed abruptly. He is young, and already it seems to him like we have been together forever. I wonder what his life was like before the attack at the river that he embraces two strangers so easily. I want to ask him if it was tough before, was his Mommy kind, or was she severe. He adapts quickly. Today, I am his mommy. If he remembers two days ago, he doesn't show it.

I am still standing at the double glass doors when Claire arrives in the passenger seat of a truck more rusted out than Gary's. She sits alongside the man who looks much older than her. She opens the door to her side of the truck, and the man pulls her back for one last kiss before she leaves. It is lingering, and just watching it makes a longing in my belly. I look away.

Billy has dropped my hand and takes up with another child. He is being chased by a younger boy, and when the child catches him, he yells, "You're it," and Billy chases him back. The boy looks to be near the age of Billy's little sister.

I feel the rush of cold air as Claire enters the building.

"Good morning," she says.

"Hi."

"Where's your husband?"

"Captain Davis helped him get an interview for a job."

"Wow, that's quick," she says. "What does Gary do?"

"Oh, about anything," I say.

"You're lucky. I see the little boy is adjusting."

"Yeah, I was just thinking that myself. He's been through so much, I don't see how he just keeps going and going."

"Kind of like the Energizer Bunny."

"Huh?"

"Never mind. Did you do okay last night?"

"I guess so. It felt pretty strange sleeping with so many snoring women."

"Tell me about it. Gary doesn't snore?"

"Not that I know," and she gives me a strange look. I add, "Grandpa used to snore so loud I could hear him from the loft."

"Where's your Grandpa now?"

I think I'd better be careful, because I bet he is out hunting for me right this very minute, but I can't say that, so I say, "Back on the farm with my Grandma."

"I need a cup of coffee before I start my duties. The little boy will be okay out here. Come along and tell me about your grandparent's farm."

I start to follow, then stop. "Billy," I call to him. He stops his running, and looks up.

"Yeah?"

"I'm going to be right in here with this lady, okay? Will you be all right?"

"Sure," he says, and we move inside the dining room doors.

"Hey, Claire," one of the men says from a far table. She calls back, "Sam, you doing okay today?"

"Never better, except a kiss from you would sure be a nice top off to my morning coffee."

"Now Sam, you know I'm taken."

Sam laughs.

"How long did you say you and Gary have been married?"

Last night, before we went to our separate beds, Gary and I went over the details of the story we will tell. I'm hunting for my folks. He brought me here, because he thought it would make me happy, and it will. We have been married for a month. I am eighteen years old. I hope I can keep all the lies straight, and I hope to God no one gets Billy to talking. Even if he is clever enough to keep the Uncle Gary straight, all the lies we have concocted are almost too much for even me.

"Just a month," I say.

"A baby on the way?"

"Good Lord, no. I'm too young to have babies."

123

"Some would say you are a little too young to be getting married."

I blush. "It's not back where we're from," and that's the truth, except for Grandma and Grandpa's perspective.

"How'd you get separated from your mom and dad?"

"I was little, so I don't remember a whole lot. I was just seven," I lie, and I think of Billy. I wonder how much of that night he remembers, and I wonder when he is seventeen will his mother's face fade like an old picture. I realize I am assuming she is never coming back, and I make a note to ask Gary what her letter said.

"Most of what I remember is what Grandma has told me. Stories about the night of the quakes, packing their truck with all that they could. My Momma and Daddy went home to get important papers and my dog. Grandma and Grandpa took me with them. It was early morning when we crossed the bridge. I never saw my Momma again. It was important to Grandma that I not forget, and yet as the years went by, the things in the present seemed to be more important," I say, but that's not true. Grandma always remembered...always. The thought of her makes me homesick to see her weathered face.

She nods understanding. "Mrs. Davis says I am to help you get settled in here, and then help you search for your parents."

"Help me find my Momma?"

"Uh-huh."

"Gary says I need to go to a hall of records, you know, to see if there are death certificates. He also says I need to get an official birth certificate, but that's in Frankfort and costs money."

"He's right. Did Captain Davis ask to see your marriage certificate?"

I stutter, "I don't know, Gary didn't say anything about it."

"Mrs. Davis was concerned. You seem so young."

Claire watches my face closely. My cheeks feel hot. "I'm not that young."

I am scared. I am sure the lady from the annex has called to see if we came here, and if she did call, I am sure she has told them that she didn't give us a marriage license. My mind races – what if they arrest Gary for what the lady was silently accusing him.

"My wedding dress is in the car," I add. "I wouldn't leave without it, and so is Gary's suit." It's the truth. We just haven't had the chance to use them yet.

"You brought your dress?" she asks laughing.

"I did."

She laughs louder, puts her cup of coffee down, and wraps her arms around me in a hug.

"Carrie," she says. "You are a breath of fresh air. First thing we'll do is check records."

"Where?" I ask. I don't have a good feeling.

"Down at the Annex Building."

"Right now?" I ask, and I can see the face of the lady at the Annex, stern and accusing.

"No," she says. "It's the weekend. Not much open on Saturday."

I feel the breath I was holding leave in a rush. She eyes me with what I think is a knowing look, and I suspect my held breath was obvious to even Sam.

"Everyone who stays here any length of time at all gets assigned chores. You have any skills?" My puzzled expression makes her add, "You are willing to work, aren't you?"

"I'm a hard worker."

"What do you think you can do?"

"Just about anything."

"Can you read?"

"Of course I can read."

"Can you do math?"

"Yes," I say, offended that she would think I wasn't educated.

"How far did you go in school?"

"How far?"

"Did you graduate, or something?"

"There weren't schools in Stears Branch. Just Grandma and Grandpa, and they knew a lot. I can read most anything. We had books."

"You said you escaped the quakes and the floods. How did you have any books?"

"Grandma had just about everything stored, like books, paper, pencils. You know, all she needed to teach me."

"Hmm. You got away just in time, and you had all that?"

"I watched the big bridge go down. We made it just in time to the other side of the river. Grandpa saw that we were safe."

"You're just a little touchy, aren't you?"

I think to myself that had she been there, had she seen the falling cars, heard the screams of people falling, she wouldn't challenge me.

She says again, "So what can you do?"

125

I think a moment, "I can cook mush, make chicory coffee, gather herbs for healing, I know most of them. Yellow root. Ginseng. Black cohosh."

"We have doctors for such things. You said you can read?"

"Yes."

"Do you like children?"

"Yes."

"We can have you help Mrs. Davis with the children in the mornings. They don't meet on Saturdays, but if Mrs. Davis approves, you can start on Monday. Tomorrow, we all go to church."

I know church. Grandma and Grandpa held church every Sunday. Since being on the road, I lost track of what day it was, and I wondered if tomorrow Grandma and Grandpa, if he's still there, will meet around the kitchen table, if Grandma will read a Psalm, and Grandpa some other passage, and then talk about what it means. Lately, all Grandpa talked about was the evils of the world. Grandma and I both knew he was talking about Gary. And, though I wasn't sure what Grandma thought, I knew Gary didn't fit the category of evil-doer.

"This morning you can help me get ready for lunch. You can wrap silverware."

At the end of a long table near the kitchen are stacks of paper napkins and piles of spoons, forks, and table knives. Claire shows me how to wrap and tuck, and then place them bottom down into circular bins. The clock on the far wall says nine thirty, and I wonder when Gary will return.

Claire takes her cup, refills it, then heads to the table where Sam is sitting. I fold and tuck. I try to hear what Claire is saying, but they speak in low tones, occasionally laughing. I wonder about Billy, but don't get up to check on him. My thoughts bring him into the cafeteria.

"Carrie," he calls and runs to where I am sitting. One of the cooks looks through a small open window and frowns.

"No running in here." And he stops.

"This is a neat place, Carrie," Billy says. "Can we stay here forever?"

"I don't think so," I tell him. "We'll get a place of our own pretty soon, and once I find my Momma and Daddy, we'll all go back to Grandma's."

Billy shrugs. "My Mom will be back by then," and he sits down beside me. "Can I help?"

126

"Sure," I say, and the same woman through the window says, "Wash your hands first."

"Over there," I tell Billy, and he runs past Claire's table.

"I said no running, young man," the faceless voice calls from the kitchen.

When Billy gets back, he begins the easy task of wrapping. We are done before lunch, and he says, "Come on, Carrie. I want to show you the play room."

"Claire, I'm done," and I follow Billy out.

She nods, and as we pass, Sam laughs and says, "I agree."

Chapter 16

Yesterday Gary didn't get in until long after lunch. He came in greasy-faced and smiling. I said, "You missed lunch. Are you hungry?" and he assured me that he had missed more than one meal in his lifetime, and he hadn't been hurt by it. He said that he would get paid next Friday a total of two hundred dollars if he did a good job. That was big bucks.

Gary went to Captain Davis and asked if we could have a room together, since Billy's mom left we hadn't had any time without the boy. I stood at the women's quarters and listened. So did Crazy Mave.

Captain Davis reminded Gary, "The main Shelter doesn't have the facilities for family apartments."

"That makes it hard, being almost newlyweds."

"That reminds me, Mr. Combs. I have neglected my duties in not checking on your arrival. I do need to see your marriage license in order to even work on getting you family housing."

Gary went out to the car and returned with a stack of papers, and apologized. "I'm sorry, Captain Davis. I have misplaced it."

"I'm sorry to hear that, because I can't assist in getting you your own place without that documentation," the Captain had said. "You need to be more careful with important papers."

Gary wasn't happy last night or this morning. All during the church service he frowned and fidgeted in his seat. For that matter, so did Billy.

After lunch, and my chore of helping clean off tables, Gary asked a young girl if she would mind keeping an eye on Billy while he and I had some time alone. She said okay, and Billy was happy enough to play with the other children. Claire doesn't work weekends, and I am glad.

It is cold out, but the sun is shining. We bundle in the coats from the Goodwill and head out. Gary takes my hand, and we meet Mrs. Davis on the front sidewalk.

"Where you two going?" she asks.

"For a walk," I say. "It's my first time in Lexington since I left as a little girl, and I think I lived only a few streets over before the quakes."

She nods, and says, "Don't be too late."

128

"I feel like we are being watched all the time," Gary says once Mrs. Davis moves beyond the sound of our voices. He adds, looking back in her direction, "The Captain asked to see our marriage license. I said I couldn't find it."

"Claire said she thought he would. Everyone is asking me questions, trying to pin down our story. I think they know."

"Know that we're not married?"

"That, and that I ran off from my grandparents."

"How would they know that?"

"I don't know. Just seems like they're awfully nosy about things. Go up this way," I say when we get to where there is a park with what used to be stair-stepped fountains. They are cracked now and empty of water. "I think I remember coming down here at night with my parents. Water would run over these curved steps and lights would shine through in blues and purples. It was beautiful."

"I suspect that replacing fountains hasn't been this city's primary concern during reconstruction. How far up here do you think your house was?"

"I don't know. I was little so I don't remember distance. My Dad would carry me on his shoulders. At Christmas time there would be a big tree covered with giant shiny balls and multi-colored lights on the corner back there."

We pass old buildings that were old even when I was little. The buildings sit flush to the sidewalk. I stand in front of one, looking up into colored windows and a spiraling pinnacle and steps leading to a heavy wooden door. A cross adorns its face. I look at Gary.

"A church," he says. "Where people go to worship."

"And pray?"

"And pray.

Stain glass windows glint in the sunlight. I pull on Gary's arm to stop, and I gaze at the massive figures of Mary and Joseph on the road to Bethlehem – Mary heavy with child, Joseph leading.

Gary breaks the solemnness, pointing to the right. "I work up this street, only a couple of blocks."

We pass a group of buildings that Gary tells me is a place of higher learning, a university. We walk up to the wide expanse of steps. "People still go to school here, after they have graduated high school," he says.

"Did you go to the university?"

"No. Just high school."

129

"Did you want to?" I ask.

"Sure. Wouldn't you?" he asks as we move beyond the school.

"I guess. I never knew about universities," I tell him, kicking at the gravel on the broken sidewalk. I look up and grab his arm. "Stop. This is where I lived."

We gaze at the large three-story house, red brick, and white falling-down porch. The front façade is grown up with ivy, and where the ivy stops are long zigzagged cracks in the brick.

"Do you think anyone lives here?" I ask.

"Probably street people. Those men who don't want the restrictions of the Shelter. Not so sure I like the Shelter's restrictions either," he says with a crooked smile.

"It's a warm, dry place to lay our heads," I remind him.

"For now."

We climb the steps. On the front door, nailed onto the wooden panels over the broken glass is a sign that says "Condemned by order of the Sheriff."

"I wonder how long it has been condemned," Gary says.

I don't answer. In the corner of the front porch, beyond two broken floor boards, stands an old concrete flower pot with dried weeds hanging over its edges. Then I remember, wondering if it is possible. I stretch across the broken boards and squat to look closely at the pot. It looks the same - like the same one Momma painted white and had petunias trailing their long spindly stems with purple blooms. The boards beneath the pot seem intact. I lift the edge, and there beneath the pot, as my memory had reminded me, is a key. I slip it from beneath the pot, and let the pot down easily, lest it cave in the remaining boards on the porch.

"Which door did it fit?" Gary asks.

"That I don't remember."

"Well, how many doors were there?"

"I don't remember that either. But I'm not sure we even need a key if the doors all look like that one," I say pointing to the front door.

"Well, it's boarded up, and if we start tearing boards down, someone is going to notice us."

"We're going in, aren't we?" It isn't a question.

"Yeah," Gary says smiling. Down the steps and around the side we find a door, its concrete stoop is separated from the main wall by nearly a foot. Gary tries the key. It doesn't work. Jumping off the top step, he takes my hand and we climb over a fallen down fence. There is a back door, with an old screen door dangling off two hinges. The wooden door hangs half open.

"You were right, we didn't need a key."

"But does it fit?" I ask.

He places the key into the lock and turns. At first it doesn't budge, but Gary jiggles it, then he tries again. The bolt closes and opens, first slowly and then more easily.

"With a little grease from the garage, it will turn with ease."

Gary holds out his hand and pulls me up the steps. He pushes the wooden door fully open, and we step inside. There is a sink, and a faucet. Gary goes straight for it, tries one handle, and then the other. The second spurts brown water, and a smile spreads across his face.

"No hot, but at least there is cold."

The walls are tall, taller than our cabin in Stears Branch, taller than the shelter where we are staying, but they are yellowed, and there is a smell of sweat and animal pee. I stand in the doorway, uncertain. Nothing in this room feels familiar.

"Come on," he says.

Reluctantly, I follow him through the kitchen into a hallway where a stairway leads upward. The railing is gone, and in the front of the house are the front windows that look out onto the street. There are ashes in a fire place, not like the one in Grandma's cabin, but smaller, and blackened soot covers smooth, painted tiles. In this room are mattresses strewn in two corners and piles of empty cans with ragged tops peeled back. Gary picks one up and laughs.

"Beanie Weenies," he says.

Gary pushes a black button on one wall, but nothing happens. He tries another, still with no result.

"No electricity, but I guess I should have known that."

This room smells worse than the kitchen, and as I identify the smell, Gary says, "It has possibilities, Carrie."

I look at him. *Possibilities for what?*

"A little elbow grease, a little cleaning."

"What about the people who slept here. They'll be back."

Gary dangles the key.

"How is that going to help?"

"First, we'll fix the door, then we'll clean it up. Let's see what's upstairs."

131

"Why'd they destroy this?" I say, placing my hand on the remnants of the railing.

"For firewood, I expect."

Second floor is as large as the first, and at the edge of the stairs is another door, a heavy bar guarding its passage to an upper floor. Gary tries the key, and it doesn't fit.

"We'll have someone pick the lock."

I move into a pink room, grimy pink walls, pink carpet stained with brown, and my heart stops. There, strewn around the floor are toys, books with the edges of the covers chewed half away. A bed, once white, with two posters left on a headboard, its mattress lays half on and half off. On the wall are pictures in broken glass frames. I pull open a closet door, but no clothes hang where I remember they hung. I turn to run, to run out of the hollow memory, but Gary is there, and he catches me.

"My room," I sob, and he pulls me into his chest, wraps his arms protectively around me. Everything that was then is no more. Childhood in this house disappeared. "Momma," I cry.

Gary lifts my face. He whispers, "It's okay, I'm here now. I'm here."

He kisses the top of my head, and runs his hand through my hair. It tangles in his grasp, and the feeling I had when I saw Claire and her husband kiss invades me. I lift my face to his, and the kiss I had longed for at the spring behind Mrs. Pendleton's house, the kiss under the walnut tree, comes sweet to my lips. *This is a kiss,* runs through my brain, and I press myself closer into his lean frame. I think it will last forever, and I do not want forever to end. Gary pulls away from the kiss first. His face is flushed. He bends and kisses me again, fleeting, controlled, but no less longing.

"We need to get back to the Shelter before dark," he whispers in my hair.

"Why?" I whisper back.

He laughs at me, and I am confused. I say again, "Why?"

"They'll send a search party out for us. We'll come back. I promise."

"Claire and Captain Davis," I say laughing.

"Them and then some. We'll come back and clean this place up, and we'll make it ours."

"Will you kiss me again?"

"Do you want that?"

132

"Yes," I say, and with that, he smiles and pulls me to him again. Another kiss, long and tender, unlike any Grandpa or Grandma kiss. I think to myself, *If this is what being married is, then I will marry you, Gary Combs.*

Our walk back to the Shelter is less direct, and we turn down the street to where the garage is located, where Gary's been working. It is large, with dark windows, and all manner of cars and trucks sit in the lot. It is Sunday, and it is closed.

"I have to be there tomorrow by seven a.m.," Gary tells me. "And, the head mechanic may keep me all day. Will you be all right at the Shelter?"

"I don't like to be there without you, but I'll be fine. Claire says she is going to help me find my parents, and talked about our going to the Annex tomorrow. That scares me." I have put the courthouse visit off for over a week. The need to know about my Momma has been overshadowed by fear of the second floor of the Annex.

"Yeah, just steer clear of the office on the second floor."

"What if it's the same office as the one for records."

"It's probably not."

"But what if it is?"

"Run," he says, laughing, and takes my hand pulling me into a run. I can hardly keep up, and I am laughing, too, my breath coming in short spurts. In front of the Shelter Captain Davis is standing, his arms across his chest and his lips a tight line. He is waiting.

"I started to worry about you two," he says eyeing us. "We lock the Shelter at dark."

"We're locked in?" I ask.

"For your safety, and had you not gotten here in time, you would have been locked out."

"Whew," I say.

"Where were you?"

I feel like I am being cross-examined and he sounds an awful lot like Grandpa, but I know Grandpa loves me.

"Carrie thought she lived somewhere downtown, and we have been going up and down streets to see if she can remember any of the houses."

"Any luck?" he says looking at me.

Gary answers quickly, "No."

"Well, I'm sorry to hear it. You both missed supper, and the little

133

boy started asking for you some time ago."

"I'm sorry," I say.

"No problem. We just assured him. We also saved some sandwiches for you. They're in the kitchen, and my wife can help you get some milk or coffee."

"That's okay, sir. I can handle it," I tell him.

As we pass through the front doors, Billy comes running. "I thought you had left me," he cries, and throws his arms around my waist.

"Leave you? Never!" I assure him.

"You missed supper."

"I know, Captain Davis told us. You know, there are going to be times when Uncle Gary is at work, and I am down at the courthouse looking for records. You'll have to stay here during those times, and sometimes Uncle Gary and I just need to be alone, but we'll never leave you. I promised. Remember?"

"That true, Gary?" Billy asks.

"Now would Carrie lie to you?"

"Naw, she always tells the truth," and I smile in relief. I can tell he believes, and I am happy that it is evident to Captain Davis as well.

Inside, in the cafeteria, we sit at a table and eat left-over sandwiches, while Billy drinks another glass of milk before bedtime. Gary is holding my hand across the table. We sit like this until the wall clock says it is nine o'clock.

"Billy, you and I need to get to our beds. I have to go to work tomorrow."

"I'm not sleepy," he says.

"Well I am, and you can't stay with Carrie, you're too old. Big boys can't sleep in the girls' room.

We get up, and Gary pulls me close for a good night kiss. Billy sighs, and says, "You guys are mushy."

"That's okay," Gary says, rustling up Billy's shock of dark hair. "It's what Mommy's and Daddy's do, right?"

"Yeah," Billy says and grins.

We are the perfect family, and the scene is not lost on Sam, who sits to one side watching intently.

In my bed, amongst the sounds of snoring women, I wonder if Gary snores.

Chapter 17

The dawn is followed by breakfast, Billy, and instructions from Mrs. Davis. My chores in the Shelter have been laid out. I am to help with clean up in the kitchen. I don't know why Captain and Mrs. Davis decided not to have me work with children, but I know clean up, and the clean up here has hot water and plenty of soap. I have never seen so many dishes in all my life. Grandma would just die if she saw them all, and if she saw how messy the cooks were, she'd scream, I know it. Cook told me breakfast serves over a hundred people, and lunch serves twice that many with stragglers wandering in at meal time. When I am rinsing plates it seems like a thousand. They put Billy into school today, took him themselves. Captain Davis said they would register him, even without papers. I promised Billy again when he left this morning that I'd be here, that I won't leave him, and he hugged me with an urgency that cried for assurances.

I whispered in his ear, half expecting him to cry, "You be brave, you hear me? Your Daddy would want you to." He looked at me with big, watery eyes, but didn't cry.

I am peeling potatoes when Claire finally comes in. Like always, she is drinking a cup of coffee.

"So, they found you a job?" she asks.

"Yeah." I am peeling from a hundred-pound bag, and the pile of peelings in the sink is growing.

"I thought they were putting you with the children in the day care. Wonder why they didn't." she says more to herself than to me, then asks, "Where's Billy?"

"In school."

"Huh. I didn't think they'd enroll him this soon, since you all don't know how long you're going to be here."

Behind my back, Captain Davis answers her, "All children need to be in school. And although the boy's mother put him in the care of Mr. Combs, he isn't the legal guardian, so we have to follow proper protocol."

I repeat, "Protocol?"

"The law dictates how to handle deserted children, Mrs. Combs, and since you and your husband don't have legal papers for the boy,

135

we have to find him a stable home."

"But Gary has a letter," I stammer.

The cook stops her stirring and turns to look at the three of us through the serving window. My face drains of color, I can feel it.

"He hasn't presented any letter."

"I don't know that he thought he needed to."

My mind is racing. I have promised Billy, and here they are telling me they're going to put him into some other home.

"As soon as Gary and me get the money, we'll be finding a place of our own. We are his family."

"We'll see," is all the man says.

The Shelter no longer feels like a friendly place. Captain Davis fills his coffee cup and moves through the dining room doors.

"Whew," Claire says. "Wonder what has got underneath his saddle. That's horse talk, honey."

"Billy's mother asked us to take care of him."

"Keep peeling," Claire says. "What happened to his mom anyway?"

I want to tell her, because right this minute she feels like an ally, but I think that Gary would kill me if I did. I decide to tell her half of it.

"We came across the river together, and well, she was a widow. I guess she just didn't feel like she could take care of him. She didn't have any money."

"So, why didn't she come here with you."

"I don't know," I say, and it is the truth.

"Well, I get the feeling that for some reason the Captain doesn't believe you guys."

"You do?"

She looks at me, tilts her head to one side while looking at me. "My Jack said he thinks you're a runaway, but I said, 'What're you running from?' Still, there's something I can't put my finger on, and I suspect that's how the Captain and Mrs. Davis see it, too."

"Well, I'm not a runaway," I say.

"Whatever. I'll check with cook to see if she can spare you after lunch dishes are done, and we'll go down to the Annex this afternoon."

"Where's the Annex?" I ask, knowing exactly where it is.

"I thought you said you stopped there before coming here last week?"

"No," I lie.

"Hmm. Well, it's just down the street."

136

"So, where do we go when we get there?" I am trying to relieve the anxiety that has been rising in my chest ever since the Captain started talking about taking Billy from us.

"Well, I believe the records department is on the first floor."

"So we don't have to go to the second floor?"

"I didn't think you had been there," she says, and she looks at me again, eye to eye, her eyes narrowing in her scrutiny.

"I haven't."

"Whatever," she says, and with that Claire turns and walks out.

The head cook, a large dark lady comes up behind me. "Ms. Carrie, I don't know what you are hiding, but you better be careful who you're trustin'. Now finish up those potatoes before you get us both into trouble."

She's smiling at me a big, kind smile. I decide she is right, and I think I'll not trust Claire with any more of my story.

The potatoes are finally peeled, and Cook and I, with hands on either side, lift the heavy pan to the stove. When the two hundred-plus men and women have eaten lunch, and pans scrubbed, Claire returns.

"Ready?" she asks.

"I guess so. Cook, anything else you need me for?"

"Not until four, then I'll need you to help me set up the line. Remember what I told you, Carrie."

"I've not forgotten," I say and nod.

"What's that about?"

I decide not to lie to her. Maybe she needs to know. "Cook thinks you can't be trusted."

Claire laughs.

The walk from the Shelter to the Annex is less than a mile, the best I can tell. It takes us 20 minutes to walk down the street to the source of my anxiety. We pass men in suits, and ladies in dresses. Past the dry fountains and empty lots filled with weeds where buildings once stood.

Disheveled men stare at us, and women in ragged coats push wire buggies. I wonder whether they have slept at my house last night, ate their beanie weenies, and urinated in the corners. I think about my house, the house where I was born, where my mother painted pink walls and laid pink carpet in an upstairs room. I dreamed for just a moment how it would look when Gary and I finished cleaning it up, and then we are at the front doors of the building. I take a deep breath.

Claire said records were on the first floor, but I am still nervous, and Claire doesn't miss it.

"What's got you so antsy little miss?"

"Just a little scared."

"Of the second floor?" she asks smiling.

"No," I snap.

"Excuse me?"

"I'm looking for word on my Momma, Claire. I don't know what I'm going to find. She might be dead. If she's dead, I don't know what I'm going to do, okay?"

Inside, we stand at a counter behind the first door.

"Excuse me?" Claire calls out.

Several workers are moving back and forth between cabinets with deep drawers. They ignore us.

"Excuse me," Claire says again. Her voice takes on a different sound, loses its sarcasm from before. "Can someone help us?"

A gentleman looks up from his desk, shuffles his papers and lays them in a stack at one corner. "What can I do for you," he says to Claire. He smiles and gets up from the desk moving to the counter where we stand. I notice that Claire turns her head to one side and smiles a broad warm smile.

"I am trying to help this child find word on her mother, and well, to tell the truth, I didn't know where else to start. I'm hoping you can help us."

I look straight at the man and say, "I'm not a child," but he is still looking at Claire with a transfixed look on his face.

Claire looks at me, then back at the man. "She lost family in the quakes. I think she traveled with her grandparents and got separated from her parents. She's down at the Shelter staying for a time, and I offered to help, you know, trying to do what I can to help her reunite with them, if they are alive."

Claire twirls her hair with a finger, lets the strand fall across her cheek, and then pats my arm. I want to shake her hand off, but she is looking at me with a warning look. She looks back at the man and smiles again.

"Well, you know we lost a bunch of records during that time, but what we do have is on the second floor. We just keep vehicle registration down here."

Claire gives a pout, and then puts her arm around my shoulder in a motherly way, "I'm sorry, honey."

I shrug off her embrace. It feels like she is playing some kind of a game. I think she knew good and well that the records were upstairs.

"Well, Ma'am, I am just about finished up here. I can take you upstairs and help you see what we can find. What name we looking for?" He lifts the counter walking through to our side of the office. He smiles a sympathetic smile at me. I feel like I'm twelve years old.

"Baxter," I say. "Emily and Jonathan Baxter."

"Come on upstairs with me."

And with that, we walk through the door to the row of stairs against the right hand wall. He leads, and Claire follows. My heart is beating double time, and I try to keep close behind Claire, hoping to all hope that I am inconspicuous.

We pass the door that says marriage licenses, and as we pass I glance through the glass window at the woman standing behind the counter. It is the same lady with the blue hair. She is frowning at a stack of papers in her hand and does not look up. I am relieved, and move quickly beyond the door, bumping into Claire. She turns to say something, and sees my expression, then looks up to the sign above the door we have just passed. She starts to say something when the gentleman interrupts.

"Well, here we are. Do you know how to use a computer, young lady?"

I don't know what he is talking about. The word holds a faint memory of familiarity, but it is lost behind mountains of a whole other world. The room is filled with several long wooden tables, and on each table are square boxes with blue pulsing screens.

"I'm sure she does," Claire says. "Which ones can we use? They all look pretty old."

"Well, I think the ones on the back table are newest. You know the city hasn't had funds to update." And then defensively adds, "There have been more pressing things than these records."

Claire smiles at him again, that charming up-turn of lips and white teeth, "I wasn't criticizing. I understand full well about priorities. What can we expect to find, and how do we start a search?"

"You can log on using my password if you don't have one, then go to birth records. Perhaps you should also check," and then he looks at me again, "obit records. If you have any questions, you can ask Sandy. She should be back shortly."

139

"Thanks," I say.

"What's your name?" Claire asks.

"Mike, Mike Brown."

"Thanks, Mike Brown."

He smiles and walks out of the room. At a back computer Claire sits down and begins typing the sign-in as Mr. Brown told us, then moves for me to sit where she has just made the blinking screen pull up a list. Before I can ask what I'm supposed to do, she moves to the computer next to mine and begins the process over. When her screen comes up with the list, she looks at me and says, "You search under births. I'll take obituaries."

"How?"

"You really don't know how to use a computer?"

"No," I tell her. "I can read the words, but I don't know what to do with the computer in front of me. I vaguely remember playing games, and I mean vaguely."

"This is going to take longer than I thought. We'll start out doing this together."

Claire scoots me out of my seat, and replaces me in front of the screen so I am sitting beside her. She fingers the flat panel, pushing the squares until the arrow points to births. Another screen pops up with dates.

"If we're lucky this thing will have a cross reference. What year were you born?"

I start to say 2012, and then catch myself. She looks at me with raised eyebrows.

"Look, Carrie, you don't have to be Einstein to know you're under age. Why do you think the Davises are watching you so closely. They don't have proof, but they're pretty suspicious that you're an underage runaway. You're looking for your mom, and if you don't let me help you, your Gary is going to be in more trouble than you ever imagined."

I still don't answer. I think about Cook's warning.

Claire can read minds. "Look, Cook doesn't like me, I know that. She doesn't approve of the things I've done in my life. I guess I can even agree with her. I've made a mess of things more than once, but I've been where you've been, and if you don't let me help you, Gary may end up in jail for a long time."

"Jail? Why?"

"You know what statutory rape is?"

140

"No," I say, and I really don't.

"It's where a guy who is over eighteen has sex with a girl under eighteen, and I don't think you're eighteen."

"Gary and I haven't had...you know, sex."

"You've told everyone you're married. What do you expect people to think?"

Then part of my story pours out, "We tried to get a license, the day we came to the Shelter. I didn't have proof of my age, so they didn't give us one. The lady thought I was under age."

"You *are* under age. Good God, Carrie."

"It's why I didn't want to come up to the second floor."

"No joke. How long do you think you can keep this up before the Davises find out?"

"I don't know."

"Well, believe me, they intend to find out, and when they do, it won't just be that little boy they'll be sending to a foster home, it'll be you, too."

"I can't let that happen."

"What year, Carrie?"

I take a deep breath, "2012."

"Jeez, you're just sixteen. You're going to get me fired for helping you."

"I'm almost seventeen."

"According to the law, 'almost' doesn't count. You're sixteen. Okay, let's get to work here. I have to have you back in an hour, and I have to think this whole thing through."

Claire typed in 2012, then asked, "Where were you born?"

"Here," I say.

She types in Fayette County births, and a list of months appear. "What month?"

"January."

The alphabet appears, and Claire presses B, and there, like magic I see my name appear. Carrie Ann Baxter, January 29, 2012. Beside my birth date there is my Momma and Daddy's name, Emily D. and Jonathan Baxter. Claire clicks on Momma's name and hits another key. The address on Broadway pops up.

She looks up from the screen, "I guess that's where you were Sunday, right? You found your old house."

I nod. No other addresses appear. "During the hard times, some

141

things never got registered. I wonder where she is now."

She clicks a button that says 'next' and the words "March 14, 2018, live birth, male, University Hospital."

"Looks like you've got a little brother."

I lean closer into her, reading the screen. "A brother?" I whisper.

"By this, it looks as if he is ten, or maybe eleven. I don't figure numbers real fast."

"I've got a brother," I say again, this time out loud.

She clicks the backward arrow and goes to the previous screen where she finds my Daddy's name, Jonathan Baxter. She clicks on his name, and stops short. She looks at me.

Beside my Daddy's name is partial date, October 2017, then the word *"Deceased."* I stand and lean over her, looking at the words.

"I'm sorry, Carrie," she says.

She doesn't have to tell me what deceased means. Her "I'm sorry," says it all. I look across the room at the line of tables, at the metal boxes with blue pulsing screens, and I can see beyond them, to my Grandpa's orchard, there among the apple trees, and I can see the trees laden with apples, and those scattered beneath the trees, the last of yellow jackets hovering over them, straining for the last bit of summer for their hives. And amongst the fallen apples and buzzing bees I see the wooden marker that says Jonathan Baxter. He is not lying there beneath the stand of trees, but he is there just the same, deceased.

"Carrie, are you okay?"

No, I am not okay, I want to say. It is a stupid question. I am away from the grandparents who love me, away from all that is familiar, in a strange city, amongst stranger people, and I have just seen the word deceased associated with my Daddy. How can I be okay? There is no Momma, no Grandma, not even a Gary here to hold on to me so that I don't fly away right now out of my skin. I want to know why all of this has happened, this unsteady earth that ripped my family apart.

A lady stands from behind a desk on the far side of the room. I haven't noticed her before this moment.

"Is everything okay?" she asks Claire.

"She'll be okay. We just found some word about her father. It's not good."

Not good? It is terrible. I stare at Claire. *I'll be okay? How does she know how I will be?*

"Carrie, sit down. Please?"

She wraps her arm around my shoulder, and I turn my face into her and cry.

"It's okay, honey. It's going to be okay. We're still looking for your momma. There's no deceased next to her name. That means she is still alive."

"Is there anything I can do?" the lady asks Claire.

"No, thanks anyway."

"Sshh..." Claire says, and I take a deep breath. "Here," and Claire offers a partially used tissue from her pocket.

"Let me write down this one thing, honey, and then we'll head back to the Shelter."

Claire writes a letter followed by a set of numbers and tucks the paper into her jeans pocket.

"We've done enough damage here today," she says.

With two clicks the screen we have been looking at for the last eternity has gone blue. "Come on," she says, pulling me to my feet.

We walk out of the records room, and pass quickly by the windowed marriage license room. Claire puts herself between me and the door, and ushers me down the stairs. At the vehicle registration she sticks her head through the open door and calls "Thanks" to Mike Brown.

Outside, we move with speed towards the Shelter. Neither of us speak.

At the double glass doors Claire asks, "Do you have it together, Carrie?" I nod.

"They don't need to see how upset you are. The less they think we know, the fewer questions Captain Davis is likely to ask. It's time for you to be at work anyway. Stay close by Cook, and look too busy to be interrupted. Let me look at you now."

She holds my face between her hands, wipes the last of my tears from beneath my eyes with a moistened thumb. It brings to memory when Momma used to clean my face with her spit, and I think I am going to start crying again.

"Carrie, hold it together now. Think you can do that?"

I nod my head again, and we enter the doors together. Captain Davis is speaking with a gentleman in his office doorway. Claire pushes me through the swinging dining room doors.

"Off to work, kid," she says. And before the doors swing shut behind me, I see her wave to Captain Davis.

Chapter 18

Since Gary worked long on Friday and Saturday, his boss gave him off today. It is our secret. With Billy in school, after breakfast clean up and lunch set up is taken care of, Cook shoos me off. I don't know where Mrs. Davis is, which is good. I don't want to explain.

Captain Davis is always involved in something else during the day, so he is nowhere to be seen. Today feels like freedom.

We walk out the glass doors hand in hand. Gary's been gathering buckets and cleaning supplies. It is going to be a work day, but not the kind either one of us is going to mind. The sky is clear, deep blue and cold. Our breath comes out in puffs of white. I pretend to smoke, holding my fingers the way Claire does.

"That's not a pretty habit," Gary says.

"Claire does it."

"You're not Claire."

"Don't you think she's pretty?"

We have almost reached the three-story brick house that used to be my home. He stops, looks at me closely, "Yeah, she's pretty, but you're beautiful, okay? You don't need to be pretending to smoke or acting like her."

With that admonition, he pulls me into a run leaving his seriousness behind. The front door looks the same. We round the crumbling driveway to the back porch where we slipped in the first time. The lock has remained unbroken; no one has snuck in since our last visit. Gary pulls the key from his pocket. It turns easily. I am surprised.

The trash that littered the corners of the first floor has been removed. The stink is gone. It is free of mouse eaten mattresses. No more empty beanie-weenie cans, no broken bottles. There are still boards on the windows, still tattered curtains, and still rusted doorknobs.

"What have you done?" I ask.

"Look better?" he asks with a grin.

"It's wonderful. No, it's beautiful."

"Well, that's a bit of an exaggeration, but it is a start. Frank and I did help it along."

In the kitchen are buckets and a mop, bottles of cleaner and rags. A broom is propped in one corner. He goes to the far wall, to a small plate and flips a switch. A small bulb flickers on.

"Lights?"

To another corner he pulls off an old but clean sheet to reveal a small running refrigerator. When he opens the door, what seems like a limitless variety of fruits and vegetables tumble out.

"Gary, you are…where did you find this stuff? Apples, where did you get them? It's winter. And this?"

He laughs, and opens his arms in a broad gesture, "With a little help from my friends. And that, my dear, is a banana," he says.

I turn, "I know. I loved them. Oh Gary, it's home."

"Yeah, that's what it is supposed to be. Come up stairs."

The banister is still in pieces and wobbles as I hold on, but the transformation has covered the worst of the damage. We pass the two bedrooms – the doors pulled closed, and he directs me into the pink room. The floor is swept clean. The toys that were repairable have been fixed and moved to a box in one corner; the pictures, in dire condition, rehung and straightened. They are priceless pieces of my childhood.

The narrow bed restored, missing pieces replaced, repainted white. A narrow mattress is topped with a pink quilt. There are curtains on the windows, and those windows have been washed so that the morning winter sun shines through and warms the room with yellow light. The fireplace, that I remember could not be used when I was little, somehow has been fixed, and in the narrow opening, a small fire is burning. No smoke is filling the room.

I turn to Gary. "I love you," I say.

I have never said that to anyone other than family. Only my Momma, my Daddy, Grandma and Grandpa have heard those words from my lips. And, I know that those feelings are coming from more than the making of this room. It is that he has done this all for me, that he has brought me here to this strange town, risked his life at my request, stopped what he was doing for himself to help me, and that he loves me. How could I not love him?

He pulls me into his arms and whispers into my ear, "I love you best."

I pull back and look at him. "What?"

He is laughing. "It is what my Mom and I used to say to each other all the time. I would say to her, 'I love you,' and she would say back, 'I love you best,' then I would say back to her, 'Well, I love you most,'

145

and, we would go on like that forever."

I look at him, "Well, I love you most."

"Best."

Our arms wrap around each other, we turn and tighten our embrace until we grow silent with the feel of the other's warmth. I can feel his lips getting close, and I curve toward him. I don't feel sixteen anymore. I feel fully grown. *I am not a little girl,* I hear myself telling me, and the message is sent from my most private places to my head. We tumble backwards onto the narrow bed. His lips are on mine, his firm body on mine, and I am choked with the urgency of it, of its power over me, of my own need. Our kiss persists, it demands until Gary breaks away. I gasp. I have not been breathing and the inward breath comes with disappointment that he has pulled away. 'Not yet,' his eyes say, and I think to myself, *'Why?'*

"Come on. We got work to do."

I am pulled up, and in pulling me he embraces me again, and whispers in my ear, "Soon, okay? Soon."

I can feel my face get red. I am embarrassed by my own response to his kiss, to his body, to my body.

By the look on his face, he feels the awkwardness as much as me. Downstairs in our kitchen, we fill buckets with cold water and disinfectant, the same kind Cook uses in the kitchen at night after the last meal.

"Where'd you get this?" I ask, holding up the pine-scented liquid.

"Cook likes me, too," he says.

"And the buckets?"

"Frank and the garage. I have to return them tomorrow."

Gary hands me rubber gloves that are two sizes too big, and I start on the high, paned windows. Even standing on a tall chair, I still can't reach the top. Gray water runs from one pane to the other, and the rag I am using quickly turns black. I rinse and rinse again until the water in my bucket looks as bad as the water that Gary is using to mop with.

"I think I need clean water."

With one toss the water is thrown out the back door. I hear a stray cat howl as it gets an unwelcomed bath.

"Did you do that on purpose?" I ask.

"It got in my way."

"Still, you could have tossed to the other side. I used to love cats. I had a yellow and white one. What color is that one?"

146

"It's not the same cat. It would be pretty old if it was."

"What color is it?"

"Yellow and white, okay? But there is no way. It isn't the same cat."

"I didn't say it was. Bring her in."

"Really?"

"Really," I say. "Please?"

I put on pleading eyes that used to work with Grandma. Grandpa said he hated cats, but that was a lie. But, he wouldn't let them in the cabin. He said they smelled. There were three feral cats that kept mice out of the barn, and Jolie kept a couple, too. Once inside, Gary wraps a dry rag around the yellow and white female. I can hear her purring from across the kitchen.

"See, she likes you."

"Sure. It's just cold. How do you know it's a she?"

"She's a calico. There aren't any male calicoes. Wish we had some milk. What can we call her?"

"We are not keeping a cat in here," he says as he scratches behind her ears. The cat pushes her head against his hand and puts her paws on his chest edging closer to his face.

"Ah, come on Gary. Look at her. It'd make it homey."

"It'll make it stinky when she pees on my freshly mopped floor."

"You're right. Can she come in when we're here?"

He nods that she can.

"So, what will we name her, Dixie? She kind of looks like a Dixie, doesn't she? "

"If you say so. I can't believe you have talked me into keeping a stray," and he says this with a smile on his face. "Now finish that window, because I am getting hungry."

I climb back on my chair with clean water and finish my last window while Gary gets the top rectangles from the other windows. When I climb down I dry my hands and look up at him wiping the last of the film away from the panes.

"What's for lunch?"

"We've got bologna."

"What's that?"

"Steak to the poor man," he says.

Gary leads me to the front room and spreads a drop cloth on the floor.

"Wait here," he says, and I sit cross legged in front of the fireplace.

It is colder on this floor, and I wrap my jacket around me. It was warmer upstairs, but I am not sure it is safe for me to stay in the pink room. Within minutes Gary is back, both hands hold sandwiches, two bottles of water beneath his arms.

"At your service, Ma'am. Steak sandwich on soft white bread spread with yellow Dijon. Cold water, and hold on, I'll bring dessert."

He disappears with Dixie on his heels and returns with a red apple and a brown speckled banana. "I suspect this banana has been stored a little too cool at some time. It's how they look when that happens, but I think it'll still taste good."

"I thought you said this was bologna?" I ask, looking at the bread and round smooth piece of meat that he has generously covered with yellow spread.

"Well, I did. My Mom used to call it poor man's steak. We ate it all the time, like this for lunch, fried for supper with potatoes, and with an egg for breakfast. When we weren't eating this we were eating brown beans."

"I know brown beans," I say, "but not bologna. What's the yellow stuff?"

"Mustard. Can't eat bologna without mustard, or at least not when you're eating it cold."

"It's sour, but I guess it's okay. Grandma made ketchup. Don't think we had this though."

I pull off a small edge and give it to Dixie, she sniffs and sneezes, then licks the edge where there is no mustard. I like the mustard and the bologna, and the soft white bread. I watch as Gary presses the bread and bologna together between his hands until it is flattened thin.

"I bet your Grandpa liked it," Gary says.

The thought of Grandpa makes me shiver. I can't help but wonder where he is, and how long it will take before he finds us. And worse than that, what he will do when he does.

I voice my fears, "Where do you think he is, you know, Grandpa?"

"I don't know, but probably closer than we think. If he came on foot, it would take him awhile to get here, but if I was guessing, I'd guess he found a ride somehow."

"Do you think he took the ferry?"

"That's a given, Carrie."

"You know he asked them about me."

"Yeah."

148

"What do you think they told him?"

"It's hard telling. They weren't about to do us any favors."

"Do you think those men know we helped Mrs. Wilson?"

"That I don't know."

I have set my sandwich down. I'm not hungry anymore. Dixie pounces on what is left of it making growling sounds. I had almost forgotten about that night, willed myself to forget the dark, the screams, the shots, the haggard face of Donna, the frightened faces of the children as Gary drove to the Holiday Inn. And then she was gone. She just disappeared and left her little boy with us.

"Do you think his body has been found?"

"I don't know that either," he says.

He has stopped eating too and is staring out the window beside the fireplace. "It's been almost a month. I thought that there would have been something on the news, you know, anything, or at least Frank might have heard something. Maybe the guys at the ferry came back and disposed of the body. Who knows. I don't think that Donna filed a complaint."

"Wonder why she didn't."

"Maybe she just wanted to forget what happened."

"Gary, she left her son with us."

"Yeah. I can't quite figure why she did that. Billy is a good kid. I can't see him being any trouble."

"Do you think she went back to her people? Billy looks exactly like his daddy."

"You know, I don't want to talk about it anymore, okay?"

"Alright, but just one more question, just in case I have to know at some point."

"And what's that?"

"The letter she gave you, what'd it say?"

"It's getting late. I need to get you back to the Shelter."

"Gary?"

"I don't want to talk about it."

"Do you still have the letter she wrote?"

"Yeah."

"May I read it?"

"No."

Chapter 19

Stears Branch
Grandma.

Upstairs in Carrie's room I found paper yellow with age, but still usable, and three good lead pencils with erasers. So, I decided last night that I'm gonna journal. I sharpened the pencils with my apple paring knife, and journaling is what I'm gonna do. I'm gonna mark time by AC – After Carrie.

Day 3 AC.

I had let the fire go out. I decided not to go to Jolie's for fire. I didn't want to explain why I needed fire and why Jim wasn't there to help. I found what few matches we stored away and decided to try to start the fire myself. I wasn't good at it, always depended on Jim, but I did know how it was done. I gathered small twigs out behind the house, dried apple branches that had fallen from the weight of a good harvest, and brought in dry wood.

I decided that when Jim came back, if he did, I'd thank him for making sure we had a supply of split logs. I never considered it before, but don't think I could split a log without splitting a foot. I gathered some fat off the crock in the pantry. It's near impossible to start a fire without it. I remembered Jim shaving off thin strips of wood and dipping it in the fat. I did it just like him, dipped them in duck grease. It took forever, but finally the fire took off, and I wondered if he'd be proud of me if he were here.

This morning looked gray, so I carried in enough wood to keep the fire going, and then carried a good pile up to the porch to keep dry, enough I hoped to last a week or more. I hadn't fed the dogs since Carrie left, and they pestered and whined until I baked a pone of bread for them. I threw on most of the fat from the duck in the bread. It was going rancid. I saved just enough in a jar in case I let the fire go out again, but I promised myself not to do that.

I almost forgot the apples we had drying in the old truck. I brought them in, lest they mold from the dampness in the autumn air. Inside the cabin, I packed them in baskets and took them up to Carrie's room, next to the chimney where they would stay dry. They were the same apples Carrie helped peel and slice the day that boy came. In the root cellar I checked the turnips and potatoes, pulled some of the turnip's greens off for later. They would soon shrivel-up. I covered them, and the beets with the tall grass Jim had cut, and then with a blanket to keep them from freezing. He'd hung the cabbage by their roots, and I checked to make sure they were still firm. All of this I did before noon. I spent the rest of the day worrying. It nearly drove me mad. It's why I am writing this down. In getting it out of my mind and on these yellowed pages, perhaps I can carry on.

Day 4 AC.

Jim hasn't come home. I went to Aries' this morning to check on her. It was nearing a week since I'd been there, and I doubted if anyone else had been back to her place. I gathered my medicine bag and jacket, and the greens from yesterday. I hated to pass by Jolie's and my dread was warranted. She was the last person I wanted to tell what had happened. Outside, Tommy was throwing dirt clods against the barn. He shouted at me that Gary had left. I said, I know. With that Jolie came running out her door. I sped up, kept walking, but she caught up with me.

"Did Jim go after her?" she asked.

My face must have shown my shock, must have registered all over, my disbelief that she knew. I stopped in mid stride, "How'd you know?" I tried to keep some control in my voice, but I knew it was shaking.

"Gary said he was going to ask her to leave with him." Then she added quickly, "Everyone knew how she felt about him."

"Everyone?" I asked, but it was more of an accusation than a question. I wanted to slap her, but instead I turned and started walking again towards Aries' place.

"Janie," Jolie called to my back.

"You best not say any more," I warned, and she didn't. I don't know how long she stood there staring at my back. I didn't turn around to see. When I got to Aries', the door was closed to the cold. I knocked. She didn't answer. I opened the door a crack, "Aries, it's me, Janie."

It was cold inside, but the fire hadn't gone out yet. Aries was in her bed, her face white. She opened her eyes and smiled.

I said, "You don't look too good."

151

"I'm holdin' on," she said, then asked, "How you doin'?"

"Holdin' on. So you know, too?"

"Jolie doesn't keep many secrets."

"Just the most important ones," I said. "Your fire's about out. You been tending to it by yourself?"

"Up until yesterday. Harold came by last night and stoked it up and brought in some more wood."

I took the poker and stirred up the embers before adding a small log.

"The day Carrie cleaned the water barrel, the boy came by and put up a whole rack of wood. Janie, he is a good boy."

"Aries, he took our Carrie away. I can't call him good."

I took her kettle out the back door and drew up some water, came back in and added another log before hooking the kettle over the flames.

"Did you expect her to stay back here in this hollow forever? Is that what you wanted for her?"

"She was too young."

"Sixteen pert-near seventeen? I was married when I was sixteen. Who was you wanting her to wait for, Tommy?"

"God, no."

"Well then, who?

I told Aries I didn't know who. Then she asked me if Jim had gone after her. I said to her, "What do you think?" It wasn't a question. "I don't know what I'm gonna do without them, Aries."

"What makes you think they're not coming back?"

I opened my bag and pulled out my teas. "What kind do you want today?"

"You decide," she said and closed her eyes.

I chose sassafras. The aroma filled the small house, sweet and warm. Aries still had china cups, and I pulled two from her cupboard, spooned honey into both cups, and then the steaming brown liquid. I carried the cup, set it down on the table by her bed and helped her to sit up. She took a sip before speaking.

"They'll be back."

"I don't think so," I told her.

"And, if they don't come back, like you think, then what?"

"I think I'll die."

"Oh Janie," she said to me, "don't be so melodramatic. You're not the only one to lose loved ones, and some more permanently than yours."

"I'll fix you something warm to eat before I leave," was all I could say.

After I peeled potatoes and onions, heated up the turnip greens, and, after I saw to it that Aries was fed and warm, I left. Until then, we made small talk, didn't talk about loss or loved ones.

Here, back in my own place, before the fire of my own hearth, I remember what I feared most before we left civilization. More than apocalypse, more than earthquakes, more than floods, I feared Jim's leaving. I feared he would get angry at me for this or that, that I would make some error, some infraction that was so severe he would walk out the door and leave me forever.

That fear hid itself, buried itself in this wilderness. Where would he go? What transgression in this desolate place would anger him so that he would walk away. And then there was Carrie. He would never leave her, never leave her unprotected. But she is gone now, and there is nothing to keep him here, and this imagined infraction, this offense he has accused against me, was worse than all others I could have conceived or committed in that other life.

Day 6 AC.

I went to check on Aries today. I couldn't go yesterday. I didn't want to pass Jolie's house, and I didn't want to hear Aries say that other folks were suffering like me, some worse. I refuse to own that someone is suffering more than me. Aries, if she heard me rambling on like this, would say I was wallowing in self-pity. She is probably right, but I couldn't handle it yesterday. Couldn't handle it today either, but concern for her outweighed the scales between self-pity and rightness. Aries must have known, because she didn't bring it up, and neither did I.

I ignored Jolie's calls, didn't even look in her direction, and finally she quit calling my name. I want to punish her for her knowing. I don't suppose that is the Christian way for me to act, but right now, can't say I care. May be that God's punishing me for my knowing.

Aries had a little more color today, but she's still too weak to get about. I washed the dishes that were in the pan, then got her up to sit in her rocker close to the fire. She rocked with her eyes closed. The fire cast a warm glow – perhaps that was the color I saw. She's old, out lived a husband and two children. I guess she has a right to talk about loss.

I changed her bed, brought clean water from the spring. There was a light freeze this morning. I emptied the barrel Carrie cleaned that day a hundred years ago, then I rolled it inside the door so if Aries needed to get a drink between visits, she didn't have to go out and break ice to get it. I finally made my way back to the spring where Aries said Carrie met the boy. I wondered how many times Carrie said she was doing something else that she came back here to be with him, and I wondered what she did when she met with him. I try to shake the image from my mind. I tell myself that she wasn't me, and she was more innocent at sixteen than I was. I am praying that she is still innocent. When I got back to the cabin this evening, I washed Aries' bed and hung it out on the line to dry. If the night stays clear, the sheets might freeze dry. The air feels like a hard freeze.

I've kept the fire alive. Cooked brown beans tonight. Will take some to Aries tomorrow. She needs protein. It'll give her strength.

Day 10 AC.

I shelled walnuts last night before I went to bed. I got two quarts. It took half the night. Didn't matter, haven't been sleeping much. I've been sleeping in Carrie's room. Not been able to sleep in the bed Jim and I shared. I've fed Aries beans all week. She's not getting any stronger. She's sicker than I've got medicine to help. If she's not better by tomorrow, I may move back there to stay with her.

Day 11 AC.

The sheets didn't dry overnight, so I brought them in and stretched a line in front of the fire place and stoked up a big fire. I have gathered together some of my things to take back to Aries' place: my medicines, teas, the nuts, and a bag of shuck beans, turnips, and apples. She had plenty of potatoes the other day. I'm writing this morning, waiting for the sheets to dry. They're gonna smell like smoke, but at least they'll be dry.

Times have changed. That's such an old line. I almost laugh as I write it down. When I was young, people were all the time talking about how times had changed. My parents' generation, and my grandparents' generation lamented over the old times, when everything was better. Funny how things get flipped pancake style. Everything old is now new again, and those new times are old. There are some parts of those old new times that I sorely miss, like a clothes dryer. Then, there are other parts I wouldn't want back if they were handed to me with a "Here you go, they're all yours." I'd say, "No thank you."

Back here in this crevice of a mountain we moved backward whole centuries. I expected folks to swarm to these hills for safety, thought the hills would be over-run with homeless families seeking shelter. Jim expected all sorts of fighting over supplies and space. For the longest time he kept the loaded gun by our bed. I thought we might have to support half the country. We were both wrong.

Little towns on beyond Stears Branch just disappeared, and we didn't know why. I often wondered what happened to the people who lived here in Stears Branch before we arrived. Who left the stone foundations, root cellars, and the falling down cabins. Just us few stayed in Stears Branch and those few over the next ridge. We became forgotten people, and it suited us.

Day 14 AC.

It's been two weeks since Carrie left. She left on the Hunter's moon. All Saints Night has come and gone. We are well into November, and winter is coming early. We already had a light freeze. I stayed at the house for four more days then decided to come back here and stay with Aries. She is sick, near death, and it gives me purpose to be here. I don't know how she did it, but she kept her fire alive, even as sick as she was. She is a better woman than me. I will take her example.

I haven't spoken to Jolie since the first day coming to Aries'. Jolie confessed the red-haired boy named Gary told her he was taking Carrie, and I count it as betrayal that she did not come to Jim and me with this information. When I walked back to Aries' last week, passed that big house we all helped to build for her, Jolie stood on her porch and called to me. I ignored her. She sent the children out to salve my anger, and I told them to go back to their mother.

Aries says I need to let it go, that Carrie needed to leave this sheltered place. I told her for the hundredth time Carrie was too young to leave. She told me she was almost a woman. Almost wasn't good enough, I told Aries. She confessed that she saw it coming, saw the light in Carrie's eyes after the boy came. She tells me she didn't tell me either, but I remind her she didn't assist in their escape. She calls me on the word escape, and asks me if I was holding Carrie hostage.

155

Aries reminded me again that he is a good boy, but I find it hard to believe anyone could be good who caused so much grief to my family. Aries tells me I am selfish. I never thought I was, but she assures me that I am acting in that manner now.

When I say, "What about Jim?"

She tells me, "You only need to deal with your own selfishness, and allow God to tend to Jim."

If I didn't love her so dearly I would leave her here alone to die, and when I tell her this she just laughs until she coughs near to exhaustion.

Aries suggests that I write down all my anger. She says to journal.

I say, "I've already been journaling and haven't seen it help redeem me yet. Besides, I don't have time to journal now, I have to work to keep you alive."

"You don't have to work so hard at it," she says.

I am going once every few days and bringing back to the cabin the items I have stored for winter, enough to carry the two of us through till spring. Once it gets colder, it will be more difficult, and in the old house, with no heat, things will freeze. I have moved greens and potatoes. Tomorrow I will bring the rest of the dried apples, and will try my damnedest to coax some ducks back here so I can gather eggs closer to my new home. I already built a shelter for them. I will bring the meal back later, because as long as it is dry, it won't matter if it freezes. It is last year's. I needed Jim to grind meal. I didn't ask Harold or Mr. Thompson for help. I didn't want to show them I needed a man. Aries says that's my other big fault - pride. I saved seed, though, and will plant when the signs are right. I'll go by an old Almanac, but it is close enough.

Jolie's little girl, Moe, came by to ask about Carrie. I can't believe that Jolie let her travel this far alone, being so young. I wanted to chase her off, but Aries' scowl kept me from it, and Aries had me make the child tea, while the two of them talked about Jolie's new baby coming. Moe said her mommy said it would be here before spring.

"Mommy's having a hard time," she told Aries. "She's sick every day."

Aries shook her head in sympathy. When Moe left, I told Aries it served Jolie right, and it should surely pass in a few more weeks. Aries told me it was past time for it to be over, and it wasn't very Christian the way I was treating Jolie and the children. Something's happened to me, because I don't feel very Godly, and it hurts me when Aries says she suspects it's always been there inside me, just coming out in adversity.

It hurts, too, to think I am losing what I lived by all my life, ever since I was a little girl, and I sit here wondering how I am going to get any goodness back. More worrisome at this moment, while Aries sleeps restlessly, are my thoughts of Carrie, and where she might be on this cold autumn night.

Day 18 AC.

Moe comes by daily. She is better medicine for Aries than anything I have in my bag. She sits up on the edge of the bed and reads the words that Carrie taught her. Aries, weak as she is, writes more words on the flat piece of slate and creek chalk Carrie fixed for the child. She smiles as Moe works to sound out new words then looks up at me with a look that reminds me that not all of Jolie's children are slow. After they finish with words, Aries puts ciphering on the slate.

"Oh, those are easy," Moe says to her. "Carrie gave me ones a lot harder than that." Then Moe looks at me with a half frightened look at having said Carrie's name.

"It's okay baby," Aries says. "She's not mad at you."

Aries is wrong about that one. I have been angry at everyone. Only Aries has been spared my wrath. I fix fried potatoes with eggs. The ducks stayed with us the very first time, and it has been a welcomed blessing.

"I wish Mommy could cook like you," Moe says to me as she gobbles down lunch. "Are you gonna make Thanksgiving?" she then asks.

"No. I don't have a turkey."

"Oh, that's okay. Daddy snared one, and now Tommy is feeding it meal. By Thanksgiving it should be good and fat."

"Hmm."

"Mommy can't cook worth a twit, not like you. And she don't cook at all now that she's sick. So will you come and cook it for us?"

With that Aries laughs until she chokes. I run to her side and pull her into a sitting position.

"Moe, get me some water," I order, and obediently the child hops from the bed and brings us a dipper.

"Granny, you okay?" the child asks.

Aries nods and I ease her back down to her pillow. The coughing spell has taken its toll.

"I think you had better go on home now," I tell Moe.

She pulls on an old sweater of Carrie's, a blue one that we had handed down back when Jolie's second child was five. It is too little for Moe now, and will probably not make it until Jolie's fifth grows into it.

"See you tomorrow, Granny," Moe says as she heads out the door. "You too, Grandma."

I would have said, "Call first," had we phones. But we don't, and so I know, like clockwork, the child will be at the door before noon and, should Aries be able, sit on her bed until after supper.

Through raspy voice Aries whispers, "I'll be waiting."

Day 24 AC.

Just as Moe promised, she has been here each day. Two days ago I took over the reading of books to the child. Aries rests back on her pillows and watches us. She smiles often, but it is getting weaker. She is barely eating at all, but the child doesn't notice. She is too young to take notice of such things. We have been reading through a book of fairy tales, one that I remember as a child, where the prince always gets the princess and everyone lives happily ever after.

I made a clear broth today from a squirrel Tommy killed, onions and greens added to hide the gamey flavor of the animal. I hate cooking squirrel. Moe turns her nose up to the greens, but I tell her she has to take the good with the bad. She loves squirrel. I feed Aries the warm broth, adding little bites of greens. She swallows slowly a few sips before shaking her head and pushing the spoon away.

"Granny's gonna die pretty soon, isn't she Grandma."

"Yes," I say.

Moe comes to the bedside, crawls up and pats my back. She has read my thoughts as if she had them written on her slate, "You'll still have me, Grandma."

There is healing in her words, and I tell her, "I know, sweetie, I know," and it is the truest thing I have felt in weeks.

Day 27 AC.

Aries died today.

158

Chapter 20

Carrie.

I was glad that Gary left early for work. It happened yesterday, the thing that I had not anticipated or planned for when Gary and I left Stears Branch. I sat on blood stained sheets with crazy Mave staring at me.

"Well, Mave," I asked. "Where do they keep the rags?" She looked at me with a puzzled expression but said nothing.

"Rags?" I asked again, pointing to the sheets. *Where is Claire when I need her?*

I woke early with cramping, should have gotten up, but then with dawn came the red flow. It was never like this, this rush of blood. I knew Cook was going to be wondering where I was, and I didn't want to go to the kitchen with it pouring. "Rags," I said one more time.

A light seemed to turn on in Mave's eyes. She took me by the hand and led me to a closet in the back of our sleeping quarters. *The closet, feminine hygiene, yeah.* She opened the door, and inside was a shelf lined with boxes.

"Rags," she said and handed me a box. I opened the box, and inside were soft oblong pads. "Rags," she said again and smiled. It was the first time I saw her smile. Her teeth were crooked and stained, but the smile was genuine. "Thanks," I told her.

I gathered my bed clothes off the cot, folded the red blanket over the naked mattress, and put them at the foot of my bed. I gathered my towel and clean under clothes and headed for the shower. Most of the women had already risen, a few remained on their beds, heads covered to keep the morning sun that streamed through the tall windows out of their eyes. I still have not adjusted to the communal showers and yesterday was glad that no one else was in the shower room. Only Mave stood and watched as I peeled off the night gown. At that moment I had lost my sense of modesty.

"Mave, let me know if Cook is coming," I said to her.

Mave nodded. I have come to appreciate warm water and bars of soap. I lathered and washed quickly and put my panties on the floor of the shower room and tried as best I could to stomp the bloodiness from them. Once most of the stain was out, I turned off the water and wrung out the panties, dried off, and looked at Mave for instructions.

"Throw away rags," she said.

"Ah," I said. "Throw away rags. I got it. Thanks, Mave. Who said you were slow?"

"Claire."

She's smarter than we think. That's when I ran into problems. I gathered the sheets on the way out and met Mrs. Davis.

"I'm so sorry. So much has been happening, I didn't realize it was my time. I'll wash these myself."

She looked at me and the sheets. They looked awful, and I was embarrassed. It wasn't like I had intended to make a mess, and I had started to explain all of it to her, about not coming prepared, but at that very moment Claire came in and I was more grateful than words.

"Claire," I cried.

"Carrie, what's up? Oh honey," she saw my sheets. "Mrs. Davis, I'll help her get this cleaned up."

"I started."

"I see," she said as we walked away from Mrs. Davis. "You're first time?"

"No. Really, Claire?"

"Well, you are acting like it."

"I just," and I was about to explain the same thing to her. I was really getting aggravated at having to go over the whole story when I heard Billy's voice.

"Carrie."

I moved quickly down the hall. Billy was the last person I wanted to see the bloody sheets. God knows how I was to explain it to him. Before I could get the story out he would think I had been stabbed, and when the actual story was told, he'd tell the whole thing to Gary, probably at the supper table. When it was all done, I imagined the men at the surrounding tables laughing like they did when I asked about feminine hygiene stuff, and Gary sitting beside me looking down at his half eaten plate, face blushing crimson. I love Grandma, and she told me about girl stuff, but she never called it feminine hygiene. She messed up with that one.

When I finally got to the kitchen, Cook didn't say a word. I figured Mrs. Davis beat me to the punch, and I was actually grateful I didn't have to try to explain. I did have to go back to the women's quarters to

160

change the disposable rags. Claire went with me and showed me what to do with them. The first time we went back, Mrs. Davis met me at the yellow doors and warned me not to flush them down the toilets.

Today has been about the same as yesterday, but I didn't mess the bed sheets. I like the pads, and I like the idea of not having to wash them out and hang them on a line to dry. Back in Stears Branch, everyone knew what time of month it was for me when they saw the rags on the line – Grandpa, Jolie, Harold, Mr. Thompson, and God-forbid, Tommy. He would make rude jokes about me and then run off laughing as I clipped the rags to the rope we strung between two poles. What was worse was when Grandpa's dogs would start sniffing at my behind, and Tommy would laugh so hard that he would fall down rolling in the grass. That's when Grandma chased him back to Jolie's with a threat to tan his hide. I made a promise to myself, when we go back home, I'm going to make sure I get a dozen boxes of these things to take with me.

Gary has accused me of being cranky, and Claire just says it out loud there at the breakfast table, "It's her time of the month."

Just like I knew it would happen, Gary's face turns pickled beet red.

If all of this isn't bad enough, Crazy Mave pipes up with her thoughts. The whole time we have been here she has hardly said two words, and now she decides she is going to be social and enter into the conversation.

"The Curse," she says with emphasis.

Billy screws up his freckled face and looks up at Gary, then looks at me, "What's the curse?"

Sam, who is almost always at the table right behind us laughs and says, "On the rag son, on the rag," at which point I stand and take my tray to the clean-up station.

I can hear Billy's voice behind me, "What's the matter with Carrie, Gary?

"Nothing," Gary tells him.

"Yeah, there is," Billy says. "She looks real angry. What did we say to make her mad?" And with that, I can hear Sam laughing all the harder. If I wasn't sure Harold was Tommy's Daddy, I would swear it was Sam.

"You okay?" Cook asks me.

"Men," is all I say, and then she laughs a big belly laugh.

"I guess you are kind of young. Just wait until you're older honey.

161

Can't say it gets much better."

Claire comes into the back kitchen. "You going to send Gary off to work, or just let him leave without a goodbye?"

"I'd just as soon not go back out there right now, if you please."

"Lighten up, Carrie. Sam doesn't mean anything by it, and Mave can't help it. If you're feeling up to it, we'll go back to the Annex tomorrow." I ignore Claire and proceed to pull out the bag of potatoes that I know Cook is going to need peeled.

"Here, that's too heavy for one person," Claire says, coming to my assistance. "You don't need to be lifting that by yourself." We lift the bag to the sink, and together we empty the bag with a loud rumble. Claire looks up and says she has to tend the laundry, and my sheets from yesterday are clean, if I want to put them back on my bed. I nod, say that I will get them after I am finished with Cook's work.

In the background I hear the big dishwasher begin and see Cook out of the corner of my eye push the first rack of plates into the channel and metal doors swish shut. I think that Cook went into the dining room, and I saw the other clean-up crew taking out trash, but I feel someone behind me. Thinking it might be Sam, I turn quickly. It is Gary.

"I'm sorry they embarrassed you," he says.

"Where's Billy?" I am trying to stay indifferent, and I don't really know why. It reminds me of Grandma when she tried to make Grandpa pay for some transgression, but for the life of me I can't think of what Gary did wrong.

"He went on to his class. He didn't know any better, Carrie."

"I know that."

"Neither did Mave," he says.

"I know that, too."

"And, well, Sam's just an asshole, and you have to ignore him. I told him so. Does that help?"

"You called him that?"

"It's the truth, isn't it? Look, I've got to get on to work. He won't bother you anymore."

"Gary?"

"Yeah?"

I want to tell him I love him, but it feels foreign to me, "Have a good day today, okay?"

"Sure. You, too."

Chapter 21

Friday, and another week has passed. We have been here over four weeks. Captain Davis has let up his scrutiny for the time being. Routine has fallen into place. I rise at six-thirty, Billy at seven. He stays with me in the dining room until Mrs. Davis comes to get him for the school bus. I see Gary for a brief moment before he leaves for work. I get a hug and a light kiss on the forehead. It is not enough. He knows it, smiles and whispers "Maybe later," but those laters have not come.

The people who came in from the cold to spend the night – bags hanging from their shoulders – drink pots of hot coffee and spoon down plates of gravy and biscuits before leaving to go back to their cold corners. They do not trust anyone, let alone the Shelter, so they only come when it has been cold like last night. Claire says on warmer nights they prefer their hidden getaways beneath bridges or when they can, inside a condemned house. I wonder, when she tells me this, how many stayed in my house, urinated in the corners of my room, or scattered bottles of cheap liquor amongst mouse droppings, and I shudder. More women stay here long term than men. Most of them leave during the day, too, but Gary, Billy, and I are different, since we have "hit on bad times," according to Gary. We are willing to work for our keep.

Gary says he is saving his money, and I know he is telling the truth. We pay a small fee to cover our food expense here. Claire has pretty much kept her distance. I have had a hard time not thinking about my Daddy, the computer boxes at the city Annex and the thought of a brother. I think about Grandma nearly every day, wondering whether she is okay and whether my Grandpa may be around the corner to drag me back, but in the last week my hunger to find my Momma has surpassed any other I have ever known, even that forbidden hunger for Gary.

"Hey, baby girl," Claire says as she enters the dining room. "You about done here?"

I look over at Cook, and she nods me to go ahead. Claire grabs two cups and fills them with coffee from the big double coffee makers. I have developed a taste for coffee, which I never thought I would back

163

in Stears Branch. I like the sweet milk she adds. Claire holds the cup up for me and motions for me to come to an empty table.

"Jack and I have been talking," she tells me. "We got a plan. Whatever you two are running from, we both think you are good kids, and it wouldn't be the first time the establishment screws someone. Believe me, I know."

"So what's your plan?" I ask in a whisper, and I look back to where Cook is watching us from the clean-up window.

"You tried to get a marriage license, why?"

"Sshh... Dumb question," I say softly.

"Not so dumb. Do you love Gary, or is there something else."

"What difference does it make?"

"Lots. If you are just trying to get away from this tyrant of a grandfather, then Jack and I can get you out of here. If you are wanting to marry Gary, well, I think that we can take care of that, too."

"First of all, I love Grandpa. Second, I can't prove I'm a legal age to get married."

"Yeah, I know the latter. Found that out at the Annex." Claire pulls out a cigarette and starts to light it.

From the kitchen Cook calls out, "No smoking in here, Claire."

"Cook, can I have Carrie for a little while today?"

"Miss Davis give you off work today?"

"Took off," she answers back. "Can I have Carrie? I promise not to teach her how to smoke or anything else sinful, okay?" Claire is serious. I can see it in her eyes. Cook does, too, and so she tells me I can have the rest of the day off, but to be back before Billy gets in from school.

"I don't have enough energy to do what I need to do here, let alone keep up with that little fire cracker." And she has said that with a bit of tenderness at the edge of her otherwise stern voice.

"Thank you, Cook," I say.

"Yeah, thanks. You won't be sorry. I promise. This is a good thing, know what I mean?"

"I hope to God you're right."

Claire takes me by the arm, fills our disposable cups with more coffee and leads me out the swinging doors. In the hall, Mrs. Davis and the Captain are talking. They look up. They both frown.

"Don't worry, I promise to bring her back," Claire says to them both as she pushes me through the door. "Here, put this on. It's cold

164

outside," as she hands me a jacket.

In the circle driveway is the truck that Claire comes to work in every morning. Jack is behind the wheel. She opens the door and pushes me up into the cab, then jumps in beside me.

"Did you talk to Gary?" she asks Jack.

"Yeah, Frank, his co-worker is going to cover for him. Their boss was okay with it, too. We need to get a move on it. We have to be back to Georgetown before three o'clock to get it all done."

"We need to be back here by three, Jack. She's got to be here for the kid."

"Like I said, we got to move it," and with that the old truck screeches out of the driveway and onto the street. In spite of it being morning rush hour, there are few vehicles on the road. We pass the cemetery, stone walls on one side of the road, wrought iron fence on the other. Claire sees to where my eyes go.

"We'll go there in a few days. We have some business to take care of first."

"What are we doing, anyway?" I ask.

"Going to Frankfort to get your birth certificate," Claire says proudly.

"And, how is that going to help?" I ask again.

"I got ways," Jack says, and he has this satisfied smile on his face.

"Carrie, this is Jack, my kind-of husband. Jack, Claire."

"Kind of?" Jack asks, and then laughs.

"Here's the plan," Claire interrupts. "We get your birth certificate. Jack changes the year on the certificate. 'Cause we're getting it straight from Frankfort, it will have an official seal. Then...we meet Gary in Georgetown, right Jack?" Jack nods.

"Jack's got friends in high places up there. We get a marriage license, and the guy there owes Jack a favor or two, so he's going to, like, make it for two months ago. Kind of prove your story to the Davises. Then we get you out of the prison there, and get you and Gary your own place somewhere, but not that dump you used to call home."

"I grew up there," I say.

"You grew up in some place called Butcher Hollow," Jack laughs, not taking his eyes of the road. We have turned onto an old service road. There are crumbling buildings, old gray stones tumbled down from tall walls. At an intersection, a sink-hole has ravaged the road.

165

"No, I grew up in Stears Branch," I correct.

"Honey, he's just giving you a hard time. He knows that," Claire says, and she glares at Jack. He shrugs.

"The quakes made the old rock quarry cave in. Was part of the reason this end of town was devastated. Most of the houses and businesses were built right on top of the excavated limestone formation. When the bedrock started to shake, what was left of the framework just gave way."

We cross a newly built bridge, and from there move to a half circle of a road where fields and crumbled rock fences stand. We cross railroad tracks, the means of transporting most of the goods, Jack continues to explain. He is rugged looking, more rugged than the men in the hollow, and since he has options, I think he chooses to look that way. I find myself judging him by his looks and am surprised by how much he knows.

When we come to the end of the road we are on, we turn right, and a whole city appears. There are more cars, and people walking and speeding by on two-wheeled vehicles. I remember Grandma's stories, and I look at Claire and ask, "Motorcycles?"

She laughs and says, "Yeah."

One passes us. A girl is on the back, and her hair is flying behind her like ribbons in the wind. I think to myself that I'm going get one of those someday.

The whole drive feels like it takes us 30 minutes, and I ask Claire if that is so. She laughs and says, "That is the shortest part of our adventure today."

"Kentucky 676 should only be a mile or so," Jack says.

"Look for the east-west connector." Claire tells him. "There, right there. Turn left."

Within seconds we turn left at a battered green sign and follow the drive up a sloping hill. At the top stands a square building.

"What time is it supposed to open?" Jack asks.

"Ten o'clock," Claire tells him.

"That means we've got a little wait. So, after we get the paper...by the way, how hard you think this is going to be?"

"Depends," Claire says. Then she turns to me, "They're gonna ask you a bunch of questions. Just to make sure you are who you say you are. They'll ask for a picture identification. Just tell them you lost your purse, and you haven't ever gotten a driver's license." I nod.

"And, for God's sake, don't act nervous. For the most part you are only telling them the truth. Minimal lying here, so you should do okay. Just not too much information, know what I mean?"

"Yeah, I'm used to that."

"True. You'll be asked who your parents are, and also it will help if you can tell them when your dad died. They will cross reference that. It's okay to tell them you were staying with your grandparents since you were little. Do you remember the street they lived on before?"

"No, but I know where my parents lived when I was born. And, I know my Momma's maiden name. "

"That should be enough."

The next fifteen minutes we wait in silence. My head is spinning with the plans for the day and what it means. Jack lights a cigarette and shares it with Claire. She acts like she is going to pass it to me, and I shake my head no, but she laughs and hands it back to Jack. In the distance I hear a clock chime, and after the short melody I hear it count off ten strikes. Jack opens the door and flips out his cigarette.

"I'll wait here for you two. You won't need me in there, and if there is any trouble, I can have the truck running as soon as I see you heading out."

"There won't be any trouble," Claire tells him. "You're gonna scare her. Nothing is going to go wrong. We have the truth on our side at this point."

Inside the building we come to a desk where a young woman directs us to another door, where inside is an older lady with blue tightly curled hair, just like the one in Lexington. My expression must have been telling, because Claire leans down and whispers to me, "Old school....they all tend to look like that."

"Hi," she says to the lady. "We're here to get a duplicate birth certificate for the young lady."

Just like in Lexington, the lady seems preoccupied with some other task. It takes her a moment before she looks up at us.

"Name?" she asks.

"Carrie Ann Baxter."

"Date of birth?"

"January 29, 2012."

"City or county of birth?"

"Uh, Lexington, Kentucky."

"Parents' name?"

167

"Jonathan and Emily Baxter."

"Okay. Found you. Do you have some means of identification?"

"She lost her purse. It's one of the reasons she is needing her birth certificate, so she can get a new identification card."

"Hmm, too bad. "

"Who are you?"

"Just a friend with a car," Claire says.

"Oh, I thought you might be a sister or an aunt, you know, who could vouch for her. So honey, do you have a driver's license?'

"I never learned to drive," I say.

"Okay. Let's see where we go from here."

"My father is dead," I offer. "Died in October 2017."

"Hmm. We'll need to verify at another computer. Stay here, I'm going to look that up over here." She moves over to a different square box, one just like we used in Lexington.

"Don't offer any more information. Only answer what she asks," Claire warns, then adds, "And, whatever you do, don't tell her you have a brother. She'll ask what your mother's new married name is, and you have no idea."

"Maybe she didn't remarry." I say.

Claire looks down sympathetically, "Maybe not, but that's a whole other story, and we don't need to go there now."

The lady comes back with a satisfied smile on her face. "I did confirm that honey, and I'm sorry that you lost your father. Times were very hard then. I also found your mother's marriage license to your step-father, Russell Jones. He didn't adopt you?"

I tell her no.

"This should only take a few minutes. I have it printing off, and I will have to put the seal on it. I need you to sign that you have received it, and since your friend is here, I will need to check her license and have her sign as a witness. Are you agreeable with that?"

Claire said yes. In less than fifteen minutes, less time than we had waited to get in the building, I am walking out with two things – my birth certificate and my mother's new name. Now Jack is to work his magic, and I didn't see how he is going to make a two into a zero on this thin paper document. The lady who issued and signed me my bond of freedom was Doris Wright.

Chapter 22

From the courthouse it is to Jack's place to pick up cash. We leave his apartment and I am glad to be out of the stale, smoky room. I am wondering what I will owe Jack for his services. Claire told everyone that she is married to Jack, but today I find that she is not. She calls it an "arrangement," that someday I may understand, but she hopes not. It is past noon, and Gary is to meet us at the courthouse in Georgetown. We have taken another back road, twisting between the hills and tree shadowed creeks. I am too nervous for it to be a pleasant drive. Claire is in the middle now, and I am looking outside the window, wondering what is going to happen next.

Just like in Frankfort, we come upon lights, and except for the few unrepaired buildings, I suspect this town looks the same as Frankfort. Just like promised by Claire, when we get to the center of town, I see the yellow El Camino parked in a pull-in space. Standing beside the door is the man I have been calling my husband, and he is smiling with this tan faced, broad grin.

I have butterflies in my stomach, and there are long, slow minutes that I am not sure I am doing the right thing. There is part of me that is excited to see him, reassured by that very grin, and there is another part, deep in the pit of my stomach, that is absolutely scared to death. I want to run back to Stears Branch where I know my Grandma is waiting. Not sure what being married is going to mean except to protect me from being sent to some foster home. I look up to see Claire staring at me intently.

"You can back out right now if you want," she says. Jack looks at both of us like we are crazy for all that we have already put him through to complete Claire's schemes.

"What the hell?" he asks.

"Shut up, Jack. It's okay to be scared, believe me," she says to me.

"I'm not scared," I lie.

"Like I said, it's okay to be scared."

Jack jumps out of the truck and approaches Gary with a firm handshake and a good ole boy slap on the back. Gary sees through me, and his grin fades.

"You okay?" he asks, then says, "This is going to be okay, I promise.

169

You've got nothing to be afraid of on account of me, understand?"

He means it, I know, but that doesn't change how I am feeling. Claire brought one of the nicer dresses from the bag we brought with us to the Shelter, snuck it out before coming after me in the kitchen this morning. She brought the light blue one, the one that matched my eyes, and while we were at Jacks, we changed. She fixed my hair, curled the edges with a hot iron, and found a little veil from some second-hand store. She put makeup on me, some lipstick and brushed on some black stuff to my eye lashes. It makes me look older.

Gary stares at me, "You're beautiful, you know that? The first time I saw you standing on that porch, apron full of apple peelings, and the wind blowing that sun-glistening hair of yours, I thought you were the most beautiful thing I ever saw. But here you are more beautiful, even if you do look like a deer in the headlights," he says, finally laughing.

"I've never been able to figure women out," Jack says, still with his arm around Gary's shoulders. "Think they know what they want, and you go to all sorts of trouble to accomplish their wishes, and then, poof."

"Yeah, thanks for all the trouble and time today. I hope this covers some of the expenses and the time you took off work." Gary hands Jack a folded stack of bills.

"No way, man. You keep that. We might have to pay the guy inside, but other than that, consider it a wedding gift from me and Claire."

"Not sure I can ever repay you enough."

"Well, you got yourself an eighteen-year-old bride here. What we're gonna do in here is have the Justice of the Peace back date this license, you know, to satisfy the Davises, and whoever else might want proof of your story. Know what I mean?"

"Now Carrie, when we get in here, we're gonna get the license from the clerk. They are good for 30 days, and he's the guy we're gonna have to pay to get him to back date it. We're gonna tell him you're pregnant, you know, so that you don't have to explain to the kid when it gets older why the dates don't add up right." Jack is explaining the strategy.

"But I'm not pregnant, I've not even..."

"I know that. Gary knows that. We all know that. But we don't want the clerk in there to know it," Claire explains.

"It's okay, Carrie," Gary reassures. "They don't put the reason on the license."

170

"Do you remember when you told Captain Davis how long you two were married?" Claire asks.

"Honestly, I don't," Gary says.

"If we're lucky, he won't either, or you can act like he was mistaken."

He nods understanding. I am there listening to the three of them.

"I do," I say. "We told him a month."

Jack interrupts, "Look guys, we're wasting time here. After the license we gotta get the preacher, know what I mean?"

We walk up long steps to the front of the courthouse. The turret on the domed top had toppled eleven years before, but the remnants still lends to the grandness of the building. Glass doors with Scott County Courthouse painted on the front welcome us. Inside the building is little different than the offices in Lexington and Frankfort.

"Ralph should still be here. Said he wouldn't leave until we got here."

A heavy young man with black beard comes out of a restroom. "Jack, I was starting to wonder if you were going to make it. I'm only working half a day. It's gonna cost a little more for my inconvenience." He laughs and adds, "Just kidding."

He looks over at Carrie and back to Jack, "This the little one in trouble?" Carrie feels her face grow hot with embarrassment.

"Honey, it happens to the best families, believe me. Come on in here. Let's look at your documentation."

We follow him into an office that has a glass front door and behind the door is a counter. He walks around behind it and pulls out a folder. "Okay, let's see what we got. Where's your driver's license."

"I don't drive," I say.

"Your ID card then?"

"I lost my purse. We just was in Frankfort and got a new birth certificate. Here."

The clerk looks over the document, then looks back at me, then at Jack. "Old buddy, you are calling in a couple of favors here."

"Look, Ralph, she's a good girl. Can you help us out or not?"

"Okay, but," and with that the clerk looks around. The office is empty except for the five of us: Jack, Claire, Gary, me, and the clerk. "This is gonna cost a little more than the $35.50, and all in cash, understand?

Gary answers, "I got what you are asking, so can we get on with this?"

171

"You lose your license, too?" the clerk asks.

Gary pulls out his wallet, letting the clerk see the stack of bills, then hands the man his license.

"Well, at least some things are as they seem," he says to Jack. When he completes the papers, signs and dates the papers, he hands them to Gary. That'll be a hundred dollars."

Gary pulls out a single bill and puts it on the counter.

"Plus, of course, the cost of the license, that's thirty-five fifty. Gary pulls out the balance, throws the two quarters on the counter with a clang.

"Nice doing business with you people. Now if you'll excuse me, the office is closing."

Outside Claire looks accusingly at Jack, "I thought you had some friends to help us out."

"I think the only one he was helping out was himself," Gary says, but continues, "Jack, I still appreciate all the trouble you have gone to for us. The money I had still stands as yours."

"Like I said, consider my part a wedding gift. Let's not keep the parson waiting."

I get in the El Camino with Gary, and we follow Jack and Claire to a small stone church halfway back to Lexington. All the way, we can see through the window, and Claire has not stopped fussing at Jack. If I weren't still nervous about the next step, I'd be laughing.

Gary says, "I hope that you don't start acting like that once we're married," and he is laughing.

"Despite what Cook has said about her, she has had my back up to this point."

"That she has, Carrie."

As we pull up to the stone church, it's steeple still pointing upward to the cloudless blue sky, a small round man with round spectacles steps out onto the front steps. He has a kindly smile. I am glad to see at least one person of authority today who is smiling.

The parson speaks first, "Welcome to Pisgah Church my friends. I've been expecting you. Good afternoon, Claire. It's good to see you again. We've missed you recently. I hope this means you'll be coming back soon."

"Parson, you know Captain Davis keeps us listening to his fire and damnation preachers on Sunday," and her smile to him is open, honest, and sincere.

172

"So is this the young couple you told me about?"

"This is Carrie Baxter and her fiancée, Gary Combs."

"Nice to meet you two. Maybe you can talk Claire here into making Jack an honest man," he says with a wink at Claire. "I could do a double ceremony right now if you like."

Jack shuffles his feet, "It's not me, Parson. It's her, and you know it."

"So she's said before, son. Well, let's go on inside and get this wedding underway."

Inside is a small, fragile white-haired lady. She is at a piano, and looks sweetly at me when asking if "she would like some music for her wedding."

"Might as well make it a proper wedding to remember." She reminds me of Grandma, and I feel tears well up in my eyes.

"Honey, don't cry," she says, and Claire looks at me with this panicked expression as if after all we have done it will all go for naught in the last few minutes of her grand plans.

"You look like my Grandma," I say. "I just wish she was here to see this day."

Claire breathes a sigh of relief.

"Parson, I have to be back at the Shelter in an hour, do you think we can get on with it?" Claire asks.

"Of course, dear."

The minister's wife begins playing a soft sweet song, and I can see that Gary is just as nervous as me.

The parson's voice booms out loud, in contrast to his small stature.

"Dearly beloved, we are gathered here in the presence of these witnesses to join this man and woman in holy matrimony, which is an honorable estate ordained by God. It is not to be entered into inadvisably or lightly, but reverently. Into this estate these two persons have come here to be joined as one. If there is anyone here who sees fit to find reason why they cannot be married, stand now and state your cause."

No one says a word. I half way expect one of the blue haired women to burst through the back door to stop the wedding, or even worse, Grandpa.

"Gary," the parson says, "do you take Carrie Baxter to be your wife, to live together in accordance to God's holy ordinance? Will you love her, comfort her, honor and keep her in sickness and health, for

173

better or worse, for richer or poorer, in sadness and in joy, to cherish, forsaking all others, keeping yourself only to her until death do you part?"

I hear Gary say, "I will."

The parson looks at me, and I feel a solemnness that I have never known. And as Gary smiles across our outstretched hands, I feel a peace that has been, up to this very moment, absent.

"And will you, Carrie," the voice is softer and tender, "take Gary Combs to be your husband, to live together in holy matrimony in accordance to God's holy ordinance? Will you love him, comfort him, honor and keep him in sickness and health, for better or worse, for richer or poor, in sadness and in joy, to cherish, forsaking all others, keeping yourself only to him until death do you part?"

I am silent, this is all new. The parson whispers, "You are to say 'I will,'" and in a stronger voice than I knew I had, I say, "I will."

"Do you have rings to exchange?" I am confused. I knew Grandma always wore a narrow gold band, but I didn't have anything. Then, Gary pulls from his pocket a small silver band.

"Gary, place the band on Carrie's finger and repeat after me, 'With this ring I thee wed.'"

I hear Gary's voice repeat the words. When the parson looks at me, I start to say I don't have any ring, but Claire tugs at my elbow and places in my hand a larger narrow band. She has tears in her eyes. *What part of this vow moves her heart?*

"Carrie, place the ring on Gary's left hand, and repeat after me." I hear him say the same words, and I repeat, "With this ring I thee wed."

Then again the parson's voice booms out, and I look towards his wife, sitting there at the piano, sweet tears running down her cheeks. *I bet she cries at all the weddings.*

"In as much as these two have consented together in marriage before this company of friends and before God, I pronounce you husband and wife. What God has joined together, let no man put asunder. Gary, you may kiss your wife."

With those words, Gary pulls me close, lifts my face to his and kisses me. We have kissed so infrequently, I had nothing to compare this magic to, because it is magic. And, in that magic I kissed him back as I had never kissed anyone, not Grandma, not Grandpa, not in the long lost memories of kissing my Momma or Daddy, and I knew that this was right.

Behind us, Jack hollered a big whoop, and Claire was laughing. The piano bangs a loud song, and we turn to go. Claire stops me, grabs my shoulder and whispers in my ear that this is all right, I will be all right. And I know she is right.

"Just a minute," the parson calls. "I have to sign the paper."

Gary pulls it out of his front pocket and hands it to the parson. He looks at the paper, and then at Gary, "You just about let this license expire son."

"I know. I couldn't get off work until today. Is it okay?

"Yes son, it's all right. Now get off, the four of you. Vivian and I have things to tend to."

Outside, at the vehicles, Claire takes Gary by the arm and instructs him regarding the last of her plans.

"You can't come back with us now. Has to look like you haven't been together today. Try to get some oil or grease on your hands, and, oh yeah, crumple this license up a little. Put it in the glove box and just wait for Captain Davis to require to see it. That and along with the letter from that little boy's mom."

"Understood," Gary says.

"And you," she says to me. "You can have that honeymoon some other day. Not tonight, and not this weekend. And, I don't think we can go around displaying that birth certificate. Jack did the best he could, but you were right about the numbers. Captain Davis won't take any bribes. Understand?"

"I understand completely," I say with the same resolve as Gary.

"Now, Gary, kiss her one more time before I drag her away from you. That kiss made my whole day, just about my whole life, except for maybe when Jack kisses me."

Gary doesn't hesitate at her offer, and the kiss that was so tender inside is more insistent than the one inside the church. I feel the same insistence and lean into the hardness of his body. The kiss flushes my face and leaves me hungry.

At the doorway stands the parson and his wife, and Claire in all her worldly wisdom changes her plan.

"Carrie in the car with Gary, at least for the next mile or so, and then Gary, you'd better stop so we can change out." She is laughing at Gary, and he gives a shrug, like maybe he will and maybe he won't. But we both know Claire is right.

175

Chapter 23

The first thing Mrs. Davis asks me on Sunday when we gather for church is, "Where did you get the ring?" I am taken aback. Maybe it is because I have admired it, held it up and examined its perfectness when I thought no one was looking. Cook noticed it right off on Friday night and warned, "Don't lose that pretty little thing in the dishwater." But now Mrs. Davis has noticed, and I must lie to keep up our ruse.

"Gary got paid Friday," I tell her, and that's probably not a lie. "He didn't have the money to get me a ring when we first got married." And I breathe a breath of relief because that's not a lie either. "He gave it to me Friday evening."

"Oh," she says.

Gary comes through the door from the men's quarters, and as he does, he is stopped by Captain Davis. I'm trying to pay attention to what Gary is saying and only half listening now to Mrs. Davis.

"Carrie, are you listening to me?" she asks.

"Oh, sorry," I say.

"Well, we got a call from social services on Friday afternoon. They got a call from the courthouse regarding a gentleman who showed up there saying his granddaughter had run away, and had they seen her. "

My attention is now fully on Mrs. Davis. She is watching me closely for any reaction, and I am trying with everything in me not to turn and run. I hear Gary saying in a raised, agitated voice, "I told you I have the papers, had put them in the glove box. Yeah, both of them."

"The clerk thought she remembered the girl from the gentleman's description, but was certain she remembered the boy. He had red hair. Apparently they were trying to get a marriage license and the girl was too young."

"Morning, Carrie."

It is Claire's voice behind me, and I have never been so happy to hear a friendly voice in all of my life. To Mrs. Davis she says, "Wow, that's really a coincidence isn't it?"

"I thought it was more than a coincidence," Mrs. Davis says, then adds, "The clerk says she sent the couple down here to the Shelter, about the same time Mr. Combs and Carrie showed up. She didn't tell the older gentleman she sent them here, because she thought he

176

seemed a little agitated and didn't quite trust him," and again Mrs. Davis focuses on my face.

"Hmm, that really is a coincidence. There really are all sorts of crazies still running around here." Then to me, Claire takes my hand and says, "I see Gary finally got you that ring. He'd told Jack that he's been saving for that ever since he started working at the garage. You guys didn't have the money for a ring back then. That is the sweetest thing, don't you think so?" she asks Mrs. Davis.

Mrs. Davis turns on her heel to walk away, then turns back, "You two girls need to get on into the meeting room. We have a guest preacher today."

Gary walks to where we are standing. Billy is in tow.

"Wow, Carrie," Billy says. "Gary got really mad."

"He wants to see our license and the letter from Billy's mom giving us custody, and he wants to see it today. Something's up."

"Grandpa's up," I say.

"That's the least of your problems," Claire says. "Because you guys are legally married, remember?"

"Right," Gary answers, and smiles at me. "But what's worse than her grandfather finding us?"

"The police finding a body on old route twenty-five."

The color drains from Gary's face, more than the tan, more than the freckles, the whole spectrum of color has vanished.

"Yeah," Claire says in response to Gary's reaction. "And, to make it worse, that scum at the ferry has pointed a finger at a young man with red hair driving a yellow El Camino."

"Oh my God," I whisper.

"Yeah, an awful lot of coincidences coming full force your way."

"It's not been made public knowledge yet, thank goodness, or the Davises would have already turned you in. Jack says we gotta ditch the car. Did you do it, Gary?"

"What do you think?" I ask.

"Well?" she asks Gary again. It is Billy who comes to our rescue. We had forgotten his presence in the midst of our terror.

"Miss Claire, Gary tried to save my Daddy, and he saved Momma and Susie and me, and if it hadn't been for him I bet we'd all be dead."

"I just needed to be sure. Well, we gotta get you three out of the Shelter today."

Captain Davis sticks his head out the door and calls in his most

177

commanding voice, "Service is starting now."

Gary, Billy and I walk to the chapel. Claire slips into the office. When she slips into the chair beside me, Mrs. Davis is leading the congregation in a lively song about getting to heaven. I have memories of Grandma's singing the refrain, but I can't pull on those sweet memories with the threat that is hanging over Gary's head.

Claire leans towards Gary and whispers, "Jack spoke to Frank. After lunch Frank is going to call here at the Shelter and say he needs you at the garage, pronto. You'll take the car, and they'll park it behind some of the projects. Frank says you can use his car."

I am glad that Billy is on the other side of Gary and Claire. He is singing loud and clear. Mrs. Davis is in her element, hands moving to the music, smiling at the residents of this Shelter – at those singing like Billy. On Sundays the criteria for getting fed is to listen to the guest preacher. They are like preachers I heard Grandma talk about. I haven't, in the four Sundays here, heard one story about Jesus's love. Most are about the evils of tobacco or alcohol, or whatever sinning the rest of us have committed. Even Grandpa, in his fury at Gary for coming into our little valley, believed in Jesus's forgiveness and love for us.

The thought of Grandpa sends shivers up my back. I turn from my seat to see if he has walked into the meeting room. I can feel his presence as real as if he is sitting right behind me. I turn and look. It is Mave, not Grandpa, sitting straight backed and wild eyed this morning. I wonder if Grandpa has taken possession of her body and is waiting, just waiting to whisk me away from Gary and back to Stears Branch.

"Carrie, we'll get you out of here after Mrs. Davis leaves for the afternoon," Claire says, seeing the panic in my eyes.

I nod, then ask, "What about Billy?"

Billy hears his name and turns his attention away from the man in the front, "What about me?" he asks a little too loudly.

Sam turns around and looks at us. "Hey Claire, whatta you up to now?"

"Don't you worry about it. I got it covered. If Carrie or I need you, you be there?"

"Have I ever not been there for you?" and he winks at me.

Mrs. Davis has turned from her front row seat to see who is talking. She glares at Sam, and he takes off his hat, tips it to her and lays it

178

in his lap. Billy waves at her, and her face warms into a smile for the child. If nothing else, she cares about Billy.

The service winds to an end with the anticipated altar call. When we begin singing, the same four men who went forward last Sunday go forward today, hats off, heads bowed in sincerity, staggering to the wooden altar rail. The preacher, one I haven't seen before, says "Hallelujah!" Thinking he is going to start preaching all over again, Captain Davis interrupts and asks the rest of us to stand for the closing prayer.

The round-faced wall clock marks the time at eleven thirty, just in time for the lunch line to form. I am so distracted, the only thing I hear of the Captain's prayer is "Amen." Music starts again, and row by row the residents and street people who have wandered in file out. One of the secretaries has come through the doors and made her way to the captain. She whispers in his ear, and he nods and makes his way to where we are waiting to leave the room.

"Mr. Combs," he says, "your boss called, and they say they need you down at the garage immediately. I'm sorry but you won't have your free time with your young wife today. One of Cook's assistants can fix you a quick sandwich. When you get back this evening I still need to see those papers."

Gary nods and thanks the captain. Claire smiles. Part One of our escape has gone without a hitch.

"I'll go and get that sandwich for you," I tell Gary.

I push my way through the line and toward the back door of the kitchen. Claire follows. We leave Gary, Billy, and Captain Davis watching our backs. At the doors, I look back to where they stand, and Captain Davis is talking, Gary is nodding.

"Gary's been called in to work," I tell Cook. "Captain Davis says to fix him a sandwich."

"Well, do it," Cook says.

She is always cranky on Sundays because Sunday dinner is always a big deal. Yesterday I peeled potatoes to mash and cut apples until my hands shriveled. Sunday is Waldorf Salad, and this afternoon I will wash the mayonnaise off the salad. Monday she will make them into apple crisp. She doesn't let anything go to waste. I decided early on she is a miracle worker when it comes to running the Shelter's kitchen.

After Gary's sandwich is made and delivered, and Billy safely in

179

line with Sam, I am in the serving line dishing up potatoes. It is getting colder, and we are nearing Thanksgiving. We have a bumper crop of hungry wanderers. I keep an eye on the door expecting Grandpa to come through any minute. I knew it was inevitable. I am sure it will be today. But, I am grateful it is not at lunch.

I am scrubbing the green bean kettle when Claire comes in. Cook is scraping down the grill, preparing to empty the grease from the catcher.

"I need Carrie today," I hear her say to Cook.

"I need Carrie today, too," Cook says back.

"No, I really need to get Carrie out of here today."

Cook stops the scraping, looks from Claire to me, and then back at Claire. "What you got going on girl?"

"Look, I know you don't like me," Claire says.

Cook put her hands on her hip and says, "I've never said such a thing."

"Okay, maybe not, but I know for sure you don't trust me. You still think I stole milk from the cooler."

"And?" Cook says back to her.

"Well, I did, but there was a good reason, and you never did ask me why."

"So, I'm asking, why you need Carrie?"

"Carrie needs me, and she needs you, too. Can you see that?"

"I'm gonna need more explanation than that."

"You need less explanation than you realize, but we have got to get Gary, Billy, and Carrie out of the Shelter while Captain and Mrs. Davis are not here."

"When you bringing them back?"

"I'm not."

"Carrie?" Cook asks looking at me.

I have wiped the large kettle and hung it on the hook over the prepping table.

"My Grandpa's coming after me."

"And you're under age."

I nod.

"Are you really married to the boy?"

"Oh yes, Cook, legally married and all."

"There's more than that," Claire adds, "but we can't go into that now, okay?"

180

"Cook, whatever you hear about Gary, it's not true. Promise me you won't believe any of it, please."

"So, Claire, what are you asking me to do?"

"Look, as soon as the Davises leave the premises..."

Cook interrupts, "They already have."

"Okay, let me take Carrie. I'll come back and do her chores. I'll do anything you want, I'll mop, whatever."

"I'll call my daughter. She'll pick up the slack here for today. I'll let the Davises worry about tomorrow. Maybe they can get that Mave to do some work around here," and with that Cook laughs at her joke.

"Cook," I say, and I go to her, hug her. "Thank you."

"Go, get your little butt outta here before I change my mind."

I know she won't. In the dining hall we find Billy, playing checkers with Sam. He is letting Billy win royally.

"Thanks, Sam, I owe you one," Claire says.

"You owe me more than one," he tells Claire. "You do, too, missy," he says to me. "Go on now with your Aunt Carrie, boy. We'll pick this game up next time, and I'll beat you then."

"Sure you will," Billy says, and we go to the hallway. Billy's bags have mysteriously been propped against the front door. Mave, wild-eyed Mave, is holding mine.

"Here," she says. Sam says you need this.

"Thank you, Mave," I say to her.

"Yeah thanks," Claire adds.

On the circle drive is Jack's old beat up truck. He is out, the truck running, and he throws our bags into the back. "Off for another adventure," he says to me, and laughs.

We pull away and I turn for one last look at the Shelter that has provided me home, food, and friendship. A dark green car, little, and nearly as rusted as Jack's truck, pulls into the circle drive as we pull out. I can see through the glass the tall man's head behind the wheel. It is Grandpa.

181

Chapter 24

We travel down Jefferson, and from Jefferson on to Third Street. I recognize our direction. We went that way to get to our house. But we cross Broadway, go on to Upper, and finally to Mechanic Alley, which is a rightful name for the location of a garage.

Outside the narrow block building is Gary, waiting with his co-worker, a dark skinned man a little older and larger than Gary. He looks familiar, something about him I should know, but can't figure out how or from where I know him. Gary meets me at the truck and lifts first Billy and then me out off the front seat.

"It's not good," he says to me before I can say anything to him. "The news broke about the body, and they are looking for the El Camino. Frank and I took the car over behind what used to be the projects. Now it is just a bunch of fallen down warehouses. We wiped it down good for prints, but I don't think anyone has my prints anyway."

Gary's co-worker is standing beside him, staring at me, his head tilted to one side like he is studying something. The something is me.

"Oh, I'm sorry, honey. This is Frank Thompson. He works here."

"Don't I know you?" he asks.

"I don't know anybody here in Lexington except for my friends here, Cook, Captain and Mrs. Davis, and I guess Sam and Mave."

"No, I know you from somewhere, I'm sure of it. I'm not from Lexington, either, and I can't say I know too many folks from here myself. My family was originally from Georgia."

"I've never been to Georgia."

"Carrie...what was your last name 'fore you married this wild man here?" he asks.

I hesitate, "Carrie Baxter."

"No, not Baxter. You had some other name. You're Janie Kelsey's grandkid, by God. You lived back on the Ridge."

"Frank? *That* Frank Thompson?"

"Yeah, Reva's runaway boy."

"Oh my God."

"Gary, you didn't tell me you up and stole her from Stears Branch."

Jack interrupts, "Hey guys, let's take this reunion inside the building."

Gary looks down the street with caution. Jack is right. The El Camino is gone, but enough people saw it coming and going the last couple of weeks, and any one of them may alert police, and that would lead them directly to the garage.

"Frank, Jack's right. We gotta take it inside. Neighbors have seen me, and it's on the news now."

Frank nods, and pulls me into a bear hug. "Come on in here, I can't believe it. Carrie Kelsey, or that's how I always thought of you. Jeez, you were always a cute kid, but man, you've grown up. What are you, about sixteen now," and his face registers the age and looks at Gary.

"Man, when you get yourself into trouble, you do it up right."

"We're married Frank."

"Yeah," Claire says, "but unless you had some private time yesterday, I don't think you've consummated the thing."

"Nobody's going to know that," he says. I am looking from one to the other not quite certain what they are talking about.

"It only takes a few minutes, and one doctor who can confirm or deny your word," she says, then adds, "and by the confused look on Carrie's face..."

"She doesn't have a clue, does she?" Jack says to Claire.

"Not a clue," Claire answers.

"God, Gary," Jack starts.

"Shut up, Jack," Claire interrupts. "Some men are gentleman, unlike a few others I know." Then she pulls me out of hearing shot of the three men, whispers, "You've not slept with him, have you." It's not a question.

"We slept in the car together the night we met Billy's family."

"No, like *slept with him,* as in the Bible, says a man *knows* a woman. You've not had sex with him?"

"No," I protest. "We just got married."

"No, you just got married a month ago, remember?"

Over Claire's whispers I hear Gary.

"Look, we can't stay here. I still have the key to the old house on Broadway. No one knows about that."

"Grandpa does." I turn and tell him, "Grandpa is here. Pulled into the Shelter just, and I mean *just*, as we pulled out."

"Jeez, what else can go wrong," he says.

"Well, the good news of the day is that the Davises are not at the Shelter today. They're not doing an evening service at the Shelter

183

tonight. They're talking at a church on the other side of town. And, anyone who knows anything won't talk," Claire says.

"Well, they will be back at the Shelter tomorrow, and I'm sure by then they will have heard the news, and your grandfather won't give up, he'll be back. You're right about the house. It's not a safe zone."

Jack runs a hand through his scraggly beard and looks at Claire, "And my place is no option. After tomorrow you are out of a job for your part in this fiasco and probably an accessory to the crime for abating and assisting a criminal."

Claire nods that he is right. "Okay, then we come up with something else."

"My place," Frank offers.

"That's as obvious as Jack's. Besides, I'm not gonna risk your family. You're gonna have to play dumb."

"I'm already implicated, I called you in to work, remember?"

"Nah, that's easy. I called pretending to be you," Jack tells him.

"Why would you do that?" Gary asks.

"Oh Jack, you are really trying to redeem yourself, aren't you." Claire is laughing.

"Hey, you do what you have to do, right?"

"It would help if we knew where Billy's mother was. She could at least resolve part of this problem," I say.

"Well, we don't," Gary answers, a little too abrasively for my liking.

Billy, who has remained quiet during all this discussion, turns his face up to me. "Is Gary mad at me, Carrie?"

"He's just worried, Billy. It's not your fault, okay?"

"Let's think this through," Claire says. We move deeper into the garage. Smells of oil and grease permeate the building. What benches line the garage walls are grease covered.

"Here, in the boss's office," Frank offers, and we enter the windowed doorway. "Leave the lights off, and Gary, catch the big door and close it. It's Sunday, we don't work on Sundays."

Gary nods, grabs the rope until reaching the handle and pulls the rolling contraption down. Inside the small office, in front of the tan metal desk, are three chairs. Frank offers the seats to Billy, Claire and me.

"It's where we give the bad news to customers," he says with a grin.

"Okay, back to the getaway plan," Claire says looking at the men who remain standing with hands in their pockets. Their eyes show their helpless apprehension.

"Can't go to Broadway, can't stay here, can't go to Jack's. What else have we got to shoot down?" Gary says.

We are silent. A clock on the wall like the one at the Shelter provides the only sound breaking the silence. It is already two pm.

"I think Grandpa probably left the Shelter right away. His next stop – the old house on Broadway. After that I don't know where he would go," I say.

"We don't know if he knows about the body, or the police's suspicions of the red-haired boy and the yellow El Camino. Lucky for you there is no one at the Shelter to tell him about this garage," Jack says.

"I wonder whether he knows about Daddy and about Momma's new name."

"Ah, Carrie. Thanks. I got it," Claire says. "Does that computer have Internet access?"

"Yeah, that's one of the ways we find out about car parts. Why?" Franks asks.

"Do you have to have the password to get in?"

"No, the boss is the first one in, brings it up, and it stays up all day until he takes it down about five."

"Well, it's worth a try."

Claire moves to the black box screen on the desk, moves Frank and Jack out of her way and begins to type on the keys. "If he had a password, what do you think it would be?" she asks.

"Lord, I don't know. Something easy to remember, maybe his wife's name. Gloria, try that."

Claire types in 'gloria' and nothing comes up. "Okay, let's try all caps, GLORIA. One more idea. Do you know her birthday or their anniversary?"

"I don't know my own anniversary," Frank laughs.

Claire flips through the wall calendar with bright colored cars with fancy women behind the wheel. December is the last month. I can tell she is getting frustrated. Her attempts are failing.

"Hey, I remember, last month they went on a trip. Maybe it's in October."

"October what?" Claire says.

"We don't have cleaning service here. No one ever empties the trash can until it is running over." He lifts the can to the desk top and

185

begins to sort through papers until he finds the torn calendar sheet, October, black car with a red-haired lady in a black skin-tight suit. "Bingo on the anniversary. They married 10/24/2023."

Claire types in again, GLORIA102423, and like magic a blue light pulses.

"Thanks," she says, and then to me, "What did that clerk in Frankfort tell you? You know, your mother's married name?"

"Emily Jones," I tell her. "She married Russell Jones."

Jack reminds her that even in this post-apocalyptic day, there are still hundreds of Joneses in Lexington. Claire pulls up births in Lexington and looks up 2017 for live births. Now it is her turn say, "Bingo."

"She was still Baxter when your brother was born. She must have been pregnant before your dad died. There is an address here. Of course, that was ten years ago, but it may be able to help us cross reference."

Claire writes the address on an invoice book, making sure to pull it off the pad before writing.

"You've watched too many detective shows, Claire," Jack says.

She ignores his rib. "Okay now. Emily Jones." The screen pulls up more than ten, ages from twelve through sixty-five. There are two that match closely to my Momma's age. She leaves that screen, and she pulls up Russell Jones, and like with Emily a whole new set comes to the screen.

"None of them are close to your Momma's age," she says to me.

"Okay, we're taking bets. Who says she married older and who says she married a young guy?" Jack asks.

"Jack, you're losing your good standing here. This is serious," Claire says. "Carrie, what do you think?"

"I don't know."

"I say older," Gary says. "She just had a kid, was by herself, and needed someone to take care of her."

"I agree," Claire says. "Three older, one fifty-four, one sixty-five, and one eighty-two."

"I rule out the eighty-two year-old," Jack says.

Claire rolls her eyes, but deletes the eighty-two year-old. "That leaves two. Let's check addresses on them to see if they match."

Neither matches. I am about to cry.

"Look," Frank says. "Doesn't Clays Mill Road cross Pasadena?"

186

"You're right. Maybe they were neighbors. How old is the one on Pasadena?"

"He's the fifty-four year-old one."

"I think that's our best bet, to side with Jack."

Claire writes down an address. She also writes down a telephone number, then closes the computer down.

"Does your boss change passwords regularly?" she asks Frank.

"Can't say I know."

"Well, this may come in handy later," and she folds the papers with password and address into her pocket.

She picks up the phone and dials, waits for the phone to ring. After what feels like an eternity, she hangs up. "Answering machine picked up. Didn't want to leave this number."

"We probably need to be getting out of here anyway," Gary advises. "Frank, you better get on back home. Your wife is going to start wondering where you are."

"You got my number," Frank says to Gary. "You call, understand? Anything, you call."

"I will. Thanks friend."

"And you, little missy," he says to me like I am still nine years old, "When you get back to Stears Branch you tell my Momma that I'm doing fine, okay?"

I nod that I will. His words have made me homesick for Grandma and Reva and Jolie and Moe. Even made me homesick for Tommy, and I never thought that was possible. I wonder if I will ever see the old walnut tree where Gary first kissed me, and I look up to see him staring at me. He knows, and I am glad that he knows.

"I love you," I mouth without sound. He pulls me to him, and I breathe in his smell, fresh like lemons, and I push out the smell of the garage. "I'm frightened," I say in his ear.

Everyone looks away but Billy.

"Gary, we need to get going," Claire says.

"Yeah," I hear him say in my hair. "I know. Give us just a minute."

Gary pulls my face to him, pulls me into a kiss that feels hot and driven. "This is going to be okay," he says as his lips leave mine, his words moving directly into me. "You have to believe this. Do you?"

I nod, not sure what to believe. This feels like a last kiss.

"Don't leave me," I say.

"Do you really think I could?"

187

I shake my head.

"Look at me," he says. "Promise not to give up."

"Gary," Jack says.

"Okay," and Gary lets go.

Frank slips out the back door to the garage after handing keys to the garage and an old white car to Gary. Gary calls it an Oldsmobile.

"Put the garage key in the mail box. I'll be here before boss. He'll never know."

"Thanks again."

"Hey, think nothing of it."

Our conversations stop, our searching over, and Billy, Claire, Jack, Gary, and me sit silent, listening to the noisy clock.

Claire, the constant thinker, speaks first. "Okay, Jack, you need to go ahead and go back to the apartment. Worse comes to worse, I'll call you there. I'll need to go with them to find this address." She is holding the piece of paper studying it as she speaks. "It shouldn't take us long. Just not sure what we're gonna find. Carrie's mom will either help us or hurt us, but either way, we can't just do nothing."

Jack nods and leaves by the same door as Frank. We can hear the truck rev up, the wheels spin out, and we hear the gravels spew as he pulls away.

"Now, for the four of us," Claire starts. "This is the plan. We're going to go to this address on Pasadena. I'm gonna go in first and talk to the lady. Carrie, if she's your mother, I'll motion for you to come on up. Gary, you need to stay out of the picture until her Momma gets the whole story, and Carrie, she deserves the whole story, the truth, you're not going to have to tell any more lies, okay?"

I am relieved.

"Billy, you need to stay with Gary until Carrie comes out and gets you." Claire looks at me with straight forward green eyes. "I'm hoping that once your Momma hears the whole story, the true story, she'll give you guys shelter. If she believes you, Carrie, she's going to be your best ally. We have to hope her husband, Russell, agrees."

"And if not?" Gary asks.

"Then you're going to have to bolt. Seriously, you'll have to run for it, leave Billy with Carrie. That okay with you?" she asks Billy.

"I wanna stay with Gary. No offense Carrie, but..."

"Why can't Billy stay with him?" I ask.

Claire gives in. "Whatever, it may be for the best anyway. Police

188

won't shoot if they are aware there is a child involved. Gary, keep Billy visible, but don't let it look like you are holding him hostage, okay?"

"What's hostage?" Billy asks.

"Like he is keeping you against your will."

"Heck no, Miss Claire. I'd go with Gary anywhere. My Mommy told me to stay with him no matter what."

"Gary, you did get your marriage license out of the box along with that letter?"

"Yeah, Claire, I did." Gary has been getting weary of Claire's overbearing directions. I can tell it from the tone of his voice, but what else are we to do? I'm glad we have Claire.

Gary opens the door to the garage for us to leave, re-locks it, and walks around the front to deposit the key in the mailbox. "Everyone must be napping," he says as he returns and starts the car.

"Well, we have had one piece of good luck then," Claire says. With that we pull out from behind the garage and move towards the next connecting street.

"Turn left," Claire says, and Gary does. The downtown streets are as vacant as Mechanic Alley. We move seamlessly between traffic lights until reaching Main. As we wait for the red to turn to green, two police cars, flashing lights on their tops, speed by. Claire glances nervously at Gary, but says nothing. We watch the two cars skid sideways and block the next street.

"That's Mill they're blocking, Go straight," Claire whispers. She has no sooner said this than two more cars speeding further to our right on Vine Street turn onto Limestone. Now there are shrill sounds everywhere.

"Drive as normal as you can. Carrie, slump down. They have a description of you both. Good. The bigger problem is your hair, Gary."

From the back seat, Billy pipes up. "Gary, here's my cap. You can wear it."

"You're a champion," he says, reaching for the cap.

We miss the speeding police officers and their screaming sirens. We move past the tall buildings turning onto an adjoining street with rows of small stores and then older houses.

"Turn at that big church," Claire says. She is reading from the scrap of paper she got from the computer at the garage. "It's not much farther up here, maybe less than a mile. I think it is just past the school.

189

Here, at this light. Turn right."

Among trees and houses that survived the quakes, there, between two old maples stands a modest brick house with black shutters and a white porch with a swing on the front. I know it is my Momma's house. I have waited for this day for weeks, no, years. I open the door and climb out of the large car. Claire is already out and standing by the front fender.

"I said to wait," she says.

"I don't want to," I tell her.

She looks at me, pauses, "Okay. Go ahead and come with me."

I watch her move to the sidewalk, and I hesitate. She turns, waiting at the end of the sidewalk, her face saying, "You wanted this. What's wrong with you, girl?" I look at Gary and he is mouthing, "Go on."

Everything is uncertain. What if she doesn't believe me? What if it isn't her? What if it is her, and Grandpa has already found her, and the police are behind the front door waiting? There are so many questions flying around inside my head.

I begin moving, and I try to imagine what my Momma looks like. It has been so long that I can't recall. I see her hair, darker than mine, kind of curly. No one knows where I got my wheat-blond hair. She was thin, I remember that, but her eyes, I forgot her eyes. I don't remember what her voice sounds like. Is that what I will be like for her? Before I realize it we are on the porch, in front of the door, and it is closed. Claire knocks. She knocks again. Finally a little boy comes to the door.

"Hi. My name is Claire. Is your mother at home?"

"We don't buy magazines."

"Oh, we aren't selling anything, I promise. I have something important to talk to her about. Is she home?"

"Are you sure you're not selling windows or something? My Dad says we don't need windows or a roof or anything like that."

"No, I promise. We're not selling anything."

"You aren't those religious people are you? My Mom says I'm not to talk to them either."

"No, we aren't those religious people either," Claire says, laughing. I don't know what they are talking about.

"May we come in?"

"Who is that guy in the car?" the boy says. "You aren't trying to rob us are you, because my Dad is a lawyer and you guys would be in

190

a lot of trouble."

"No, no one is going to hurt anyone. We will stay outside here on your porch until you get your Mom. We'll sit right here on this swing, okay?"

"I guess that's okay."

The door closes, and Claire looks back at Gary and shrugs. Within a couple of minutes the door opens, and a thin woman in her early 40s with short graying hair is standing at the door. She looks suspiciously at Claire. We stand as she speaks.

"May I help you?" Her voice is soft, and I know it.

"Momma?" I ask before Claire can say anything else, can prepare her for the shock. She looks at me then, and the face, though older, is the same face, the same green eyes, the same mouth, and I remember. The years are chased away, and I am five years old again. I say it again, "Momma, it's me, Carrie."

My Momma's face turns ashen, her knees buckle and Claire grasps beneath her arms to keep her from falling to the floor of the porch.

"Emily, what's the problem?" Russell Jones comes to the door. In an instant he has his wife's arm and has pushed Claire away.

"What's going on here?" he demands.

"Carrie?" Emily whispers. "Is it you?"

"Yes, Momma. It's me, really."

"Mr. Jones, can we go inside? I had wanted to better prepare your wife, but Carrie...she has been trying to find her mother for so long. I'm sorry. We didn't mean to upset her."

"Who's in the car?" Russell Jones asks.

I say "My husband," and Momma says, "You're too young to be married."

"It's a long story, Momma. I've got to tell you about it. I need your help."

The boy comes back to the door and stares at the commotion on his front porch and then at the face of the little boy staring at him from the back seat of the car.

"Mom, who are these people?" he asks.

"Jon, this is your big sister," she tells him, and his eyes get saucer round.

"That's her?" he asks.

"Yes, honey. That's her," Emily tells him.

"He knows about me?"

191

"Of course I know about you," the boy says. "We got your pictures everywhere!"

"You never forgot me?" I ask looking at her. I am crying. She is crying, and her husband has ceased to have his 'I'm going to throw you off this porch' expression on his face.

"Come in," he says.

"Gary's in the car." I turn from my mother and look back at the car where Gary sits nervously at the wheel. Billy has his face plastered at the back window looking at us.

It is then I see the white cars pull up, their wheels squealing as they whip perpendicular to the Oldsmobile. There are no sirens this time. *How did they find us?*

The uniformed men are out of the cars with guns pulled before I can call out to Gary, but he has seen them before me. He is out of the car looking between me and the officers who are surrounding him. I think he will try to make a run for it, but he doesn't leave Billy. An officer grabs Billy from the back seat holding him by both arms as Billy strains against his grip.

"Don't move any farther, Mr. Combs, or I'll have to shoot."

"Gary," I scream and run down the porch steps toward the commotion. My mother starts to run after me, and then her husband stops her.

"This is the girl," one officer says to the one holding the gun.

"Take her along with the kid."

Billy is trying to pull free from the officer's grip, and releasing one hand from Billy, the officer reaches out for me. Billy pulls free and runs for Gary. He is between the officer with the gun and Gary and grabs Gary by the legs. He is crying.

"Damn it," the officer with the gun says to the officer who lost hold of Billy and me. "Can't you keep a hold of one little kid."

"Let go of me," I yell at a third officer who grabs me and pulls me towards his cruiser.

"You Carrie Baxter?" he asks.

"No."

"Who the hell are you then?"

"Carrie Combs. I'm married to him," I say pointing to Gary.

The two police officers in charge look at each other, then back at me. "We have it from your grandfather that your name is Carrie Baxter and that this man here has taken you from his custody."

192

"That's not true. I left on my own."

"Your grandfather says you are under age. You are too young to have gotten married." And to the other officer, "Get the kid and get him into the car. We'll take the kid and the girl back to the Davises for now."

I watch as they pull Billy off Gary. I hear them say words to Gary about having the right to remain silent and having other rights that I don't understand. Billy is pushed into the back seat, and I want to run. Gary is knocked into the side of the car, a knee is shoved into his back, and his face is rammed into the frame of the window. His nose is pouring blood. Russell is holding my Momma back; she is straining against him. Claire is standing helpless beside them.

It is when the officer that put Billy in the car with blinking lights grabs my arm and yanks hard enough to make me fall that Momma breaks free of Russell. She jumps at the officer and begins hitting him with all the strength I ever saw. He lets go of my arm to protect his face from her onslaught. Russell is there and holds her arms.

"I'm sorry, officer. She is distraught," he says.

I look at Momma's face, and I think she is going to turn on her husband at any moment, but he keeps talking in a quiet calm voice. "You see, Emily is Carrie's mother. It seems they were separated when Carrie was five, back when the floods and earthquake separated Lexington and those lands south of here. Mr. Kelsey, Carrie's grandfather, raised her, that is, until Mr. Combs and Carrie, well, the way I understand it, fell in love and wanted to get married. Gary promised to help Carrie find her mother, and well, that's what he has been doing. Carrie's grandfather did not approve of Gary and Carrie's relationship, but she left on her own accord. I think there has been a big misunderstanding here that my wife can address with her father."

The two officers with hand cuffs and guns drawn look at each other. The other two officers from the second car look away, and then back at their sergeant.

Russell says, "You can leave the kids under my supervision. We can handle this from here."

"Mr. Jones, that would be all well and fine if that was the only problem we had here. Mr. Combs here is also being brought in on suspicion of murder."

Gary turns quickly from his position, is pushed back against the car. "That's ridiculous," I hear him say from where his face is pushed

193

into the window of the car."

"Shut up," the officer says to him. "A body was found, badly decomposed on US 25 up from the river. The ferry men described the boy here as following a family of four: man, woman, a little girl and a little boy about the age of the boy there. We haven't located the other bodies, but the Davises confirmed that Mr. Combs arrived about the time that the murder took place with Ms. Baxter here, and the little boy. He was driving a vehicle that matched a description they gave. We've got to take him in. The evidence is overwhelming."

"Gary didn't kill anybody. I can't believe you believe those thieving ferrymen over Gary. He saved their lives. Just ask Billy," I scream at them.

"We have no idea what you and Mr. Combs have convinced the child of, Miss Baxter. If you are not careful, you may be indicted for complicity."

"Are you threatening my stepdaughter, officer?"

"I'm just saying there are a lot of unanswered questions, and I need to get this boy down to the jail, and the child and Miss Baxter back to the Shelter. The Davises have said they will be responsible for them until the arraignment, or until we can find a foster home for the child." With hearing that, Billy opens the door trying to escape. He is screaming.

"No. You promised."

I struggle to move toward Billy. Again the officer takes hold of my arm, less aggressive than before. Billy is attempting to reach Gary but is grabbed before reaching him. Gary is shoved into the back seat of the first car.

"Officer," Russell says. "Will you let me take charge of Carrie and the child? Emily here is her mother and is more capable of dealing with her daughter, and it has been eleven years since they have seen each other."

The officer steps away from the group to call, returns announcing that Billy must return to the Shelter, but I can stay with my mother on the condition that if I run, Mr. Jones will be held responsible.

"May I speak to Gary?" I ask.

"No."

"To Billy?"

"For a minute, no longer."

"Thank you," I say, but I don't feel grateful. The youngest officer,

194

the one who stands farthest back from this crazy scene, opens the back patrol car door.

"Am I coming with you?" Billy asks.

"They won't let you, Billy. I'm sorry."

"You promised."

"I know. But these are the police. They think that Gary hurt your Daddy."

"I'll tell them different."

"Billy, they just think that we told you to say that. They don't understand. It is going to be okay."

"You promise?"

"Oh Billy, I want to promise. I am going to try real hard to make it okay."

Billy begins to sob. I wrap my arms around him, and he buries his head in my blouse. I wish I could keep his request for this promise, but I don't know. I wish his mom would show her face, and I wonder where she is now. I can see the younger officer watching Billy and me. He looks to be Gary's age.

I can see Momma's husband talking to the officer. They are talking low, and I hear him say stuff about an attorney. And I hear him say that he has a right to speak to Gary, because he is his attorney. I see the officer shake his head. Momma's husband is standing at the police car, the window is down and Gary is telling him something, and Russell is listening, nodding, looking at the Oldsmobile, then looking back at Gary. I see Russell reach his hand in and shake Gary's.

"That's enough time," the sergeant says to me. Billy's crying has slowed to quiet sobs. I kiss the top of his head and slip out. The younger officer moves in beside Billy and says something to him. Billy nods.

The window to where Gary sits rolls up automatically and Momma's husband steps back. The car with Billy turns around and heads back the way we came. The one with Gary turns it's siren on. Before it speeds away, Gary's face presses against the back side window, and I see his lips mouth "I love you most."

195

Chapter 25

Mr. Jones takes my Momma by the arm, smiles at me and says, "We should probably take it all inside. We've given the neighbors enough to talk about as it is."

Claire nods, and we follow up the narrow sidewalk. My brother, and it sounds strange to say that, is standing on the porch watching us.

"Come inside son," the man says, and the boy obeys.

My Momma looks shaken, but I can see there are a thousand things running through her mind. Mr. Jones is looking at both of us, and runs his thick fingers across his face and through his hair.

"We've got a lot of things to figure out and some work to be done before tomorrow. Carrie, I need you to tell me everything that's gone down since you left your grandparents, and I mean everything. Don't leave out any detail, and you have to be completely honest with me. Your friend's life depends on it. Do you understand?"

"If your son will show me, I'll go make some coffee while Carrie fills you guys in on the details, if that's all right?" Claire says.

"Thank you. I don't I remember your name with everything that has happened in the last hour."

"My name's Claire."

"Jon, take this nice lady to the kitchen and show her where the makings are for coffee, okay?"

"Okay. It's this way."

I watch them as they move down a hall and into another room. Mr. Jones, my Momma, and I just look at each other. I'm not sure what to say. Mr. Jones must be reading my mind. He smiles, and says, "Just start from the beginning, when you first met Mr. Combs, Gary, is that right?"

I nod, and then begin. I tell them about Stears Branch, and how Grandma and I first saw Gary in the car on the old four-lane highway, and how in a few days he showed up at the cabin looking for his Daddy. I tell them how Grandpa had been suspicious ever since we had been there in the hollow, and never did take to anyone, and how he drew a rifle on Gary, but Gary didn't have any kind of weapon at all. I told how Gary stayed. I told Momma how I told Gary I was wanting to come to Lexington to find her, and he said he was going south to see

196

if he could find his Daddy who had left before the quakes ever started, gone looking elsewhere for work.

I confessed Gary and I kissed, but that was all. We started meeting behind Aries' house at the spring that flowed from beneath the rock. Grandpa got even worse and forbade me to see Gary at all, and Grandma got worried. Even though she didn't say so, I think she knew I was falling for him. I told them about Jolie and how she encouraged Gary to ask me to come with him. He offered to bring me to Lexington, and I wanted to come.

"Since Grandpa got so crazy, I snuck out in October, and we pushed Gary's car out past the cabin, until we reached the road, and then headed north." I look down at my hands. I feel my deceit is written all over me, like a sign around my neck that says LIAR.

"We got as far as the ferry where the old Clay's Ferry Bridge used to stand. Some rough men were running it, and that's where we met Billy's mommy and daddy. We had already paid our fare and we were waiting to cross when they showed up with a mule. Billy had a little sister. The ferry men did them dirty, Mr. Jones," I say.

Mr. Jones smiles and says, "Why don't you try calling me Russ, okay?"

I look at Momma and she smiles and says, "It's okay, baby. He's your step-father."

"What happened to Daddy?" I ask.

"Your Daddy died not long after the trouble, but I'll tell you about that later. We need to know what to do to help Gary right now," she says.

I nod, and continue, "Like I said, they weren't very honest men. The one old man had a wife who was younger than me and even had a baby by her. I couldn't believe it, but Gary told me to hush and not draw attention to us. Gary told them we were cousins."

I told Momma and Russ how the ferrymen told Billy's parents how much it would cost. It was all Mr. Wilson had. Then they raised it because they said the ferry was sitting low in the water and made it harder to cross. They wanted the mule, but Mr. Wilson said that was all they had.

Then I tell them, "Donna, that was Billy's mom, pulled out some bills she had hid and gave the men the money they wanted, and those men's eyes lit up. We made it to the other side. We were in the car and were first off the ferry. I watched the Wilson's get off, and Gary

197

offered them a ride, but they said no. After that we headed on up the road."

"So, you don't know what happened to Mr. Wilson?"

"Not exactly."

"What do you mean, Carrie?" Momma asks.

By this time Claire and Jon have brought in the coffee.

"Claire and me made some peanut butter and jelly sandwiches, too," Jon says.

Emily laughs, "I'm sure you convinced her of that. It's your favorite."

Jon smiles a sheepish smile, and Claire adds, "We thought you guys might be hungry."

"Thanks, Jon," Russ says, and he picks one up. "Why don't you show Claire your room?"

Once Jon leaves the living room, Russ nods for me to continue.

"About half way up, through a clearing, I saw the ferryman head back over the river, and then we heard a commotion near the bottom of the road. When we heard screaming, Gary put me out of the car and told me to hide in the bushes and said not to come out until he came back. He repeated his instructions making me repeat it back to him so he knew I understood how important it was that I not come out for anyone else but him." I feel myself begin to tremble at the memory of what happened.

"I know this is hard, Carrie, but I have to know what happened down on that road. The police are saying that Gary killed a man, and they are implying that he killed the woman and the little girl, and did worse to both of them." Russ's face is stone cold. His tone is as cold as his face.

"Why would they think that?"

"It's what the men running the ferry have told them. Apparently, they are saying that Gary saw the woman's money and was trying to rob the man. They said they got there in time to see him murder Mr. Wilson. And the woman and little girl were nowhere to be seen, and Gary was speeding off in his yellow El Camino. It was a cut and dried description."

"They're lying."

"You may know that, and I may believe you, but the police have no evidence to support what you are saying."

"Okay. Okay. Well, I stayed in the bushes for what seemed like forever. I finally climbed out and started walking down the road in the direction that Gary had gone. When I got a little ways, maybe less than a hundred yards, I saw headlights. It was Gary. He was so mad at me. It was the most angry he has ever been at me, before or since, or ever. He had Donna in the seat with him, and Billy, and the little girl. Billy's eyes were as big as saucers, and he wasn't talking. Donna wasn't talking either. The baby girl wasn't crying or anything. Donna's clothes were torn near off her body, her arms scratched and her face bruised up. There was no sign of the mule. Once Gary was done yelling at me, he squeezed me into the El Camino, and we headed north and ended up at the Holiday Inn a short ways up the road."

"Okay. Then what happened?"

"Not much really. We got them food. We spent the night in the El Camino. She kept the little girl and boy with her in the back of the El Camino. It was the way she wanted it. Gary wanted her to stay inside the cab, but she wouldn't."

"When we woke up in the morning she was gone. She left a letter asking us to take care of Billy. She took the little girl with her. I think her name was Susan or Susie. I don't quite remember."

"One thing more I remember, when she got into the back that night, I saw that she didn't have any panties on, and she was bleeding."

"Gary told me where two things were before the police took him. He said the letter from this Mrs. Wilson was under the front seat of the Oldsmobile along with your marriage license. Do you know what the letter says?"

"I don't. Every time I asked Gary about it, he told me no, or he told me he didn't want to talk about it."

"Claire," Russ calls. "Have they come and impounded the Oldsmobile out there yet? I have been negligent in not collecting those papers."

Claire moves to the front door and opens it. The sky is darkening. Evening is nearly upon us.

"Not yet," she says.

"Do you mind?" then adds, "If they don't get it now, they will have it by morning. Who owns it anyway? I suspect who does will be hit with complicity or at the very least tampering with evidence."

Claire moves with lightning speed and returns with two separate envelopes. She hands them to Russ who opens the first. He looks over the license and then to me.

199

"When did you decide to get married?" he asks.

"The next day, when I woke in Gary's arms. He asked me then. I told him I hardly knew him."

"Did you wonder why he would ask you then, after what happened on the road?"

"No, why would I?"

"Well, if he had been guilty of anything, and if you were married, you couldn't testify against him."

"Russ," my Momma says in disgust at him.

"Well, I am just trying to understand why he asked her then."

"I don't understand what you are saying…he was just trying to find the best way to protect me."

"If I may interject something here," Claire interrupts. "If Gary had done anything to hurt Donna Wilson, her son, Billy, wouldn't have had such a strong trust in Gary. You saw how he was out there a few hours ago. Also, while we are trying to help Gary, does anyone here know how we can keep the Shelter from placing him in a foster home and us losing all contact with him? If he is placed, then Carrie will have no way of getting records to get him back. And, even if Gary is exonerated, with all that has happened, I don't think the Davises will give any assistance in finding the boy."

"I understand your concern, Claire," Russ says, "but at this moment, my first concern is for my stepdaughter's husband. And, I see that perhaps you lied on her marriage license about her age?"

"That, and in getting her a new birth certificate, thank you."

"Alright, we will see what we can do about little Billy."

Russ opens the second envelope and reads silently the handwritten parcel, looking up at Carrie between sighs.

"It follows your story," Russ says. "It is on Holiday Inn stationary and is dated October 27, 2028. It is smudged with dirt and bloody fingerprints. It is written in a fine female slant hand writing. Whether it is enough to free Gary is questionable."

Then Russ looks at me, "It does give Gary temporary custody of Billy, and that may be enough to keep Billy out of a foster home and bring him here. I have one problem. Gary doesn't want you to read the letter. He said as much when we spoke. I'm sorry, Carrie."

"Why won't he let me see it?" I ask.

"I'm not sure. I'm also not sure it will be enough to get him out of jail. We'll just have to see. The DA may think you wrote it after the fact, which implicates you."

Russ gets up and goes to the kitchen. I can hear him on the phone. He is talking to someone, and I think he is talking to Captain Davis, because he is referring to Billy. I hear him saying he represents Gary and Carrie Combs. Then I hear, "Yes, Mrs. Combs' maiden name was Baxter, we are speaking of the same young lady. I understand that her grandfather has been looking for her. I am not talking about that issue. I am speaking regarding the young man named Billy Wilson. Sir, it is a separate issue entirely. I am holding a letter in my hand at this moment by the under-aged child's mother giving Gary Combs legal temporary custody."

Claire, Momma, and I all three get up and go to the kitchen where Russ is pacing as he speaks, moving the full extension of the telephone's cord. He is rolling his eyes and his lips mouth "bureaucrats."

"I understand sir, that Mr. Combs has been arrested for the murder of Mr. Wilson, but the letter in hand will likewise exonerate Mr. Combs on that matter as well. No, I don't know why Mr. Combs did not share this letter with you. It could be that he did not trust you with it."

Claire is holding her side laughing.

"Where is the boy now? Hmm. I understand that he was quite traumatized by the whole event this afternoon. Yes. No, you are not, and I emphasize, NOT to implement finding foster care for the child."

"If you must know, Captain Davis, I am Mrs. Combs' stepfather, and I am here with her mother, Emily Baxter Jones, at this moment. Would you like to speak with her?"

There is momentary silence at the Jones' house while Russ listens to Captain Davis.

"I can bring Carrie's mother to the Center this evening with a driver's license to prove her identity, if that is what you want. No, I am not sure that Carrie wants to see her grandfather at this time, based on all the turmoil that he has put her through with this erroneous accusation of kidnapping and statutory rape. He has made her life quite miserable."

"Momma," I say. "I don't want to hurt Grandpa."

Russ puts his hand over the receiver of the phone, "He has a right to a little discomfort based on what he has put you through. The least he could have done is to help you find your mother, from my point of view, Carrie. It would have saved a lot of grief." Then, back into the phone he says, "It is getting late, but I would expect you to have Billy Wilson ready for me to pick up tomorrow at eight a.m. and have his

201

belongings together as well. I will be there with this letter in hand. If you do not comply I will have to take further legal steps to obtain the legal rights of my clients. Goodnight."

Russ has no sooner hung up than he is dialing again. I hear him speaking to someone at the police department. "Yes," I can hear through the phone, "the suspect has been processed and taken to a holding cell."

"When will he be arraigned?" I hear Russ ask. "Okay. Do you know which judge he will be before?" Silence, then Russ asks, "When will it be posted? Okay."

"Good news and bad news," Russ says as he looks at me.

"What does that mean?" I ask.

"Bad news is, the judge is tough. He doesn't play games, and he can't be gotten to by sappy stories or bullying. Good news is, he can't be gotten to by sappy stories or bullying. In other words, I think he is a pretty fair man. We'll just have to wait and see what comes of it. It would be real nice if we could find this Donna woman by tomorrow. Where do you think she is?"

"I have no idea."

"Where were they from, or where were they coming from when they were crossing at the ferry?" Momma asks.

"Well, Gary fussed at me for talking to her, but she did tell me they had lived in between Clark and Estill County, originally, and when the floods came, she and her husband were caught out in them and headed across a river just like us. They ended up in a little community called Red Lick. They hit on hard times and were heading back across the river at the ferry in order to get to Clark County. "

"Where to start, is the question," Russ says.

"Maybe I can help a little," Claire interrupts.

"How?" Emily asks.

"Jack. What do you think, Carrie?"

I smile. Jack has friends all over. "He's already done too much," and I look at Momma and say, "He changed the birth date on my birth certificate and got the guy at the court house to issue us a marriage license, changing the date so the Davises wouldn't raise cane…it's asking too much."

"Carrie, this is like really important now. Mrs. Jones, may I use the phone?"

My Momma nods, and I hear Claire talking to Jack.

202

"You okay?" she asks. "Police just about met us here. Yeah, they got Gary. Her parents are great. Her step-dad is a lawyer for God's sake. Can you believe it? Someone's looking out for them. I need your help, honey. This time, if it works out I'll say 'yes'…we'll go to that same little preacher, and I'll do the whole thing, I promise. Yes, I promise. You'll make an honest woman…yes."

I can hear Jack whopping it up on his end. Russ is laughing at Claire's side of the conversation. Momma says, "I am glad Jon doesn't understand this part of the conversation," and my brother walks out of the room. I think he understands it quite well. Momma just doesn't know.

"Jack, the lady that Gary saved might be in Winchester or somewhere there abouts. What? It's on the news? Okay. Her name is Donna Wilson. She will have a two- or three-year-old little girl with her named Susan or Susie. Husband's name was Bill. Oh, they are giving his name on the news. Are they giving hers, too? Good, otherwise, it would scare her off. Call me at this number as soon as you find something."

I see Claire's face get worried. She looks at me and then says, "Have you called him? Okay, I'll try."

Once off the phone Claire runs to the front window. The Oldsmobile is gone. At some point during our story, a tow truck has impounded the car, and they are sure to trace it to the garage, and from the garage to Frank.

"One more call?" Claire asks.

"Call as many as you want," Momma says.

"Do you have Frank's number?" she asks me.

I pull the paper from my pocket and hand it to her. "Turn on your TV," she says to Russ. "Jack says this is all over the news, every station, all over."

The Shelter had television sets, but I was always so busy, either with Cook, or with Billy, or Gary, or so dead tired, I never paid too much attention. Now, Russ, Momma, and I sit in front of the screen while Claire talks in whispers to Frank.

Jon keeps to himself in another room until he hears me start crying, and he runs out thinking it is Momma. He looks at the two of us and he is spooked by how alike we look, except for our coloring – both small, both delicate features, both leaning forward, holding on to every word that comes out of the mouth of the man on the small screen.

203

They are accusing my Gary of all sorts of crimes, of murdering Billy's father, his mother, his little sister. Of his kidnapping me and brainwashing me, and finding any number of other crimes that have gone unsolved in the last two or three years, some having taken place while he was at Stears Branch. And then there is Grandpa, standing there shaggy-bearded, clothes hanging loose on his lean body, being interviewed, saying I was taken against my will, being practically child-robbed from my crib. I wonder what has happened to my Grandpa, what has made him a madman in his old age. He knows damn well that Gary was not in Irvine or Red Lick three months ago. He was in Stears Branch driving Jolie's three kids through fields and apple trees, gathering walnuts with Tommy, kissing me at Aries' fresh-water spring. He is lying. Then I realized in that same instant, that I have sounded just like Grandma.

When Claire has left and Russ has gone to tuck Jon into bed, Momma and I remain on the couch. I lean my head on her shoulder and speak.

"Momma, I found you. I knew you were alive. Grandpa told me and Grandma that you and Daddy were dead. I just couldn't, no – I wouldn't – believe him."

She doesn't say anything. She just keeps running her hand through my hair, like Grandma used to when she had something on her mind.

"You know, he put up crosses for you and Daddy. You should've seen Grandma. It wasn't a pretty sight, her tearing around like a wet hen."

I thought that would make her laugh, but she looks at me with sad eyes, removes her arms from around me. There is something that isn't said, that she can't say, doesn't want to say. I watch expressions change on her face – move from sadness to confusion and then to something I don't recognize.

"I didn't know what happened to you," she says to me. "So much occurred here all at once, so fast, so many interruptions, that we didn't make it to the bridge that day. We never made it to the bridge at all. We never even tried – not that day or in the weeks that followed. Oh, Carrie, I'm so sorry."

"There wasn't a bridge, not anymore. Grandpa was the last one to make it across before it went down."

"Still...Carrie. Still, I could have tried."

A silence rests between us. It wasn't like Grandpa and Grandma tried to get me back to her either, even when the water went down. Grandpa went to the river, knew there was a way across. Like finding what happened to his own flesh and blood wasn't more important than reciting a long list of names on Sunday? What is it about keeping things the way they are that swallows up hope?

When Momma breaks the silence, it isn't about loss. When she ceases to stare at her hands, she looks at me and asks, "Do you love him, this Gary?"

"Oh, yes."

"What do you know about love? You're only, what, seventeen?" and I see it strikes her hard that she has to think about how old I am.

"He's all I know about loving, except for Grandma and Grandpa," I say.

Her eyes widen and then begin to tear.

"Oh, and you and Daddy, too," I add.

"That's not what I meant."

All the hidden meanings about loving gets confusing – pushes around between my heart and my belly. I look at her again, frown as I puzzle about the indictment of her words.

"Is this about kissing?"

"Kissing and … the other stuff. Oh, Carrie, I am too tired for this conversation right now. I'm just happy to have you back. Come here." And with that she pulls me back into a hug.

"Grandma never talked about kissing or the other stuff."

"Really?"

"Yeah. I guess before Gary there wasn't a reason."

I yawn and feel my eyelids get heavy. The last thing I remember before falling asleep on her shoulder is wondering if Gary will get out of jail and if I will ever know about the other stuff.

Chapter 26

Grandma.

Day 30 AC

Thanksgiving is just about on us. I find little to be thankful for except for Moe. Though the temperature has been below freezing for some time, the ground had not frozen through and the men did not find it difficult to dig Aries' grave. Reva thought I should be the one to say words over Aries, but I couldn't. Mr. Thompson wouldn't. I couldn't see Harold doing it, and he didn't want to either. Jolie would have jumped at the opportunity but was not well enough. Mr. Thompson fashioned a casket from dark walnut he had been saving for a table. He said it seemed only right to use it for Aries, and any rift that was between Reva and him was mended a bit by that act of kindness. Tommy crossed the ridge to the next settlement to seek help. There was a preacher there, and enough of those people knew Aries or had heard of her. Enough came on that day to make it a decent funeral.

We opened Jim's and my cabin for the funeral dinner. I cooked, but the ladies from over the ridge brought food as well. Jolie's oldest girl, Kathy, was helpful, cooking and helping to clean out the cobwebs that had grown quickly in the corners of my house. There were no fresh flowers to honor Aries, but I had gathered lavender last summer for making soap, and the ladies from over the ridge brought bouquets of dried Queen Ann's Lace and Butterfly Milkweed. The old cabin smelled a sweet mixture of burning applewood that Harold had gathered and the dried bouquets.

After the words were said and prayers made, Aries' small body, wrapped in her favorite quilt and encased by the polished dark wood, was lowered into the grave. I am always amazed how in the face of grief, when food is placed upon a table, grief is replaced by party. I can be easily offended by such joviality, but in the memory of Aries' life, its beauty and honesty deserved celebration, so I put my sentiments aside.

Jolie did make it to the funeral. When she greeted me, somewhat hesitantly, she said she could not forego attending regardless of how she felt. And, it was obvious she was not well. Little Moe said the baby was to come in early spring, but Jolie looked larger than that, and her movements were encumbered and pained. Both Harold and Tommy were solicitous of her every move, especially Harold, keeping an eye on her the entire time of the funeral. Kathy confided while she helped that her mother had been hurting almost since the beginning, and had been bleeding, off and on. Aries, although just buried beneath the apple trees beyond the back porch and cold these three days, seemed to be speaking from her grave that I must give up my grudge. In looking at Jolie, I was hard pressed to agree that she was right. Though the mind was willing, this dark heart was slow to follow.

The funeral was held in the morning, the funeral dinner at noon, so neighbors began to leave by mid-afternoon. Much of the leftover food was boxed up and sent home with Jolie. Her girls stayed behind and helped me, working as hard in cleaning up as they did in making the place presentable before. My opinion of both of them was changing. I even thought that Tommy was growing up.

When the fire died down, and we had scattered the ashes to be sure the fire was out, we walked out the back door. The old dogs waited, and Kathy threw them what was left of the cornbread. When we got to Harold and Jolie's, Kathy peeled off towards their house, but Moe stayed by my side. I asked her if she shouldn't head on home. She told me her Mommy said that maybe I would need some company, since I had always had someone to take care of, first Jim and Carrie, and then Aries, and that I would be all alone now. I told her that her Mommy might need her, and she said her Mommy had told her that she would have Kathy, that Tommy would come get her if she was needed. Then she asked me, "Do you miss them?"

"Aries?" I asked.

"No. You know, Mr. Jim and Carrie." I looked at her, and there was no sign of nosiness in her voice, no evidence of coyness in her eyes.

"Yes, Moe. I miss them more than…than anything," and I felt tears start to well up in my eyes. I looked away before she could see them coming.

"It's okay, Grandma."

That was two days ago. Moe has been with me since. We get up every morning, stoke up the fire, gather duck eggs, check the wood pile that mysteriously gets replenished every night, and check the water barrel. I ask Moe what she wants for breakfast, and she always says,

"Whatever you want." We spend time reading, and I have forgotten to journal. We are using Carrie's pencils to practice writing letters and numbers.

This morning we are eating mush. I have sweetened it with honey and covered it with some milk that Mr. Thompson has given us. It is good and warm and nourishing on this cold day.

"When is your birthday, Moe?"

"I don't know," she says.

"You don't know?" I ask, disbelieving. I think to myself, what child doesn't know when her birthday is. "Well, do you celebrate your birthday at some time? You have a birthday party?"

"I don't think so," she tells me.

"Hmm," I say. "Well, how many years have you been born?" I think I am asking a simple question.

"What?"

"You know, like, I think Tommy is about fifteen, Kathy is maybe eleven, and Joey, well, I thought he might be eight or nine. So are you six or seven years old?" I am trying to count back the years myself, because I helped to deliver her, but have lost count myself.

"Oh. I guess I am six years old or maybe in between six and seven. Something like that."

"I thought you were born in May, is that right? I didn't remember the year."

"I don't know years, Grandma."

"Well, I guess we had better start learning, so you can teach your new baby brother or sister about years. Carrie taught your sister."

"Really?"

"She did. Today is Wednesday, November 27, 2028. We'll write that on the top of your paper for today. "

A knock on the door startles both Moe and me from our discussion of years. I open, and it is Tommy. His face is flushed from the cold. He is in shirt and pants only, no coat. Joey behind him is looking scared.

"Dad asked me to come get you. Momma's sick. Something is wrong. He told me and Joey to stay here with Moe. He doesn't want her there. He asked you to bring your medicine basket."

I can feel Moe's eyes on my back.

Tommy whispers, "Miss Janie, she's bleeding real bad."

"Moe, will you show Joey and Tommy where the rest of the mush is. I'm gonna see what's ailing your Mommy, and your brothers are going to stay here with you until I get back in just a little bit."

I am trying not to act worried, smiling while I get my jacket and basket of herbs, making sure that I have red trillium, yellow slipper root, and red clover. The roots are already pulverized into powder and packed in little bags, the clover dried in a small lidded basket. I pull a stack of sheets that I had used for Aries and a small bar of strong lye soap that sits on the shelf with the sheets, and another pouch – partridge berries, that I wish I had given Jolie weeks ago. It helps prepare for labor.

"Don't you boys let that fire go out," I admonish, smiling, hoping that it diminishes the alarm that I feel in my gut.

I rush towards Jolie's house running over in my head what needs to be done. I have been present for the births of Kathy, Joey and Moe, but Moe nearly slid out. I don't know how or what to do with complications, and I know waiting for me at Jolie's house is her husband and daughter who are expecting me to know. I am counting months backwards from what Moe has told me. If Jolie is due in late March or early April, then she is between four and five months. I don't know if a baby can live outside the womb in a hospital at that gestation, let alone at Stears Branch with no doctor.

I don't knock at Jolie's door. Kathy meets me. She has heard me on the steps. I tell her, and it sounds so much like an old TV show, to stir up the fire and put on some water. If this wasn't so critical I would laugh at the picture we make. Harold opens the door to the bedroom and from the doorway I can see Jolie. She isn't making a sound, and it is not a good sign.

"When did she start bleeding?" I ask.

"Early this morning I suspect. I have been sleeping in the loft with Tommy so as not to bother her. She was already like this when I got up. I sent Tommy after you right then. The bed is soaked, Janie. Is she gonna live?" Harold asks.

I don't answer, because I don't know. I go to where she is lying. She opens her eyes and manages a smile for me.

"I didn't know if you would come or not," she says.

I am ashamed of myself, as well I should be. "I'm here, aren't I?"

She nods.

"How long have you been this bad, Jolie?"

"On and off for a while. I've been trying to hold on till the baby got bigger."

209

"Are you sure about the date? You look farther along than what Moe says."

"Pretty sure. I think I had the curse in May or June, I'm not sure. I don't keep up with it too much. Didn't have one in July at all I know. The boy came in late September." With that she turns away, not wanting to look at my face. "I didn't have any periods then, but I had started getting morning sickness."

"You know you could have been pregnant and still had a period," I say.

She shakes her head that she didn't know.

"Morning sickness usually starts pretty quickly and ends by three months, but it doesn't always hold true. Are you having contractions now?"

"Some."

"How painful are they? You know on a scale of one to ten, ten being the worst you ever had, when you birthed Kathy or Joey."

"Some are in the middle. Right now they're not too bad. They slowed down some."

I'm not sure if that is good or bad. I think if she has gone this far, the baby needs to be born regardless of how big or little it is. She doesn't need to go on losing as much blood as what the bed looks, and she needs to be cleaned up so I can see what is going on.

"Harold, let's try to get some clean straw and sheets. Kathy, has that water got hot yet?" I ask from the bedroom.

I get up and head to the main room, unload my bag and hand the sheets to Harold. The cups sit on the mantel, and into one I add the powdered yellow slipper root for the pain along with the red clover to hopefully thicken her blood. I leave the red trillium out of my bag in case we have to restart the labor. The medicinal smell of the tea is strong, but I think it is needed. Inside the bedroom I watch as Jolie grimaces in pain.

"Can you sit up?" I ask Jolie. She nods that she can, and with my free arm as a support she takes both hands and pulls herself into a seated position. "Does that hurt worse?" I ask.

"A little."

"Drink this. It should help the pain. We need to get fresh bedding underneath you. You've lost a lot of blood already Jolie, and the tea will make it easier to move you."

She takes small sips. It is hot and tastes bitter. She makes a face.

210

"Drink it," I say, and she obeys without further complaint.

Once the cup is drained, I unbutton her gown and ask Kathy to get a clean one. Together, Kathy and I pull the bloodied gown over Jolie's head. She does not bother to cover her enlarged breasts. Harold has returned with one of the children's bedding from the loft. He gently lifts Jolie while Kathy and I pull the soiled mattress off the rope-knotted bed and replace it with the clean one and wrap the sheets from Aries' house over it. With the same level of care, Harold lowers Jolie to the clean bed.

The tea begins to take effect, and stress lines on Jolie's face ease. Her eyelids become heavy and close in a light sleep before I begin to wash the drying blood from her thighs. Harold sits by the bedside holding her hand while Kathy brings basin after basin of clean soapy water into the bedroom.

"Is she going to make it?" Harold whispers.

I still don't know the answer to his question. He has asked it twice now, and I wish I had the answer for him. Once she is clean, I can look, can feel. I wash my hands, wash them with water as hot as I can stand and with soap as strong as I have. I roll my sleeves up above my elbows. I have never reached inside of anything, not animal or human. Jolie's other youngest, Moe, came out on her own, just slid out like Jolie was made for birthing babies. Jolie had said that's how Tommy had been, too, but this time is different, and I know if I don't reach inside, I won't know what is going on. I don't want to do this. It goes against everything I know. It has nothing to do with Jolie anymore. I feel ignorant. I am ignorant. I don't know what I am looking for or what to do if I do feel something out of whack. I look at Harold.

I say it out loud, "I don't want to do this, Harold."

"Will it save her?"

"I don't know, but I know we can't not do it, Harold. That baby is stuck in there, and if it doesn't come out, I'm afraid she'll just bleed to death. Then they'll both die." *Oh God, forgive me my trespasses. Help me in my hour of need. Please God, please.*

I reach between her thighs, and lightly spread them apart. I can't see anything. Carefully, I put two fingers inside of her and put my other hand on her belly, reach inward with the rest of my hand and hear her groan. I can feel a contraction start at her belly, hear her cry out more loudly. Harold places his hand on Jolie's belly and rubs it gently. A new rush of warmth on the hand that is inside of her runs

211

down my arm. Her water has broken. I feel a small foot and I think, *Oh my God. What do I do now?*

"Harold, the baby is upside-down, turned the wrong way. I can feel its foot, right here in my hand."

His eyes nearly pop out of his head, "What you gonna do?"

"I think it's already too far to turn it."

"Push it back up," he says.

I look at him. The foot feels like it is only as large as my thumb, so little. When the contraction ends, the womb relaxes. I don't know if he is right or not, but it seems the only option. I push, and the small foot moves easily back into the safety of its home. I call to Kathy.

"Kathy, get a basket and start warming blankets. Get some bottles and put warm water in them and cork them up. Line the basket with them. Hurry, Kathy."

"Now?"

"Yes. Now!" To Harold, "I think we are going to have turn the baby around whether we want to or not, but I can't do it by myself."

He still has his hands on Jolie's belly. "Can you feel anything there that feels like a butt or head or anything?" He moves his hands over the soft roundness, looks at me hesitantly.

"Not sure if it is butt or head."

"Is it hard or soft?" I ask. I am thinking if we push against the head, we may break the baby's neck. The head should feel hard.

"I can't quite tell," he says. "I think it is soft though. I think there are two bumps, one bigger than the other."

"Where do you feel the littler one, up at her ribs, or down lower?"

"Lower."

I can feel her uterus tightening up and I know another contraction is about to begin. Jolie moans again. I begin counting to myself, one-thousand one, one-thousand two, and get to sixty before her uterus begins to relax. The contractions aren't lasting very long – not long enough. Kathy comes back into the bedroom looking helpless. I ask her to begin counting like I just did, but out loud, and not stop until I tell her to.

"How high can you count?" She shrugs.

"Just keep counting to sixty and keep track of how many times you count to sixty. Can you do that?" She nods that she can. I turn back to Harold. "If you push against the soft bump lightly counter clockwise, what happens?"

He puts light pressure to the lower mound on Jolie's abdomen. He looks at me and smiles, "It gives and shifts a little bit."

My hand is still inside of Jolie. I can hear Kathy counting. There is still no contraction.

"Okay, let's try it again, a little more firm, but don't muscle it, okay? We need to get it done before the next contraction. I'll see if I can feel something other than a foot."

I have moved my hand farther into Jolie. Harold uses both hands now and holds the rounded bump like it is a soft tomato. I see him applying pressure and turning at the same time, and I can feel the foot move out of my reach. I look at him. Now Jolie's belly looks like a football shape, and I am starting to have some hope. I can see hope on Harold's face, too. I hear Kathy say "Five times, Miss Janie," when the abdomen tightens again.

"Hold off, Harold," I say, and instinctively he knows.

This time Jolie screams out, and more blood and water have gushed out and onto my arms. My expression changes from hope to fear. I have counted during this contraction, and I have counted to ninety before Jolie stops her crying out and the uterus begins to relax.

"We're too far to quit now," Harold says. And I know he is right.

"Okay, do you have the butt?"

He nods.

I say under my breath, "Turn, baby. Turn, please."

Another flow of blood comes out and I think that Jolie must have none left. The clean bed we had placed her on is soaked through, but when the next contraction comes, I don't feel a foot, I feel a small hand that seems to reach out of the womb and grab hold of me. I can feel the place where the baby should come from and it seems wide open.

"Kathy, when I tell you this time, hold your Momma up a bit, like she is sitting forward, and tell her to push like she is going to the bathroom. It's very important. Don't let her quit until I say so, okay?"

Kathy nods. She moves behind her mother's head. She is fearful, but so are Harold and I.

"Harold, when I tell Kathy to have Jolie push, you need to be at her belly and push against that butt and help push the baby out. If I can get a hold of its shoulders I'll pull, but we gotta be careful not to break anything, understand?"

It feels like an eternity before I hear Kathy say "Three times." I

213

didn't realize she was still counting the minutes between contractions, but I am grateful.

"On the count of three," I say, feeling the womb tighten on itself and draw downward. I am amazed at how the body knows instinctively what to do. It is just that Jolie is too weak to help it. "Push," I call out.

I watch Harold as he is pushing against Jolie's belly. Jolie is groaning, but not screaming at the same time. Kathy is shouting, "Push Momma, push. Don't stop. No, Momma, don't close your eyes. Push. Keep pushing."

I hear myself say, "Good job, Jolie. Rest just a minute." And then to Harold, "I can just almost feel it's shoulders. It's little head is right there. Come, look before another contraction," but before I can finish, a contraction has leaped hard and heavy upon Jolie.

"Push, Harold." Kathy takes up her mantra without being told. I look up and she is holding her mother's shoulders better than any midwife I ever saw on television. I can see the little forehead slip through the canal. I think I am going to have to pull the shoulders, but I am wrong. As the head is through, the delicate shoulders slide easily and I have in my hands the tiniest little thing, whole and beautiful.

"Harold, a towel, quick, one of those warm towels."

I had thought of a lot of things, but I must not have thought a living baby was going to come forth. I don't know what I had expected. I wrap the baby in the towel, umbilical cord still attached. Kathy lays her mother back down and brings the basket, warm with its bottles. I cannot bring myself to turn this fragile person upside down to smack its bottom. She is blue, she hasn't taken a breath, but I see this little pulse at her chest, know her heart is beating. She is alive. In the towel, I lift her to my neck and pat her back, once, then again. I whisper in her ear, "Breathe little girl, breathe." I hear a hiccup and then a whimper, and finally a soft mewing sound like a kitten. The blue is replaced with pink, and the small chest is rising up and down with air. When I finally look at Harold, he is crying, big man-tears rolling down a stubby-haired face.

I shall never in all my days, from this day forward until the day I take my last breath, forget this picture.

I am brought to the present with Jolie's moan. "We gotta do something about the cord," I say.

Harold, too, is brought out of his reverie, and by memory knows what is next. In the kitchen he is heating a knife over the flame in the fireplace. He gathers string, dips it in the still steaming tea water, and comes to where Jolie is lying. I unwrap the baby. Close to the tender skin, Harold ties one knot and a few inches farther, ties the other string. With a quick movement, the cord is severed. I re-wrap the baby and hand her off to Kathy and wait.

"Is she alive?" a weak voice comes from the bed.

"She is," I say. "How did you know it was a girl?"

"I always know. Always have known with each one," she says with half a breath.

"We've still got the afterbirth to come," I tell her.

"I know."

I ask Harold to stay with Jolie while I go after tea to stop her bleeding and more herbs to ease her pain. I can hear them talking from the kitchen, Harold telling her how pretty the baby is, and how brave Kathy was and what a help. It is true. Kathy is holding the basket now, humming to the infant. I go and take a peak, think that after Jolie is settled, I will have Kathy help me clean her up and take her to her mother to nurse. I wonder if the baby has come too soon for Jolie's milk to come in. I look through my bag and sort through the teas and herbs that Carrie and I had gathered in September. The bag is as well stocked as it can be. Aries used quite a lot of them, but not the red clover or the lady slippers. The pink slipper is stronger than the yellow so I use it now that the baby is here. I consider though, that Jolie will need something to give her strength.

"Kathy, does your Momma have any bone broth from where Harold got the deer?"

Kathy looks at me blankly, as if she doesn't know what it is. I ask it in another way, "Did your Momma make any soup from the deer your Dad got the other week?"

"Momma hasn't been able to cook. Daddy and I made jerky."

"Get me a little of that so I can make some broth for your Momma. I'll show you how so you can do it later. We'll make enough now to last until tomorrow when I come back to check on your Mommy and the baby."

Together we tear the jerky in small pieces and then pour the herb scented tea over top. With bowl in hand, I go back to where Harold and Jolie have been talking. He has cleaned the bed again, removed the bloody sheets, and found fresh straw for the mattress. He has crawled in beside her. There is a basin beside the bed, and in it is the afterbirth.

215

Jolie's eyes are closed. He looks at me and explains, "She was so cold. I thought I could warm her up. She wants to name her Aries."

"This will give her strength," I say. "Jolie needs to try and nurse Baby Aries. If she doesn't have any milk, have Kathy come get me. Maybe Reva can give her some milk. The baby's sleeping now. It's been a long day for both of them. You, too."

"Janie?"

"Yeah?"

"Thanks."

I smile. "Jolie and Aries did all the work," I say, motioning towards where Kathy is now standing in the doorway holding the baby. "You and I just manipulated things a little."

I pick up the bloody sheets and towels, the basin full of afterbirth, and head home. Back at Aries' cabin I send Moe home with Joey and Tommy. She will be anxious to see her new baby sister. I set about soaking the sheets in a tub of water. It will take more than one washing to get all the blood out. I bag up the afterbirth and go to my cabin, to the orchard where freshly lays Aries and the empty graves of Emily and Jonathan. It seems only right to bury the leavings of Baby Aries next to her namesake. The sky has grown pink with evening. It gets dark so early this time of year.

This new life came on Wednesday, November 27, 2028.

Chapter 27

Carrie.

Gary's arraignment is today. Russ told me that I don't need to go if I don't want to. He says it may be hard on me to see Gary in the orange detention uniform, shackled and hand-cuffed. He is probably right about that, but I need to see him, hand-cuffed or not. Momma and I sat up most of the night talking about the last eleven years, and Russ was on the phone trying to get Billy back and Gary out on bail. The police won't let him out. I am hoping today, after the arraignment, he can come home, but I don't know where home is.

I am also hoping that we can get Billy out of the Shelter before the Davises put him in a foster home. Russ left early this morning with the letter from Billy's mother and hasn't returned yet with Billy. Claire promised that Jack is hunting for Donna, and I am worried about Frank. Again this morning the news ran the details about Gary's supposed crimes along with the interview with Grandpa in front of the Shelter.

"Your Grandpa looks tired," Momma says. She looks sad when she watches the screen and listens to his talk.

"I suppose so," I say. After hearing what he said about Gary, I can't feel sorry for him, but I have to remember he is her daddy.

"He was just doing what he thought was right," she says. "He thinks he is protecting you."

Again, I say, "I suppose so."

We have eaten breakfast, and I have helped to clean up the dishes. Jon has headed off to school, and Momma and I sit in a strained silence. During last night's long talk about life in Stears Branch, about Grandma and Grandpa, about what the escape from the ridge was like and about running away, there is one question she hasn't asked me, and I know that it is sitting heavy on her. She is sipping on a third cup of coffee, and the news about Gary has gone off. There is little on television, she tells me, even with many of the conveniences returned to what she calls normal, national and world broadcasting still has not caught up to where it was before. It gets heavy again, the silence between us, and she looks into the cup.

217

"You and Gary," she starts. "When did you get married, really?"

"Only a week ago," I tell her.

She looks at me, surprised. I feel there is no need to lie to her. She is my Momma.

"Your license says a month ago," she says.

"I know," I say without explaining further.

She hesitates to ask further, but can't keep from wanting to know. "Why?"

"Because of the Davises," I tell her. "We wanted to get out of the Shelter and get our own place, a home for Billy until his mommy returned, and for us."

"And, that was the only reason?"

"No," I say, then more emphatically, "No! We wanted to get married. Gary had wanted us to get married right away, to protect me from things like what happened at the ferry, and then everything got complicated. There was the lady at the courthouse Annex. And after that, we didn't have a chance being at the Shelter. When the Davises got suspicious about me and Gary, Claire and Jack helped us get the papers we needed to get a license. Claire planned a nice wedding for us, really nice, at a little stone church with a preacher and all."

Momma looks at me with a strange expression, and asks, "What would the lady at the annex have to do with anything?"

I think she just missed the whole nice wedding thing, but I answer her question. "She insinuated I was under age, and that Gary would get accused of something called statutory rape. The same thing that Grandpa is trying to pin on Gary."

Momma's face gets red. She doesn't know what to say.

I go on, "I didn't want Gary to get into trouble, you know."

Momma is silent, and she is trying to think through this. She finally says to me, "You got your license illegally, Carrie. He could still be charged with that crime. You are still under age, and you got your license with a forged document."

Now it is my turn, but I don't turn red, I turn white. I can feel the blood drain from my face. "How can they prove that?" I ask.

"Your Grandpa will say that he can vouch for your age, that you are not old enough to sign for your own license. He can also say that you signed under duress, which wouldn't help Gary's case."

"Great. And, I suppose that is exactly what Grandpa will do if given the chance."

"Carrie?" Momma asks me, and again her face is red. She pauses before the rest of her question comes out. "Have you and Gary had sex?"

"Momma," I tell her, "when have we had the chance? And, it's not that I haven't wanted to. Gary was the one who said we had to wait, wait until the right time."

"Carrie."

"What?"

"How do you know about sex?"

"Momma, I don't."

Momma begins to laugh, and I start to ask her what's so funny when Russ comes in.

"We need to get to the courthouse. Gary's arraignment starts in about an hour."

"Where's Billy?" I ask.

"They thought they would get around releasing him to me by sending him on to school. I have contacted the school where he is going, and I have his things in the car now. After the arraignment we will go to the school and pick him up. The Davises no longer have any legal jurisdiction over him. I have a legal document that appoints you as legal guardian for the time being."

I am glad Momma and I are both dressed. It only takes a few minutes to get into the car and a few minutes longer than that to get to the big courthouse downtown. It is an imposing building that was untouched by the earthquakes and sits across the street from the Annex that still haunts me. I remember it as the first one Gary and I went to on our first day in Lexington. At the front door stand Claire, Sam, and Jack. Jack reports he doesn't have any leads yet on Donna, but says not to give up.

"It'd help if I had a picture to go by," he tells us.

"We'll see if we can do something about that," Russ says. "I have someone who might be able to help."

Claire let me know that she has been banned from the Shelter.

"That's not such a bad thing. Not sure I'll be going back," Sam says as he spits dark juice onto the sidewalk right in front of Russ.

As we go through the doors, Frank and Gary's boss from the garage show up. Inside, and near the double wooden doors where Gary will be brought before the judge, stands Grandpa. He stands with his arms folded across his chest, imposing, as if his presence will somehow

219

bring me to my senses or to my knees in repentance. It does neither.

"Carrie," he says sternly.

I ignore his call.

"Carrie, come here," he says more loudly, and I turn to Russ.

"Mr. Kelsey," Russ says. "I don't believe that Carrie wants to speak to you at this time."

"Who the hell are you?" my Grandpa yells. His voice echoes across tile floors and between tall wooden doors. I have never heard him curse.

"Mr. Kelsey, this is a courthouse, and I think you should lower your voice. I am your daughter's husband, Russell Jones. I am representing Gary Combs in this situation. I am sorry that it has come to this."

"You are who?"

"Emily's husband. Emily, come here honey," and my Momma comes from behind the group and moves to Russ's side to where Grandpa can see her.

Grandpa's eyes widen, his mouth opens to deny it, and he looks at her more closely, then back at me. Her hair is streaked with gray around her face, her eyes have fine lines at the corners, and she is thinner than she was eleven years ago, but he can see it is so.

"Hello, Dad," Momma says. "Carrie found me."

I am not sure what I expected from this man who buried my Momma and Daddy behind the cabin, and who refused to invite Gary into Stears Branch. I didn't expect him to run and hug her. That's what Grandma would have done, but I didn't expect him to turn and go into the court room without another word, either.

"Go figure," was the only thing said, and Sam said that.

We followed Grandpa, but we sat on the opposite side of the small room. To be such a big building, I expected something more. Russ looked at his watch, and then at me.

"I am hoping that they will allow me speak to Gary for a few minutes before the judge takes his seat," he says.

A man in gray pants and shirt opens a door and says in a loud, formal voice, "All stand, Judge Herndon presiding."

Momma whispers, "That's the bailiff."

I don't understand what is going on, but the judge comes in, wearing a long black robe and a serious expression on his face. He nods at Russ and says, "You are here for this case?"

"Yes, Your Honor. Personal reasons."

220

"I didn't think you took on criminal cases."

"I don't typically. This is an exception."

The judge nods at the man on the other side, and Momma tells me he is the prosecutor. Grandpa is sitting behind the prosecutor.

"Bring the accused in," the judge says.

Russ is right. I don't expect to see Gary in an orange suit. His hands are cuffed, and his legs are chained together. He has to shuffle to walk. His face looks bruised, and Momma takes my hand and whispers, "It's all right, Russ is going to get him out."

"Who hit him?" I ask.

The judge says Gary's full name. Then he begins with asking the man that Momma called the prosecutor to state the case against Gary.

Russ stands and addresses the judge, "Your honor, may I have a few minutes to speak with my client. He was arrested yesterday evening, and I have not had the opportunity to meet with him.

The prosecutor stands up and says he doesn't want Russ to be able to do that, and tells Russ he will have plenty of time to develop his defense. "This is just an arraignment," he reminds both Russ and the judge.

"By appearances, Your Honor, it would seem that my client has had a rough evening."

The judge interrupts Russ and asks the prosecutor to get on with the charges. Russ sits down.

"Mr. Combs, please stand,"

I listen to the charges. "On October 26, 2028, kidnapped underage Carrie Baxter and Billy Wilson, statutory rape of the underage, Carrie Baxter, robbery with deadly weapon, murder in the first degree of William Wilson, Sr., Donna Wilson, and Susie Wilson.

I want to vomit. Momma takes my hand. I say, "None of that is true." The judge looks at me and says, "Quiet, or I will have to ask you to leave, young lady."

Gary turns and looks at me. I think he was more prepared for the lies than me.

Russ stands, "Your Honor, may I address the charges?"

"How so, Mr. Jones?"

"I have proof in my possession that Donna Wilson and her daughter, Susie Wilson, were with Mr. Combs after Mr. William Wilson was murdered, not by Mr. Combs, but by the ferry runners at Clays Ferry, and that Donna Wilson wrote a letter giving Mr. Combs temporary

221

custody of Billy Wilson until she got back on her feet and could come back and get Billy."

The prosecutor stands and says, "Objection." And the judge tells him to sit down since this was just an arraignment, as he had so willingly reminded Mr. Jones earlier. And the judge reminds Russ of the same again.

"In addition, Your Honor," Russ continues, "If I may provide further information that is relevant to this arraignment and the charges, Mrs. Combs, aka Carrie Baxter and Mr. Combs are married, legally, and I have their marriage license to prove that."

"Is that so, young lady?" the judge asks me.

"Yes sir," I tell him, and with that my Grandpa leans over and says something to the man at the other table who pipes up and says, "I don't know how that could be since she is under age, and couldn't have gotten a license without a guardian signing giving permission, and Mr. Kelsey adamantly informs me he didn't do that."

"If that is true, Mrs. Combs you would have needed a guardian's signature. Did you have someone sign as giving permission for you to marry this young man?"

I want to slink into my seat. Now lots of people are going to be in trouble, and Gary is going to be in more trouble. Grandma's words of one lie reaps a thousand sorrows are coming to haunt me. I hear a rustle next to me. My Momma is standing up.

"Your Honor, I am Carrie's mother, and she came here to Lexington with Mr. Combs, against her grandfather's wishes, in order to find me. Find me she did, and I gave her permission to marry Gary Combs, and I would do it again, Sir."

The judge is quiet and looks back over his papers, looks over at my grandfather and shakes his head, then to the prosecutor says, "The charges of kidnapping of Carrie Baxter Combs and statutory rape of same are dropped from these charges. However, Mr. Jones, you are going to have to come up with more than this so-called letter from Donna Wilson to get him off the murder charges. Do you understand?"

"Yes, Your Honor."

"Now, Mr. Combs. You are being charged with robbery with a deadly weapon, murder in the first degree of Mr. William Wilson, Sr., Donna Wilson, etc., etc."

"A preliminary hearing will be set for two weeks from today. That should still give you enough time, Mr. Jones, to get the names of witnesses and time to speak with your client even with the Thanksgiving holiday tomorrow and Friday."

The prosecutor stands and requests the case go to the Grand Jury.

Russ stands and immediately objects. "Your honor, I would ask that you deny that request. We have individuals that will impact your decision regarding this case. To go to the Grand Jury would deny our presence to present that to you. To go to a Grand Jury pushes these trumped up charges further than necessary and costs the State unnecessary expense."

"This office does not feel that the charges are trumped up or frivolous." The prosecutor stands at his table looking at Gary.

"Sir," Russ shoots back. "No one said this was a frivolous case. It is a matter of a vindictive grandfather and unscrupulous ferrymen who have pointed their fingers at an innocent man, and I would like to have the opportunity to provide that information. If you take it to a Grand Jury first, I will be denied that chance."

The judge looks at both men, then at Gary and at me.

"Mr. Blanton, on this point I agree with Mr. Jones. We will proceed with a preliminary hearing as afore mentioned."

"Your Honor, one more thing. We would request that you would allow Mr. Combs be released to my custody during the time between now and the preliminary hearing."

The prosecutor stands up and objects to any such thing, and when Russ asks for an amount of bail the prosecutor again objects to this. Grandpa, all during this time, is whispering in the prosecutor's ear.

Momma whispers, "Bail means your step-daddy and I will put up money to promise that Gary won't run away."

The judge calls both Russ and the prosecutor to his platform, and both men argue, exchanging harsh words in low voices and shaking their heads. Finally, both return to their tables. It doesn't look good, because Grandpa has a satisfied smile on his face.

The judge asks Gary to stand again. "Mr. Combs, the prosecutor has argued that you are a flight risk based on your history, and I am inclined to agree with him. I understand Mr. Jones' concern for your safety, based on other inmates' feelings regarding felons who are suspected of harming children, so you will be placed in an isolated cell. You will be allowed one hour of isolated exercise time and one hour for visitors, i.e. your wife and your attorney, and those approved by the court, but you will remain held in jail until the preliminary hearing. Do you understand that this is done for your safety?"

"I do, Your Honor."

"This court is dismissed."

"All rise," the man at the door says, and the judge walks out the same side door he entered. We stand together as Gary is removed, still handcuffed and still with the chains on his ankles, still shuffling on the wooden floor. I only have a moment to say goodbye and tell him I love him. He tells me he loves me most, and for what he is going through, I believe him.

Outside the big doors, Grandpa stands, gloating it seems to me, waiting for something. I move past him without speaking.

To Jack, Russ says, "I have a friend who works with the police on suspect drawings. He is coming by our house this afternoon when Billy gets in from school. I'm thinking we might be able to get a composite picture of his mother between Billy and Carrie."

"That should help. Carrie, if you were guessing, where do you think Billy's mom would have gone? I mean, what kind of woman do you think she was?" Jack asks.

Russ looks around the lobby of the courthouse. "Why don't we take this down the street? There are a couple of places where we can get some coffee and get away from the crowd that is starting to accumulate here."

"I'd like to get away from Grandpa," I tell him.

Grandpa is still watching us, and I wonder what kind of damage he might do if he could hear what Jack and Russ are discussing. At this point, he is a stranger to me. He has ceased to be the man who helped raise me, and he has become the enemy. I can see the hurt in Momma's eyes when I say this, and I think she wants to go talk to him, but at the same time I think she sees the danger that he is posing to Gary.

"What time would be a good time to come over tonight?" Jack asks.

"Do you feel like cooking up your Thanksgiving feast tonight?" Russ asks Momma.

She looks at Frank and Gary's boss, Lloyd, "You're welcome to come, too. Tonight is as good a Thanksgiving as tomorrow."

"We need to get back to the garage. We're shorthanded now that Gary's sort of indisposed. Maybe some other time. See you later, Carrie." And with that Frank and Lloyd leave.

The rest of us load up in Russ's car and Jack's truck. We ride the few blocks to a little café that serves coffee and the sodas that Gary first bought for me at the Waffle House. I have adjusted to good coffee, but not sodas, so when the waitress comes, I ask for coffee with sweet cream. Russ orders a basket of sweet rolls, and Sam puts away two cups of coffee in the span of time it took to fill everyone else's cups once.

"The arraignment went fast," Russ says. "The charges were as expected based on what the police told me last night. Apparently, some travelers found the body of Mr. Wilson, and the ferry owners pointed the finger towards Gary, and your grandfather's accusation of kidnapping set the stage for penning the murder on Gary. Then, of course, the Davises' suspicions of Carrie being a runaway didn't help once the police began to ask questions. What isn't clear is why the prosecutor has ignored little Billy's account of the story as an eye witness."

"They questioned Billy?" I ask.

"They did with the Davises present, and a very quickly appointed court psychologist."

"Why won't they listen to Billy?" Sam asks, and it is exactly what I am thinking, but he asks it before I can get it out.

"I'm sorry, honey," Russ says to my Momma. "Apparently your grandpa says that Gary has a way with children, that he saw it while he was staying with people in Stears Branch before he took off with you. Based on that and the interview with the psychologist, they think Gary has brainwashed the child."

"Grandpa said what?" I ask. "He barely looked at Gary, let alone paid attention to what he did with Jolie's kids."

"Well, he seems to have axe to grind with the boy."

"That he does. He never gave him a chance," I say.

I look at Claire. She hasn't said a word almost the whole morning. I don't know if it is the loss of her job or something else that has closed her lips. I think those lips are almost never silent. She never told me what happened to her before Jack or what made Cook so mistrust her. And I wonder why she has stepped back, or what is going on here that has sewn her mouth closed. She watches me with guarded eyes even now, as she sips her coffee. I don't think she is listening to what Jack and Russ are saying, and I am distracted by her change, confused. I see that Sam is so consumed with sweet rolls that for once he is not noticing Claire, otherwise he would be drawing everyone's attention to it. Russ brings me back to the table.

"Where do you think Billy's mother would have gone? What was she like?"

I try to piece together what I hope might help. "While we were waiting for the ferry to leave, she was friendly. She talked about when she had met Mr. Wilson and the floods, and how they got separated from her family. And then, when we got across, they unloaded their stuff and the mule. The ferrymen wanted the mule for their extra trouble with getting across the river, but Mr. Wilson wouldn't give it to them. Gary told the Wilsons to head out fast, because those men were not to be trusted. He was right."

"Like I told you last night, part way up the road, I saw the ferrymen come back across the river. They had a vehicle with them that Gary said could go up the side of hills. Gary went back down to help the Wilsons. He didn't come back....he took so long. Then I heard shots. Gary didn't have a gun. Was Mr. Wilson shot? Did the police say that? Grandpa knows Gary didn't have a gun, Russ."

"I haven't seen the autopsy report to know the cause of death. The body was badly decomposed, but that's a good point. It's just whether your grandpa would lie."

I think about that, whether in his hate for Gary he would stoop to lying. He may have created an enemy of Gary, painted him in the worst possible light, but would he lie? I look at Momma, and she is shaking her head. She doesn't think so either.

"That's good information, Carrie. I wonder if Mr. Wilson had a gun. Maybe Billy will know that."

"I don't think so, but I know the ferrymen had guns. Shotguns. They looked like the one that Grandpa had."

"That's more good information, because we can find out whether there were any bullets found. Okay, back to Mrs. Wilson, Donna, right?"

"Yeah. Afterwards she was very quiet. Her clothes were torn, and there was blood on her arms and on her ..." I look around the table, then down at my hands. "You know, like someone had done something bad to her. She hardly talked at all. She wouldn't sleep inside the cab. Gary offered. She kept the children with her under the tarp in the back. I think she knew right when we got to that Holiday Inn that she was going to run off. She talked something about her family living on a road, somewhere on State Route 460. She named another road, but I can't remember."

"Does that give any sense of where to look?" Russ asks Jack.

"Well, it narrows it down a little, but 460 is a long road. Could be anywhere between Mt. Sterling and Paris."

"All right. For now I'll see what I can find out about a cause of death. Too bad we don't know a maiden name to look up Mrs. Wilson's family. We will meet tonight to get a composite picture, and maybe have a little turkey. How does that sound?"

"I like the way it sounds," Sam says, and I have to laugh, because I have no idea what kind of help Sam will be.

"Claire," Momma says. "You will come with Jack, won't you?"

She doesn't say anything, and again I don't know what's happening inside her. Jack wraps an arm around her and answers for her, "Sure she is."

"We'll see you later then," Momma says, and then to me she says, "You have a lot of potatoes to peel young lady."

"Oh, I know how to peel potatoes."

Chapter 28

Grandma.

I went to Jolie's this morning to check on Baby Aries and Jolie. It is Thanksgiving, and I have not forgotten Moe's request for cooking the turkey Harold killed on Tuesday. It is dressed and hanging in a bag high enough that their dogs can't get it. Inside, the house is warm, and the children's faces are filled with smiles. They have been passing the baby between them, and since the baby is not crying, I assume she will be a good baby. I can see Jolie through the bedroom door. She is sitting up. Harold is sitting beside her and she is sipping from a cup.

"I made broth just the way you showed me," Kathy tells me. She is proud of what she has done. "But, I don't know what to do with the turkey."

"It's okay. We'll do it together. How does that sound?"

Kathy's smile reaches across her freckled face. "Great."

"You'll soon be the best cook in Stears Branch," I say.

"You're just saying that."

"Not really. Now go gather that bird in here before the dogs find a way to get to it, and we'll start."

Kathy goes out to the porch, and Moe and Joey move closer to the table.

"We're hungry," Joey says.

"You've not eaten?"

"Kathy just got Mommy soup. We're starved," Moe adds.

"Well, let's see what we can find."

Harold comes out from the bedroom after taking the baby from Moe and giving her to Jolie. He stands at the door watching without speaking. Jolie has wrapped the baby in swaddling and puts Baby Aries to her breast.

"Does she have any milk?" I ask him.

"I reckon. She is taking her breast and seems satisfied. And she already made a mess. We had to hunt something up for a diaper."

"Well that's a good sign. Where do you keep your corn meal?"

"I'll get it. Need anything else?"

"Hmm. What do you children want with turkey?"

"Everything," Joey says.

"Harold, how about potatoes? Did you get yours in?"

Harold says that he did. I send Joey out after potatoes with a large basket. Moe goes back to Aries' old cabin with another basket in search of duck eggs. In the meanwhile, I am cooking mush and making a pone of bread.

When Tommy shows his face I ask him to go over to Reva and Mr. Thompson's to see if they want to share Thanksgiving dinner and the big turkey. He comes back with word that they will come, and Reva will bring honey and apple bake.

I send Harold to my old cabin after the big old black kettle I use for such occasions. By the time he gets back, Kathy and I have pulled the last of the black pin feathers from the bird.

I am glad that Jim found a salt lick because we have plenty of salt, and without it the bird would be gamy and flat. I wish I had black pepper, but we don't, but do still have red peppers from the seeds we brought, so we use that to season, along with the wild onions we have dried.

Once the big bird is settled in the kettle and over the fire, we all are around the table eating hot mush with the wild honey Harold had gathered from the bee tree before Carrie and the boy left. I try not to think about their leaving as I taste the sweetness, but it wears heavy on my heart.

I look at Julie, and she has lain back with the baby in her arms. Both are sleeping peacefully.

"Young lady," I say to Moe, "have you ever peeled a potato?"

She shakes her head that she hasn't.

"Well, you are going to learn. Can you be careful with a knife?"

"You're gonna let me use a knife?"

"If you promise to be careful. Kathy, do you have a small paring knife, and can you show her how to keep from cutting off her fingers?"

Kathy pulls two small knives from a drawer. "Like this," Kathy says, and together they start on the bag that Joey has brought into the house. I pour hot water into the mush pot. I hadn't expected to stay and cook. I haven't brought anything with me. I look at Joey, can tell he is ready to hit the door to play. He sees me eyeing him, has a "What now?" look. Harold has left to gather in more wood, and Tommy is helping.

"Joey," I ask, "would you do me a favor? I need you to go down

229

to my cabin. I forgot to ask your Daddy when he got the pot. I bet we still have a bunch of greens in that root cellar and some cabbage, too, and onions. Do you think you are strong enough to bring some of that back in just one trip?"

"Well, yeah."

"And, if you want, you can go inside and up to the loft where Carrie kept her stuff. There might still be some paper up there and I bet you can maybe find some colored pencils that you could make some pictures if you like."

With that Moe's head snaps up. "Me too?" she asks.

"Oh course," I tell her. "Once that big basket of potatoes is done. But I imagine you will be done by the time Joey gets back. Have you lost any fingers yet?"

She holds up both hands to display all ten fingers. Joey heads towards the front door.

"Your coat," I remind. "It's cold, isn't it?"

By the time Joey returns with the greens and cabbage, Harold has a new stack of wood on the porch. Tommy has filled the water barrel on the front porch and the small barrel that rests inside on the work table against the wall. Turkey smells begin to permeate the room. The eggs Moe gathered are boiling in a smaller kettle next to the kettle with the big bird. When they are done, everyone is anxious for them to cool enough to peel.

The morning mush has worn off their stomachs, and empty bellies are waiting for fresh cornbread and boiled eggs. Feeding a family with growing children takes more work than feeding two or three. I begin to feel wore out, and turkey dinner is a long ways from being done. Kathy and I wash the greens. Sandy soil rolls off cold crinkled leaves, and each motion reminds me of a memory I have been trying to forget...gathering greens on a day of angry words. Pearls of remembrance were once a promise of keeping hope alive. They are now a remembrance of loss.

Later, after the bird is cooked tender, cabbage is chopped into narrow slices and pickled with apple cider vinegar, potatoes mashed down and mixed with milk from Reva, and greens mixed with red peppers, we sit around Jolie's table, the whole family of Stears Branch. All of us: the Thompsons, Tommy, Kathy, Joey, Moe, Baby Aries, Harold, Jolie – up the first time since the birth – and me, bowed heads giving thanks for what God has given us, his blessings. I am glad that Harold gives this Grace. I am unworthy and not fully thankful. But I do give thanks.

Everyone pitches in with clean up, and when it is all done, and night has fallen, Moe comes home with me. In the small cabin, the fire has almost died out. I stir it up, lay logs to mount a fire, placing a guard to protect the house from flying sparks. Finally, the two of us fall exhausted into bed. Before I fall asleep with Moe curled up in my arms to keep me warm, she whispers in my ear, "I love you, Grandma."

"I love you too, Moe."

"I know, Grandma. Granny Aries said you would someday."

Chapter 29

Carrie.

I am holding Gary's hands across a small table. A guard stands at the door. Russ has already talked with Gary, and I only have a few more minutes before my time is over. We have been holding our breath waiting to hear from Jack. Claire called once to see if I was okay. She didn't say much. She told me Jack had started out with the pictures at Paris and was moving south. I tell Gary, and Gary isn't holding out much hope on finding Billy's mom.

I say, "We can't give up hope."

"Russ says we have to be prepared."

"Gary, we should have done what married people do," I whisper, "you know."

The guard steps nearer to the table. I know he is listening to our conversation. I look into Gary's eyes. They are big and blue. No, they are more a pale turquoise today. His eyes are the color that shows up near the horizon that comes just before the sun blazes in the evening sky with orange and red.

"We did right to wait. What would you do if you became pregnant, and I wasn't here to protect you?"

"Where would you be?"

"In prison or worse."

"Worse?"

"Don't ask," and he takes my hand and kisses the palm. The guard clears his throat and tells us that we have two more minutes. I want to scream, "It is too short." These last two minutes we don't speak. There are too many words to say and too little time left today.

"Time," the guard calls.

From a thick metal door, another guard enters and leads Gary out. Momma is at the other door waiting when the guard opens the door behind my chair to let me out.

"Russ had to leave," she says as we walk out of the jail to her car.

"Momma?"

"What?"

"Thank you for what you did, you know, at the arraignment."

232

She leans against the steering wheel and looks at me. "I think Gary is a good boy, and I didn't want your impulsivity to get him into more trouble than he is already in, Carrie."

There is a sharp edge to her voice that I am uncertain of how I am the cause and there is a question that I have wanted to ask, and this may not be the time to ask. I go ahead.

"Momma, did you love Daddy?"

"Of course I loved your Daddy."

"But you married Russ."

She stops and looks at me for just a moment, "Carrie, I don't want to hurt your feelings, but that is a stupid question. Let me repeat, I loved your Daddy."

"I saw the registration of your license at the Department of Records. How could you have married Russ so soon after Daddy died?"

"How can you ask a thing like that?" There is anger in her voice, but then she takes a deep breath, "I want to show you something. I'm taking you to see where your Daddy is buried."

We drive over bridges and past store fronts. She keeps her hands on the steering wheel and her eyes focused on the road until we drive through heavy iron gates supported by stone pillars.

"We're here," she tells me, finally looking at me again.

We follow a faded yellow line on a paved road, past a stone monument that has King Solomon cut in deep letters, and then we follow a white-lined narrow road bordered with stone crosses and bending angels, some so ancient they are covered with a black and white substance akin to lichen so their names and dates are indistinguishable. Where the road ends are hundreds of new shiny rectangles, row after row of pink, gray, and black. The grass lays brown amongst the stones with the cold weather, but I imagine it in summer, lush and green amongst the dead.

Momma parks the car and says, "This is our row."

I get out and follow her. We walk through the row until we come to a tombstone shaped like all the rest, but on the front is a heart with ribbons entwined held in place by tiny flying birds. I see the name Jonathan Baxter, and the dates B-October 19, 1986, D-October 5, 2017. Beside his name I see my mother's name, Emily Baxter, and the date B-June 6, 1987, D- .

"I have asked Russ to bury me next to your Daddy when I die, Carrie. I loved your Daddy. And yes, I love Russ, too. He saved my life more than once."

Momma directs me to a bench that overlooks a large pond with ducks paddling around in fussy circles. The sun glistens off their white backs as they paddle towards us looking for handouts. When they see we have none, they paddle back towards the children who throw bits of bread onto the water on the far side.

"I'm not sure where to start. What do you remember?"

"Grandma never wanted me to forget you and Daddy," I say. "We went over memories all the time. You, Daddy, important parts of my life here. I remember some about the day we left, but not much. Gary took me to the bridge, and it brought back the memories of that day and of the horrors of people falling off the bridge into the water below – their cries for help, and the screaming."

Momma starts, "After we left you with Grandma and Grandpa, we went back to our house for documents and the dog, and then tried to get to your Nanna and Paps. Do you remember them?"

"Kind of," I lie. Their names echo faint familiarity.

"It wasn't good. The earthquake so frightened Nanna that she had a heart attack, and we tried to get her to the hospital. Roads were jammed with cars. After that, we missed getting to the bridge, not that it mattered by then. The earthquake took it down, and the flood that followed took out every other standing bridge. We didn't know what happened to you or your Grandma and Grandpa. For all we knew, you were swept away with all the others. We were isolated. Nanna died. Your Daddy gave up, losing you and his Mom. Work was scarce. Food, within a few weeks, was even more scarce."

"We took what we could from the old house on Broadway and moved in with Paps. He and Nanna are buried two rows up from your Daddy. Your Daddy took a job in reconstruction and was killed in a large equipment accident. There were too many deaths all at once."

I look at Momma. She has a faraway look in her eyes. I think she is going to cry, but she continues.

"That's when I met Russ. He helped me get a settlement, and helped me get on my feet. I worked in his office as a secretary after that. I was pregnant with your brother when your Daddy died. I don't think I would have been alive for you to find me if it hadn't been for Russ."

Momma paused. The children on the other side squealed as the ducks paddled and bobbed after the sinking bread. She looked down at her hands, and then over at me.

"We need to go now."

In silence, we follow the same colored lines, except in reverse, out of the cemetery, and I'm not sure why she is angry with me but I am certain she is. On our way home, we pass the Shelter, and she slows down as we pass. In the parking lot Grandpa's rusted green car sits ominous in the front row.

"You are going to have to patch up this quarrel with your Grandpa."

"Momma, none of this needed to happen if Grandpa had been more reasonable. He became irrational in his fears, and his suspicions were unwarranted."

"Perhaps not, Carrie. You did run off."

"Still, his behavior towards Gary was unprovoked. I just wanted to find you, that is all."

"Really? Be honest."

"Okay. I was falling for Gary. But I don't think he would have left at all had Grandpa and Grandma not treated him so poorly. It was the same as chasing him off, and had he not left, I wouldn't have left."

"So what about finding me?" I don't know how to answer that. What about finding her? I don't say anything. There is nothing for me to say. She is right about everything she has told me today, about Grandpa, about running off, and finding her, and about love. Grandma would say I wasn't being honest with myself. I think that is what Momma just told me, too.

Chapter 30

Momma said that it is good that the judge denied the prosecutor's request for a Grand Jury. She said she isn't an attorney like Russ, but if that had happened, it would have gone automatically to a full trial, because Russ wouldn't have been able to submit any evidence to the judge in Gary's defense. We still haven't heard from Jack.

Billy said the picture looked just like his Mommy. Russ made copies of it for Jack to take with him, and Billy has kept one here. Jon taped it on the wall of the bedroom they are sharing so Billy can see it every day. The days are as routine as possible under the circumstances. Jon catches the bus, and Momma and I take Billy to the school he was attending before the arrest so he can have some stability.

I see Gary every day for thirty minutes, and so does Russ. I have told what happened so many times, I don't ever want to tell it again, but Russ makes me tell him over and over in case I left something out. Russ got the autopsy report, and indeed, Mr. Wilson was killed by a single shotgun wound, although he was severely beaten as well. No shotgun casing was found. The second shot may have been at Gary. Russ is going to check the El Camino to see if there are buckshot holes lodged in the car that can prove the second shot that I heard was at Gary.

The ferrymen are holding to their story. No one has talked to the little girl at the ferry or the little girl's mother. Russ is considering calling on the mother to testify that the men crossed back over. That is a long shot, however, because if she does, her life is over with them. That's what Momma told him. The prosecutor is sure to call the ferrymen themselves. They will be his chief witnesses. Russ says even at best, the prosecutor's evidence is circumstantial.

"They were not actual witnesses," Russ tells us. "They are only saying they saw Gary and you follow after the Wilson's. However, it is what the police are going on."

I say, "No, they didn't. They were half way over before we left."

"You sure?"

"I'm positive," I tell him. "We stood there and watched them push off."

That was four days ago. Tomorrow we go to the preliminary hearing.

Russ continues to work on Gary's defense. What we need is for Jack to get back with Donna. Jon and Billy have gone to bed, and Russ is at the dining table spread with papers.

"What happened to your friend, Claire?" Momma asks. "She has only called that one time, and not been over since before the arraignment."

"I don't know," I say. "She just kind of zipped up and disappeared."

Russ looks up and puts his pen down.

"I thought she looked familiar that first day. I knew I remembered her face from somewhere."

"Really?" Momma says.

"Uh-huh. It finally came back to me. She got into some trouble back when I was doing pro-bono work down at legal aid. I consulted, but didn't actually handle the case."

"Was it bad?" Momma asks.

"She was young," is all Russ says, and I am left wondering.

"What did she do?" I wanted to know.

"She has been good to you," Russ says to me, and Momma agrees.

"Without her, things could be a lot worse than they are now," he says.

"What's going to happen tomorrow?" I ask.

"Well, we have the letter from Billy's mother, but the judge already said that was not enough to exonerate Gary. But we also have Billy. Hopefully, he will allow his testimony. The psychological evaluation goes against us, but I think Billy will be a strong witness if allowed to speak. I'm not sure how the prosecutor will handle the information he got from the psychologist. I'm hoping that he doesn't deny us using Billy for examination because of that report. Then we do have you and the character witnesses."

"What about Grandpa?"

"Oh, I am sure that he will testify against Gary regarding character, but I have enough witnesses to counter that. Of course, it is a no-brainer if we can get Billy's mother here. I really prefer not to have it be at the last minute."

Russ goes to the phone and tries Jack's number. He shakes his head – still no answer.

"What happens if Donna Wilson doesn't show up and they don't let Billy speak?"

"Then we hope they believe you, but your information is as

circumstantial as the ferrymen's. You didn't see what happened either."

"And if they don't believe me?"

"Gary doesn't get out and it goes to a full trial."

"What do you mean?"

"Just what I said. We can only do our best, and we might fail. But Carrie, that's not the end of the world. Gary would just be in jail until a full jury trial is convened."

"How long does that take?"

"Depends. The trial wouldn't be set for months. Depends on the docket. Then they would have to seat a jury. After that, it depends on whether we have any more witnesses. If Jack doesn't get back with Mrs. Wilson, it gives us more time, up to a year, to find her. That's a good thing. The bad thing is that Gary remains in jail during that time."

"A year?" I feel sick. It sounds like an eternity.

"That is probably the longest. If it comes to that, I'll fight to get an early trial date, but finding Billy's mom is the most important thing."

"What happens if it goes to trial and we never find her?"

"It could be bad."

"Gary said prison, or worse. What's worse?

"You know, there is no need to go there. Let's get through the hearing first, and if we lose that, then we will talk about what is next."

"Russ, we can't lose. Momma, are you coming with me tomorrow?"

"Carrie, I will come with you, but I have to tell you something. You need to begin acting like Gary's wife and adult instead of like a sixteen-year-old. He needs you to be there for him. Do you understand what I am saying?"

"One more thing," Russ says to me. "If need be, I am going to ask you to tell the judge what happened at the house, at the ferry, and also what you saw when Gary came back with Mrs. Wilson and the children."

I freeze right there. *Me? I can't do that.* And then I look at my Momma. She has just told me I need to grow up. I nod.

"It will be okay. Just tell the judge like you have told me," Momma says. "How many times?"

"A hundred at least."

"I'll be there."

*****

238

Tomorrow came quickly. I didn't sleep. I am glad that Russ waited until last night to tell me about testifying, elsewise I would've worried about this for days, and had I told Gary he'd have said no, I know that.

Billy is at school for now. Frank is to get him when Russ calls. He feels there is no need to expose Billy to more trauma than necessary. I am relieved when it is time to leave. The ride to the courthouse seems to take forever, and in my head I rehearse the events, relive them like it was yesterday. I have forgotten how long ago that night was – *is it a month or is it two?* I no longer remember, and to my distress the face of Grandma has started to fade. In these moments it feels like the pearls of remembrance, those jewels strung together at Stears Branch, have broken and are rolling helplessly out of reach.

Inside the courthouse, there at the same dark wooden doors, stands Grandpa, his arms folded across his chest just as they were two weeks ago. He has been waiting for our arrival, I can tell.

"Good morning, Emily," he says.

"Good morning, Daddy."

He nods at me, and I can't smile, but I try to remember what Momma said to me the other day, and I say, "Good morning, Grandpa." It is all I can say, and his eyes widen with surprise.

Russ nods as he opens the door for us to enter the courtroom. We pass two armed police officers. I see Claire, and I want to run and hug her, to tell her how much I have missed her. But all I do after taking her hand for one brief moment is go and sit behind the long table where Russ has guided Momma and me. When we are seated, I turn and look at her again. There is a faint smile on her lips. Behind Claire, Sam, Cook and Crazy Mave are seated.

On the other side, behind Grandpa and the prosecutor, are Captain and Mrs. Davis. I look at them. Captain Davis frowns at me, but Mrs. Davis looks down. She refuses to make eye contact with me. There are no other people sitting on the prosecutor's side. I wonder where the ferrymen are.

I lean forward and ask Russ, "Are the ferrymen coming?"

"The prosecutor supposedly took a deposition. I don't think he wanted the judge to see the type of men who are condemning Gary."

Russ is studying his papers. It seems like an eternity and no one is speaking. The room is quiet, haunted with fear. At times I catch Grandpa watching me. I try to sit straight, keep myself composed, and again go over what I will tell the judge if need be. I wonder if the

239

prosecutor will question me about my marriage, and I lean forward and ask Russ.

"Maybe," he says in a low voice.

"What am I to say?" I whisper back.

"You'll have to tell the truth because you will be under oath."

"Oh," I say, and I get a giant size knot in my throat. I try to swallow it down, but it remains.

"Don't worry. I'm here to protect you from his questions that don't apply to this case, and I don't think the details of your marriage apply to the charges against Gary. If he brings up the legality of your marriage, I can say your mother has already settled that question during the arraignment."

"Whew."

Russ smiles. The side door opens and the guard brings Gary in, just like before, in the orange jump-suit and chained feet and handcuffs. He looks back at me and smiles a worried smile. I stand up and hug him and whisper "I love you most," in his ear. He smiles and his shoulders relax. He whispers back, "Best." A gentleman comes in and sits at a table with a narrow machine that he types on during the hearing. It is only a few minutes more when the bailiff opens a door and instructs us to stand.

"All rise. Judge Herndon presiding."

We stand, and afterwards the judge informs us that the preliminary hearing is in session. The prosecuting attorney stands and again states the charges against Gary, and tries to put in all of the charges that were made at the arraignment.

"Your Honor," Russ stands and addresses the judge. "These charges have previously been amended at the arraignment. I don't know what my associate is trying to do here, but I respectfully ask him to review his notes on the matter."

The prosecutor clears his throat and starts over with the charges. They still sound horrible to me, but I think it makes the man look conniving and I wonder if that will work in our favor. When he is done, the judge asks Gary to stand.

"Mr. Combs, how do you plead?"

"Not guilty, Your Honor."

"Mr. Blanton, what evidence do you have to bring this man to trial on these charges?"

"Your Honor." With that the prosecutor brings a packet of papers to the judge. "We have depositions by the ferrymen who took Mr. Combs and the deceased and his family across the river on October 26, 2028. As you can see, they clearly describe the young man's vehicle, a yellow El Camino, and a clear description of the young man himself and his female companion. According to the deposition, these ferrymen were the last to see the deceased alive."

"Your honor," Russ interrupts. "If I may inquire. Do these men say in said deposition that they actually saw a crime being committed by my client?"

I watch the judge as he flips through the pages not saying anything and then looks at the prosecutor. "Mr. Blanton, Mr. Jones has a point here. There is no witnessing a crime here, only a supposition and comment that the two traversed the river at the same time."

"Judge, however, this area is operated only by this one ferry and they run twice a day. No other travelers crossed over the river after Mr. Combs and Mr. Wilson and his family crossed. Therefore, Mr. Combs was the only likely individual to commit the crime."

"Likely, and the one who actually committed the crime, are two very different things, Your Honor. It negates the fact that the ferrymen themselves, and they are known to be unscrupulous individuals, could have committed the crime, and their deposition is not to be trusted."

"Your point is made Mr. Jones. What else do you have Mr. Blanton."

"Character witnesses who can testify to Mr. Comb's deceitfulness your honor."

"Let's hear what you have."

"Captain Davis of our city's Homeless Shelter."

"Captain Davis, this is not a full trial, but a pre-trial where we are attempting to get information to determine whether this young man should go to trial. You need to understand that the information you provide us today is to be held to the same standards as if you were in a full court. Information given here will be held to the same standards. Do you understand?"

Captain Davis is sworn in, and I listen as Captain Davis paints Gary as a secretive and deceitful person. He brings up the fact that Gary did not give him copies of the letter from Donna or our marriage license when initially requested, and the judge took all of this in. Mrs. Davis does not go on the stand. She still refuses to look at either Gary or me. I get the feeling she is not convinced that Gary has done anything wrong. Next, the prosecutor calls Grandpa. I hear the big doors open

241

behind us and I look back in hopes that it is Jack, but it is Frank, and he has Billy in tow. Billy runs down the center aisle and through the rail that separates the rest of us from Gary and Russ. He looks at Gary, perplexed. "Uncle Gary, why they got you all chained up?"

"Order in the court," and the judge hits his desk with a wooden hammer. "Someone get control of that little boy now or I will have to ask that the courtroom be cleared immediately."

"Billy," I say. "Shh... You are going to get Gary in trouble. Come here and sit down."

Obediently he does, and whispers, "I don't want to do that, Carrie. What's going on?"

"Shh...," I say again. "Just listen and don't say anything until you are asked, okay?"

Grandpa goes up to the seat beside the judge and the judge tells Grandpa the same thing he told Captain Davis. The prosecutor starts asking him questions about when Gary was at Stears Branch and, true to form, Grandpa is telling him that Gary came barreling in on his El Camino and started trouble. Then Russ takes over, and I love Russ right now.

"Mr. Kelsey," he says. "What kind of trouble did Mr. Combs cause?"

"Well, he was driving his car all over the fields."

"Was he destroying anyone's property?"

"Well, no."

"Was he bothering you personally?"

"Well, no. But he was bothering Carrie."

"In what way?"

"He filled her head full of ideas about the outside world, about finding her Momma and Daddy, and all of that."

"And, may I ask, being a father myself, what was so wrong with wanting to find her parents?"

Grandpa stutters.

"That's okay, Mr. Kelsey. Let me ask you another question. Who was he driving around in the car that you said was causing problems?"

"Jolie and Harold's kids."

"Carrie?"

"No, I wouldn't let her be around the boy."

"Did this Jolie and Harold mind Mr. Combs driving their children around?"

"No, they liked having those kids out of their hair."

"Oh, I see. And, regarding Carrie, why didn't you want her to be around Mr. Combs?"

Grandpa stutters again, and then he blurts out, "'Cause I knew something like this might happen."

"Just one more question for you, Mr. Kelsey. Did Mr. Combs have any kind of weapon on him at all at any time when he was at Stears Branch? A knife, a shotgun, hand gun, a rifle, anything?"

Grandpa hesitates as if he is thinking, and then says, "No, I don't believe he did. No, he didn't. I'm sure of that."

"Thank you, Mr. Kelsey."

"Mr. Kelsey, thank you for your insight. You may sit down."

"Your Honor. We do have one witness to the incident in question," Russ says. "That is Mr. Wilson's son, Billy. He is six years old. We would like for him to tell you what happened."

The prosecutor stands and objects. "Your Honor, you have the psychological evaluation in front of you and the attached report. According to the psychologist, Mr. Combs has, in layman's terms, brainwashed the child. You saw his response to the accused when he entered the courtroom a few minutes ago."

"Is this the child you are referring to, Mr. Blanton?" the judge asks, pointing to Billy.

"It is."

"The report does indicate psychological trauma present, Mr. Jones. I am not sure it is in the child's best interest to have him retell the events of that night."

"Judge, this little boy is the only one present who can exonerate my client."

"Mr. Jones, this report suggests that the child may not be able, at this point, to distinguish what actually happened based on your client's influence."

"Your Honor, that evaluation was done immediately after a traumatic arrest of the only guardian Billy has known since the death of his father and his mother's leaving. I showed you the letter written by his mother. He has been in the care of Mr. Combs and Carrie since that time. I ask that you consider the effect of seeing the police grab the only one who has been taking care of him and separating him from that source of stability since the trauma of his father's murder."

"Your Honor. The child needs to be removed from the custody of

243

Mrs. Combs until the case is solved, and put into foster care, which is what Captain Davis was trying to do when Mr. Jones interrupted that process," the prosecutor says, interrupting Russ.

Billy starts crying out loud at that moment, "Carrie, you promised to not let them take me away anymore."

"Mr. Blanton, this is not the time or place for that issue, and you have upset the child. He is obviously attached to Mr. and Mrs. Combs. Mr. Jones, I will take up the consideration of hearing the child's story of what happened that night. In the meantime we will recess for lunch. This court will resume at one-thirty and I will give you my decision about the little boy."

With that Judge Herndon rises and the bailiff has us rise again. Gary is ushered out before I can say goodbye, but it will only be for a couple of hours.

Captain Davis storms out. Mrs. Davis stops, "Billy, are you doing okay?"

"Sure am, Mrs. Davis."

"Are you in school?"

"Yeah, Carrie makes sure I go every day. I'm only out today to help Gary. Did you know it's almost Christmas? "

"If you come to see me, I might have you a present."

"Really?"

"Yes, really."

I say, "I don't know."

"It's all right. I won't take him from you. I can see he loves you both. I'm sorry about all of this. I really am."

"Me too," I say.

Grandpa is standing at the edge of our railing. I'm not sure what he is waiting for. He finally speaks.

"Carrie, I'm sorry. I don't know what else to say." With that Grandpa just walks away and through the tall doors.

Chapter 31

Except for Russ saying that the morning went pretty well, and it is a good sign that the judge was considering hearing Billy's testimony, lunch is strangely quiet. Claire and I briefly share a word, and she leaves for her new job, which is a part time evening job waiting tables at a hotel dining room. Even Billy is quiet. Frank went back to work. When the big church chimes tell us it is one o'clock, we make our way back to the courthouse. I have grown accustomed now to the statue of the man on the horse on main street, and the one in front of the courthouse proper, but Billy is still amazed at the massiveness of the monuments. I don't see how they stood in the face of the earthquakes.

Inside the courtroom, Captain Davis has returned and sits behind the prosecutor. Mrs. Davis and Grandpa did not return. Gary is not brought in, but when the judge enters, we all stand just the same. He calls Russ and Mr. Blanton up and speaks to them while the rest of us wait, impatient to know whether he will hear what Billy has to say. When both men sit back down, the judge addresses all of us, including Captain Davis.

"I have gone over the evaluation done the evening Mr. Combs was arrested," he says, looking at both the prosecutor and Captain Davis. "And, as Mr. Jones indicated in his argument, the events of that evening were traumatic for the child. It may have affected how he responded to questions and his emotional state at the time of the evaluation. The timing of the evaluation was unfortunate and should have waited until a more appropriate time."

"I am, therefore, taking it under Mr. Jones' advisement to hear what Billy Wilson has to say about the night in question. However, I intend to do that in my office, without either Captain Davis or Mr. and Mrs. Combs present."

Billy starts to cry at that point.

"Young man," the judge advises Billy. "If you want to help your Uncle Gary, you will stop crying right now and be brave. Do you understand? Mrs. Combs will be right here waiting for you when we are finished talking."

Billy nods that he understands.

"Do you see this nice lady here at the typewriter?" he adds.

245

Billy nods again.

"She will be with us, and she will write down everything you say. You need to understand that you must tell me the truth, no matter what. That is very important. Are you willing to do that?"

"Oh, yes sir. I always tell the truth."

The judge smiles, and then speaks to the rest of us, "When we are finished I will bring the boy back to this room. Please remain here."

The judge stands.

"Billy, come along with me now."

Billy gets up and goes with the judge. To the bailiff the judge requests cookies and milk be brought to his quarters.

From that point, the rest of us sit and wait. At three-fifteen the judge and Billy still have not returned. Russ is writing and making calls. The prosecutor continues to check his watch, and frequently sends an associate to check the status of the meeting with Billy. Captain Davis leaves within 20 minutes of Billy going with the judge. He informs the prosecutor in a booming voice that he has other things to attend to.

A little after four o'clock, the side door opens, and without the formality of the bailiff, the judge and Billy enter the courtroom. We stand, and with an informal wave the judge seats us.

"I like him," Billy says to me as he moves behind the railing, sitting next to me.

"I will consider what young Mr. Wilson has told me this afternoon," the judge says. "However, Mr. Blanton, you will need to have all three ferrymen who accompanied the Wilsons and Mr. and Mrs. Combs across the river here in the courtroom tomorrow morning by nine a.m. At that time I will give my decision on the child's testimony."

"Your honor, that is short notice, and they run a business. I may not be able to get them to agree to that."

"Well, Mr. Blanton, their testimony is the only evidence you have that provides probable cause to bring this case to trial. If that is not possible, perhaps I should dismiss the case now."

"No," he stammers. "I will have the men in question here as you order. If I may ask, what is your decision about the boy's story?"

"If you were listening, I said I will let you know tomorrow at nine a.m. as to Billy Wilson's testimony."

"You honor, I was not given the opportunity to cross examine the child."

"You were the one who said such an experience might be too

246

traumatic for him. We have his side of what happened fully recorded, Mr. Blanton. This court is dismissed until nine o'clock tomorrow."

Russ turns to me, "This is good news. I need to meet with Gary and let him know what has transpired. Emily, would you get Carrie and Billy home? I am sure Jon is wondering where everyone is."

Momma nods, and we leave. When we are back at the house, I call the school and let them know that Billy has to be absent again tomorrow because of the hearing. Next, I call Frank and let him know. He says he will be there, along with Lloyd. Everything seems to depend on Billy, because we have yet to hear from Jack. Claire is at work, and I don't know how to reach her tonight. I try their phone, but there isn't an answer, but I leave a brief message that the judge will rule on Billy's story tomorrow at nine a.m. I don't say anything about the ferrymen.

Chapter 32

Friday morning. I am saying my prayers, praying that this will be the end of the nightmare that we have been living the last few weeks. Russ went over with Billy last night what the judge asked him. Billy being Billy, it was hard to tell. It was a jumble of telling us about how nice the judge was, about chocolate cookies with chocolate milk, and asking if we had ever had chocolate milk. He repeated to Russ how he told Judge Herndon how good Gary and I had been to him, getting him clothes and seeing that he had food and a safe place to sleep.

When it came to the night on the road, Billy refused to talk. Russ enlisted Jon to see what Billy would tell him, but he was no more successful than Russ. Billy has not breathed a word of what happened that night. Gary told Russ – made him promise not to tell me. Russ honored his request.

I enter the courthouse alongside Billy, knowing no more than I did before. Billy is pensive, and he holds my hand in a tight grip. The prosecutor is at his desk when we enter through the heavy courtroom doors. Captain Davis is two rows behind him.

There are two differences about the courtroom this morning from the previous occasions. The first thing is that there are four armed officers at the back doors. There were only two yesterday, I'm sure, and I don't remember four being there two weeks ago at the arraignment. I am not sure what that means. When I ask Russ, he doesn't know either. The other difference, and it is a big difference, when Grandpa comes in he does not move to sit behind the prosecutor. He sits near the back of the courtroom, and he is sitting on Gary's side.

Momma leans over and whispers in my ear, "Your Grandpa doesn't look well at all today, Carrie."

"Do you see where he is sitting?" I ask back to her observation.

"Yes, and I am glad that you noticed."

The courtroom is formal again today. The guard brings Gary in. The bailiff follows.

"All stand, Judge Herndon presiding. Court is in session."

The wooden hammer strikes the desk, and we sit down. Billy has put his hands over his ears in response to the striking of wood upon wood.

248

"What is it?" I ask, and he just shakes his head.

"Jon said he didn't sleep well last night," Momma whispers.

I understand.

The judge sorts through the papers before him, looks at Billy and at Gary, followed by a long slow survey of the courtroom.

"Mr. Blanton, have your witnesses arrived?"

"Your Honor, they are on their way."

"You have fifteen minutes, then we proceed without your witnesses, and I will make my decisions without their input."

The courtroom remains silent except for Russ's hushed whispering to Gary. "I'm going to have you tell what happened. I'll put you on the stand. We don't know what Billy told the judge. He hasn't said a word about it. The judge needs to hear an adult's version."

Russ looks at his watch. Mr. Blanton looks at his watch. The judge looks at the clock at the back of the courtroom and at Mr. Blanton. He lifts his gavel to continue without the witnesses when three disheveled ferrymen, and I recognize them from the night we crossed the river, enter escorted by a fourth gentleman in a dark suit.

"Your Honor, my witnesses have arrived."

I can see that Mr. Blanton is noticeably relieved. If Mr. Blanton is relieved, his witnesses are noticeably agitated. They scan the courtroom and see Grandpa, Gary and me. Billy has crouched behind me. I don't think they see him hiding between Momma and me. The display does not go unnoticed by the judge.

The back door opens again, and I turn to see who has entered. I see only Claire's thin face before the men from the ferry begin to cause a commotion at the prosecutor's table. The judge hammers his gavel again, and he tells Mr. Blanton to get his witnesses under control.

"Mr. Blanton, are all three men going to give their perception of the event on October 26th?" the judge asks.

Two of the men are shaking their heads that they refuse to go on the stand. I recognize the old man, the father of the little girl, the man who demanded more money from Gary and Mr. Wilson. I hear him tell Mr. Blanton that he will tell "that damn judge what he needs to know."

"Please, Mr. Harrison. This is a court of law," the judge reminds the ferryman.

"Whatever. I just need to get this over so me and my sons can get back to the river."

"Your Honor, Mr. Harrison will represent the other two with his

249

testimony. He was present at the crossing of the river, and the ferry belongs to him and his sons."

"Mr. Harrison, please take a seat." The bailiff escorts the ferryman to the chair beside the judge's tall desk.

The judge gives instructions, just like he did to Captain Davis and to Grandpa, but he emphasizes the penalty for falsifying his statements, informing him that in doing so he risks the full extent of the law. It doesn't seem to bother Mr. Harrison, until he looks and finally sees Billy. He glances at his sons nervously, fidgets, and then licks his lips. Billy draws tighter into himself and pulls further behind my shoulder.

The bailiff swears in Mr. Harrison, and I hear him say, "I will."

"Mr. Harrison," Mr. Blanton says in his most professional voice. "Just tell the judge what you have told me as to what happened the night you ferried Mr. Combs and the deceased and his family over the river."

I listen in disbelief while the man on the stand lies – lies about Gary, lies about me, and lies about the whole ride across the water. And, I want to stand up and scream when he says he saw Gary with a gun and that Gary and I followed the family up the road. He says we were going to rob them and asked for the ferrymen's assistance. Even as frightened as Billy has been, he sits up and looks at me with a puzzled expression on his face. When Mr. Harrison finishes with his lying, Mr. Blanton sits down with a pleased look on his face.

Russ turns and looks at me and says, "That last bit of information wasn't in their deposition. I think they were coached to say that."

"Mr. Jones, if you have anything to say, you need to address the court," the judge says.

"I do, Your Honor. Mr. Harrison, the last part of your statement was not in your original deposition. May I ask when you decided to add that last part?"

"What part you speakin' of?"

"The part about Mr. Combs requesting your assistance to rob the Wilsons and that he had a gun."

"I just remembered it."

"And, when did you remember that?"

"Last evening, when me and my boys there were going over stuff."

"You didn't have any assistance with your memory from Mr. Blanton or anyone from his office, did you?"

"Your Honor, I object to the implication," the prosecutor replies

250

before Russ can get another word out.

"Your Honor, I don't have any other questions for this man. I don't expect him to answer honestly, regardless of what I ask."

"Mr. Blanton, do you have any other individuals to call in regardsto bringing this case to trial?"

"No, Your Honor. I feel this testimony is sufficient to bring this case to trial as it stands now."

"I see. However, as a hearing, Mr. Jones has the opportunity to bring supporting evidence to support or refute your findings. Mr. Jones, are you ready?"

"I am, Your Honor. I would like for you to hear Mr. Combs' side of the story, if you would permit."

"Go ahead. Mr. Combs. I leave you with the same warning that I have given all other individuals, both today and yesterday, regarding information being provided. You are to tell the truth, and in the event that you do not, you will be prosecuted for that failure. Do you understand the ramifications of those laws?"

Gary has moved to the same chair that Mr. Harrison has vacated. He is standing when he answers, "I do," to the bailiff's swearing in.

"Sit down Mr. Combs. Do you still, based on Mr. Harrison's testimony, claim to be innocent?"

"Yes, Your Honor."

"Well, then, let's hear what you have to say."

"Carrie and I arrived at the ferry station several hours before it was time to leave. I had crossed several weeks before, and they knew I was hunting family. I had to say something, and I knew that they were a devious and rough crowd. I told them she was my cousin."

When Gary calls them devious they begin to get loud, and the judge pounds the gavel again warning the prosecutor to keep the men under control.

"Go on, Mr. Combs."

"We were about to leave when the Wilsons showed up with their two children. Carrie started talking to the lady, and I became irritated, because I felt we needed to keep to ourselves. She's not that way. She doesn't know a stranger, if you know what I mean. We paid our fare, and the Wilsons paid theirs, then Mr. Harrison asked for more because of the mule, said it was more trouble. Mr. Wilson told Mr. Harrison he'd already named his fare, and they didn't have any more money, but Mrs. Wilson said it was okay, she had it. She had this little bundle

251

in her dress, and she pulled out what Mr. Harrison asked.

"It was rough going over, because the ferry sat low on the water, and it was a fast current, but Mr. Harrison and his boys made Mr. Wilson and me help, so we made it over. On the north side, he demanded more money again from both Mr. Wilson and me. I refused to pay. Mr. Wilson said he didn't have any more money. Mr. Harrison said he'd take the mule as payment. Mr. Wilson said 'no'.

"The Wilsons got off the ferry along with their mule, and then Carrie and me with my car. I offered to take them on up, but I didn't have any way to get their mule up the road. That's all they had, and said they'd be fine. I said they had better head on up fast because I didn't trust Mr. Harrison or his sons. Carrie and I watched the ferrymen part way over, seeing they didn't have any trouble getting back on the other side empty, and then headed up ourselves."

Gary stops here. He looks at me and at Billy, and down at his hands.

"Go ahead, Gary. The judge needs to know what happened," Russ encouraged.

"We passed them on the road, the Wilsons, and when we got to a bend near the top where we could see over the trees, Carrie saw the ferrymen heading back over to this side."

"That's a lie," one of Mr. Harrison's sons shouted out over Gary. Gary looks at him and Gary's face takes on a hard expression, like the night it all happened.

"Your Honor," he says, once his expression comes back to normal. "Carrie wanted to go back right then, and I didn't. I said 'What could we do?' but she just kept hounding me. So I made her hide in the bushes and I went back, but I was too late. I should have gone right when Carrie saw them. Maybe it would have been different, I don't know." Gary has put his head in his hands, and when he raises his head, his face is wet with tears.

"Can you continue?" the judge asks.

Gary wipes his face and nods.

"I had turned my motor off, so I rolled down the road to where they were, made my way half-way down without being heard with all their rutting. The youngest Harrison, him," pointing to the one who interrupted, "had Mrs. Wilson down. He had ripped her skirt, panties at her ankles and had the money pouch from her waist. He was on top of her, his pants down to his knees. He was pumping over and over – pinning her arms with his greasy hands. She was facing where

Mr. Harrison had already beat Mr. Wilson with the butt of his shotgun and if he wasn't already dead, he was near so. She whimpered like a whipped pup."

I watch Gary's face, but he won't look at me, he only stares at the back of the courtroom.

"Billy had his little sister and had scrambled to a pile of leaves part way up the ditch. I grabbed both of them by the arms and pulled them the rest of the way up and threw them into the car and went back to where the two brothers had started to lead the mule back down the side of the hill. I saw Mr. Harrison raise his shotgun and shoot Mr. Wilson full in the face. Mrs. Wilson screamed with that, and I grabbed her by the arm and dragged her up the ditch until she gained her footing and climbed with me. Mr. Harrison saw us. He started up after us and when we got to the car, he was not far behind. I was pulling away when he fired a shot at us, but he didn't hit us."

"Carrie was waiting in the middle of the road. We fled to Lexington and spent the night in a parking lot. Mrs. Wilson wanted to stay in the back of the El Camino with the children. The next morning she was gone. She left me a note and Billy. Carrie, I didn't want you to know about what happened."

Mr. Harrison stands up, "He's lying. He's a lying son-of-a-bitch, Your Honor."

"Sit down, Mr. Harrison, or I will have you arrested for contempt of court."

"Mr. Combs, you can step down now. Mr. Jones, do you have any other witnesses to give support to Mr. Combs' story?"

"Your Honor, Mrs. Combs' story picks up where Gary's leaves off, at the top of the hill. I am not sure that is necessary. She also has verification of the ride across the river, if you feel that will provide additional support, but based on the behavior here, I think that may not be needed."

The judge nods.

"You do have Billy's side, and you said you would advise us today whether you use it in this proceeding. If I may ask, have you come to a decision?"

The judge looks back at the police officers at the door and at Mr. Harrison and his sons.

"I have. Mr. Combs, will you stand, please?"

I turn to the back of the courtroom at the commotion at the doors.

253

They have been blocked by the police officers, and someone is pounding on the doors to gain entrance. Russ rises and goes to the judge and speaks in a low voice.

"Officer, please let the gentleman who is requesting entry in."

I turn to see the doors open, and Jack is standing there with Donna. She looks nothing like she did on the night of the ferry. Russ turns in synch with Gary, but our expressions are all that he needs to see to feel our elation.

I don't think Billy recognizes his mother, with her hair grayer, her face thinner. She is dressed not in the mountain garb he remembers, but dressed like Momma. His little sister is not with her.

Mr. Harrison and his sons do not recognize her either. There is confusion in Mr. Blanton's eyes as to why Russ is bringing this woman in as a witness, since a character witness would have little effect at this point. I think he is still hoping that Billy's story will support the ferry owner's story, and the psychological evaluation will hold. It is wishful thinking on his part. I know it is.

"Mr. Jones, introduce us to your witness."

Russ turns towards the police officers, and Jack whispers to one, who in turns whispers to the other. I see them both stand shoulder to shoulder with their hands on their weapons.

"Your Honor, this is Mrs. Wilson, the wife of the deceased."

"Mommy?" Billy jumps up from in between Momma and me, and with hearing those words, Mr. Harrison and his sons quickly rise to leave the courtroom.

"Gentlemen, I suggest you be seated until this story is complete. Please come forward and give your full name?"

Donna walks by herself up the center aisle, without looking at the ferrymen. In a clear voice she says, "Donna Marie Wilson."

"Please have a seat Mrs. Wilson."

"Mommy. It's me, Billy."

"Billy," the judge interrupts. "I need you to wait just a few minutes until your Mommy here can tell me what happened that night your Daddy died. Then you can have her all to yourself. Do you understand, young man?

"Yes sir."

"Mrs. Wilson, Mr. Combs is accused of the murder of your husband, and of you and your little girl. This is a hearing to determine whether he should go to trial. The men here," he said pointing to the ferrymen, "are the ones who have made this accusation. Is this true?"

"Your Honor," Donna says with a half-smile on her lips. "Obviously I am not deceased. Neither is my daughter, Susie. Mr. Combs saved our lives. We crossed the ferry together. After crossing, the three men sitting there," and she points to where Mr. Harrison and his sons are sitting, fidgeting and glancing toward the available doors, "came back across and ambushed my husband, two children, and me. They robbed us. That one," pointing to Mr. Harrison, "beat my husband and then shot him in the face with his shotgun, and that one there, he raped me. I don't know what he would have done to Susie had it not been for Gary."

"Officers," Judge Herndon says, and he says nothing more than that for the officers to move towards the three men. A fifth officer moves through the door, and all three men are subdued. It comes fast with no opportunity to escape.

I hear the same phrases read to them that were read to Gary, the right to remain silent.

Billy breaks free and through the railing to where his mother sits. He bounds into her lap wrapping his arms around her neck. She is holding him tight.

I have a thousand questions, but the judge is banging that gavel on his desk again, and crying "Order, order," but he is looking at Billy and his mother and there is no severity in his words.

"Mr. Combs, will you stand please."

Gary stands.

"The charges against you are dropped. You are free to go. Guard, remove the handcuffs and the ankle chains."

It is at this moment that I realize one other change in the courtroom today. They didn't make Gary wear the orange suit, and I look at the judge and he sees that I have just now realized that. He smiles at me.

"Now, Mr. Blanton, I appreciate your zeal in solving and resolving crimes in this county. However, in the future you would be well advised to check the character of your witnesses and if I find you have coached your witnesses to lie, as it is obvious you did in this case, I will personally see to it that you do not practice law in this state again. Do you understand?"

"But Your Honor, that is not…"

"No excuses, Mr. Blanton." Judge Herndon stands, and the bailiff announces that court is adjourned.

255

Donna and Billy are still on the chair by the judge's desk. Russ, Momma, Gary and I are standing as in a daze. I don't know what anyone else is doing. It is then I feel liberating tears rolling down my cheeks.

Chapter 33

Russ, Gary, and I are sitting in the living room. This morning is a blur. The television is tuned to the twelve o'clock local news, and the reporter is telling the story of the events from the morning. No one is being interviewed this time. There is a short clip of the Harrison men being shoved into patrol cars heading off to jail, fighting the officers every step of the way, cussing, claiming their innocence. There are no pictures of Gary, no one asking how it feels to be acquitted for a crime he didn't commit. Captain Davis left the courtroom without a sideways glance after the judge announced the charges were dropped. He didn't apologize for his accusations. Gary's story is sandwiched between a report about a house fire in Winchester and the upcoming shopping frenzy for Christmas.

I stand and go to the window looking through the curtain. The yellow El Camino sits in Momma's driveway. Russ got it out of the impound lot within the hour after we left the courthouse. Donna and Billy will be here in a little while.

At the courthouse, a social worker appeared after the judge's decision. She thought Billy and Donna needed time with her to talk about what happened. Jack said he found Donna in a little town beyond Mt. Sterling. She was living with a family and trying to find a place of her own. The family assisting Donna owned a five and dime store. She was working there. She said she intended to go back. While we waited for Momma to bring her car around to take us home, Billy kept asking Donna over and over why she left him.

"Billy," she tried to explain. "I knew Gary would take good care of you until I could get a place for us to stay."

"But you took Susie and not me," he said.

"I thought it was too much for me to leave the both of you."

"Why didn't you leave Susie?"

"You were a big boy. She was a baby."

"She was over two."

I thought to myself as she spoke, even as much as he loved her, it was going to be a long road to rebuilding trust.

"Are you going to take me with you?" he asked.

"Do you want to come with me?"

257

Billy looked at Gary and me. "Carrie always keeps her promises. Are you gonna keep your promises, Mommy?"

Donna looked at me at that moment with pained eyes, "I'm going to try Billy. I'm going to try really hard."

With that the social worker led the two of them back into the courthouse.

*****

I think as I look out the window at the yellow vehicle that I will miss Billy. I wonder what it will be like for Gary and me without him. All our married life has been with a child, and now it will be just us. I can hear Momma and Grandpa arguing in the kitchen. Momma is putting together some lunch, and she pushed me out saying she needed to speak to her Daddy alone.

"You can't just keep holding on," I hear her say. Her voice has risen from a whisper, and I look to see if Gary and Russ are listening. They are engrossed in their own business.

"Daddy, she is married for God's sake."

I can't understand what Grandpa says, but I know he answers, because I can hear his familiar grunt at the end.

"No, they haven't. When would they have?" and I think Momma realizes that her voice has risen to a higher pitch, and she lowers it so I have to strain to hear her. "They haven't even been married for seven weeks yet. And for all of that time they were either in the Shelter or he was in jail. Now when do you think they would have had the opportunity?"

I hear Grandpa mutter.

"Really, Daddy? I can't believe you think that."

I finally hear him again, and he says, "She's just too young."

"Maybe," I hear Momma say. "But if you hadn't chased her off with all your craziness, none of this would have happened." And in a much louder voice, so that Russ and Gary stop talking and look up, we all hear Momma say, "Don't you walk away from me. You come back and hear me out."

"That's getting a little intense," Russ says. "I'd better go in and referee." Russ moves into the kitchen where the argument continues. Gary gets up and comes to where I stand, pushes the sheer curtains back.

"No worse for the wear is it," he says, looking at the El Camino.

"I guess not. Did you ever think you would see it again?"

"Some days I wasn't sure, but it wasn't the car that kept me up at night worrying." He wraps his arms around my waist. "Were you worried?"

"Every day."

"If it didn't work out, what were you going to do?"

"I don't know. Do you know, I feel like I have said that far too often."

"It's okay. Would you have gone back to Stears Branch?"

"How could I?"

"Oh, now I don't know," he laughs.

"I don't think I could live without you."

"That is a little melodramatic don't you think? You could have found someone else to marry."

"I'm married to you."

"That you are, Mrs. Combs. Russ is trying to get us a place for our honeymoon."

"Honeymoon?"

"You know, where we can be alone for a first time. I had thought maybe we'd go to your old house on North Broadway, but your Momma said that wasn't good enough. So they want to put us up in a motel. That's probably what she and your Grandpa are fighting about."

"Gary."

"Huh?" His voice is raspy and his breath is warm against my neck. He smells like lemon soap and I lean into its sweetness. His body has grown taut against me. I can feel him hard against my back.

"Gary, I don't know anything about honeymoons."

"Ssshh…" he whispers into my hair. "You know your hair smells like springtime. Have I ever told you that?"

"A couple of times."

We have not heard the front door open. Jack clears his throat.

"Okay guys, save it for later. Glad it was me that interrupted and not Grandpa, huh?"

I break from Gary's embrace. I think Gary's face is redder than mine, and he instinctively untucks his shirt, and I wonder why. Jack just laughs and winks. And, if Gary's face could get any redder, it does at that moment.

"How long were you in jail, buddy?"

"Too long, Jack. Glad you came to the rescue."

"I was beginning to wonder if it was going to happen. Donna and Billy are on their way in and Claire is helping. We've kind of got an announcement, but I'll let her tell you."

Momma comes through the swinging kitchen doors smiling. Her face says she has won the argument. She hugs Jack as if they have known each other all of their lives.

"The hero of the day," she exclaims, and Russ right behind her nods in agreement. Grandpa follows, looks at me and shrugs. It is no mystery as to what that means.

Around Momma's table, we enjoy conversation and early dinner. Jack is taking Donna and Billy back home tonight. Billy will enroll in school in Mt. Sterling. He will not have missed a beat. We laugh about the ferrymen's expression when they realized who Donna was, and Mr. Blanton's expression when the judge reprimanded him for his unethical behavior. Billy tells again how good the cookies were that the judge gave him and raved on and on about chocolate milk until Donna promises that she will get him some when they get home. When the boys' antics end, Jon and Billy leave to pack Billy's clothes.

Jack stands to make a toast of iced tea, since Claire is not partaking of alcohol. Momma and Russ seem to understand more about that than Gary or me. They are smiling.

"I'm gonna make Claire an honest woman," he announces in a booming voice, and Jon and Billy stick their head out from the bedroom to see what that means. "I want to invite all of you, and that means you too, Grandpa, to Claire's and my wedding. A week from today at that same little church where you and Carrie got married. Same preacher, the one Claire likes. Won't be fancy, but we'll be doing it right."

Claire looks happier than I have ever seen her. Her face glows. I start to say that I thought they were already married, and Gary kicks me under the table.

"What?" I ask, responding to his kick.

"It will be more than 'kind of' married, Carrie," Claire says.

"Oh," I say.

"And if that isn't enough," Jack says, and now he is glowing. "We got a bun in the oven."

Momma laughs, and Grandpa chokes on his iced tea. I am absolutely confused, but as long as the bun makes Jack happy, and Claire is happy, then I am happy.

"I thought you were going to let Claire give the good news," Gary says.

"Ah, guess I just can't help myself. Don't know when I have been this happy."

Curiosity gets the better and I ask, "What's a bun in the oven?"

There is a pause around the table, and finally Grandpa answers, "She's gonna have a baby, girl. Guess you're just a little... "

I look to Gary, and changing the subject ask, "Claire, would you like to wear my wedding dress? I know it is used and all, but if Gary doesn't care…is that okay with you?"

Gary looks at me. I know he bought it for me, but we are already married, and we aren't going to do it again, not with Grandpa hanging over us. He nods that it is okay.

"Carrie, that's your wedding dress," Billy pops up.

Billy's gonna blow the whole wedding cover. I swallow hard.

"Hey buddy, you were in school when we got married. Remember? Mrs. Davis had you in school the second day," Gary says.

"Oh yeah. You got married right away. "

"Claire, I want you to wear it. You will be a beautiful bride. Do you think Cook will bake a cake?"

"To make her an honest woman?" Jack says laughing. "Bet I can get her to do it… if I can just sneak past the Davises and into the Shelter." And then he and Gary are laughing until tears are rolling.

"It's settled then," Momma says. "Carrie can stand up for you… that is, unless you have someone else in mind already."

"There's no one else I would rather have, Mrs. Jones."

"Grandpa, will you stay?" Jack asks.

"I'm not sure what I'm going to do."

"Are you going back to Stears Branch, Daddy?"

"Not sure your Mom will take me back."

"Why ever not," I ask, and I can see from everyone's expression there are a lot of things that I don't know about being married. A lot more than buns in ovens or honeymoons.

*****

When the celebration is over and the dishes are cleaned off the table and put away, it is time for Donna and Billy to leave. Jon and Billy have dragged the black plastic bags to Jack's truck. We are standing on the same porch where more than two weeks before I stood with Claire waiting for my Momma to come to the door and Billy sat with Gary in Frank's Oldsmobile. With everything that has happened, it seems like two years. Jack loads the bags in the back and ties them down, then starts the truck. He stands at the truck door and waits.

"Jack said you were working, but how you doing with money?" Gary asks.

"We're making it," Donna says.

"Do you have your own place?"

"I've been saving for that. Maybe in a few more weeks."

I watch Gary pull out his wallet, the same one he used at Waffle House and the Good Will, and the same one he used to help pay our way at the Shelter. He pulls out two hundred silver certificate bills and hands them to Donna.

"I can't take that."

"Sure you can. You lost everything, and well, if this just..."

Billy interrupts "Gary, that's a whole lot of money. Where'd you get all that money?"

"Billy," I say. "Gary has a job, remember?"

"Yeah, but that's a whole lot of money."

"It is. You remember what Gary told you once?"

"It was the only time he told me to shut up."

"You just let Gary worry about his money, okay?"

"Okay. Carrie?"

"What?"

Enormous tears fill his eyes and spill down childish cheeks. He reaches and encircles me with thin arms. His face buries in my blouse, and I hear his sobs. We have both been country newborns in this, seeing and sharing a new world. I am going to miss motherhood. I am going to miss Billy.

"Billy, your Mommy is waiting," I say loosening his arms.

I kiss Billy on the top of his scruffy brown hair. Gary has come to stand by my side. He encircles my shoulders with one arm and takes Billy's hand with his other.

"You be a big boy for your Mommy and take good care of your little sister, you hear?"

"I will Uncle Gary. I love you, too, you know."

"I know."

"Will you all come and see me?"

"Sure Billy. Jack knows the way now. We'll be able to find you."

"You promise?"

"Promise."

"Carrie?"

"I promise, too."

With that he takes the steps in one jump and runs to where Donna was waiting.

"Buckle up," Jack orders, and through the window to Claire, "I'll be back after you in a few hours. You'll be okay?"

"We'll take care of her," Momma says loud enough that all of her neighbors are sure to hear.

The six of us watch the truck disappear. Evening is coming. A chill is in the air. Inside the house we sit and look at each other not certain of our next move. It is like chess, except there are no winners or losers. I am wondering where we will stay. There are no more bedrooms here at Momma's. Jack will be back by nine-thirty to get Claire, but there is no place for Gary and me. I had been in the spare bedroom, but Grandpa is there now. I think he could share with Jon, but there is awkwardness about Gary and me sharing a room under the same roof as Grandpa. I am looking at my hands. Grandpa is looking out the window. Jon and Claire are watching television. Russ is reading a newspaper.

Momma clears her throat. "Russ," she says. He looks up and glances towards Grandpa who is not distracted from the window.

"Carrie, your Mother and I thought you and Gary needed some privacy, being that you are newlyweds, sort of, based on what you told us."

Gary looks up from his hands and looks at me with a "What did you tell your Momma?" look. I shrug, and Grandpa gives a quick look at Gary and then turns his attention back to the scene outside the window.

"Anyway, we have secured you a room for a few nights."

"In a motel?" Jon pipes up.

"Yes," Emily says.

"Wow, we never get to stay in a motel. Does it have a pool?"

"I think so, why?" Emily asks.

"Man, can I come?"

"No, Jon," Russ says. "This is for Gary and Carrie's honeymoon. That is enough questions. Time for you to turn in."

"It's only eight o'clock. I never go to bed this early."

"Carrie, I'll help you get some things together," Momma says.

She gets up and I follow her to the bedroom. She doesn't say a word as we pack jeans, undergarments, and night clothes. At the bottom of one of the Goodwill bags is a nightgown the clerk picked out, she said for that special night. I pull it out and fold the transparent whiteness carefully with the other things Momma has folded. She looks at me with questions.

"I never wore it," I say in answer to her eyes.

The small bag is closed and latched. Gary is standing by the front door waiting. I hug Russ.

"Thank you," I say.

Momma hugs me. Russ shakes Gary's hand. Grandpa stands at the window now, looking out at the El Camino.

"Dad?" Emily says.

Grandpa turns. "Don't forget who loves you," he says.

"I never have," I say to him.

*****

We load our bags into the El Camino and back out of the drive. Jack left Gary a wrapped package on the seat. As we pull out Grandpa is still watching, a shadowed shape through the curtains. We ride to the motel in silence. It is the same motel where we slept in the parking lot two months ago. This time we go inside, and Gary stops at the counter and gives them our name. The clerk smiles and hands us a key, points us in the direction of the room. "No smoking," he calls as we head in the direction of room one-twenty-one.

The key catches in the lock, but Gary jiggles it, and on the second try it turns. The door swings open, and inside the darkened room warm air rushes to greet us. Gary flips on the light, and I am met with a vision of a huge bed that takes up the major portion of the room. In a far corner is a chair with a small table and a lamp. To the right is a closet with double mirrors for doors. I stare at the scared expression on the face reflected back at me. For one moment I want to turn and run, but above my own reflection is Gary's face, and it comes into focus. He is smiling. His expression says, *It's okay, it's me.*

Gary picks up our bags and sets them inside the door. With his hand on my back he ushers me in and shuts the door behind us.

264

Chapter 34

I am standing in front of the full length mirror that covers the closet doors of our room. I am naked. I don't think I ever stood naked in my life except when I was little and Momma or Grandma bathed me, but especially not like this. Gary lies asleep with the sheets twisted at his hip. He is beautiful, and I am not sure that is a description he would appreciate, but it is true. I look back at my own reflection. My hair is a tangled furl around my face. I move closer and stare. Turning half way I study my profile then turn back full frontal. One hand touches my breast, the other the fine mesh of gold hair, and I laugh. My laughter wakes Gary. He shades his eyes from the light filtering through the partially opened drapes and smiles. I drop my hands.

"What are you doing?"

"Looking at myself."

"And what do you think of what you see?"

"I'm not sure," and I turn, twisting my neck so I can see my back side.

"I am looking at your butt, and I like what I see. Come here."

I leave my reflection and walk to the giant bed. We have only used a corner of it. Gary kicks the sheets away and opens his arms to welcome me. His interest is obvious. I lie down beside him, and he moves to his side laying an arm across my belly.

"Did you notice, you're developing womanly curves now, like these," and he reaches his hand to brush my breast, and it makes me draw in my breath. I turn to face him rising on my elbow.

"No one told me it was going to be like this," I say.

"What'd you have done had you known?" he asks with a smile.

"It might have been a dangerous thing. I wonder if this is what Grandpa and Grandma were afraid of?"

He has lost his coyness and has become serious. Gary lifts on his elbow, and now we are face to face.

"'What they feared came upon them.' That's what the Bible says."

"I didn't know you knew the Bible."

"See, there are some things you don't know about me."

With that he rolls on his back and pulls me on top of him. I position myself on my elbows and his hands are on my bottom. I can feel his thigh against mine and the urgency that I have learned to know. I feel the same urgency. His eyes grow dark with intensity. I need to continue, but I already know what he is going to say before he says it.

"Carrie, hold on. Wait."

"I hate this part," I say.

He laughs, and opens the drawer next to the bed. I roll off temporarily while he opens the square pack. There is no fumbling now. We have it down pat. Within moments he pulls me back to him and our movements are in cadence until he tightens, and in that I feel my own longing fire, tighten, and release.

Resting my head on his shoulder, I take in the stillness of the aftermath – the slowing of our breathing. I like when he runs his hand up my back and tangles his fingers in my hair.

"Were you saying I am getting fat?" I ask under my breath.

"What?"

"You said I was getting womanly curves. Did you mean you thought I was getting fat?"

"No." Gary runs his hands down my side, stretches his hands lower to feel my thighs, and then back up to feel my shoulders and arms. "There's not an inch of fat on you Carrie, okay?"

I roll off. He has slipped off the protection to keep me from having babies. "I hate these," I say as I go into the bathroom and flip on the lights. "Do you know how many we have gone through in the last three days?"

"I hate them more than you, and I think I am more aware than you of how many we have used."

I lean out the bathroom door to see him laughing as he opens the drawer next to the bed where there is a half empty box of the things. I wrinkle my nose at him.

"Let me see. I believe you are the one who keeps telling people you are too young to be a mother," Gary says.

"I am too young."

"Well, this is how we are trying to prevent it. Do you want children?"

"Yes, but I won't be seventeen until next month. Is there another way?"

"My mom used to take pills," Gary says.

"I wonder what Claire uses?"

"Whatever it was, apparently it didn't work," and he isn't making a joke.

266

I go back into the bathroom to shower. It is our last day here. It has been a wonderful gift from Russ and Momma. It is hard for me to imagine Momma ever doing what Gary and I have done, but it seemed important to her that we have this time. I turn the water on in the shower and wait for it to grow warm. *It is one of the luxuries I will miss if we go back to Stears Branch.* I look at the illuminated face in the mirror, small breasts, blue eyes that no longer reflect a child but a woman, and I like what I see. I square my shoulders, reach behind the curtain to check the temperature, and step into the water.

After washing with lilac smelling soap, shampooing, and finally turning off the water, I can hear Gary. He is whistling, and I realize I have never heard him whistle before. He placed clean clothes on the sink, my toothbrush and toothpaste. I open the bathroom door a crack, and in spite of the steam I can see the room is picked up. He has already made the bed, and he sits on the edge waiting his turn in the shower. His back is turned from me as he watches the morning news. There is one pile of clothes at his feet, and the suitcase Russ gave us is packed and next to the front door.

"Your turn."

He gets up, and the look in his eyes seeing me wrapped in a towel makes me think we are going to mess up the bed again, but he kisses me on the top of my wet head and goes into the bathroom and closes the door behind him. I knock.

"I forgot my clothes," and he opens it a crack and hands out the undergarments. When he shuts the door again, I push on it.

"What?"

I open the side drawer and the box to keep me from having babies has been removed.

"Gary? What did you do with those things, you know, what did you call them?"

He opens the door, the shower is running, and steam is sending up clouds obscuring his nakedness.

"What things?"

I am pointing to the empty drawer.

He smiles, "I packed them."

"It's Monday, right? I think I will see about finding something else, okay?"

Gary is starting to step into the shower when he asks, "Who are you gonna ask?"

267

When I say, "Momma," he stops mid-step and turns, slipping on the water that dripped on the tile floor from where I dried off.

The bathroom in the motel is one of the biggest I ever saw except for the one at the Shelter, but Gary's sprawling body on the floor fills the space between the toilet and the long sink. I watch his eyes flutter then close.

Oh my God, I've killed him. I've only been with him three days and I've already killed him.

"Gary, wake up."

I squeeze into the bathroom between the door and the sink where he is lying. The shower is filling the room with more steam. Blood is on the floor. I reach behind the curtain and turn the shower off.

What would Grandma do? Get cold water Carrie. Get ice from that bucket. Get the washrag. Good girl.

I am kneeling beside Gary, holding the cold rag on his forehead. *Head wounds bleed lots. It's not as bad as it looks.*

"Gary, can you hear me?"

His eyes open, a hand immediately reaches for his head.

"You're gonna talk to your Momma about this?" is the first thing that comes out of his mouth.

"Gary Combs, Jr., you've just busted up your head and are about to bleed to death, and you are worrying about who I am going to ask about not having babies? Who else do I have to ask?"

He touches the back of his head, sees the blood and sits up. He is laughing, and at this very moment I want to smack him in the face, or better, in the back of the head where the big lump is forming. He stretches his hand back again and rubs the spot, pulls it away with another handful of blood.

"Whew, that hurt." He reaches up and touches my bare breast smearing me with his blood, and laughs again. "I wonder if your Grandma ever doctored your Grandpa butt naked."

I ignore his joking, but he is right – two naked people on the floor of the bathroom, in a motel room, one bleeding from the head. I get ice from the plastic bucket and wrap it in the washcloth and examine the gash on the back of his head.

"Gary, I think you need stitches."

"No, I don't."

"Yeah, you do. It's a pretty big gap back there. I'm calling Russ."

"No Carrie."

268

"No, you're going to listen to me. Hold this while I get help."

I hand him the washcloth with ice. The towels on the floor are red with Gary's blood. I go to the phone and dial Russ before helping Gary clean up and put on clothes.

****

"Carrie, what happened?" Momma says.

We are sitting in the emergency room at the hospital that is down the street from where she and Russ live. Holiday Inn allowed us to leave our things in the room until we can get back. They were apologetic, telling us not to worry about cleaning up the mess.

"Momma, it's a long story."

"Well, I am just a little confused by what Gary was saying. He really wasn't making a lot of sense on the way here."

Russ is sitting patiently on the opposite side of the waiting room. Grandpa is here, too.

"If only Grandma was here," I say under my breath, "I'd say it was a family reunion."

"Carrie."

There are five rows of seats, one row against each of three walls and two in the middle back to back, and every seat is filled with someone needing help. Flowing blood seems to take priority over the others waiting to be seen because Gary was taken back immediately, and because he was talking nonsense when we walked in, the nurse took me into the room where they examined him. By the time the doctor finally arrived, Gary had his wits about him, but the doctor didn't want his version. As I told what happened, the doctor had a hard time not laughing, and Gary stared at the floor. Gary got ten stitches, and a good two inches of that shock of red hair was shaved off. When the doctor left, Gary very quickly informed me that I was giving way too much information.

"Well, he asked me what happened."

"He didn't ask what led up to what happened."

"But Gary..."

"It's okay, come here."

Gary was giving me a hug of assurance when the nurse came in to tell us, for precaution, they were going to x-ray his head to make sure there wasn't a concussion.

269

That was three hours ago, and we haven't laid eyes on Gary since. Momma asks me if Gary has insurance, and I ask her what that is.

"Insurance, it's what people have to help pay for hospitals and emergencies like this. Does the garage provide insurance for Gary?"

"I don't know. Gary never talked about it. I can ask Frank."

"Don't worry about it," Russ says from across the room. "Sometimes it is just as good not to have anything, and it's a rarity in these times anyway."

With that, the lady at the desk looks up from her papers, frowns and calls, "Mrs. Combs? Step up to the window please."

I look at Momma. She doesn't look happy, not with Russ or me.

"Yes?" I say as I approach where she is sitting behind her window.

"Mr. Combs needed emergency care when you first came in, and I neglected to get some pertinent information. I need to get that now, if you don't mind filling out some paper work."

She hands me an ink pen and papers. I look at the questions and realize I don't know the answers to most of the questions.

"Well, can you at least put your husband's name, date of birth, and social security number?"

"He has his wallet with him, Ma'am."

"Surely you know your address and telephone number."

"No Ma'am. We don't have an address."

I go back in time to two months ago, the Court House Annex, and the gray haired lady who was drilling me about my age, my identification. I am ready to run out through the hospital's magic doors that open without pushing. There is a quick pa-pound pa-pound in my ears, my heart beating double time.

"Ma'am," I hear a man's voice behind me. I expect it to be Russ coming to my rescue as he has all the times in the last three weeks, but it isn't his voice. It is the prickly voice I know so well. I turn, and I hear Grandpa saying, "This is my granddaughter, recently married and not from around here. I'll help her fill this out."

"Who is going to be responsible for the bill today?" she asks.

"You needn't worry about that. It'll be taken care of. Carrie, sit down."

Grandpa takes my elbow and moves me to where he was sitting. I am looking at the words, and I don't know half of what they are asking.

"Grandpa, what am I going to do?"

"Start by putting down his name, Gary Combs, Jr."

I print his name, then look at Grandpa. I don't know an address, and I already told the lady I didn't know an address.

"Just put Stears Branch, Kentucky, for now. You can ask Gary the other things when he comes out."

I nod and fill out as much as I can, where Gary works, my name. I leave my birthday blank, and I watch Grandpa from the corner of my eye. He notices and looks up and away. The heavy doors that separate us from the examining room open, and Gary is wheeled out in a rolling chair into the waiting room. He is pale but smiling.

"I think he might live," the nurse says. "We didn't have any clean clothes to give him. He looks worse than he is."

She is talking about the T-shirt, the red blood turned brown since his arrival. In the time between his arrival and his appearance now, the waiting room is empty except for Momma, Russ, Grandpa, and me.

"This was a lot of trouble for nothing," Gary says.

The doctor follows through the doors. "Not really, Mr. Combs. You have a concussion. You need to take it easy for the next few days and watch slippery bathroom floors. As well as no surprises that catch you off guard. Oh, and Mrs. Combs, I have a prescription here that can help that 'no baby now' situation."

The doctor is looking directly at me when he says this, and I look down to avoid his knowing gaze. Gary's face turns redder than the blood that gushed from his head, and he puts one hand over his forehead like he has a headache. He doesn't look up.

"I've written a small prescription for pain medication. You will need it for tonight. Don't take it for any longer than a day or two," the doctor says to Gary.

Gary takes his hand off his forehead, and looks up at the doctor who is smiling. He hands the small paper to Gary and to the lady at the desk, hands a larger paper. She begins to type on her keyboard.

Grandpa takes the registration paper to Gary and is talking to him, but I continue to watch the lady at the desk, her pursed lips and fast fingers. She looks up on occasion to see if we are still there, and then returns to her typing. No one else enters, and she is still typing from that same paper the doctor gave her when Gary came out.

I hear Momma ask Gary if he brought a coat. I hear him say "No."

"It's cold out," I hear Russ say.

"I'll be okay. We need to go back and get my car and our things,"

271

Gary is now sitting beside Momma, and the rolling chair has returned to the other side of the heavy doors. All the while I watch the lady typing, and Grandpa is beside me, watching me.

"Mrs. Combs?"

I have been waiting for her to call my name, waiting for this to happen.

"Yes?"

"I have your bill ready."

Gary turns to where I am standing, rises wobbly-legged and feels for his wallet.

"What do we owe?" he asks and moves to where Grandpa and I are standing.

"With the emergency room charges, the x-ray, radiologist, ER doctor's charges, and lab fees you have a total of $2,318.59. How do you want to pay for that?"

"I don't have that much."

"What do you have?" she asks.

Gary opens his wallet. He has another $200 left after giving Donna the $200 on Friday. Even if he hadn't given the money away, it still was not enough. He lays the cash on her desk and she looks at him.

"Is that all?"

"Yes Ma'am."

She sighs. Grandpa has reached into his pocket. Onto the counter he places a long strand of pearls. Grandma's pearls.

"This cover it?"

"Grandpa!"

"Sir, this hospital does not accept barter as payment. When an individual does not have insurance, we accept silver certificate bills, pure coin, or a credit card that is backed by a government certified bank. The hospital cannot accept merchandise in exchange for services."

"Mr. Kelsey, I can't let you do that," Gary says.

"Well now, boy, I don't see that you have any say in the matter."

"Grandpa, those are Grandma's pearls of remembrance. Great-great-grandma, Meona's. It's family."

"Girl, if this here man you up and married isn't family, I don't know who is. This hospital won't accept barter, so I gotta trade some of these old family members in for some cash. Russ, can you help me do that?"

Russ is liking Grandpa. You can see it in his eyes .

272

"You accept the boy's $200 as down payment?" Grandpa asks.

"I'll have to have you sign a note to the fact," she says, and with that she pulls a set of papers from her desk and begins filling them out. Russ looks over them and nods approval. Grandpa and Gary both sign.

Gary, Russ, and Grandpa head to a pawn shop on the west end of town. Momma and I go home. Momma looks very satisfied with herself.

"So what do you think of your Grandpa now?" she asks.

"I think Grandma is going to kill him when she finds out what he did with Grandma Meona's strand of pearls."

*****

Against doctor's orders, Gary went ahead and worked Tuesday and Wednesday. His boss paid him today, and Jack said he would help pay for my dress, since part of Gary's pay went for the pills to keep me from having babies. Tuesday night when Gary got in from work we had an embarrassing family conference with Momma, Gary, and me around the kitchen table. I was pretty sure that Grandpa listened at the kitchen door. Gary didn't say a word while Momma and I talked about how long I should wait until having babies.

Gary and I agreed to take the pills the ER doctor prescribed for two years, and then have babies. Momma said she thought that was a good idea. It took one whole day's work to pay for three months of that stuff. Momma helped with another three.

Gary was embarrassed that he didn't have the money for all of it himself. When Grandpa burst into the kitchen from his eavesdropping and offered another pearl to pay for the rest, we both refused to allow it. He finally agreed, allowing Gary his pride in taking care of me.

273

Chapter 35

My dress didn't fit Claire. Her baby bump, as she called it, kept the dress from zipping up, so she searched for another. When I offered, my heart was in it, but seeing Gary's expression that afternoon at the table gave me second thoughts. Once given, I couldn't take it back though I regretted giving it. Now my dress rests in a box, pressed between sheets of white tissue paper so, as Momma says, it won't turn yellow, and someday, if I have a daughter, she can wear it at her wedding. I just smile. *I had wanted to wear it at my own wedding first.*

Today the sun shines bright but cold for Jack and Claire's wedding. She found her dress, and Jack found flowers. No one knows how he pulled that off in December, but he did. He traveled to Mt. Sterling and brought Donna, Billy, and Susie in for the wedding. They stayed with Momma last night.

"Carrie, you're prettier than before. How'd you do that?" Billy asked.

Billy jumped from the car and is now pulling at my hand dragging me to where his Mommy is standing. He is beside himself with excitement for coming to see us. I can't say that Gary and I are any different with seeing him. I kneel down beside him and draw him into my arms.

"Jack said you went on your honeymoon after we left," Donna says.

"We did."

"What's that?" Billy asks.

"You'll find out someday." Gary says and smiles a knowing smile at me.

"What happened to your head, Uncle Gary?"

"Carrie pushed me down."

"Did not," he says, and then with questioning eyes, "You didn't did you?"

I rise, keeping my hand on Billy's shoulder. "Billy, you know better than that. I'd never hurt Gary. Not on purpose anyway."

"Uncle Gary, quit teasing."

"Just look," and Gary kneels down to show Billy the bandage at the back of his head.

Susie eyes us with caution from behind her mother's legs, looking

274

from Gary to me. Our joking with Billy does not ease her nervousness. We move to the front of the old church's stone steps.

Hopeful that the elderly reverend does not recall when Gary and I were married, I open the front doors and peek inside. He is bustling from pew to pew greeting what guests have already been seated. He doesn't see me. I'm afraid he'll say something to Grandpa in casual conversation.

Billy and Jon edge past me into the church, while Momma waits for Russ.

"You two behave in there. It's a house of God," Momma says to the boys' backs.

"I'll go on in with them," Donna says, and she enters carrying Susie.

Jack pulls up just as Russ and Grandpa do. Claire waits in the truck until the last three guests enter the ancient stone church and then she gets out. Her beaded slippers peek out beneath her snowy white gown. Her hair normally hangs loose, but it has been tied up high on her head and falls down her back in long curls. She reminds me of long ago, of the princesses in the fairy tales Grandma used to read on snowy nights.

"Claire, you're beautiful," I say.

For that one moment there is no other sound – no spoken words, no whispers from inside, no coughing, no clearing of throats.

The four of us: Jack, Claire, Gary and me, stand on the stone steps that lead into the sanctuary. Music drifting through the doors breaks the silence.

"That's our sign," Jack says. "Gary, you and I go in first. Carrie, when it gets louder, you start coming in. Remember to go slow. And Baby – you know what you're supposed to do."

Claire nods. She holds the white flowers with both hands. They're shaking.

"Baby, you nervous?"

"A little."

Jack takes her face in his hands, kisses her gently on the lips. "I gotcha Claire, don't worry. Us guys gotta go in now, okay?"

She nods. Gary and then Jack go through the wooden doors. I look at her. I take hold of her hands, wrap my fingers around the fingers grasping the bouquet.

"It's okay, Claire, really."

"I know," and she smiles – rose colored lips drawing up at the

275

corners. The smile reaches her hazel colored eyes.

The music gets louder, and I open the door, prop it with a rock that sits to the side, and then enter. At the front of the sanctuary, I see Jack's big smiling face. This is the day he has been waiting for. Then, there is Gary, my Gary, and it is his face that I long for. I glance at the Reverend. *He remembers our wedding. He knew the truth even then.* The understanding in his smile tells me our secret is safe.

To my right, Jon and Billy fidget in their seat. I can see Momma and Russ. Momma blinks back big tears. She is crying like this is *my wedding.* Grandpa watches her, and then looks across the church bench into the aisle at me. His eyes mist up. *I wish Grandma was here. Grandma, can you feel this going on right now?*

As I get to the front, I hear the Reverend's wife hit the piano powerfully with the music. I turn to see Claire, all in white, start down that same aisle – walking amongst friends: Momma, Russ, Jon, Grandpa, Frank, Donna, Billy, Susie, Cook, Crazy Mave, Sam, and even Mrs. Davis. Family.

Chapter 36

Grandma.

I sit here on Aries' front stoop wrapped in one of her wool shawls. It is nearly Christmas, and the cold comes early. This is the first snow to come in December since our arrival in Stears Branch – first since the time of the earth change. Flakes fall soft but steady. Already the children in this hollow wait for Santa and his sleigh. Stears Branch has not hid from that excitement. The sun sets behind the far hill, the one that encamps the ancient walnut tree, co-conspirator with the boy who stole Carrie away. Even in the dark, the snow laden ground illuminates the hollow.

The night is filled with ought-to's for me. There is not enough time to make the special gifts for Jolie's children. I don't know where the days escaped to. They are good children. Moe won't expect anything, and neither will Kathy. The baby is too little to know, but I know.

Perhaps I can go tomorrow to the cabin, find one of Carrie's dresses for Kathy, wash and make it look a little new. Get one of the fairy tale books for Moe. Get a gourd... fix a rattle for Baby Aries. It is a plan, and it is the best I can do.

From my vantage point, I see a winding wisp of smoke from Jolie's chimney. It is past dinner. My beans wait on the edge of the hearth, bread baked, apples roasted with honey. It will make a filling supper, but I'm not hungry. Food doesn't satisfy the empty places. Moe did not stay tonight. It will be lonely.

I've tightened my belt another two notches since Jim left, not that it has hurt anything. I stand to go inside. The cold invades the shawl and the woolen shirt beneath. At first I think it is a mistake. I shade my eyes from the snowflakes and stare into the night. I see smoke, a distant turn of curl that vanishes and re-appears. *It can't be Reva's. Wrong direction. Too small for a forest fire. Too wet. Someone's in my cabin. Who?*

"Damn, coldest night of the year, and I gotta get out and chase someone out," I say to no one. "Need that rusty shotgun."

Inside the cabin I get boots and heavy coat. I grab the little axe. On the front stoop, I take both steps and stop. In the distance is a

277

shape moving in the direction of where I stand. The shape is vaguely familiar, but I can't place it. It is humped over but walking steady in the deepening snow. When the body is within ear's reach I call out.

"Harold?"

The figure doesn't answer. I can't tell if he just doesn't hear me or if he chooses not to answer.

"Just stop where you are," I say.

"You propose to stop me with that dang thing?" the body asks, pointing to the axe in my hand.

"Jim?"

The axe drops with a clunk at my side.

"You came close to taking off a toe."

He raises his head and pushes his hat off his face. He is thinner, his belt pulled in as many notches as mine. He is trying to smile but there is an uncertainty in his eyes.

"You scared the shit out of us. There's three crosses back behind the cabin," he says.

All the years we been married, I'd never heard a cuss word out of his mouth, and the first thing he does is fuss at me about not being at the cabin and saying 'shit.' *Go figure.*

"Well?"

"Well what?"

"You gonna let me in before I freeze to death out here?"

"Us?"

"We have some talking to do before I talk about the 'us'. Can I come in now?"

I nod and turn. He follows. Up the two steps and into the warmth of Aries' small cabin. *I think I should run into his arms, cry, welcome him home, say all the things that I have thought for the last two months, but at the moment I am angry for all the agony I went through while he was doing God knows what.*

And all that can come out of my mouth is "Have you eaten?"

"No."

I go to Aries' cabinet and pull out her plates and dip up beans, apples and break off bread. I hand him the plate and spoon.

"Got any coffee?"

He is acting like nothing has happened, that things are the way they were two months ago, that he didn't leave me to fend by myself while he traipsed off angry.

"No. I haven't been drinking chicory. I ran out."

"Oh."

"Did you find her?"

"Who?"

"Damn it, who do you think? Carrie."

He has his head down, and he is grinning. "You shouldn't be cussing like that Janie. You know how Carrie feels about that."

"If you don't tell me what's going on I'm going to get that little axe from the porch and use it on you. I am about tired to death of your games." I get up and go into the kitchen, lean over the dry sink and feel sobs wrench from my chest.

"Sorry. It's just too easy to get you going. Carrie's not at the cabin yet. They should be back in a day or two. In time for Christmas Eve." He comes into the kitchen standing at my side, one hand on my shoulder. I straighten my back against his touch.

"They?" I struggle to say and pull away.

"Yeah, that's part of what I need to talk to you about. She's married, Janie."

I walk back into the little room and sit on the edge of Aries' bed.

"Married? To that boy?"

"To Gary."

"So you've had a change of heart." I am looking at him dumb-founded. Of all the people to have a change of heart, he is the last one I expected to have a change of heart about Gary Combs, Jr.

"He's a good boy. He loves her."

"When did you decide this? Did you sign the papers for her to get married?" I accuse him.

"No. Her Momma did."

"Emily?" and I feel my heart begin to race. It beats at double time, starts to skip, and my head begins to get light. I take a hold of the poster at the foot to keep myself erect. It doesn't work. I feel myself start sliding to the floor. Before my head hits the foot board, I sense rather than feel Jim's arms catch me. He lays me on the bed. The room has become hot. He opens the doors, both back and front, and cold air blows through. I feel a wet cloth on my face. His words feel like a hallucination.

"Janie, can you hear me?"

I open my eyes and Jim is still here. It is not my imagination. It is real.

279

"There's more."

"Is it bad?" I hear myself ask.

He is smiling. He is no longer playing games. There is concern in his face.

"I'm sorry, Janie. Before I go any further, I have to tell you I was wrong. Wrong for a hundred, maybe a thousand things. I am so sorry. I have learned so many things on this journey, done so many hurtful things. What I did to you was one of the worst. Will you forgive me? I have a lot of stuff to make up for."

'I'm sorry' is not a phrase I am used to hearing from Jim, and I don't know how to respond. I don't say anything.

"It's okay. I know it's going to take time. Are you up to hearing some more news?"

"Is Carrie pregnant?"

"No. She tells everyone she's too young to have babies." Jim is shaking his head when he tells me this. "You should hear her. It embarrasses Gary to death."

"What?"

"Oh yeah, one more thing I have to confess. Carrie said I had to."

I look at him wondering what else he has to tell me.

"I stole your strand of pearls."

I open my mouth, and he interrupts me, "Before you say anything, I didn't use all of them, just some. You still have the strand, it's just shorter. It was a necessity, believe me."

"Jim, Grandma's pearls?"

"You'll understand when Carrie gets here. Let's take those beans and bread down to our cabin, okay? You have some company."

"Who?"

"Someone you've been waiting a long time to arrive."

I want to run out the front door, forget the food, forget the fire, forget the coat, forget the pearls, forget everything else. I know who is at my cabin. I have waited for this day, this moment, for eleven years. Jim stops me.

"We need to stoke the fire. We'll come back here later. You need to get a hot pad so you don't burn your hand on the bread pan, and I'll take the beans and apples. Put out that lamp."

We walk in silence to our cabin. The dogs who moved to Aries' with me follow us in hopes that we drop our parcels. The lights to Jolie's house shine onto the snow in yellow strips, but no one is watching

280

from the windows. The smoke I saw before was from our chimney. In front of the porch sits two unfamiliar cars. There are shadows crossing in front of the windows, three, and I am confused.

"Three?" I ask.

"Yeah, just one of your surprises."

I push the back door open, holding the hounds back with my leg, allowing Jim to enter first with his load.

"Sorry we are late," he says. "Had a little trouble with your mother."

"Mom?"

Jim sets his pots on the wooden table and grabs the bread pan before I drop it. I can't speak. Words are stuck somewhere between my brain and my mouth and they refuse to come. Years of words, years of 'I love you's' are stuck in emotions that are too fragile to let go. I hold on to the tears, order them by will to be stayed.

Emily, who rarely cried as a child, is crying for both of us. The boy in the corner, next to the fireplace is watching us, large brown eyes, his young brow creased with questions. Emily sees to where my gaze has gone and lets go.

"Mom, this is Jon, your grandson."

"Jonathan's little boy?"

"Grandma?" he says.

"I have a grandson," I say to Jim. "Where's Jonathan?"

"He's gone Mom. Died before Jon was born. This is Russ," and Emily takes the older man's hand and draws him to where we are standing. "He is my husband. He adopted Jon."

"Mrs. Kelsey, I am so happy to finally meet you. Emily told me so much about you, I feel that I already know you."

"Mom," Emily is saying, and it is almost too much for me to take in at once, "Thank you for taking care of Carrie, of raising her to be the young woman she became. She is truly wonderful, Mom. Really."

"Grandpa, did you bring that food? I'm hungry."

"Jon," Emily says.

"It's okay, Emily. The boy's gotta eat," Jim says.

I watch Jim pull a plate down from the shelf, hand it to Jon, and set three more plates on the table along with cups. On the fire hangs a pot, and it is then I smell it, the sweet smell of coffee. He pulls the pot off, and Emily goes to a cooler that is against the wall next to the wooden sink. She pulls out a glass bottle and a small wrapped square.

"Grandpa said you were going to love this," Jon says.

281

"Sit down, Mom. You too, Russ. Jon, you need to wait until Grandpa says grace."

"Yes Ma'am."

We bow our heads, and I hear the solemn words that come from Jim's lips.

"Thank you Lord for this good food, and the blessings of family together. Amen."

"Kind of short, Dad."

"Jon is kind of hungry, right buddy?" Jon nods as he scoops beans into his mouth.

I sip on real coffee, lightened with milk. The butter on the bread was sweet butter, not the soured type we made from Reva's milk, and it ran off the bread in yellow globs.

"Any honey left?" Jim asked.

"Maybe. If it is, it may be sugared. I took some back when Aries got sick, but not since her funeral dinner here last month."

"Sorry she died. She was a good woman."

"She was that and more," I say.

"Aries lived at the very back of the hollow. Your Mom went back to take care of her when she got sick, right Janie?" I nod and take another sip of the strong liquid.

"I ended up staying there when she died. It was smaller and easier for me to keep up by myself," and with that I look at Jim. He looks away. He acknowledges guilty as charged. Jon gets him off the hook.

"Did Carrie sleep up there?"

"She did," Jim says.

"Can I sleep up there?"

"I don't see why not. Grandma," he asks looking at me, "is the bed still there?"

"I haven't done anything to it. Jon, I just need to get a fresh sheet on it. If you're through eating, you can help me."

I get up from the table and go to the cabinet. Inside is what is left of linens, close to thread bare, but still usable. I take two sheets and motion for Jon to lead the way up the ladder and through the square opening that leads to the space that was Carrie's room. His head has no sooner cleared the opening when his voice calls down to Emily.

"Jeez Mom, you got to see this." He moves one step down almost catching my fingers in the process.

"Sorry, Grandma. I didn't see your hand."

282

"Jon," Emily says, "you need to watch what you are doing."

"I said I was sorry," he says. "You have to see this. It's awesome."

Jon continues to climb, and I follow. Once through the opening we stand. Jon circles the space examining each item that Carrie touched. At the marks on the wall above the bed he looks at me in question.

"It is how long we have been here. Carrie marked the time with those lines."

"You've been here a long time, Grandma."

"We have."

Emily climbs the ladder and enters this sanctuary. She too surveys the room, taking in the months and years that she has missed. The pictures tacked to the walls, pictures of birthdays and Christmases. All memories that she was left out of. I see a sadness fall over her.

"This is so cool, isn't it Mom?" Jon breaks the spell, and I am grateful for his presence for it wipes away the onslaught of regret.

"It is," Emily says.

I remove the stale sheet, the one that has not been touched since Carrie's leaving, and shake out the clean. Jon and Emily are looking at the books and papers that Carrie learned to read from.

"You brought all of these?" she asks.

"It's all your father allowed me to bring. Remember? I had another box, but…"

"Who taught her algebra?"

"Your father."

"Really?"

"Really. Neither of us knows another language so we fell short there."

"Still, Mom. You two did a wonderful job."

"Carrie's been teaching Jolie's children, which has been no small task," and I laugh at my assessment. "She's really good with children." I stop with that, catch myself in my own noose.

"Janie, we need to be heading back to Aries' cabin so Russ and Emily can get some sleep. It's been a long day," Jim says from below the ladder.

"Goodnight, Grandma," Jon says.

"Goodnight sweetie. I'll see you in the morning."

"Okay."

"Jon?"

"Yeah?"

283

"Don't let the bedbugs bite."

"Grandma, you have bedbugs?"

"No…it's just something we always used to say."

"Sleep tight."

"Okay. Grandma?"

I step my feet one rung down the ladder before descending further. "What Jon?"

He is smiling as he answers, "Don't let the bedbugs bite."

I climb back up the ladder and give my new grandson a hug; he bear hugs me back.

*****

In Aries' cabin Jim stokes up the fire. The two rooms warm quickly. I go to the back porch and break ice to bring in a bucket of water. Our wet shoes sit next to the hearth to dry. Coats are removed and hung on pegs. I return from the kitchen to see Jim removing his shirt. He hangs it on the back of Aries' rocker. He begins to unzip his pants, and I turn away, folding down the quilt on the narrow bed. When I turn back he is holding my nightgown that hung on the poster of the bed. There is uneasiness in our solitude.

"I'm not asking anything of you, Janie. I'll sleep on the floor if you want."

I pull my shirt over my head. I can't help but wonder what his life has been like in Lexington, whether he spent it with any other woman, and I am embarrassed by my lack of proper underwear. I pull the drawstring on my pants, and they fall to the floor. I step out of them, and I take the gown he is holding out and pull it over my head. His face shows the same uncertainty that I feel. I crawl into the bed, move to the far side, leaving him room.

He hesitates, and then crawls in beside me. For a long time there is silence between us, both measuring the breaths, waiting for sleep of the other before relaxing. At last I think he is asleep, and my mind wanders.

"Janie," I hear him say in the darkness.

"What?"

"I love you."

With that he pulls me to him, and I don't resist. He kisses me on my forehead, and we both fall asleep in that embrace.

284

Chapter 37

Jon, Russ and Jim went into the hills, cut a cedar tree and pulled it down to the cabin. Around the fire we have strung berries and popcorn into long strands. Emily thought of everything, bringing colored paper and small bottles of white glue. I have watched with pure joy while our grandson and his Grandpa have made strings of multi-colored chains. It has been a long time; I had forgotten such small pleasures.

"When will they get here?" Jon asks. He is asking the same question I want to ask, and he can get away with it because he is young,

"I don't know," his mother tells him.

"Are they bringing presents?"

"Jon," Russ says, "you are too old to be asking questions like that."

"It's Christmas," he says. With that he goes back to the window and looks out again.

Jim and I have had little time to give thought what to give a young man from the city. We talked about it in whispers last night, and decided to give him the bow that Jim made early in our sojourn in Stears Branch. Jim made it out of a single piece of walnut, scraping and shaping the long slender bow. Today, before coming to the big cabin, he went to the barn and brought back the bow, asked Harold for fresh gut to restring it, and I used the fat we had left to rub it to a shine. New feathers were attached to the arrows, and to the bow's upper limb. We worked side by side to clean the old quiver. It was a good time, a healing time, a time of learning about his search for Carrie.

As I stand with Jon at the window, I revisit our words.

*****

"I caused her a world of hurt, Janie," he said to me as we used a smooth stone to soften the deer hide again after it had dried. "I thought I was protecting her, but I wasn't."

"You did what you thought you had to do."

"But I was wrong. I wish you could have seen them. We were both wrong. I'm not sure we could have kept her here, but it wouldn't have been like it was."

"How was it?"

"I had him brought up on charges. Kidnapping, rape, murder."

"Jim, he took her away from us."

"No, he didn't. I didn't see it at first either, but he didn't."

I was being dishonest with him. Warred within in myself whether to own it.

"She went of her own free will, Janie. And he didn't rape her. They didn't, you know…and he didn't murder anyone either. That little boy they took care of proved that. I almost had him put way for something he didn't do."

"You're giving yourself a lot of credit there."

"Maybe. But when they get here you need to give him a chance."

So, am I going to give you a chance for running off and leaving me?

I thought of Aries and fumbled into the truth, "I watched her leave that night, when they were pushing the car down the road. I knew it was too late to go after her and I was too scared to come tell you."

"Why?" He looked at me in disbelief.

"For the very reason you took off. I knew you were gonna say I knew."

"Did you?"

"No. But I knew you wouldn't believe me. We were both scared it was gonna happen, and it did."

*****

The snow is still heavy on the ground. The only evidence of the city is Russ's and Jim's cars. Even they defy civilization with their mound-like appearances. Supper is waiting. A ham sits on the hearth side sending scents of smokiness into the air. Dried shuck beans bubble over the fire with sputters and snaps at the flames and real coffee crowns it all. I am sipping on a mug, and I enjoy each drop of its richness.

When Jon hears loud tail pipes he looks at me in expectation. The sound brings back a whole host of memories. Headlights weave through the trees, and I am surprised at seeing two sets. The El Camino curves around the barn first, followed by a truck that backfires at the rise in the hill in front of the old bridge. I hear the motor rev, see it speed up and backfire again. One pulls beside the other in front of the porch shining their lights into the cabin where Jon and I fill the window.

286

A large burly man opens the truck door getting out first and pulls a woman alongside. Through the partial light she looks to be older than Carrie.

"That's Claire and Jack," Jon tells me. "They're Gary and Carrie's best friends."

"Oh."

"Jack's the one who saved Gary's life at the trial. He got Donna back in time to point the finger at the real killers."

"Oh," I say again. "I guess someone's gonna have to fill me in about that."

"Grandpa hasn't told you?"

"Just a little."

Gary climbs out of the El Camino and goes to the other side. I am watching, my eyes straining against the dark to see Carrie's face as she steps outside of the car. Their friends are already on the porch, but I can still see Gary and Carrie. They have stopped, are looking at each other. She has a ball of yellow and white fur under one arm, and I see Gary pull her to himself, and I watch as she draws close, moving the cat to her other side. I see him kiss the top of her head, and then he looks straight at the window where I am standing. We make eye contact for just a moment, and he leans down. I know he is saying something to Carrie because her head jerks toward the window. Carrie pulls from his embrace, grabs his hand and pulls him to the porch.

"Grandma, we're home," and to the other two strangers with them she says, "Come on in, you all. It's too cold to stand out here waiting for someone to answer. This isn't Lexington."

I hear a strange voice bellow deep with laughter, "Jim, you're not packing that shotgun are you?"

Jim pulls the door wide open. "Get you and your little lady in here before you freeze to death. Gary, get my baby girl in here, or I'll be pointing that old twelve-gauge at you again if she gets a fever."

The fur ball jumps from Carrie's grasp and races across the floor. Jon chases it and grabs the cat before it gets to the table.

"You need help getting your stuff in?" Russ asks.

"We've got quite a load, but I think it can wait." Gary looks at me, "Mrs. Kelsey, I brought her back."

I'm not sure what to say. *Do I say thank you? Do I curse you for all the grief you caused me?* Then I look at Carrie's face, and I have never seen her so happy, so full of love.

287

"Well, I suppose, since you are married, Mrs. Kelsey seems a little formal. I guess you might as well call me Grandma. That's what Carrie has always called me."

"Grandma," Carrie says, "the tree is beautiful. Did you do it?"

"Nah, Jon and your Grandpa did most of it I think. Jon picked the tree out, and your Grandpa and Russ cut it. Took all three of them to drag it back to the cabin."

"We have supper ready, if you four are hungry?" Emily asks.

"Jack is always hungry," Claire says. She pats his protruding belly. "I'm not sure which of us is pregnant."

"I think it backfired," Jack says.

Claire blushes. I watch everyone but Jon laughing. It is a funny thought, and in my day I might have thought to say it myself.

"Don't pay any attention to him," I say. "How far along are you?"

"Grandma, you haven't changed a bit," Carrie says.

And with that, everyone but Jon and me are laughing, laughing so hard that they are practically rolling on the floor, and Carrie and Grandpa are the worst.

"What's so funny, Jim?" I ask.

"Oh nothing. Carrie hasn't been gone so long that she has forgotten you or your ways."

"Like I asked before, what's so funny?" and this time I am trying to hide my own laughter, because they are both right about me.

"Well, before I have to begin arbitration between Jim and Janie, we'd better get your coats off and get you around the table. I am starved," Russ says.

"Jon, put Dixie down and wash your hands," Emily says.

Jon drops the cat, watching her move to the warmth of the hearth, and after washing in the basin of cold water, takes his place next to Jim. Gary lifts his fork to the ham, and I hear Carrie's voice loud and clear.

"Gary?"

"Billy and Carrie made us say grace every meal at the Shelter. Still does even with Billy being gone." He raises one eyebrow as he looks at her, "You can be proud of her, Mrs. Kelsey."

"Grandma," I remind.

Gary smiles and nods.

"Grandpa, will you bless the food? Jon, bow your head," Carrie says.

Jon looks at Emily, she motions him to obey, and he lowers his head after picking a piece of crisp fat off the ham. Grandpa looks at him with a wink.

"Good Lord, thanks for the food. Let's eat. Amen."

"Really?" Carrie asks.

"I gave thanks, didn't I?"

There is a conspiratorial look between Jon and Jim. Emily looks at Carrie and shrugs.

"I hope God was listening closely because that went by so fast, if he wasn't, he missed it."

Even with the crowd, there is elbow room. No one speaks while food is being scarfed down. As I watch three grown men and one growing boy, I think had they been with us in the beginning, we would have run out of food before the growing season started that first year. It feels good, this crowd at the table, and I wonder how long it is going to last.

When bellies begin to fill, Jon pipes up, "Gary, did you bring presents?"

"What did I tell you earlier?" Emily says.

"Let the boy alone," Grandpa says.

I am wondering what all happened to Jim in Lexington. He has been transformed from a cranky old man to someone I don't recognize. I think I am going to like what I see, and he catches me smiling at him.

"What?"

I ignore his question. "Let's stack these things in the sink and put some water in the kettle to boil for later. I think Grandpa wants to have Christmas."

Carrie is observing the transformation, too. I think she has been a part of it.

"We can use some help in getting things in from the trucks now, if I can get some volunteers." Russ, Jack and Grandpa all get up with Gary and put on their jackets.

I go to the water bucket and fill the kettle. Emily helps me move it to the fire. Before I realize it, Carrie has gone to the wood pile in the corner of the kitchen and pulled a log and placed it into the fireplace.

"You don't need to do that," I say.

"Yeah I do. I'm home now. We all have to do our part, right?"

"But you're guest."

"Since when?"

"I don't know, since you went and got married."

"Oh, Grandma. What's got into you? I'm still Carrie."

The front door blows open with a gust of wind and the first load of packages come in with it. Jack is carrying a suitcase in one hand and a cooler under the other arm. He has a reach like a brown bear. Jim is carrying one cooler with a suitcase stacked on top, and Russ has three black plastic bags. Gary is the last to enter, and he carries a tall stack of brightly wrapped packages. With him, one of the tamer dogs manages to scuttle around his legs and rush towards the table.

"Grab that hound," I say to Jon, and he rushes the dog amid Grandpa's calls to the hound. The dog slobbers and licks the boy's face to Jon's delight and Dixie takes the ladder to the loft in a single bolt.

"Jon."

"It's okay, Mom."

Jon is hugging the red and brown neck, scratching between his ears.

"He's always wanted a dog," Russ says.

"He's not taking that thing home with us," Emily says.

"I've two more boxes in the back. Jack you help me get them?"

As they exit, Jon escorts the dog out the same way he came in. When Gary and Jack re-enter, Jon is standing guard to keep the dog out.

Packages are placed beneath the sweet smelling cedar. Now that scalding water has been set over dirty plates and the leavings of the ham, a lone shank bone, is wrapped and stored in the pantry, the cedar's scent begins to permeate the cabin with its earthy perfume. The men grab ends of the giant table and move it to one side of the great room. It is time for tradition, and I move into the bedroom and gather Grandma's Bible.

This company of family moves to the fireplace and sits cross-legged style in the light of the blaze while Grandpa reads the Christmas story, as he did for Carrie each of the Christmases we have been at Stears Branch. And as we have done for each Sunday after the reading of the Word, I recite the legacy of family. Grandpa stands, digs into his pocket and lays the remnants of the pearls on the hearth, a shorter strand but still connected, intertwined, unbroken.

After a long silence, Jon whispers, "When are we opening presents?"

I smile as his mother answers, "Christmas morning."

Chapter 38

"Grandpa, I thought you would never get here," Jon says.

"He's driving us all crazy all, Grandpa."

Jim is carrying the bow in a long slender wrapping. I am carrying a small square box with a makeshift bow on the top.

"Sorry honey, we don't have much in the way of ribbons anymore."

"Grandma, I didn't expect anything. You didn't know we were coming."

"That's true. But it's Christmas morning."

"I know, but I'm not a little girl anymore."

The truth of that runs all through me. The fire has been stoked up and coffee is already on. A skillet is over the fire getting hot and a kettle is spewing grits in bubbles and popping bursts. Emily sticks her head out of Jim's and my room. Her hair is a tangle, and it is easy to see she just woke up. The cat wiggles past her legs and out of the bedroom.

"I think Jon was up every hour to see if it was morning yet, and if it wasn't Jon, it was that stupid cat on the bed."

Russ enters through the back door, kicking the dogs back. He is carrying a load of wood. I didn't see him as we entered.

"Where's Gary?" I ask.

"He has a mission," Carrie says.

"Mission?"

"Yeah. Remember when Mrs. Thompson's son ran off? He went to Lexington. When Grandpa caused all his rip-roar," Carrie looks at Jim, "and you know you did."

"Guilty as charged," he says with a contrite smile.

"Go on, what about Frank, Jr.?"

"He came in early this morning, and Gary took him to his mom and dad."

I wonder if Reva can survive the shock. I look at Jim. He reads my mind.

"She'll be okay. She's got a bunch of grandchildren to revive her. Give Frank Senior a jolt, too, I suspect."

"Well I'll be d...."

"Grandma."

291

"Carrie, you don't know what I was going to way. I've cleaned up my mouth since you've been gone." I look at Jim, "Well, kind of."

Gary comes in with a big smile on his face.

"How'd it go?" Carrie asks.

"Almost as good as it was here. Grandma, you have breakfast ready?"

"Barely got here."

"You know, Carrie was right. All the way on that road to Lexington she kept hounding me that you were the best cook in the world. After last night, I have to concede, she's right."

Carrie has laid slices of bacon in the skillet. The smell works through the house and wakes Jack from the loft.

"I smell food."

"His alarm clock is his belly," Claire answers from behind him.

"Where'd you get bacon?" I ask.

"Just something we brought to fill out your larder. Merry Christmas," and she turns from the skillet to the box that is sitting on the shelf and sets it on the table. "Gary, do the honors while I keep the skillet from catching on fire."

"Let's see, flour and yeast. How about some baking powder and regular salt. Carrie said no one needs sugar, but I picked some up, a little, just in case. Here's some cocoa. Thought we might have some tonight. And a bucket of lard, for the biscuits I hope you'll make for breakfast."

I think I am going to cry with the treasure trove that is being placed on the table in front of me. Before I can say anything else Gary goes to one of the big coolers, opens it, and pulls out a turkey, big enough to feed the five thousand.

"Think we can manage this for Christmas dinner?" he asks. "Oh yeah, just one more thing," and with that he pulls a small six-ounce bottle of Pepsi. "I couldn't get diet, so I hope this is okay."

Gary pulls a can opener out of his pocket, and with ice cold water dripping off his elbow and onto the wood floor, he hands me an ice cold Pepsi. Carrie has this wide grin on her face, and I have yet to see her so proud of an accomplishment. I take a deep swallow and my eyes water. I can feel it fizz back up and enter my nose. I choke.

"You all right?" she asks.

I choke again and manage out a "Yeah."

"Ice cold, just the way you like it, right?"

I nod, and hate to tell her it isn't as good as I remember, but I take another sip.

"I hate the stuff, Grandma. I don't see how you stand it."

I drink half, and tell her I'll save the rest for later, and put it back down into the cooler.

"Gary, put the lid on so it doesn't spill," she says.

Emily has finally emerged pulling her dark hair into a ponytail.

"Gary's back from Frank's Mom's," Carrie tells her Momma, "and we've started unloading the boxes and coolers."

"She sent down some butter, but since there are a bunch of children at her house at the moment, she thought she'd better keep the milk. But don't worry, we brought some ourselves."

"Did you bring the hen eggs like I asked," Jim says.

"Yep."

"And the ice cream?" Jon asks.

"It would have melted, Jon. Sorry, buddy."

"Guess I'd better get to working on your biscuits if you want them for breakfast," I tell the men.

I pull out a bowl and start with the flour and lard. I put a cast iron Dutch oven at the fire's edge to heat. Biscuits will taste awfully good with butter. The men move to the table and their conversation goes to the future. I want to listen, to eaves drop on what they are saying, but Carrie and Emily's chatter prevents it.

I hear Russ say, "It can be a partnership, Gary…" and then he turns, crosses his legs and I lose the rest of what he says.

"Do you think a garage can make it this far from.." and Carrie is laughing so hard I can't hear the rest of what Gary is saying. I want to tell Emily and Carrie to tone it down, but then the men would know I was trying to key into what they are saying.

Jim is speaking louder than the rest, "Well, I think it will work, not just because of Carrie either."

Carrie hears her name and looks at the four men. She gives them a "You want me?" look and Gary says, "No, we're just talking about the garage." She nods like she knows exactly what he means.

"What's that all about?" I ask her.

"We'll explain later," and she gives her Momma a knowing smile.

"I really don't like people keeping secrets."

"We're not keeping secrets, Grandma. "

"Feels like it to me."

293

"Your dough is looking a little stiff. You'd better start laying those biscuits out or they'll be tough," Carrie says to me, and she knows she is changing the subject.

Emily stirs scrambled eggs. Carrie lifts crisp bacon, and spoons grits into the wooden bowls, topping each with a spoon of Reva's butter while I fret. I rush the biscuits and burn them on the bottom, but no one seems to mind since I found a jar of wild honey in the back of the pantry. Jon, even with his urgency to open gifts, takes his time with the sticky stuff and the dark bottomed bread. He splits the biscuits and sandwiches them with the crisp bacon, and I am reminded of golden arches and biscuit egg sandwiches, but these are better.

The men agree to do dishes, and once again they are discussing futures. I hear Jim say, "With all of us working together, we can have Jack and Claire a cabin by summer's end. In the meantime, they can stay here with you and Carrie, and Janie and I can continue to stay in the cabin at the far end of the hollow. "

"I wouldn't want to push you out of your home," Gary says.

"You won't be. I know Janie will agree."

All four men are in agreement. There is a consensus. My heart races. I look at Carrie, and she acts like there is nothing going on. Emily doesn't blink. I look for Claire and she is nowhere to be seen. If Carrie and Emily hear, they don't let on.

Are you deaf, I want to ask?

Jon and Claire have come in from feeding the dogs. Jon has muddy paw prints on the front of his pants, and he is smiling.

"Is it time now?" he asks as he spoons leftover gravy in a saucer for the cat.

Jim looks at him, "It's time."

"Janie, sit down," he says to me, and then to Gary, "Do you want to start?"

Gary smiles, "Grandma, Carrie and I are moving back to Stear's Branch."

"Claire and me, too," Jack adds.

"Jim says we can have this place. Jack and Claire will stay here with us until we can get them a place built, maybe out beyond the garden."

"You won't mind will you, Grandma?" Carrie asks.

My mind is zipping back and forth between *"Take this house. Take the little house. I'll live in the woods, I'll live in a cave. Is this a brutal prank you are playing? Please let this be true."* I pull out of myself to see everyone, every single pair of eyes, even the dog that followed Jon and Claire into the house and the cat sitting with her saucer of gravy on the table, are staring at me waiting to hear me speak, waiting for some response.

"Janie?"

"I'm sorry. I'm just…there is so much. No, I don't care. Take the place, Carrie. You really are coming home?"

"Yeah, Grandma. I'm home."

"That's what you boys were whispering about?"

"Sorry, Janie," Russ says. "We have been talking about opening a garage. Building a concrete block building down at the forks of the road. No one has claimed it. We're going to double check out deeds to be sure. Gary and I are going to go in as partners, and Jack is going to work for us."

Russ looks at Jim and continues his announcement, "We believe there will be a demand for it as the bridge and roads are rebuilt, and people begin to work out of the area and cars are used again. With Gary's connection to Ashland, we may even be able to add a gas station, but that will have to wait."

"They'll start out in the old barn," Jim says. "We'll fix the four by four. It'll give them something to work on."

I laugh, "I'm sure it will. And you're okay with this Emily?"

Emily looks at Carrie and back at me. "Would I like to have her next door? Yes. Do I think this is a better place for her and Gary? Maybe. Is this what she wants? That is evident."

"That's not what I asked."

"Yes, Mom. The final thing is, I want her happy, and she will be happy. The big thing is, she found me, and we can see each other now any time we want. She can come to Lexington. You can come to Lexington. I think it is settled for everyone."

"Well, is it settled that Jon here can finally open his presents?" Gary asks.

"I suppose so," Emily says, and she grabs Jon and squeezes him.

"Get that dog out of here," I say. "No presents until the dog goes out."

*****

295

Once everyone has opened their gifts, Jim goes to the pantry and brings out the bow.

"Jon, Grandma and I want you to have this."

The yellowed magazine pages that acted as wrapping fall away from the bow, and Jon's mouth forms a perfect O. His eyes widen at the gift.

"Wow."

"Dad, what have you done?"

"I made it, Jon. Your Grandma decorated it with turkey feathers. It's made in the tradition of the Cherokee, people who lived on this land long before we did."

"Really?"

"It's true. My ancestors settled here, but Cherokee hunted here before that. When the Cherokee were herded off their land in North Carolina, some escaped to 'this dark and bloody land'."

"Your great-great-great grandmother was one who ran away," I say.

"Grandma Meona?" Carrie asks.

I nod.

"Wait until my friends see this," Jon says, and he holds the bow, turning it in his hand, then pulling on the gut string with one eye closed, he aims at the back door.

"Jon, that is not coming home with you."

"Mom!"

"It's a dangerous weapon. You can get in trouble in town with that."

"Emily," Russ says.

"No, I mean it."

Jim glances at me.

"I'm sorry, Dad. It's not safe."

"Emily," he says, "it has been one of the ways we have endured out here. Once I ran out of shells, it was how I was able to bring game down. It's a legacy of our lives here in Stears Branch." He spreads both hands palm up motioning around the cabin.

"Dad."

Jim walks to the front window looking out at the snow covered cars and then turns back to Emily, "I don't think you understand. Our way of life here is getting ready to change. I don't want it forgotten."

Russ moves to Jim's side. "We can't take it to Lexington. Emily is right. But when Jon comes and stays with you during the summers, you can teach him how to use it, show him how to shoot. Make sure

296

that all of this isn't forgotten."

Jim agrees, but not without reluctance. "Your Grandma has one more gift. It's for you and Gary," he says, looking at Carrie. "Janie?"

Gary sits beside Carrie, has one arm wrapped around her waist. I go to the window sill where I had set the small box. It sits soft in my hands, ruby colored velveteen faded to pink at the edges, old, older than me, older than my Grandma. I hand it to Carrie, my wrinkled, blue veined, weathered with age hands, to her young, soft, smooth hands.

"Grandma?"

"Didn't you just tell me a few hours ago you weren't a little girl anymore?"

"Yes, but…" She knows what is in the box even before slipping off the make-shift bow and snapping open the case. Carrie looks up at Gary, then back into the satin lined box. I watch his arm tighten around her waist, his lips brush her hair. She closes the lid, and they look at me.

"It's a little shorter. I think you both know about that, but it's time to turn the stories over."

"What is it?" Jon asks.

"Pearls." Carrie says.

About the Author

Joy Chrisman Welch was born in Ohio and moved to Kentucky where the craggy rocks of ravines and mystery of rock shelters held her until she took root. Her love for folklore, the old ways of mountain medicine, and the stories of outrageous heroes have molded her way of understanding story, and she believes that in writing, you must be driven by story.

She attended Sue Bennett, a small junior college in London, Kentucky, in 1968, then transferred to Eastern Kentucky University, where she graduated with an undergraduate degree in elementary education. Since that time, she has studied creative writing at the University of Kentucky and earned a Master of Arts at EKU with a concentration in creative writing.

Her goal in *The Road Builders*, as well as other projects currently underway, is to tell a story of loss, love, forgiveness, and restoration.

Joy currently lives in Lexington, Kentucky, where she writes at her "Nikky's Cubby," so named for Nikky Finney, a 2013 National Book Award winner, at the Carnegie Center in downtown Lexington. She was Ms. Welch's first writing instructor at UK in 1989.